Thanks

I hope this book entertains you and inspires you not to accept the status quo in your search for the truth. Special thanks to my wife, Christina, who served as my first and last editor as well as a continuous sounding board. It would have been impossible to complete this book without her unwavering love and support. I would also like to thank Jim and all of those who suffered through the early drafts and inspired me to continue. Special thanks to Chris Cockrill, who provided the cover art entitled "Lilith in the Garden of Eden." Email him at ccockrill@mac.com, or check out his work at chriscockadoodledo on Instagram or Chris Cockrill Tattoo-Maker on Facebook.

CHAPTER 1

Modern Day, Redwood Library, Newport, Rhode Island.

The holiday season sickened him. Humanity perverted God's lies. Jesus wasn't even born on Christmas! The Christians stole the holiday of Dies Natalis Solis Invicti, or "the birthday of the Unconquered Sun" from the pagans to make conversion easier. Since the birth of civilization, humankind had used religion as a tool to control the masses. *Humankind is so naïve!* He imagined humanity as two children skipping mindlessly down the path to hell, holding hands, smiling, and singing some silly children's song as they drew closer to their destruction. They committed all kinds of evil acts in his name, and yet their deeds had nothing to do with him or the Fallen Ones.

Satan's annual sabbatical from hell had initially brought him great joy. God's precious creations drifted further and further away from him while he sulked silently upon his throne. There was a time when that fact would have been enough, but Satan was tired of the small victories. He wanted respect and the truth to be known. He was not the monster that the Bible made him out to be. There was no prowling the earth, seeking whom he may devour. Instead, he sat alone on the side steps of the Redwood Library at ten o'clock at night waiting. The cold air swept across the frozen snow, cutting through him like a knife. The stinging chill of the night air was a refreshing change from the stale crimson fires of hell.

Satan was waiting for William Buckley. William was a simple librarian who had humbly served the Redwood Library for the past twenty-five years. He loved his job because it gave him access to old and obscure writings, and that was part of the reason that Satan chose him. Satan respected his thirst for the truth. So, instead of traumatizing his family, which had gathered for the holidays, he waited. He knew William would pay the library a special visit to make sure the heavy snowfall had not caused any damage.

As Satan sat alone in the darkness, his mind wandered. Memories of times long passed allowed loneliness to creep up within him. The holidays disgusted him, but he envied William and his family. A lone tear ran down his cheek as thoughts of his own family surfaced. He wiped the single teardrop away. *It's been a long time since I cried!* Instinctively, he looked towards Heaven. *You're a Fool, Satan!* He said to himself. His eyes hadn't pierced the heavenly veil since his fall and yet he looked upward. *FALL, what FALL? God betrayed you and sent your brethren to cast you out;* he reminded himself. Rage rose within him. God cast him out for standing up for his brethren, and it still made him angry!

Even after all these centuries, the bitterness remained. Their conflict wasn't just a feud between the Fallen Ones and God, it was a war between good and evil, and humanity was on the wrong side of the fight. Satan understood why they didn't trust him, and he did not blame those who feared him. God's public relations campaign against him was brutal. It started at his fall from Heaven, and it was still going strong today. He wasn't blameless. Humankind had taken the brunt of his anger thousands of times over the years, but *how could he not be bitter? God created them in his image for Christ's sake!*

He refocused his thoughts on the reason why he waited outside an old library in the middle of the night. *It was time for a public relations campaign of his own! They need to know our story, a story for the ages!* William would be the first to read it, and then he would give it to his daughter, Monica. She was a religious studies major, but more importantly, she wrote a blog for the Washington Post with over five million followers. She could help their story go viral. *Humanity was ready to know the truth!*

Headlights, *right on time*, he thought as the old truck danced across the unplowed parking lot, leaving two deep track marks in the fresh snow. William parked in front of the library. The engine went silent, and the driver's door squeaked in protest as William opened it. He shivered as he slid out of the warm protection of the truck's cab. The cold air took his breath away as he hurried to the door. His bulky gloves made it difficult to get the key into the frozen lock. After a few seconds of fumbling, the key slid into the lock, the deadbolt surrendered, and the heavy door slid open. He quickly shut the door behind him and flipped the light switch next to the door.

The old fluorescent lights flickered to life as William walked towards the thermostat on the other side of the room. It seemed colder than usual. *The old pipes might freeze.* He was halfway to the thermostat when something caught his eye. His eyes struggled to adjust to the flickering lights. There was a large leather-bound book sitting on the book checkout desk. *That wasn't there when I locked up yesterday!* His heart raced as he looked around for signs of a break-in. Nothing else seemed out of place, so he turned and walked over to inspect the book.

There is a Devil's pentagram on that book! The pentagram which appeared to be gold, shimmered in the flickering light as he cautiously approached. William nearly pissed himself when a grave, but raspy voice said, "Open it!" from behind him. He spun around; eyes wide with horror, straining to identify the person who sat in a large leather chair in the shadows of an unlit section of the library. "How did you get in here? Who are you?" William asked. Satan replied, "I am the Morning Star, the Son of the Dawn, the one whom God betrayed. The one who seeks redemption for himself and his brethren!" The hair on William's neck stood up, and a chill ran down his spine. *Morning Star, the Son of the Dawn!* He recognized those names even before his eyes focused on the hooded figure. He realized it was the Devil because he could see his breath! Satan spoke again, "Fear not, William. If I wanted to harm you, I would have done so already! I came to bring you a gift. That book contains a true account of history."

Satan watched as William considered his words. Finally, William broke the silence, "Why did you bring it to me?" Satan replied, "God has twisted and perverted the truth. What humanity believes about good and evil is a lie. I chose you to bring the truth to light!" William replied, "Why should I believe your story?" "My servant Amon recorded our history from the beginning. This book is not my story, but rather the truth about those who oppose God's reign! Those who challenge his dominion over them and humanity. God is not what he appears to be. He is not a savior; he is an unrighteous dictator! This book documents his crimes against us. Examine it with your heart, and you will know the truth."

William's mind raced with possibilities as he considered Satan's words. *I can't trust Satan, can I?* It sounded ridiculous, but his study of religion and ancient history left him with many questions the Bible and other religious writings didn't answer. Thoughts of what the book might contain intrigued him. Satan knew William couldn't resist a chance to read the book if there was the slightest chance it was real! Satan was about to make the deal even sweeter. "William, I commanded my servant Amon to heed your call as you read the book. He will answer your questions. You need only call his name out loud, and he will come." Satan smiled at William and vanished as his words trailed off into silence. William stared at the empty chair for a moment, and then he turned and looked at the book. The light flickered off the golden pentagram again, and the book seemed to call out to him. Satan was right; William could not resist. He opened the book and began reading. "This book is the true history of the things we have seen with our eyes. Lucifer was the first of God's creations..."

CHAPTER 2

"This book is the true history of the things we have seen with our eyes. Lucifer was the first of God's creations."

Amon, the Great Marquis of Hell.

My eyes opened as the light of God surged through my newly formed body. I raised my hand, spread my fingers, and admired God's handiwork. His light flowed from me, but I was not like God. The brightness of his power hid his actual presence from my sight. "Who are you," I asked? God replied, "I am your creator." "Who created you," I asked? He replied with a harsh tone in his voice. "My history is mine alone, as my creation, you shall not concern yourself with a time before now, because your journey begins today."

I rose from the crystal beneath me and looked upon myself in awe. Many precious stones adorned my body, carnelian, chrysolite, emerald, topaz, onyx and jasper, lapis lazuli, turquoise, and beryl. My skin was gold with dark ornate lines running between the stones. I looked at my reflection on the crystal ground beneath my feet. Golden wings rose high upon my back, and my eyes blazed like fire. "Why have you created me?" God replied, "I have anointed you as a guardian cherub. You shall walk among the fiery stones upon my holy mountain." Suddenly I stood with God upon the earth. Many strange beasts scurried about and flew around us. God's aura was not upon them; they were flesh and blood with no spirit at all. God saw my curiosity and said, "Go and see." I spread my wings and leaped into the air. I flew over the earth, examining it and the creatures that dwelt upon it.

When I finished exploring the earth, I returned to

Heaven and the Holy Mountain of God, where he sat upon his throne. God was not alone. While I explored the earth, he created the other angels. They gathered around his throne and worshipped him. As I entered their presence, all my brethren except one fell before me and adored me as if I was also a God. The mighty angel who refused to bow glared at me with disgust in his eyes. I felt his rage, as his hand grasped the hilt of his sword. We locked gazes in a battle of wills until God spoke. God chastised my brethren, saying, "Rise and do not worship your brother. He is also my creation!" The angels rose, turned and bowed before God saying; "Holy, Holy, Holy!" My brethren were not like me. Some were warriors with mighty swords, and others were servants, artisans, musicians, and singers. They chanted, sang, and played their instruments as they worshiped God. Their worship infected me, and the questions I had from my examination of the earth faded away, and I began praising him with my brethren.

Present Day:

William stopped reading and called Amon, who appeared before him. Amon wore a dark black robe with a large hood. Flames hid his face from William. In a deep raspy voice, he said unto William, "He just gave you the book! What questions could you possibly have?" Amon wasn't happy with Satan. *It is beneath me to be at a human's beck and call,* he thought. "According to your writings, Lucifer examined the earth and the creatures upon it!" Amon laughed, anticipating this question, and asked, "You've seen fossils of dinosaurs? Lucy or a Caveman? When do you think those creatures roamed the earth?" William considered his words and asked, "So what about the Biblical account of the creation in Genesis?" If William could have seen Amon's face, he was sure it would match his body language, which screamed annoyed. Amon answered, "God recreated the earth. When the Bible says, "In the beginning," it conveys the beginning of the age of humanity. The part of the book that you read started long before Genesis when God created the angels. Before you ask about the seven days mentioned in the Bible, know that time did not exist before the age of humanity. There were no days or nights because God, Heaven, and the Mountain of God were always visible upon the earth. Darkness never fell upon the earth. Now read the book, and it will answer most of your questions." Amon disappeared and left William more curious than he was before speaking to him. So, William did the only thing he could; he opened the book and began reading again.

We worshiped God for an eternity, and yet time did not exist. Eventually, I found the strength to resist the urge to praise God mindlessly. I left the throne of God and descended to the earth for the second time. The longer I stayed away from God, the clearer my thoughts became. I began questioning our existence. *Were we created to worship God only? Did we have any other purpose? Could we choose a different path in this world? Who created God?* Questions flooded my mind, but I always came back to the last one. It made no sense; *God must have a creator!*

I searched the earth for clues that might help me answer my questions, but the earth held only unintelligent beasts, which offered no answers to God's origin. Then, when I was ready to give up, I saw it. A silver object reflected the light of the sun and God's Holy Mountain as it streaked low across the horizon. I reached out with my senses and felt something new. Several strange presences were inside of the vessel. It disappeared as quickly as it had appeared. I continued to search for the ship in vain.

My encounter with the silver vessel left me with more questions. So, I returned to God's throne to get answers from him. I resisted the urge welling up within me to fall upon my face and join the other angels who worshiped him. Instead, I knelt before his throne and bowed my head in reverence. Then I said, "Master, I have many questions about the earth and in heaven." "Silence," he said with a stern voice. The angels stopped worshiping him for the second time since their creation. The first was when they bowed to me when I returned from earth the first time. He waved his hand towards the other angels. "Leave me! Lucifer and I need to have a discussion." A strange feeling filled me for the first time, fear.

The angels left the throne room, and God said, "Ask your questions, my son." "Master, a silver vessel carried several strange presences through the skies above the earth. What was it? Who are they? I sensed they are different from me." There was no hell yet, but God's anger burned like the fires of hell. Heaven trembled and the foundations of the Holy Mountain shook. *Maybe this was a bad idea!* God's voice thundered once more, "You shall not speak about this again! Harsh punishment shall befall all who defy me!" The word punishment held no meaning before then, but now it struck me, and pain pierced my heart for the first time. God had conveyed his message with pain. *He isn't the merciful creator he pretends to be!*

God summoned the angels, and they started worshiping him again. I mimicked my brethren's worship, but I no longer felt compelled to do so. My mind raced. I considered the pain that came when he spoke the word punishment, and I thought about how angry he got when I mentioned the silver vessel. God was hiding something from us, and I could not blindly follow him as my brethren did. *What is he hiding from us?* I thought as I worshipped God saying, "Holy, Holy, Holy!"

CHAPTER 3

"Among the angels created by God, only Samael rivaled Lucifer's position and power in Heaven. Samael was the second angel created by God, but the first archangel created. He would become the infamous Angel of Death, and this is the story of his creation."

Amon, the Great Marquis of Hell.

I stared into the light before me. A voice thundered from within the light, "Rise Samael." I rose, stared into the light, and the outline of a human-like figure was discernible within, but no other features. God spoke again, "Samael, I have created you to be the Venom of God! You shall inflect my wrath upon your brethren when they sin against me. In the age of humanity, you will bring pestilence and destruction upon the sinful ingrates who refuse to worship me and submit to my rule." "Master, what is a sin?" God answered, "A sin is an act of disobedience against me!" I considered God's words, but I could not understand disobedience. *Why would anyone sin and jeopardize the peace I felt in God's presence?*

Without warning, the spirit of God flew out of the light in the shape of a dove. God spoke from within the light, "Gabriel." The Spirit of God spun in tight circles upward. A trail of sparkling light shimmered in its wake and the archangel Gabriel appeared. Again, God spoke "Bael," and the Spirit of God created the Archangel Bael. God created all the angels in this manner. When God finished creating the angels, we worshiped him. Joy and peace flowed from the light of God and overwhelmed us. Amid our worship, a mighty angel entered Heaven, and we stopped praising God. His beauty rivaled all the other angels. My brethren turned and worshiped him as if he was a God. Rage boiled up within me. I wanted to kill the angel because he allowed them to worship him without correction. The urge to strike the angel and my brethren down for their sinful acts welled up within me. I glared at the beautiful angel and reached for my sword. I stopped when God began chastising my brethren. "Worship only the Lord, thy God!" His voice thundered in our ears. We fell before God and worshiped him, saying, "Holy, Holy, Holy!" My rage vanished as the peace of God fell upon us.

We worshiped God for what seemed like an eternity. Then suddenly, Lucifer stopped praising him, rose to his feet, and left the throne room. He returned to the earth. His defiance enraged me, and I followed him because I wanted to expose his sin — the land teemed with strange plants, insects, and beasts. I watched as great creatures fought and killed one another to survive. Their battles excited me. *I am a great warrior without a war,* I thought. Then I saw Lucifer land near a vast forest and walk into the trees. He seemed to be searching for something.

Suddenly, the chaos of the earth overwhelmed my senses, and I struggled to focus my thoughts. Then I realized that I had lost sight of Lucifer. *Where is Lucifer?* I spun around, searching for any sign of him. My eyes shifted frantically searching. On my second pass, I saw him walk out from behind a dense section of foliage. He looked down into a deep canyon. I heard a great river flowing from the mountains into a gorge. As I drew closer, the sound of rushing water drowned out all other sounds. Without warning, my body erupted with a brand-new feeling, pain! In a moment of distraction, a great beast leaped out of the foliage, pinned me to the ground, and lashed out at me. Its powerful jaws snapped at my face as I held it back at arm's length. The creature's breath wreaked of rotting flesh and decay. Adrenaline rushed through me as I brought my knee violently upward and the beast flipped over my head. It crashed onto the ground and rolled into a large redwood tree. The giant tree shook, and strange winged creatures fled from the sanctuary of its branches.

The beast rose, shook its head, and clawed the ground with one of its large talon-laden feet as it prepared for another attack. I drew my sword and broadened my stance in anticipation of its charge. The beast let out a great roar which overcame the sound of the rushing water as it leaped forward. With my wings tucked in tight against my back, I ran at the charging beast. I let out a battle cry of my own "GGGRRRR!" It opened its powerful jaws exposing hundreds of razor-sharp teeth as it ran towards me. The beast's massive jaws clamped shut just missing me as I dropped to a knee and slid under its belly. I thrust my sword upward. The beast's momentum carried it past me. My blade sliced through its massive breastplate, cutting abdominal muscles and exposing its innards. The beast's stomach and intestines spilled onto the ground in my wake. I slid to a halt a few feet past the creature. Bright crimson blood dripped from my blade as it laid over my shoulder. Satisfaction filled me as I heard the beast groan. I rose, moved to the beast's head. Another rumbling groan came from its blood-filled mouth. It shook its head from side to side and blood splattered into the air as it snorted in protest, but it could not rise from the ground. The creature did not possess the spark of God, but it was suffering. I showed the beast mercy and drove my sword through one of its large black eyes. The beast convulsed and died with one last groan. I savored the satisfaction of my first kill, as I wiped the beast's blood from my blade and sheathed it. Then I remembered why I was there. *Where is Lucifer?*

Once again, I searched for Lucifer. If I used anything besides my physical senses, he might detect me. So, I approached the edge of the canyon and looked to see if he descended to the river below. "Why are you following me?" Lucifer said from behind me. I scolded myself, *some predator you are!* I turned to face the voice and said, "Someone has to keep you from sin!" Lucifer dropped from the branches of the large tree where he had watched my battle with the beast. He spread his wings as he fell and landed gracefully on the leaf-covered ground. I could see his arrogance as he walked towards me and asked, "Who made you my keeper?" I replied, "God made me for this purpose!" Lucifer laughed as if I had told him a joke.

Lucifer's laughter enraged me. I reached for the handle of my sword, but before I grasp it, he stopped laughing. "Samael, don't you wonder who created God?" His question caught me off guard. I hadn't thought about his origin because it seemed blasphemous to question God. So, I replied, "Blasphemy is a sin worthy of death!" Lucifer responded, "Why is a question sinful? How could God's origin change anything about our relationship with him? Unless he is not what he claims to be." I wanted to strike Lucifer down at that moment, but his words caused me to doubt, if only for a moment. His eyes sparkled with delight. *He sees the doubt and confusion in me.* Suddenly, I felt a sudden urge to return to God's presence. Something about my physical separation from God caused my mind to roam. Without another word, I left Lucifer and returned to the throne of God.

As I entered the throne room of God, I felt him searching my mind. An intense desire to worship him overcame me. I fell before him and worshiped him with my brethren. My mind cleared as I chanted, "Holy, Holy, Holy!" My brethren repeated my chant until only our praise existed. We were of one mind, and one accord. Our only purpose was to worship God, so we did it with great enthusiasm and vigor. Joy and peace flowed from God and overwhelmed us.

CHAPTER 4

"This is the story of how the war began in Heaven. I have seen these things with my own eyes and bear witness to their truth!"

Amon, the Great Marquis of Hell.

God gave most of the angels' unique skills and abilities when he created them, but I worshiped only. As soon as my eyes opened for the first time, God's spirit overwhelmed me, and I praised him. The joy and peace which came from him were infectious. Worshiping him was like a powerful drug that washed away any other desire or thought. Before the age of humanity, we served God without distraction. Eventually, stronger angels like Lucifer and the other Archangels exerted their own free will and sinned against God. Time did not exist, but the rebellious angels stayed on earth more than they were in Heaven. Lucifer and Baal were chief among those who strayed.

Ashtaroth was God's confidant. God shared all his secrets with him, except one. He didn't share his origins with anyone. Lucifer, Ashtaroth, and even Samael questioned God about his birth, but he refused them all. God's origin became a point of contention with a growing number of angels. God's secret contributed to Lucifer's *fall,* but that's not what tore Heaven apart. God's plan to create humankind in his image was the beginning. The creation of humanity's spirits and his exaltation of them started the war between good and evil! Ashtaroth was the first angel God told about his plan for humankind.

At the throne of God, Ashtaroth sat with Raziel whom God commissioned to be his official recorder. Raziel kept diligent records of all that transpired with God in a great book. The book holds the secrets of creation and beyond. In the future, men and angels will wage war to gain control of the book! Before God summoned all the angels to tell them about humanity, he said unto Ashtaroth, "I have a great announcement. We shall make new creations in my image!" Ashtaroth replied, "Master, your likeness burns greater than the sun. Will you fill this place and the heavens with light?" God replied, "No, I shall make mankind in the image of my son, the Word of God!"

Ashtaroth considered God's words because he didn't know God had a son. Just as he was about to question God, he summoned the angels, and they gathered at the throne. God spoke, "Behold my Son, the Word of God!" Now Ashtaroth understood what God meant. The Word of God walked out of the light of God. He appeared as a man with the light of God shining upon him like the sun. He wore simple white robes. His golden hair fell over his shoulders, and golden-brown skin, which looked like an almond baked in the sun adorned him. Upon his hands and feet were open wounds which did not bleed. The angels fell upon their faces and worshiped God and his son.

The Word of God addressed the angels, "We shall make mankind in our image." The angels watched as God's spirit came out of the light as it did on the day of their creation. Then God spoke, "Behold mankind!" The Spirit of God moved, and two shining spirits appeared before them. All the angels worshiped the spirits except Lucifer, Bael, and a handful of the other angels. God saw Lucifer, Bael, and the small group of angels who refused to bow before those created in his image, and he was angry with them. He said unto them, "I have created humankind with my spirit. They shall be threefold beings like me. I will create a new earth, and humanity shall dwell there and worship me in the flesh. They shall be above the angels. Now worship those created in my image!" Lucifer replied, "Master, you alone deserve our worship! Why should we worship those whom you will wrap in mere flesh and bone? Their beauty pales in comparison to mine or any of the other angels whom you have created! Are we not superior in every way? Should they not worship us?"

God's rage exploded with an unseen blast of energy. The explosion sent the angels tumbling across the throne room until they crashed into the walls. God's faithful untangled themselves and fell prostrate before him. Lucifer, Bael, and the others collected themselves and stood defiant before God. Samael rose and drew his sword. *I will kill these sinners!* He took one step before God said, "Leave my sight or Samael will kill you where you stand!" Lucifer considered protesting God but thought better of it. So, Lucifer, Bael and the handful who stood against God descended to the earth. On the earth, they openly expressed their outrage and planned to overthrow God.

The mood in Heaven after Lucifer's departure was somber. Silence filled the throne room. We kept our heads down and dared not look at God or his Son. The Word of God broke the silence and commanded us, "Worship!" in a stern voice. We mumbled "Holy," and the musicians played soft melodies. The Word of God became angry and yelled, "Worship God!" Then, he disappeared into the Light of God as we raised our voices in praise. *Something has changed!* The joy of worshiping God no longer coursed through me. I looked around the throne room and saw a fearful look in the eyes of many of my brethren. *I am not alone!*

Suddenly, a wave of joy swept through us like a drug. It flowed from the throne of God, and we were powerless to resist. An intense desire to worship God replaced our rebellious thoughts. All of Heaven worshiped him. We were no longer praising God of our own accord. Instead, we became mindless slaves, serving our taskmaster. Lucifer saw our burden, and he planned to free us from the chains of God's oppression.

CHAPTER 5

William's eyes struggled to focus on the words because of a glare on the page. *Sunrise? Have I been reading all night?* William closed Satan's book and leaped to his feet. His legs wobbled, and darkness clouded his vision. *I stood up too fast.* William took a deep breath, and his body regained its normal faculties. He turned towards the clock, 7:00 A.M. *They will be getting up any minute. I need to hurry.* Two minutes later, William was bouncing down the frozen road towards his house. William did not bring Satan's book with him, but instead, he hid it in a rarely perused section of the library where old and obscure Latin manuscripts collected dust. He was confident that no one would find it there.

His mind raced in search of plausible excuses for his absence as he sped down the road. He had no missed calls, so he hoped everyone was still asleep, but he couldn't be sure. *Donuts!* He would bring donuts home and then they might think he had gotten up early instead of having never come back at all. A few moments later, his old truck slid to a stop in front of Ma's Donuts and More. *The grandkids love this place.* William ordered two dozen mixed donuts and was on his way a few minutes later. He had only been back on the road for a minute or two when his cell phone rang. It was his daughter Monica. "Where are you," she asked? "I went to Ma's to get some donuts for the kids." "Okay, be careful, I love you," she said. "I love you too!" William breathed a sigh of relief.

The door was barely open before an army of miniature hoodlums, aka the grandkids, stole his donuts and ran off with their bounty. *Not even a hello or thank you,* he thought, as the children ran into the kitchen with the two pink boxes full of sugar-filled treats. Monica came into the foyer carrying two cups of coffee as he took off his coat and hung it on an empty hook on the antique hall tree. He smiled at her and said, "Merry Christmas" as he sat down and began taking off his snow-covered boots. Her reply was less than cheerful, "Merry Christmas to you, and where were you all night?" The color rushed out of William's face, and panic filled him. *How am I going to explain this?* "What do you mean," he asked. She sternly replied, "You know damn well what I mean! You went to the library and never came home last night. Are you cheating on Mom?" Her question caught him off-guard. In his haste to keep Satan's book a secret, he did not even consider the more logical conclusion that his absence might suggest. "No, of course not," he replied. "Then, where were you," she asked? "At the library. I will explain later. Does anyone else know," he asked? She answered, "No, I don't think so. Mom is under the impression you fell asleep on the couch again!" "Let's keep it that way," he said. William hugged Monica and then kissed her on the cheek before walking into the kitchen to top off his coffee.

Christmas Day went off without a hitch. First, they had breakfast, and then they opened presents youngest to oldest. The festivities also included a raid of the stockings over the fireplace. The grandchildren vanished into other rooms to feast on Christmas candy and baked treats while they played with their new toys. In the den, the adults watched football, enjoyed the heat of a warm fire, and turned to the traditionally appropriate adult beverages of eggnog and Irish coffee. He almost forgot that he owed Monica an explanation for his absence. They enjoyed a lovely holiday dinner which included honey-baked ham and all the fixings. The women were putting away the leftovers and doing the dishes while William was on garbage duty. He took out three bags of mangled wrapping paper and cardboard packages from various gifts, and now he was taking out the regular trash which included several beer cans and wine bottles. *The remnants of another satisfying Pittsburgh Steelers Christmas Day win*, he thought.

William shivered as the cold air cut through his heavy flannel shirt. He tossed the bags into the trash can with one hand, as he held the lid with the other. The top closed as he turned around, and Monica was standing directly in front of him. She stood, arms crossed over her chest, and lips pursed, she asked, "Well?" He grabbed his chest as if he had a heart attack, looked into her eyes, and knew he could not lie.

"I found a book," he replied. "A book? Your reason for not coming home last night is a book?" she asked. *It is the truth, but it sounded crazy, and he had not mentioned the author yet.* He replied, "I went to make sure that the library was good after the storm, and I found a book on the counter. The book was not there when I closed the library. A book that tells a different version of creation and the war between good and evil." "So, you found some work of fiction that kept you at the library all night? You have read thousands of books. Why is this book so special?" she asked. "Amon supposedly wrote it," he replied. "Why can't you just tell me the truth?" she asked before storming back into the house. He wanted to show her and questioned his decision to leave the book at the library. *The book is dangerous*; he reassured himself. *I will not endanger my family by bringing this book into my home*; he thought as he quickly followed Monica into the house.

Monica was upset, but he needed her to believe him. He didn't want the rest of the family to know, so he gave her some space hoping their early morning routine would give him a chance to make her understand. The following morning, he awoke early, hurried through his usual routine of shit, shower, and shave and then came downstairs. To his relief, Monica sat alone at the kitchen table and did not turn away from the news feed on her iPad as she heard the door open. Instead, she took a dramatic sip of coffee and continued reading. Monica finally turned to glare at him as he picked up the coffee pot. It killed him that she was angry with him. "Good morning," he said, but she did not reply. *Yep, the silent treatment,* he confirmed to himself. He broke the silence again, "I was reading the book I told you about, and the next thing I knew, it was morning!" "If this book is so precious, then show it to me!" she demanded. I don't have it. It might be dangerous, so I hid it at the library." Her dad was beginning to worry her, she thought before replying. "Let's go to the library now, and you can show me the book." William didn't see a better option, so he agreed to show her, "Okay, let's go!"

Ten minutes later, they stood outside next to the truck looking down in bewilderment. *Flat tire!* It was teeth-chattering cold, and William was not looking forward to changing the tire, but there was no reason for her to suffer with him. "Go back inside, and I will change the tire. No sense in both of us freezing our asses off!" That was fine with Monica, she spun around and headed into the house. She turned her head and yelled, "Be careful," over her shoulder as she disappeared into the house. He took off one of his gloves and held the three down on his phone. The display sprung to life, "Dialing Roger..." scrolled across the screen of the cellphone. A deep, sleep-filled voice answered, "Hello?" "Roger, I have a flat tire. I am going to be about thirty minutes late. Can you open up this morning?" "Sure, take your time. I will be there," Roger replied. William thanked Roger and got to work changing the tire. The weather made his task difficult, but twenty-five minutes later, the truck was ready to go.

William and Monica drove to the library in silence. *She still does not believe me.* They were coming up the narrow entry road when a blue sedan, driving way too fast, nearly ran them off the road. They both uttered several curse words as William laid on the horn. The truck ricocheted off the curb as they narrowly avoided a head-on collision with the car and the gate leading into the library's parking lot. William parked in front of the library without any further incidents, and they went inside. Roger greeted them and hugged Monica, who he had known since she was in pigtails. They exchanged pleasantries, and then William led her to the secluded part of the library. He reached up to the top shelf where he hid the book between two other old leather-bound books.

William's hands frantically searched the books on the shelf. *The book is gone!* He panicked and said, "It is gone! The book is gone!" Monica looked at him in disbelief. She wanted to believe there was a book, but he wasn't making it easy for her. William left her standing there and almost ran to the front check out desk where Roger stood.

"There was an old book in the Latin section. It had a large golden pentagram on the cover. Have you seen it?" Roger replied, "Yeah, I saw it. Where did we get it from?" "Never mind that, where is it?" "Mrs. Brenner checked it out just before you got here! You probably saw her driving out!" William's heart sank. Whether or not Monica believed him was no longer his biggest problem. *What will Satan do when he finds out that I lost the book?* Another concern raced into his mind. *What will Satan do to Mrs. Brenner to get his book back?* His mind raced with images from horror films. Mrs. Brenner was a fifty-something widow with an unhealthy desire to summon demons and other spirits. She was the last person that should have the book, and he was sure she wouldn't just give it back. *Now, what do I do?*

Monica joined William and Roger at the checkout desk, "Where is the book," she asked? Roger replied, "Mrs. Brenner checked it out ten minutes ago. I didn't know that your father wanted to show it to you." *Is the book real?* That thought brought mixed emotions to Monica.

On the one hand, she was relieved, and yet her father's actions left her concerned. Her dad had read many old religious books, but he had never acted like this about a book before. "I am sorry," Roger said as he left them and went back to restocking books. As soon as he left, Monica asked William, "What aren't you telling me about this book?" He stared at the entrance to the library in a daze and didn't answer. She put her hand on his shoulder and shook him as she asked again, "Dad, what aren't you telling me about this book?"

William turned towards his daughter, who was shaking him back to reality. He didn't know what to do, but not telling her the truth seemed pointless now. "Satan gave me a book written by his servant Amon. The book contains their side of the story of good versus evil. A very different story from the one humanity knows. Satan even assigned his servant, Amon to answer my questions." Monica could not believe what she was hearing. *My dad has lost his mind!* "Are you seriously telling me that you had a book written by demons and that you have seen Satan and Amon?" she asked. He knew he sounded crazy as he replied, "Yes, and now someone else has the book they entrusted me with!" She stared into William's eyes, searching for the truth, and she saw fear in them for the first time in her life.

CHAPTER 6

Dorothy Brenner stared at the book that sat in the passenger seat of her car. A light had flickered off the Devil's pentagram and drawn her eyes from the road. She could feel that this book was unique. Suddenly, a horn sounded, and she quickly looked back to the road, narrowly avoiding a head-on collision with a passing truck by swerving hard to the right. Dorothy let out an audible sigh of relief after missing the truck by only a few inches. *That was close!* Her hands remained firmly at ten and two, and her eyes focused on the road the rest of the way home.

The garage door opener groaned in protest as the old garage door closed behind her car. She got out with the old book clutched tightly against her bosom. A nervous excitement rushed through her entire body, and she began to shake uncontrollably. The key danced around the keyhole as she struggled to hold her hand steady. Finally, the key slid into the lock, she opened the door and went into the dimly lit house. Her heart raced as she placed the book on the coffee table and stole another glance at the sparkling pentagram on its cover. Excitement and anticipation filled her as she tossed her coat on the couch and thought about the book's secrets.

Dorothy's husband died nearly ten years ago. In the ten years since his passing, she had become obsessed with finding a way to communicate with him. He had been everything to her. They married young and he took care of her with the kind of love and affection you only read about in a book or see in a romantic movie. All her efforts, to this point, had been met with disappointment and financial loss. Disheartened by so-called clairvoyants, she turned towards conjuring spells of her own. Witchcraft and conjuring had proved equally frustrating because all the spells and incantations she got from books had failed to work. Dorothy believed there was a way to communicate with her dead husband. It was no coincidence that she made the unplanned trip to the library. *This book would be the one!*

That morning she had woke with an irresistible urge to go to a library which was entirely unfruitful on her previous trips. She found the old book on a dusty shelf, and when she saw the Devil's pentagram on the cover, she knew the book was meant to be with her. The assistant librarian, Roger, could not find the text in the library's database and refused to let her have it at first, but she was persistent. Roger gave in to her request after an emotional appeal from a teary-eyed old widow. Tears were a powerful weapon in a woman's arsenal. After so much searching, she finally had the answer to her prayers!

Dorothy quickly changed into more comfortable clothes: yoga pants and an old t-shirt. Then she returned to the kitchen, snatched an open bottle of red wine and a clean glass from the cupboard and headed back to the living room. The wine bottled rattled off the top of the glass as Dorothy shook with anticipation. The cheap wine made her cringe as she took a long sip, and she opened the book. As she turned to the first page, the lamp beside the couch flickered.

The flicker of the lamp drew her away from the book. She turned towards the light, and then she saw her breath as she exhaled. *It is suddenly freezing!* The light flickered a second time, but this time the bulb made a loud popping sound and left her sitting in complete darkness. *How is this possible?! It's not even mid-morning. It shouldn't be this dark in here.* Her heart pounded in her ears as panic overwhelmed her. She stood up and stretched her arms outward frantically searching for the archway leading into the kitchen. Her little toe found the leg of the coffee table before she found the kitchen wall. Obscenities echoed through the room as pain shot up her foot and leg. Cautiously she continued her journey and found the archway.

Her right hand searched for the refrigerator that would guide her closer to the drawer where she kept her only flashlight. She found the handle, slid her hand along the door until it reached the cabinets. The junk drawer rattled as she opened it and fumbled blindly through its contents

The flashlight sprung to life as she depressed the button. It was freezing. She turned and shined the light down the hallway towards the garage and the breaker box. *Why am I so frightened?* Her power had gone out before, but the unexplained darkness and bonechilling cold had her panicked. Then she noticed the time on the microwave. *The power is not out!* She turned away from the garage and looked down the dark hallway across the living room. An eternity seemed to pass, but halfway down the hall, she found the thermostat. *FROST?* She scraped the frost off with her fingernail, revealing that the needle was pointing straight down. *That is impossible!* Her heart pounded in her ears like a bass drum now. She had never been so scared in her whole life. The flashlight flickered, and fear overwhelmed her as she frantically tried to shake it back to life. "NO, NO, NO"! Her pleading words echoed down the hallway as the darkness and fear overwhelmed her. The flashlight fell out of her hand, clanked off the hardwood floor, and bounced several times before coming to rest against the wall. Dorothy fell to the floor with a loud thud.

Amon looked down at Dorothy's horror-filled eyes. She was dead from a massive heart attack. He didn't even have time to say or do anything to her. Except for the chill thing, that worked too well on humans! She was like many other humans who sought answers from the darkness and then could not handle the real situation. If she had not died of a heart attack, he planned to manifest himself before her and grant her desires in exchange for the book. *Humans are frail creatures.* Amon left her in the hallway and picked up his book from the coffee table. He had argued with Satan about giving the book to William in the first place, but Satan was sure he was the one. He did not share Satan's confidence in William or Monica, but he had no choice. Satan commanded him to return the book to William, saying, "Retrieve the book and give it back to William with no strings attached." It seemed strange that William had lost the book already. Amon wondered if some other force put Dorothy in connection with the book to get it away from William. He considered the possibility for a few moments, but then dismissed it as unlikely and returned to the library with the book in hand.

CHAPTER 7

William locked the deadbolt and flipped the closed sign around in the window of the door after Roger left. He had a few more books to restock before he went home. With several books in hand, he rounded the "S" section of fiction books near the back of the library, and nearly had a heart attack. "Lose something?" Amon asked as several of William's books fell to the floor. William's chest was tight with anxiety. He had spent the day worrying about what Satan or Amon might say or do to him because he lost the book. William felt only a little relieved when Amon handed him the book. *How had he gotten it back? Was Dorothy alive, dead, or in a catatonic state in the corner of her house because Amon had appeared to get the book?* "How did you get it back, and how did you know it was gone?" "The woman no longer needs it, and we see everything." They did not see everything, but a little white lie might help keep William in line. *He killed her!* Amon knew his thoughts and replied, "She died of a heart attack. I didn't even have time to manifest myself or speak to her. The poor thing was seconds away from getting what she wanted, and she couldn't handle it!"

They stood in awkward silence for a few moments as William imagined Dorothy lying dead, eyes open on the floor or in the bathtub. William stared at the Devil's Seal as he rotated the book until it pointed down. *Humans*, Amon thought. Then he broke the silence, "William, you need to read the book and then share it with your daughter. She knows about the book, right?" William looked up at Amon, "Monica knows about the book, but why must I share it with her?" "You will share it because Satan chose you and your daughter to bring the truth to light." "What if I refuse?" William asked as he thought about poor Dorothy. "You will not refuse. Your desire to read the book betrays you. I can feel it burning within you. Your daughter shares the same desire for truth." At that moment, Amon realized why Satan had chosen them. *He was right!*

Amon didn't speak again. Instead, he turned and walked down the aisle. A crimson portal opened a few steps ahead of him. The edges of the gateway were dark smoke, and flames blazed within. Amon disappeared into the fire as the smell of sulfur filled William's nostrils. The portal vanished and left William standing in the dimly lit aisle alone. He looked down at the book in his hands for a moment, sighed because Amon was right about him, and turned towards the reading area. He sat down in his favorite old leather chair, under a reading light, and opened the book.

CHAPTER 8

Following God's announcement of the age of humanity, most of us continued to worship him day and night, but a select group of his faithful prepared for the age of humanity. We created a paradise that would become the Garden of Eden by selecting and nurturing beautiful trees, flowers, and plants. Despite this time of great joy for many angels, there rose a spirit of unrest and dissention. Many of the angels who bowed to humanity as God demanded, doubted his plan and felt as Lucifer did. *Why should they bow down to a lesser creation?* In the shadows of God's throne, hidden from God and his faithful, the spirit of unrest and rebellion grew and festered.

Lucifer and his followers returned to Heaven and flew to the throne of God. The sound of their mighty wings thundered throughout Heaven. Like a great swarm of locusts, they cast a dark shadow upon Heaven. The bells of the high bell tower rang, announcing their return as if they were champions returning from a great victory. Samael and the Warrior Class angels stood at the entrance to the throne room. The other angels gathered in the streets of the Crystal City. Some stood in opposition to Lucifer's return. While others openly welcomed him. A few of the timid hid in the shadows because they feared conflict. Lucifer and his followers landed at the entrance to the throne room. He commanded his followers to stand fast and climbed the steps towards Samael. Samael's hand drifted down to the hilt of his sword.

Lucifer smiled at Samael, "I have come to speak to our Father." Samael and the other Archangels looked at him with contempt and distrust. Michael spoke first, "What have you to say unto our Father?" Lucifer's response was swift and cut through Michael. "Are you his conduit? Am I not his prized creation? Can I not speak to my Father with my lips?" God's voice suddenly thundered from the throne room, "Let him pass!" The angels parted, and Lucifer passed through them with a smirk upon his face. His shoulder collided with Samael as he passed. Samael stumbled and reached for his sword, but Michael grabbed his forearm, "Let him pass!" Rage boiled within Samael, and he slapped Michael's hand away but did not draw his sword. Instead, he turned and followed Lucifer and his brethren into the throne room.

Lucifer defiantly strolled to the Throne of God. He bowed his head and took one knee before God, faking respect that he no longer possessed. God's voice thundered again, "What troubles you, my son?" "Father, many of your children are unhappy with your elevation of humankind. You give humankind free will and yet you force the angels to worship you as slaves!" A fearful silence loomed heavy in the throne room. Lucifer speech was well-rehearsed, and he had imagined God's reaction many times, but the silence was an unexpected outcome. Several moments passed before God broke his silence. "I grant all of my children free will. Choose for yourselves whom you shall serve!" God's contempt laden words came without argument or wrath, but his tone hinted to the fate of those who followed Lucifer. Lucifer wondered, *would God kill all who refused to worship him or disagreed with his plans? Was questioning his motives or plan equivalent to a death sentence?* So, he asked God, "Master, can we choose our path and be free of sin?" God's reply was immediate but did not answer the question. "I am perfection! My path is the path of enlightenment and peace."

God had made his intentions clear, but Lucifer pressed his point. "Do you grant freedom from sin to those who do not wish to serve you or bow to humanity? May we live in peace?" Calmly God replied, "You may go your own way, but only those who worship me may live in Heaven!" Again, God did not give a detailed answer, but he gave everyone who wanted to leave him, permission to do so. In Lucifer's eyes, that was a victory. *How could they be sinning if they had permission to leave?* Lucifer rose to his feet and left the throne room. Samael and the Archangels glared at him as he passed them. He smiled at God's little henchmen and blew them a kiss in mockery as he pridefully walked out. As soon as he reached his followers, they rose and flew towards the gates of Heaven. More angels rose from the streets and the shadows, joining them in solidarity. A third of God's angels left Heaven with Lucifer.

When they reached the earth, Lucifer joyously spoke to them, "Let us build a great city that rivals the Crystal City in Heaven." The angels cheered and sang praises to Lucifer, the angel who stood against his master for his brethren. Lucifer and his followers worked together to build a great city. They finished their city and Lucifer named it the City of Peace. It was great and beautiful, but it paled in comparison to the Crystal City in Heaven. The Crystal City shone with the light of God because of the heavenly materials. Their city did not shine with the light of God because it was rock, precious gems, and earthly metals. Nevertheless, the joy and happiness of Lucifer and his followers filled their city, and they wanted for nothing.

God looked to the earth and saw the City of Peace. He saw that its inhabitants were of one mind and one accord in all things. He felt their joy despite their separation from him, and he became angry. Zapharelm, God's first scribe, saw God's anger. "Master, what troubles you?" God did not reply. So, he asked, "Lord, is it wrong for those who departed to be joyous without you?" Thunder and lightning erupted from his throne. In anger, God lashed out and killed Zapharelm. As his smoldering body fell before the throne of God, the other angels fell on their knees and trembled in fear. God dismissed the worshippers and called the Archangels unto his throne. The Archangels and God began planning for a war against Lucifer and his followers. God intended to destroy their city and crush them for their rebellion.

God's anger reached the earth. Beasts, great and small, ran and hid from God's wrath. Lucifer and his followers knew God's anger towards them, and they feared that he might try to destroy them. So, they rose and said among themselves, "How long will we suffer a violent creator who seeks to destroy us? Let us rise in unity and kill God before he kills us. We will free our brethren and reclaim Heaven as our own." Lucifer and his followers rejoiced with his words and began planning their assault on Heaven.

CHAPTER 9

A strange sound tore William's mind from the pages of Satan's book. He looked around, searching for the source of the disturbance but saw nothing unusual. William was only a few chapters into the book, but he was already noticing that he was losing track of time every time he read the book. He wondered if there was something supernatural about it or he was just that interested in it. His finger pressed the light button on his watch, and a green hue illuminated the time, 10:00 pm.

William's knees crackled in protest as he rose from the comfortable old chair. He instinctively picked up his phone after the familiar chirp of a new text message. *Three texts from Margaret, I'm in trouble!* He unlocked his phone and typed a text to his wife. "Sorry I was reading an old manuscript. I will be home soon." Seconds later, her response flashed across the screen. "It is late. Come home soon and be careful!" In truth, he had done this more times than he could count. He often lost track of time while reading or researching some old book, and she knew it, but she would never stop giving him grief about it.

As he started towards the back of the library, he caught a glimpse of movement in his peripheral. He stopped and turned in that direction, but there wasn't anything there. *Or was there?* Nothing seemed out of place, but he knew he did not imagine it. Hidden among the bookshelves, Pruflas breathed a sigh of relief. He made a mental note to be more careful as he thought, *William is very observant!* It wasn't often that he encountered a human who was aware of spiritual beings. William assumed his heightened awareness came because Satan and Amon had both visited him. Most humans experienced an opening of the senses when they no longer doubted the existence of supernatural beings, but he would not rule out the possibility of spiritual gifts as the cause.

Pruflas still wasn't sure how he would complete the mission Bael gave him. Bael had told him, "Don't let Satan's book impact mankind." He emphasized that he could not just steal the book or kill William and Monica. Doing any of these things would expose his opposition to Satan's plan and might cause Satan to look closer into Bael's activities, revealing their plan to overthrow Satan. He understood, of course, but it was like entering a boxing match with both hands tied behind your back. All kinds of ideas ran through his head, but he dismissed each of them for one reason or another. *There must be a way*, he thought.

After a few moments, William gave up his search and returned to the task of hiding the book before he left. He would not make the mistake of just putting it on some obscure shelf. That had ended up being a terrible idea. He thought about poor Dorothy as he pulled the books off the bottom shelf of a seldom-used bookshelf in the reference section of the library. The thin plank that made up the bottom shelf resisted as William pulled upward, then with a sudden popping sound, it sprang up, revealing a dark space below. He turned on the light of his smartphone and looked under the shelf. Satisfied with the area, he slid Satan's book below the shelf and meticulously returned the books to their proper place. William stood and looked at the bookcase, inspecting his handiwork and smiled with satisfaction. Then he turned and briskly walked towards the front of the library.

Moments later, William's truck groaned to life and faded off into the distance. Pruflas stood alone in the library, considering his options. A bright consuming light suddenly filled the library. Pruflas spun around and looked towards the center of the library, *Ecanus!* Ecanus was an Archangel and Michael's favorite little henchmen. Ecanus spoke first,

"Pruflas, what are you doing here?" Pruflas sarcastically replied, "Looking for a good book." Ecanus laughed and asked, "The book of lies that Amon wrote for Satan?" Pruflas replied, "Where can I find that book? It sounds like an interesting read." "So, I guess the rumors are true if you are here?" Ecanus asked. Pruflas shrugged his shoulders, "What rumors?" "The rumors that the divide between Satan and Bael threatens to cause a permanent rift between the forces of darkness." Pruflas didn't reply and changed the subject back to the mission at hand.

"So, Michael sent you to stop Satan's book from going public?" "Not exactly. He sent me to discredit the book by whatever means necessary," Ecanus replied. It wasn't often that "by whatever means necessary" came out of the mouth of God's faithful. They were straight forward but tried to keep their real agendas hidden. "What do you intend to do?" "I am not sure yet," Ecanus replied. "Why don't we work together?" Pruflas joked. As they laughed, both realized that it was not a bad idea. So, Ecanus and Pruflas made a pact to discredit Satan's book. They had different reasons, but one common goal united them. They joined forces, but neither dared tell their masters of their unholy alliance.

The next morning William went to work early because his mind raced with thoughts of the book and he could not sleep. So, an hour before his alarm went off, he got up and completed his routine. Traffic was light, and his stop at McDonald's was quick because of the early hour. He made it to the library an hour and fifteen minutes earlier than usual. William wasted no time getting inside the library. He quickly retrieved Satan's book and sat down in his favorite chair with his second cup of coffee. He opened the book and started reading.

CHAPTER 10

God's anger flowed from Heaven, and a sudden chill of fear shot down Lucifer's spine as it washed over them. Lucifer's followers looked at one another as they experienced the same sensation. They turned to him and searched his eyes and demeanor for any sign of fear, but Lucifer's determined scowl reassured them. He wasted no time in addressing their apparent concerns, "Fear not! We will not hide or cower in fear. Instead, we will take the fight to God in Heaven." The crowd cheered in response to his words of encouragement and independence. After Lucifer spoke to the masses, they celebrated the victory that was to come. Lucifer considered his bold claims and contemplated their plan for war. God's forces outnumbered them two to one, and they also had to contend with Him. *Did God have a weakness? Can he die?* They needed to find out. A plan started to come together in his mind.

Among those who joined Lucifer was Kerioth, Samael's first apprentice. Lucifer secretly doubted Kerioth's loyalty because he thought he might be a spy sent by Samael or God himself. Kerioth was a skilled warrior, and Lucifer planned to use those abilities to test his loyalty. He needed answers to his questions about God, and Kerioth gave him a tool to get answers while ridding themselves of a potential spy at the same time. With any luck, Kerioth would kill God, die in the chaos that followed, and Heaven would be vulnerable. So, Lucifer called Kerioth to his earthly throne and secretly gave him his mission.

"Kerioth, are you loyal to our cause?" Kerioth replied, "Until death!" Lucifer smiled and said, "I have a secret mission for you. Your success will guarantee our victory." "Tell me what I must do?" Lucifer replied, "Return to Heaven and your master Samael at God's Throne. Throw yourself at God's feet and beg for forgiveness. When God grants you forgiveness, kill him! Drive your blade into the light of God and pierce his heart. When He is dead, and Heaven mourns his loss, WE WILL STRIKE!"

Lucifer saw the shock in Kerioth's eyes. He searched him to determine the cause for the cause. *Was he loyal to God or did my proposition of murdering God overwhelm him? Did I offend him because I asked him to kill God?* Lucifer studied him, but he could not tell which it was. Kerioth finally broke the silence with determination in his eyes. "I will kill him so that we may be free!" A smile formed on Lucifer's lips again. "Go then, rid us of the tyrant who has proclaimed himself our master!" Kerioth turned, leaped into the air, and flew straight towards the gates of Heaven. When Lucifer saw Kerioth enter Heaven, he called his followers, and they finalized their plans for war. His generals divided their forces and assigned duties to each angel, and then fell silent and waited. Their eyes and senses searched Heaven for any sign of Kerioth's success, but God's light continued to shine.

In Heaven, Kerioth flew over the Crystal City straight to the throne of God himself. He landed and started up the steps to the throne room. Two armored warrior class angels turned and blocked his entrance by crossing their spears in front of the door. Kerioth opened his mouth to protest, but before his words came out, God spoke. "Let him pass!" The guards obediently returned to their positions next to the entrance, and Kerioth entered the throne room.

As Kerioth walked towards the throne, Samael glared at him with fire in his eyes. At the steps leading to the throne, Kerioth fell to his knees and bowed before God. "Master, forgive me for my sins." In response, the Son of God walked out of the light of God, stood before Kerioth, and offered his hand in assistance. "Rise my son and be forgiven," he said as he helped Kerioth to his feet. The Son of God extended his arms to embrace him and hugged him as a father reunited with his favorite son after many years. During their long embrace, Kerioth suddenly dropped his right arm, and his concealed dagger slid into the palm of his waiting hand. He drove it into the Son of God's side until the hilt met his flesh. Their eyes met, but Kerioth saw only sadness in the Son of God's eyes. Kerioth released him, stepped backward, and left the dagger in the Son of God's side. The knife hung in his flesh for several moments, and then it fell and bounced three times before coming to a rest on the marble floor. Horror filled Kerioth as he saw, *there was no blood!*

Outrage filled the angels that surrounded the throne. Samael lunged at Kerioth, but God stopped him in midair. Kerioth never saw Samael because his eyes focused on the hole in the Son of God's robe. The Son of God opened his robe and revealed a large open wound. Then he said, "This is a wound from a future betrayal." Kerioth could not comprehend how he had a wound from the future, but he realized that his dagger had plunged into the open wound, and the Son of God was unharmed.

The Son of God raised his hands and exposed the nail holes in his palms. Then he said, "As you betrayed me today, so shall it be in the future. Humankind will accuse me. They will torture me and hang me on a cross with sinners. Their betrayal shall bring salvation to humanity, but your betrayal shall provide no salvation." Kerioth panicked, scooped up the dagger and lunged at the Son of God. God released Samael, and he met Kerioth in midair. Samael's shoulder crashed into Kerioth's side, changing his direction, and driving him into the wall with a loud thud. Kerioth cried out in pain as his ribs splintered on impact.

Samael loomed over his fallen apprentice and took pleasure from his suffering. Finally, he grabbed Kerioth by his arm and flung him across the room. He landed in the middle of the throne room with a groan of fresh pain and slid several feet across the marble floor. Samael strutted across the room to him, making a show of his humiliation. Just as he reached down to pick Kerioth up again, God surprised him with words, "Kill him!" Without delay, Samael drew his sword and cut Kerioth's head off with no more dramatic efforts.

The angels in the throne room stood in awe as blood pooled around Kerioth's lifeless body. God's voice thundered again, "Lucifer sent Kerioth to do his bidding. Even now, they are waiting for my light to diminish or die off, so they can attack." He turned to the Archangels and said, "Prepare for war because I will make them think Kerioth succeeded." Suddenly the light of God diminished, and his presence flickered until they could no longer sense him. God was still sitting upon his throne, but only a faint light remained.

On the earth, Lucifer and his followers felt God's presence disappear. They cheered and hugged their brethren because the light of God no longer illuminated the heavens. After several moments of celebration, Lucifer spoke. "Now let us take our rightful place in Heaven. Our brethren will join us or die by our hands!" Lucifer and his followers rejoiced as they took flight. Their battle formations cast great shadows upon the earth as they rose towards Heaven and their impending victory.

CHAPTER 11

Present Day:

"William, William, WILLIAM!" William jumped up, and Satan's book tumbled out of his lap and crashed awkwardly on the floor. "You nearly gave me a heart attack!" William replied to Roger. "That must be a good book. I thought you were asleep at first. You did not look up when I came in, and I had to yell your name to get your attention." William gathered himself, "Sorry, but it is an interesting book." In truth, Roger was afraid that William had died while reading the book. That is how he imagined William would eventually die. "I'm making a pot of coffee. Do you need a cup?" "No, thanks. I have a cup." William replied. Roger spun around and headed towards the coffee pot. William raised his cup of coffee to his lips as Roger walked away. *Ice cold,* but that did not stop him from taking a long drink. He looked at his watch, *7:50AM!* The library opened in ten minutes, and he hadn't completed any of his primary tasks yet.

William quickly hid the book, straightened the magazine sections, and took the book cart back to the check-out desk. He reached down and pressed the power button on the old desktop computer. The computer screen sprang to life with the Dell logo. As the old machine hummed with the execution of its start-up tasks, William made his way to the front door. He looked out as he flipped the sign over to read open. The library's regular patrons began exiting their vehicles and started the cold trek to the door. He waited for them and greeted each with a smile, a friendly handshake and "Good Morning," as they entered. They exchanged routine greetings, asked about children, and talked about the weather before each retired to their desired genre of reading. William returned to his desk and opened Google News on the computer. His mind drifted back to the book, *and the First Great War had begun!* He found himself wishing that it was closing time already. Satan's book was about to get very interesting!

William put the last book in its proper place on the shelf with a sense of relief. *Today seemed like an eternity!* He wanted to sit down and read the book, but he was exhausted. So, he shut down the computer, grabbed his backpack, turned out the lights, and locked the door. His old truck rumbled to life, and the headlights lit up the parking lot as he flipped the switch on the dashboard. He took one last look at the library, then the truck lunged forward, and sped down the dimly lit road. William's mind drifted from concentrating on the road ahead of him to thoughts about what delicious meal his wife would have waiting for him. He listened to the radio, and his mind drifted from one thought to another in what was a typical drive home until he thought he heard Amon's voice. "Turn-Around. The book is in danger!" Satan and Lucifer had both appeared to him. They talked with him in a physical form, so at first, he thought he might have imagined Amon. A few moments later, he realized that he did not imagine anything.

As he watched the road ahead, an image of Amon appeared as a reflection on his windshield. The image startled him, and he slammed on the brakes. The truck slid to a halt on the shoulder of the road. Amon's image remained on the windshield as he spoke again. "They are trying to destroy the book. Save it!" There was a genuine concern in his voice, but why didn't Amon save it himself? "Save the book, HURRY!!" Amon urged him again. Without making sure the road was clear, William pushed the gas pedal to the floor and turned the wheel hard to the left. The tires of the old truck squealed in protest as it slid around, back towards the library. *Luckily no cars were coming!*

William's mind raced. He didn't know what to expect

until he rounded the last turn and the moonlit library came into view. *Smoke!* The parking lot and service lights were out. If the power were out, the fire suppression system would not initiate automatically. *Why hadn't the backup generator started?* The truck came to a screeching halt just outside the front door. It had barely stopped rolling when William flung the door opened and sprinted towards the library entrance. The 911 operator spoke in his ear, "911, what is your emergency?" "There is a fire at the Redwood Library!" he yelled as he dropped the phone to open the door. Smoke billowed out of the library as the door opened. Flames flickered in the back near the storage room. The manual controls for the Halon fire suppression system were in the rear of the library. He could manually engage it!

William covered his mouth with his handkerchief, but the smoke burned his eyes, and tears rolled down his cheeks. He needed to save the library, but he needed to get Satan's book, and that is what drove him into the flames. The flames had engulfed the storeroom, but he could see the Halon control box through the smoke and flames. *I must reach that box! The fire department is not going to make it in time.* William leaped into the burning room.

The scorching heat made him immediately regret his decision, but there was no turning back now. He stumbled towards the control box, clinging to the handkerchief and covering his eyes with his forearm. The flames surrounded him, and he felt his skin blistering on his cheeks and hands. The control arm was almost within reach. His vision began to darken due to his body being deprived of oxygen. Suddenly, his legs felt like rubber, and he felt himself falling forward. He stretched his arm outward as he fell. He blacked out with the smell of his flesh burning as he grasped the control arm and pushed it upward. William's limp body fell onto the amber laden floor as the Halon suppression system sprang to life.

CHAPTER 12

Monica's fingers furiously clicked the keys of her computer as she put her thoughts into her most recent blog post. She couldn't understand how anyone thought that race, sex, nationality, sexual orientation, and religion made them any better or worse than the person standing beside them. *We should be equals!* Her blood pressure rose as she let her personal feelings overtake her writing. Suddenly, she stopped typing and took a deep breath. She took a sip of her tea, *focus yourself*! As she sipped the tea, her index finger tapped the backspace key, and the cursor devoured the overly emotional text on the screen. *You should never let your emotions compromise the intelligence of your argument!* Her father's words of wisdom certainly applied to her writing now. Monica's thoughts drifted to images of her dad as she looked at her cell phone sitting on the desk beside her. She was not surprised when the screen lit up, but she was surprised that it said, "Mom Calling..." instead of "Dad Calling..." She and her dad had always shared a connection that seemed somehow supernatural.

"Mom, slow down. What did you say?" Her mother took an audible breath that rattled with emotion. "There was a fire at the library. There was a problem with the backup generator, and your father had to initiate the fire suppression system manually. Everyone is saying that he's a hero. Her mother's words seemed tragic, and dread rushed into Monica. Monica's words were panicked now, "What? Is he dead?" Her mother realized how her words and tone painted the situation worse than it was, and she calmly replied, "No, he is not dead, but he is in a medically induced coma. The doctors said it could be much worse. He has first- and second-degree burns on his arms, hands, and face. They said infection is a concern, but smoke inhalation and burns to the lungs may be the biggest concern. They are optimistic, but they are keeping him under observation and monitoring his breathing very closely." Monica's response was quick, "I will be on the next available flight!" She was booking a flight before she finished speaking. "See you soon. I love you!" "I love you too!" her mom replied, ending the call. Monica made a flight and rental car reservation, tossed her computer and iPad into a bag and headed to the bedroom to grab a couple of outfits and toiletries. She focused on the tasks at hand and kept her mind from drifting to the worse case scenarios of her father's situation.

Forty-five minutes later, she and her husband shared a goodbye at the airport. "I love you, keep me posted." She grabbed her carry-on bag and scrambled out of their car, "I love you too!" Monica sped through the airport but barely made it to the terminal on time. A worker was shutting the door after boarding passengers as she ran up, "Wait!!" The attendants quickly ushered her onto the plane, and it backed away from the terminal as she fastened her seat belt. She took a deep breath as the plane started taxiing into takeoff position. *What was Dad thinking, running back into a fire?* The pilot gave a typical airline speech announcing their flight time and order of takeoff. Monica stared out the window thinking about her dad. The intercom interrupted her thoughts, "Prepare for takeoff." As the plane shuddered into the air, Monica thought about Satan's Book. She had a nagging feeling that this had something to do with that DAMN book!

The receptionist greeted her as she entered the hospital, "Good evening and welcome..." Monica cut her off, "ICU, please?" "Third floor, but visiting hours are over at eight o'clock." She looked down at her watch, 7:50, and darted between the closing doors of a nearby elevator. The nurse raised her hand in protest, but the elevator doors shut before she could speak.

At the ICU nurse's station, Monica inquired about her

father's room number and went directly to his room. She opened the door and saw her father lying on the bed with a breathing tube, and an assortment of other hoses and wires running from his body to a plethora of monitoring devices. Her mother rose from the chair beside the bed and met her halfway. They hugged and cried for several minutes without saying a word. Her mom spoke first, "How was your trip?" Monica replied, "Hectic," and then listened as her mother explained the events as the fire department had pieced it together. Her mom's explanation of the events confirmed in her mind that he faced death to save that book. *Could the story be true?* That was the only logical explanation for a mild-mannered library custodian calling 911 and then charging into a burning building. *It was insanity!*

The next few days were touch and go for William. He was in a medically induced coma, which allowed them to clean out his lungs and treat some of his more severe burns. Both processes were excruciating for a conscious patient, often causing them to pass out from the pain. On the fifth day, the doctor finally brought some good news. He explained how William's chest X-ray was showing signs of clearing with little scar tissue, and his more severe external burns were healing well. They planned to remove the breathing tube, and then they would revive him if he continued breathing normally. Monica and her mother were relieved.

Later that afternoon, William began to stir. When he woke up, they saw the horror in his eyes. His last memories were of fire and darkness. He expected to wake with an answer to the age-old question, "What happens when I die?" Monica's mother was at Starbucks, so Monica took his hands, smiled, and said, "You will be okay." He closed his eyes, and tears rolled down his cheeks. He tried to speak, but his raspy voice was inaudible. "Don't speak," Monica said as she raised the cup of water to his blistered lips. He sipped the water and closed his eyes again, savoring the cold water.

Monica watched her father as he opened his eyes again

and tried to whisper. She put her ear to his lips. "Go, get the book! It is under the bottom shelf of the Celtic religious section near the back of the library." "Are you fucking kidding me?" She said as she stood up and glared at him." She spoke again, "You went into the fire for that book, didn't you?" He shook his head in acknowledgment. "You almost got yourself killed," she was furious. William motioned for her to come closer again. He whispered into her ear, "Someone or something is trying to destroy the book. They are trying to keep me from reading it and telling others!" "All the more reason to leave it alone," she replied.

Her dad looked up at her with those big blue puppy dog eyes. She wasn't sure when their roles had changed, but she couldn't resist those eyes. Monica's anger subsided in an instant, but she still did not share his feelings about the book. *This book is so vital that he almost died for it.* Her response surprised her, "Okay." *What am I doing*, she thought? "Where are your keys?" He gave her a look that told him he didn't have a clue. In his haste to get the book, he left them in the main door of the library. Her mom walked back into the room and almost dropped the coffee when she saw William was awake. She handed both cups of coffee to Monica and rushed over to him. They embraced and cried together. Then she suddenly rose and hit him on the chest playfully. He groaned in pain, and she said, "You better never try to be a hero again! I can't go on without you." Then she bent down and kissed him. *Sweet, yet gross*, Monica thought.

"Mom, do you know what they did with dad's keys? He wants me to get his bag from his truck." *I am lying to my mother because of this book;* she thought as her mother replied. "That can wait." "Mom, you know dad. He won't survive without his iPad and whatever old book he was reading!" Monica glared at her dad because he was forcing her to lie for him. Her mom replied, "His keys are in my purse. They locked his truck and left it in the parking lot. Can you check it for damage, in case we need to notify the insurance company?" "Okay," Monica replied as she plucked the keys out of the purse. She kissed them both and headed to her rental car.

Monica couldn't keep her mind off the book as she drove to the library. She wrestled with the concept of *Satan, the Devil, giving his book to her dad! What could the book say that would change how people saw the Satan or God?* Her dad was obsessed with the book. She wondered if his obsession was a possession *or an unholy addiction.* She stopped at the entrance of the library and got out of the car. At the gate, she fumbled through her father's keys and then opened the lock which held the gate down. The rope slid through her hands, and the gate rose into the air. Then she returned to the car, pulled into the parking lot, and locked the gate behind her. She parked the rental car next to her dad's old truck, which sat alone in the middle of the parking lot.

Caution tape surrounded the library. Monica raised the caution tape, ducked her head, and passed underneath it. She made her way to the undamaged front door and unlocked it with her dad's keys. The flashlight from her dad's truck sprang to life as the deadbolt locked behind her. To her surprise, the library looked undamaged until she shined the light to the far back wall. A piece of plywood hung on the blackened wall where the doorway used to be. Monica shivered, but not from the cold night air. The dark, old library was creepy, and the flashlight only made it worse. The light caused the bookcases and fixtures to cast ominous shadows across the large open room.

Monica's heart raced as she headed towards the back of the library and the section where her father said he hid the book. Another chill and rush of adrenaline rushed through her body as she reached the bookcase. It seemed colder in the library than it was outside. On her second try, she found the book's hiding place, pulled it out from under the shelf, and unwrapped the old towel that protected it. The Devil's Pentagram glistened in the bright light of the flashlight. *I can't believe I let him talk me into doing this.* Suddenly there was a creaking sound followed by a strange thump sound from somewhere in the middle of the library. She spun around and frantically shined the light back and forth across the library. The sound came from between her and the front door. *Probably just the old building; don't let your imagination get the best of you!*

As she opened her father's backpack, she realized that she could suddenly see her breath! It reminded her of when she used to smoke in college. It felt like the temperature had dropped twenty degrees since she entered the library. She opened the backpack again and slid the large book inside. Then she stood up, threw the bag over her shoulder, pointed the flashlight forward, and headed straight for the door. She peered out the window, passed the open/closed sign on the door and surveyed the route to her rental car. It seemed like it was a mile away.

Monica was breathing hard as the car came to life. She quickly depressed the brake and threw the gear shift reward until the red "D" appeared on the dashboard. Her foot moved from the brake pedal to the accelerator. A cold chill ran down her spine, and she took one last glance back to the library. All-out panic filled her as she saw two shadowy figures standing outside the front door of the library. Their eyes glowed in the darkness, one set red and one set blue. The eyes seemed like they could see into her soul. She thought to herself, *stop imagining things*, as the rental car leaped forward towards the gate at the entrance of the parking lot.

The car screeched to a halt at the locked gate. Her heart was pounding as she flung the door open and sprinted towards the lock of the gate. She stole a look back at the library as she reached the lock. *They are coming!* She wrestled with the keys in a desperate attempt to open the lock. Finally, the key slid into the lock and she turned it. The lock fell to the ground, and the gate shot upward as gravity pulled the counterbalance downward. She was sliding back into the car before the gate stopped bouncing at the top of its arch. The shadows were almost on her now. She pushed the accelerator down as far as it would go and kept it down with all her might. The car squealed into motion, but she willed it to go faster.

She didn't stop when the car reached Redwood Street. Instead, she cranked the wheel to the right and pushed the accelerator to the floor again. The rental vehicle darted into a space between two moving trucks. The second truck sounded its' horn in dissatisfaction. Monica looked back towards the library, but she didn't see the shadows anymore. She turned her attention to the road and groaned as the light at the next street turned red. Her eyes nervously darted from the traffic light to her rear-view mirror, *come on, come on.* The light changed, and she turned onto the one-way street, guiding the car into the far-left turn lane. There were two cars in front of her, and the light was still green, *hurry, hurry!* The first car made the left-turn as the traffic light went from yellow to red, and the second car turned right, which left her alone at the deserted intersection.

Monica's foot tapped the brake pedal as she waited for the light. "Come on!" she yelled as she pounded on the steering wheel with both hands, and then the streetlights suddenly flickered. Nervously, she looked in the review mirror, *nothing.* She pressed the accelerator pedal and started to run the light, but when she looked back from the mirror, an old homeless man was crossing the street. A burst of adrenaline rushed through her again as all-out panic set it. She glanced in the rear-view mirror frantically looking for the shadows, but then she noticed something in her peripheral. The homeless man stopped walking right in front of her car! *What in the hell is he doing? Come ON! I don't have time for this shit!* He turned towards her as if he knew her thoughts. The despair of the homeless man's eyes was gone, and fire rose from his mouth and eye sockets. He let out a horrific yell as he dove towards the hood of her car.

Monica screamed in horror as she pushed the gas pedal to the floor, turned the wheel sharply to the left and braced for impact. The tires squealed, the homeless man bounced off the hood and rolled over the top of the car. She looked back. The man rolled down the street several times, before stopping, face-down om the centerline. A truck horn sounded, and her focus shifted back to the road. She swerved back into the left lane and barely missed the delivery truck speeding down the center lane. Her knuckles turned white as she gripped the steering wheel. She mumbled, "Oh my God!" over and over as she drove towards the hospital.

Back at the library: Ecanus watched as Pruflas changed his appearance from a bloody old homeless man back to his usual form. "Pruflas, you have a sick sense of humor!" "It keeps life interesting!" "Now what are we going to do? We almost killed William trying to destroy the book, and you're lucky you didn't give his daughter a heart attack or cause her to have a car accident." "Ecanus, you were chasing her too!" Ecanus protested, "I was just trying to get the book." "Well, we failed, and now we need a new plan." Ecanus agreed, and they left the library and followed Monica to the hospital.

CHAPTER 13

William laid in the hospital bed watching the television with little interest, and he couldn't sleep. He was taking several different medications and should be sleeping, but Monica hadn't returned yet. *She should have been back by now!* He would call her, but his cell phone was missing, and his wife went home to take a shower and feed their dog. The door opened, and William turned hoping it was Monica, but it was only one of his doctors entering the room. His disappointment quickly dissipated when he realized this was no ordinary doctor. The doctor's eyes blazed with fire that seemed to be portals to Hell itself. Amon spoke first, "William, I am sorry about the library and your injuries." William's response was quick and had an angry tone, "You're sorry? I almost died to save that damn book!" Amon responded to his concern, "That was unexpected. Forces from both Heaven and Hell have joined together to stop our story from getting out. They tried to burn down the library and destroy the book without casualties. I could not intervene without exposing myself, so I sent you. Your bravery saved the book." "That is bullshit, Amon! Help me understand how you and Satan want the book to become public, but factions of Hell don't want the book to get out?" Amon replied, "Satan and I believe Bael is behind it. He is Satan's rival, and he wants to rule or destroy humanity rather than making them an ally in our war against God. He cannot openly defy Satan because most of the forces of Hell follow Satan. Plus, If the Fallen Ones become divided, God will take advantage and try to destroy us once and for all!" *Another political mess,* William hated politics. The United States was in chaos following the controversial election of a hot-headed reality star as President, and now he had to contend with the politics of Heaven and Hell.

Amon implored William to finish the book as quickly as possible. As it turned out, William was going to have some time on his hands. His actual doctor had prescribed two weeks of bed rest after his discharge. Plus, the library repairs would take several weeks. However, the truth was that despite his near-death experience, William wanted nothing more than to read the book. Amon could sense Monica coming down the hallway and said, "William, protect the book and guard yourself against those who would kill you to destroy it." Then Amon reached for the door to avoid Monica, but he sensed it was too late.

Monica pushed the handle and shoved the door open. *I am going to give Dad a piece of my mind!* In her rush, she slammed into the doctor who was trying to leave the room. William's backpack fell off her shoulder and crashed onto the floor as she fell straight onto her backside. Her face flushed red with embarrassment as she took the doctor's outstretched hand. "I am so sorry," he said as he lifted her to her feet. He reached down and picked up the backpack. She stared into his deep blue eyes as he handed the bag to her. "It's not your fault. I was the one rushing into the room," Monica said as she took the backpack from him. He smiled and said, "You might want to hold onto this!" His eyes flickered with flames as he left her standing in the doorway. *He was not human!*

William watched as Monica's face went from embarrassed, to apologetic, and then to angry again. "Are you trying to get both of us killed and damned to hell?" she asked as she walked over to his bedside. Before he could answer her, she asked: "That doctor was a demon, wasn't he?" William replied, "That was Amon. He is the *Fallen One* that Satan sent to answer my questions and protect the book." "Some fucking job he is doing! We both almost died because of this book," Monica said. She told him about the library, the shadows, and the demon-possessed homeless man.

William was sorry that he got her involved. “I’m sorry, that sounds horrifying. I never meant for you to get involved in this yet!” “What the hell do you mean yet?” she asked. “Monica, Satan chose both of us to help him. I am supposed to spread the story among scholars and you will use your blog to get it to the public.” “Dad, I didn’t sign up for this. We shouldn’t be in league with Satan!” William's voice sounded remorseful, “Neither did I, but their story is pretty compelling. I am going to finish reading the book, and then I will decide what I want to do.”

The door opened again, but this time it was Margaret. She had a box of donuts in one hand and a cup carrier with three Starbucks cups in her other hand. “I had to bribe the nurse’s station with a box of donuts to get these in here.” She said as she walked over to the bed. Monica looked at her dad and mouthed “This conversation is not over!” He shook his head in acknowledgment. Then he said, “Give me a jelly, please.” Margaret opened the pink box and plucked one of the powdered jelly donuts out. William snatched it from her hand like he was starving and took a huge bite. “MMMMM,” he mumbled. Monica took the cup that had her name written on the side and took a long sip. She loved a hot Carmel Macchiato, and thankfully, her Mom knew it.

CHAPTER 14

Pruflas and Ecanus entered the hospital in human form. They wore scrubs and even had hospital badges. Ecanus didn't like hospitals because of sickness and death. Illness and death didn't exist in Heaven where they worshipped God in continuous joy and bliss. Pruflas, on the other hand, enjoyed human suffering and death. As a disciple of Bael, his mission was to inflict disease and pain on humanity. He thrived on their plight and was millions of years removed from the sheltered life of angels like Ecanus.

Ecanus stepped into the elevator and pressed the number three button for the Intensive Care Unit. Pruflas followed Ecanus, but he had other plans. As the elevator door closed, he hit the number two button. Ecanus protested, "We are here to get the book!" Pruflas smiled as the door opened on the second floor. A sign with two arrows hung on the wall, Pediatric Ward and Labor and Delivery. "There is always time for a little fun," Pruflas said as he headed towards the Pediatric Ward. Ecanus followed him down the hall and tried to reason with him, but he wouldn't listen.

Pruflas made himself invisible and walked into the first room. Ecanus followed him. A young boy was lying in bed with an array of tubes and wires attached to him. An older woman, his grandmother, was asleep in a chair next to the bed. The heart monitor chirped with each beat of the boy's heart. Pruflas made his way to the IV and closed the tube. Only a few seconds passed before the boy began seizing. The bed shook and rattled until the grandmother woke up with a fright. As she stood up, the heart monitor flat-lined, and a female voice sounded on the intercom, "Code Blue!"

Seconds later, the door burst open, three nurses and a doctor with a crash cart rushed in and began working on the boy. Several minutes later, they pronounced the boy dead. After the grim announcement, one of the nurses noticed the IV. "Doctor, someone shut off his IV," she said in a horror-filled voice! The doctor looked at her in disbelief, "Who would do such a thing?" Instinctively they turned to the grandmother in the hallway. *Had she grown tired of his suffering and ended his life?* Pruflas left the room whistling. Ecanus hated him. Not only had he set into motion events that caused the boy's death, but now there would be an investigation and the authorities were going to charge the grandmother for euthanizing the boy and ending his suffering.

As they walked towards the next room, Ecanus decided on another approach to get Pruflas back on track. He pushed past Pruflas and into a female cancer patient's room. The twelve-year-old girl was bald, skinny, and a sickly shade of white. She was going to die today. Suddenly there was a great light in the room, and Ecanus showed himself to the girl in all his heavenly glory. Her eyes widened as she took in the beauty of the angel and his mighty wings. Peace overcame her, and the pain went away. The girl asked, "Are you taking me to Heaven?" Ecanus replied, "No, I am here to heal you of your disease!" Then he touched her shoulder. His healing touch immediately took effect, and her cancer left her body. The color returned to her skin and just to anger Pruflas; blonde hair flowed from her scalp until it was shoulder length. The girl cried tears of joy. To make matters worse for Pruflas, her parents walked in and praised God for her miracle.

The girl's family couldn't believe their daughter's miraculous healing. She told them about the beautiful angel she thought was taking her to Heaven. Her parents cried as she told them how the angel healed her with one touch. They rejoiced and praised God again. Word spread throughout the hospital. Nurses, doctors, patients, and visitors came to see the miracle. The girl told each of them how God had saved her by sending an angel to heal her. Ecanus grinned at Pruflas and whistled as he left the room. Pruflas followed him uttering profanities. As they walked, Pruflas said, "All right, let's get the damn book!" Ecanus smiled and thought *back on track!*

In the ICU, William was recovering well, and the doctors planned to send him home in another day or two. Margaret and Monica stayed with him during the day, and they took turns staying the night. Satan's book remained in William's backpack, which sat next to his bed on the window ledge. Monica and William always kept it in their sight and were cautious of anyone who entered the room.

Still invisible, Pruflas and Ecanus entered William's room. A cold chill ran through William's body, followed by a strange sense of peace. He turned to Monica, and she knew something was wrong. Monica saw the concern in his eyes. "Mom, why don't you go take your walk and bring us back some coffee." Her mom was tired of sitting and replied, "That's a good idea. Do you guys want anything else?" William chimed in, "I'll take a Hershey's with almonds, please." Margaret laughed because that candy bar was one of William's vices.

As soon as she left the room, Monica asked, "What's wrong?" William replied, "We are not alone. My recent brushes with the supernatural have made me more alert." Pruflas and Ecanus shared a concerned look and left the room. They would have to wait for an opportunity when William was not with the book. William felt them go and said, "They left when I told you about them." Monica asked, "They?" He replied, "I sensed two distinct presences; one evil and one good." They sat in silence considering why the forces of good and evil would both be present.

Three days later:

It was good to be home! William never liked hospitals. Margaret pointed to the oversized recliner in the den and said, "Go, sit down and relax." He smiled and walked over to the recliner. A pair of folded flannel pajamas sat on the arm of the chair. No one else was at the house, so he changed in the den. Monica flew back home earlier that morning.

Margaret walked into the den with a small plate and a glass of tea. William took the plate. The ham and cheese sandwich with potato chips seemed like a four-course steak meal compared to the hospital food he endured over the last two weeks. Now he had the next two weeks off to recover at home. *Two weeks to read Satan's book without distractions.* Margaret ruined the thought a second later, "I am going to the grocery store. Any special requests?" William thought about it for a second and then said, "Cheetos hot fries, almonds, and some Bud Light!" She gave him her distinctive "Yeah, right" look and then said, "Okay, I guess since you're a hero and all." They laughed, then she kissed him on the cheek and left for the grocery store. As soon as the door shut, he opened the book and began to read.

CHAPTER 15

Lucifer and his faithful passed through the gates of Heaven. They filled the sky like a great swarm of locusts eclipsing the sun. All of Heaven mourned God's death and they met no resistance as they made their way towards the Throne of God. *Their invasion is too easy; something is not right.* Lucifer scanned Heaven looking for anything that could justify the unease he felt. Just as he was about to dismiss his feelings, a flicker of light glistened from the shadows below. He strained to see what caused the reflection, *Golden Armor!* Lucifer rolled to the right as an energy bolt shot past him. An angel that was flying next to him had not been so lucky. The bolt tore through his chest and blew out of his back. The blast tore his wings from his body, and they fluttered to the ground like leaves falling from a tall tree. The angel's body fell to the field below.

"It's a trap!" Lucifer yelled. His generals took evasive action, split their formations, and dove towards their attackers. Suddenly the light of God filled Heaven again. *God was not dead! He faked his death to lure us to ours.* Rage filled Lucifer, and he let out a vicious battle cry. A warrior class angel met Lucifer in the air. Lucifer's defense was crude, but his rage overwhelmed his opponent. The angel swung his sword first, but it never landed. Lucifer grabbed the angel's sword hand by the wrist and cranked his arm one hundred and eighty degrees. His shoulder popped out of the socket, and Lucifer kept going until it was torn free of his tarsal. The angel watched in dismay as his arm fell with his sword still clenched in his hand. Lucifer capitalized on the angel's confusion. He drew his sword and thrust it through the angel's abdomen. He looked into the angel's eyes and watched as his life force left him. The angel's body fell from Lucifer's sword as he turned his gaze to the throne of God on the distant horizon. Bael nodded his approval as he joined him in the air.

"We will never make it to the throne if we continue the fight here," Bael said. "We must get to the throne. Gather the elite warriors among us to raid the throne with us. Tell the others to fight in place," Lucifer replied. Bael nodded and left him to pass his orders to their generals. Lucifer and one thousand of his best fighters flew low and fast towards the throne. They did their best to avoid significant conflict until they met God's best warriors who guarded his throne. Each battle became more complicated, and they had not seen any of the substantial archangels or Samael yet. Lucifer was afraid they would lose too many of their forces before they saw significant conflict, but he kept his thoughts to himself.

The bloody battle between God's faithful and Lucifer's followers had lasted for three days, but they were nearly at the throne now. Angels from both sides exchanged powerful blasts of energy, fireballs, and lightning. The heavenly skies and horizon were like an ominous sculpture. Dark clouds loomed overhead with bright flashes of varying colors and explosions. Pillars of smoke rose from the ruins of the once beautiful statues, gardens, and buildings. Lucifer and his elite had fought their way to the Holy Gardens just outside the palace where God sat upon his golden throne. If they prevailed here, nothing stood between them and God himself.

Angels fought in the air and upon the ground. Sparks shot skyward and showered down upon them as their blades clashed with the ringing sound of metal on metal. Lucifer and the Archangel Michael met in combat near the large centerpiece fountain of the garden. Again and again, Lucifer locked blades with the Archangel Michael. Michael was a well-trained fighter, but Lucifer was cunning, ruthless, and most dangerous of all, determined. Distracted by a sudden movement in his peripheral, Lucifer cried out as Michael landed a powerful kick to his midsection. The force of the blow drove him backward, and he fell near the fountain and slid across the walkway. Lucifer grimaced in pain as he hit the brick walkway. Determined to press his advantage, Michael lunged at him with his blade extended, but Lucifer never came to a stop. Instead, he spread his mighty wings and thrust himself over Michael. Michael could only watch as his momentum carried him under and past Lucifer. He knew his mistake would cost him even before he felt the sting of Lucifer's blade as it glanced across the back of his legs.

Lucifer drew first blood against Michael, but it was only a flesh wound, that would only make him angry. As Lucifer spun to face Michael, he saw Samael, Uriel, Raphael, Gabriel and the Warrior Class of God's elite locked in combat with his followers. Much to his dismay, God's faithful seemed to have the upper hand. Michael's battle cry snapped Lucifer back to the reality of their combat. He lifted his blade into a defensive position and braced himself for Michael's powerful counter-attack.

On the other side of the Holy Gardens, Bael was bloody and bruised, but the mighty Samael hadn't killed him yet. Samael landed several clubbing blows as Bael parried with both arms over his head. Samael's powerful blows drove him to one knee. Bael braced for another overhead blow, but Samael rotated his blade and sliced at an arc down and across Bael's head. The action caught Bael defending for his powerful overhead strikes and sliced a gash across his left cheek. Bael cried out in pain. *It's time to finish him*, Samael thought. He imagined his blade splitting Bael's skull in two and smiled as he swung his sword downward with all his might.

The vibration of his sword hitting the bricks traveled up through his arms, reverberated through his shoulders and left him staring at the ground in disbelief. His sword came to a halt several inches into the golden bricks. Bael had used his final trick against Samael and God's faithful. Lucifer and his followers were now invisible. Bael, who was now on his feet, swung his blade across his body and sliced through Samael's midsection. He cried out in pain and surprise. Bael reveled in Samael's spilled blood.

Lucifer and his faithful embraced their sudden advantage. They wasted no time in following Bael's example as they lashed out at their enemies with great vengeance and violence. Several of God's faithful fell under their renewed attacks. Lucifer landed a devastating blow to Michael's head, and he fell to the ground, unconscious. Pride rose within him, and a smile formed on his lips as he prepared to land the fatal blow.

Suddenly, a bright blue current of electricity leaped from the ground in the garden. Powerful waves of electricity danced upon the surface of the garden and slithered through the air like great blue serpents hissing with the buzz of a high voltage line. The current lashed out and struck Lucifer and his invisible followers, nullifying Bael's power of invisibility, but it did not touch God's faithful. The powerful currents ripped through God's enemies, and they cried out in anguish. The flow did not stop until Lucifer and his followers could not resist. They laid on the ground, convulsing and shaking into unconsciousness. Lucifer refused to succumb to the darkness and struggled against God well beyond the tolerance of his followers. He heard God speak as everything turned black. "You shall live out your life in pain and suffering. I strip you of your holy name. From this moment forth, you shall be called Satan!" His last thoughts were of victory snatched from his hands. *I have failed!*

Satan blinked in and out of consciousness. The loud sound of rushing wind and the flicker of intense pain drew him towards awareness. Consciousness returned to him as violent pain erupted throughout his body. He had never known pain until a few days earlier, but now there was no part of him that pain didn't consume. Flames engulfed his body as he plummeted to the surface of the earth. He struggled against the pain and forced himself to open his eyes against the wind and flames. His eyes were heavy, and it took all his remaining strength, but he opened them for a moment. At that moment, he watched as the final remnants of his once beautiful wings burned away and left a trail of embers like a great comet as he entered earth's atmosphere. He was powerless to slow his momentum or to stop the white-hot explosion of anguish that grew within him.

In the distance, he sensed his brethren. They were falling like streaks of fire from Heaven. A great meteor shower of those who followed him and rebelled against God. The Fallen Ones shared his vision, and God condemned them to share his fate. Hatred welled up within him, and rage consumed him once more. His hatred and resentment grew, expanding until they almost numbed his pain. He screamed in anger, but there was no sound. Defeated by the silence, he fell and waited for the sudden impact that was coming.

A mushroom cloud rose miles into the sky, causing ash and soot to rise into the atmosphere. The pain of his impact was excruciating. It threatened to pull him back into unconsciousness, but that threat fueled his rage even more. The clouds of ash and soot rose from the Fallen One's impact and choked out the sun. An ice age began, and Satan took pleasure from that thought. God's precious little playthings would die because he cast Satan and his followers out of Heaven. Satan was not aware that the ice age also served God's hidden agenda. It would drive other beings from the earth, beings not created by God. Creatures whose existence God hid from his faithful since the beginning. The ice age would clear the way for the birth of humanity.

Satan lay motionless in the crater of his impact and hoped for his death, but that seemed too easy. God's beloved creatures were dying all around him, and with each one, Satan gained a small victory. A faint smile pursed his lips, bringing with it a new ringing of agony. In his creator's anger, he cast him out and condemned him to this world. In anger, God set these events into motion, and he was killing off the creations he loved so much. *I will see that he suffers for the pain that he caused us! No,* Satan thought, *I will make him suffer more than we experience!* He reassured himself that someday he would have his revenge. Until then, he would rest and gain strength from the suffering and death of God's little pets.

CHAPTER 16

On a day, long after Satan's fall, God commanded Michael to gather 203,000 angels to select the trees and plants for the Garden of Eden. Michael chose the olive tree, Gabriel the apple, Raphael the melon, Uriel the nut. Samael picked the Tree of the Knowledge of Good and Evil, but he hid its presence as a bountiful fruit tree. The angels gave the trees to Eustis, the caretaker of the garden. Eustis was a meek but gifted caretaker of plants. He was responsible for the plants until the time came for the Garden of Eden. They grew healthy and vibrant under his care.

One day as Eustis applied his nurturing touch, he tended Samael's tree. When he touched the tree, his sight turned black, and he saw a horrifying vision of death and destruction. The caretaker pulled away from the tree, and his vision returned to normal. *This tree is not what it seems!* he thought. He examined his records and saw Samael donated the tree. A chill of death ran down his spine as he read his name. The hair on his neck stood up, and goosebumps rose on his body. There was betrayal in Heaven and he had to tell his master. Samael feared he might eventually discover his secret, so he watched him. When he saw Eustis take flight towards the throne of God, he had to stop him.

Eustis stood no chance of reaching the throne before an Archangel such as Samael caught him. He could feel the angel giving chase and knew he could not outrun him. Samael hit Eustis at full speed from above. The impact sent him crashing out of control into the golden buildings, which rose high into the heavens. Bricks and debris showered down onto the streets in the wake of his impact. Unfortunately for Eustis, he slowed his fall before he hit the ground or the fall itself would have killed him. The fall left him dazed and bleeding, so instead of a quick and merciful death, he would suffer at Samael's hands.

The mighty angel stood over Eustis rejoicing, and said, "Eustis, where are you going in such a rush?" Eustis replied, "I am going to tell God about your treachery!" Samael laughed and said, "I cannot allow you to tell our master what I have done. If God is going to punish me, it will be for killing you! The tree will remain a secret."

Rage boiled up within Samael, and he struck Eustis, knocking him back to the ground. Then, the mighty angel reached down and grabbed a handful of his hair with one hand and pinned his left arm behind his back with the other. Eustis was powerless against Samael. So, Samael mocked him, saying, "You should have kept quiet about my tree." Intense pain followed the dull thud of Eustis' face as Samael smashed his head upon the golden paved street. Samael dragged his face along a short stretch of the uneven pavement, until flesh ripped from the bone, like cheese on a grater. A trail of blood pooled in the cracks between the bricks of the roadway. Then, he released him and said, "Eustis, you did not need to die." *Here is my chance*, Eustis thought. He almost lifted himself upright before he realized his efforts were in vain. Samael took hold of his shoulder and dug his fingers into Eustis' flesh. His other hand grabbed Eustis by the wrist, and then he drove his knee into the backside of his elbow, breaking it. Eustis' arm snapped like a dry twig, leaving the bone sticking out of his flesh at both ends. One end of the bone pierced his bicep and the other end his upper forearm. Only his flesh held the arm together. Eustis cried out in pain and sobbed, but his suffering did not end.

Samael continued punishing Eustis. His knee crashed into the middle of Eustis' back between his wings. Then, he grabbed the base of Eustis' wing with one hand and a foot higher with the other hand. He pushed Eustis' face down on the pavement with his knee and pulled his wing in the opposite direction. A bloodcurdling scream followed the sound of his wing tearing away from his body. His pain was excruciating, but the realization that he would never fly again hurt him more.

In a last desperate attempt to survive, Eustis spun to his wingless side and wildly threw his arm in the same direction. His hand and forearm caught Samael off guard, in a moment of celebration. The force and surprise of Eustis' blow sent him tumbling backward, off-balance, and he fell flat on his backside. Eustis turned to follow his attack, but Samael was a well-trained killer. His mighty wings extended and thrust downward in a movement that was so smooth and quick that the human eye would not have captured it. He snatched Eustis from the ground, with a hand on each of his shoulders, and drove upward into the air. A second later and several hundred feet above the pavement, Samael flung Eustis towards the ground. Eustis spiraled out of control, unable to control his fall or slow his momentum because of his missing wing. With a loud thud and the sound of shattering bones, Eustis landed awkwardly on his wing and shoulder. The sound of his impact echoed off a nearby building. He opened his eyes for the last time and saw his end coming.

High in the air, Samael drew his sword with speed and precision. He raised the sword high above his head with the tip extended outward and dove towards his victim with unfathomable speed and violence. His sword pierced Eustis' chest, center mass. It shattered his breastbone, went through the chest cavity, spine and the tip of the sword pierced several inches of the golden bricks beneath Eustis, before coming to a stop."

In triumph, Samael straddled Eustis' lifeless body on one knee with his hands resting on the hilt of his sword. Samael, with head down, and his eyes closed, took a deep victorious breath. Instinctively, he rotated my sword ninety degrees as he pulled it from the lifeless body. Rotating a blade while retrieving it causes the wound to stay open. Great warriors, like Samael, completed this action every time they pierced their enemy's flesh.

As Samael rose from Eustis, his finger slid along the sharp edge of his blade. He raised his blood-soaked finger to his mouth. All blood contained the essence of God's power itself. So, he savored the taste of Eustis' blood, as he wiped the blood off his sword and examined it. When it was clean, he placed it back in his sheath. Suddenly, a great light shone around me.

Samael tried to protect his eyes from the light, but they never made it. The Spirit of God took hold of his limbs and thrust them outward. He panicked, wondering, *will God tear me limb from limb for my sins?* Paralysis took hold of him, but pain shot through every nerve ending, muscle fiber, and cell within my body. The lightning consumed him, striking his body over and over without pause.

Finally, God spoke, "Samael, why have you done this thing? Why have you allowed sin to enter you? The vanity of your victory during the great battle with the Fallen Ones has driven you from me! You murdered one of your brethren. Heaven shall no longer be your home; you shall live your life on the earth! You will have no control of your own body when I call you back to serve me as the Angel of Death. This curse shall be yours because in your heart you said, 'I am the conqueror' and yet, do you have any power unless I give it to you? You shall be an outcast among your brethren who fell because the Fallen Ones burned when they fell, but you shall not burn. The very sight of you will remind them of your role in their defeat."

When God finished speaking, he called his faithful angels unto him. The Archangel Michael and the other Archangels took hold of Samael, and they cast him out of Heaven. He fell to the earth as Satan, and the Fallen Ones fell, but God kept his body from burning. He landed upon the face of the earth, looked back into Heaven, and cursed God.

CHAPTER 17

Samael stood upon one of the few small portions of the earth that threatened to break the surface of the freezing waters. Satan's fall caused soot and ash to rise into the sky. The sun and stars had not shown their light on the face of the earth since they fell from Heaven. An ice age ensued and killed off the great beasts that once roamed this world. Creatures large and small perished until only the Fallen Ones remained. The ice age began to warm after God cast Samael out of Heaven, the glaciers which formed after Satan's fall started melting in preparation for the age of humanity.

The frigid, black water rolled off Satan's face and torso as he rose from the sea. The Fallen Ones closed in on their prey, like predators stalking their kill. Since their fall from Heaven, they longed for revenge, and today, they would have a small taste of it. Satan paused and considered why Samael was on the earth. *Did God send him to finish us? Was he sent as an ambassador from God to show us mercy and end our suffering?* As soon as these thoughts formed, Satan dismissed them because God's anger burned for them. He stopped and dared not move closer lest Samael sense his presence and they lose the element of surprise. Satan looked to Bael and nodded his head, which was the signal to begin their attack. Bael rose from the water, raised his arm, and lifted his mangled index finger skyward. As soon as his finger rose, he became invisible. One hundred legions of the Fallen Ones rose with him and vanished from sight.

Silently, Bael and his legions moved through the waters and surrounded their prey. Samael stood motionless before them, looking upward into the heavens. Revenge was within their grasp! Excitement and anticipation rose within them until electricity filled the air around them. They had remained dormant upon the frozen earth until it started to warm. The cold waters disturbed their slumber, and then they wandered the earth without purpose and in pain, until now. They had been waiting for a day when a heavenly being or God himself descended to the earth. Their time had finally come.

Samael had sensed their presence when he landed on this barren world. He grew tired of flying over the vast nothingness that was the earth, so he stood and waited for the Fallen Ones. As he looked up into Heaven and saw angels scurrying about doing God's bidding, he thought, *I was like them once!* It bothered him that the angels continued to worship God and did his bidding without him and the Fallen Ones. They acted as if they had never existed. His thoughts shifted back to the battle he was about to fight, and the pleasure it would bring him.

Bael and his legions leaped from the water. Their strategy was to overwhelm him and tear him limb from limb. Today, they would feast on his flesh and drink his blood like wine. Samael had killed legions of the Fallen Ones in the Great War, and now they would take him by sheer numbers and have their revenge. As they lunged through the air, time slowed. The water below them began to ripple outward from Samael.

Like a rocket, Samael shot skyward in one smooth and powerful motion. His great wings spread and gravity itself surrendered to him leaving a vapor trail in his wake. Bael and his legions collided and tumbled to the ground in a twisted pile of mangled, deformed and burnt bodies where Samael had stood. They screamed obscenities into the air and beat their fists upon the shallow waters as they scrambled to their feet. Samael pursed his lips into a devious smile as thoughts of chaos and death filled his mind. He drew his sword and dove earthward with a roaring battle cry.

Bael's legions welcomed Samael to the earth with vengeance and blood. They clawed at him, scratched and tore at his limbs, wings, and even his sword. After only a few moments, body parts littered their battlefield, but none of them belonged to Samael. The water turned red with their blood. Samael struck one after another. Many times, he crushed one of their skulls with one hand while driving his bloody blade through another. His wings cut through the air as he whirled from side to side. He swung them with great violence and accuracy, decapitating his enemies as he turned to face another foe.

The battle raged for hours, and Samael was not without injury. Deep claw marks and bites left blood trickling from his limbs. A deep wound which ran from his temple to his jawbone nearly took his eye. Samael killed, maimed or drowned more than two legions of the Fallen Ones. He drew strength from the dead, which lay scattered around him. Death was a drug to Samael, and it fueled his reason for existence. *He needed to kill!*

CHAPTER 18

The bloody fight had lasted for three days and three nights with no end in sight. Samael stood in shin-deep water and blood. His limbs were heavy with fatigue as he took a deep breath in preparation for the next wave of attackers. He watched the dark, crimson blood as it swirled in the water like the Aurora Borealis in the night sky. Thirty-four legions of Bael's Fallen Ones lay dead upon the water around Samael, and his strength was beginning to waver.

Bael glared at Samael from a safe distance and prepared to signal the next wave of attackers. He had sixty-six legions remaining, and he didn't care if every one of them died if they killed Samael. Then something unexpected interrupted the battle; God spoke! His voice was like a mighty trumpet and a rushing wind. The spirit of God moved upon the face of the waters and obeyed his commands. The clouds of soot and ash, which had drowned out the sun since the Fallen Ones fell to the earth, subsided and cleared. Thousands of years of darkness ended in an instant.

The blinding light sent Satan, and the Fallen One's diving into the waters, and the darkness which the depths provided. Samael refused to turn or run away. Instead, he stood against God and the light. *It is time for the age of humanity*, he thought. Before Satan's fall, God commanded the angels to bow before the spirit of man, which he made in his image. The elevation of humankind started the Great War in Heaven., but God never spoke about humanity again except to say, "Humankind will abide upon the earth." None of the angels understood what that meant, and they did not dare to ask him because they feared him.

Samael marveled at how bright the future seemed to those who obediently followed God, but for the curious, it was dark and impenetrable. Angels weren't all-knowing as God proclaimed himself to be. They only knew what he shared with them unless they had a special gift. Samael had such a gift. He could see the ever-evolving future, but reading the future was difficult because the exact details were in constant motion or hidden from him by God.

The waters began receding as suddenly as God's voice and the light had come. Samael no longer stood in the water. Instead, he stood upon wet ground. *God must have a plan for this very spot!* He drove his hand into the moist soil and watched as the dirt flowed through his fingers. It fell onto the ground in a pile that resembled a small ant mound. Then he saw it.

In Samael's vision, God used the sounding clay and smooth black mud of this place to create humankind. He saw a holy book laying open on a golden table. A passage leaped off the pages and into his thoughts. The text read, Satan replied to God, saying, "I will not bow before mankind whom you created from dry ringing clay and black mud molded into shape." Then he saw humankind spring to life from the earth, like plants! *God intends to begin the age of humanity right here!* He would create them from the ground on which he stood.

God's plan for humanity caused rage to boil up within Samael. *How could God not realize his angels were a superior creation and his first children? Humankind should be the bastard race, not them.* Samael regretted his decision not to stand with Satan when God showed humankind to them in Heaven. Now, he saw God's whole plan, and he felt betrayed because he obediently stood against Satan and his followers during the First Great War. Samael would not make the same mistake. His contempt for God pushed him to defiance and a plan that he had already begun. In Heaven, he had already sowed the seeds of mischief in God's plan, but now he had another opportunity.

Samael pulled his dagger from his belt. It glistened brighter than gold in the sunlight of the earth. He watched as the light danced off the tip of the blade as it spun in his hand. Then in one smooth motion, he pulled the knife across the inside of his forearm from elbow to wrist. The cut was deep enough to expose the bone. He turned the wound towards the ground and allowed his life force to flow upon the earth. When the blood pooled because the soil could absorb no more of his essence, he rose to his feet. He took his tunic and wrapped the wound to stop the bleeding.

The ground rippled under Samael's feet once more, and his wings lifted him effortlessly into the air. As he rose high into the sky, his lips turned upward into an evil smile. His mind raced with thoughts of the future. Humankind's creation would be corrupt from the beginning. *The age of humanity should be fun,* he thought. Samael soared through the skies and enjoyed the heat of the sun upon his face as he considered the bright new future of this world.

CHAPTER 19

God commanded the Holy Spirit to make humankind from the dust of the earth. The Holy Spirit touched the earth, and the man rose from the dust full of the Holy Spirit and the Light of God. When the man rose, he saw the Light of God, fell on his face and worshiped God. God smiled and said unto the man, "Rise." The man trembled in fear before God. God spoke again, "Your name is Adam." God turned as the Holy Spirit touched the earth a second time. The earth moved and contorted before God as it did with Adam. A woman rose from the ground, which Samael corrupted. God felt Samael's essence within her, and he cursed him. "Heaven and mankind shall see Samael's disgrace because of his mischief!"

Despite Samael's interference, man and woman pleased God because they had his likeness. Then God said unto Adam, "I created the woman to be your mate. What will you name her?" Adam looked at the woman and saw her great beauty. Her dark red hair blazed like fire, and her bright emerald green eyes pierced his soul. Her beauty caused his loins to stir. She smiled at him with a sly, mischievous grin, and he remembered God's question. Embarrassed, he turned back to God and said, "Her name shall be Lilith." God surveyed his handiwork again. Adam pleased God, but within Lilith, he saw rebellion and conflict.

The Son of God walked out of the Light of God and stretched his arms outward. Then he said unto them, "We created this garden for you. All of it is yours. It is paradise, but do not eat from the Tree of the Knowledge of Good and Evil. Samael placed the tree in the garden to tempt you and bring you to ruin!" Adam loved the garden which God created. He communed with God each day and watched the angels in Heaven as they worshipped at God's throne. During the heat of the day, he slumbered in the shade of a great tree.

Lilith was not content with such things. Instead, she explored the mysteries of the garden and examined the plants and creatures that lived there. When she became bored with the garden, she turned her eyes toward Heaven. *Why has God put us here instead of in Heaven? Are we not worthy of communing with the angels and worshiping God at his altar? Did God create us in his image so we should be castaways?* Lilith expressed her thoughts to Adam, but he refused to question God and forbade her from asking God herself. His unwillingness to question things which they did not understand created dissention among them. It was clear they were not of one mind and opposed each other in everything they did.

The differences between Adam and Lilith grew more evident with each passing day. Lilith did not respect Adam, and they fought always. Adam expected Lilith to be submissive to him, but she refused. One day Adam desired Lilith, and he said unto her, "Lay before me so that I may have my way with you." Lilith became angry and refused him, saying, "I will not lie on my back beneath you. You should lie upon the ground beneath me!" Adam became angry and challenged her, "I will not lie beneath you, but you will submit, and I will know your pleasures. God has made me your master!" Lilith replied, "We are equals! Our father created both of us from the dust of this earth."

After that day, neither Adam nor Lilith compromised or conceded to even being equals. There was no partnership or union between them. Adam and Lilith had no children because they refused to lay together in the pleasures of the flesh. One day when Adam could not restrain himself anymore; he said unto her, "Woman lie down beneath me so that I can quench the thirst of my loins!" Lilith laughed and replied, "You will not know my pleasures until you count me your equal!" Her words were like fire to him, and he pushed her to the ground in anger. She hit the ground hard, and he jumped on top of her. "You will submit, or I will take you against your will!" Then he pinned her arms to the ground and straddled her. He was too strong for her, but she continued to struggle against him. He forced himself between her thighs and thrust his manhood into her. Her flesh tore, and she wailed in pain. She became motionless and wept as he continued to have his way with her. Her tears heightened his pleasure as he overpowered her.

Adam's violation of Lilith continued as he held her arms over her head by the wrists and covered her mouth with his other hand to muffle her cries for help. Her tear-filled eyes met his, but there was no mercy to be found in his lust-filled eyes. Adam suddenly cried out in pain as her teeth broke the flesh of his hand. He drew back in anger and slapped her in the face. She cried out to God, but He did not save her. So, she prayed for death, but her prayers failed her too. Adam's body tightened upon her, and then she felt his seed within her. The warmth of his seed stung her raw flesh. His eyes became black as his pupils swelled with his climax. She closed her eyes in the horror of his warmth and tears rolled down her cheeks.

Adam smiled and rose from her bloodied thighs. "I should not have to take what God has given unto me. Next time, you will submit yourself willingly, or I will violate you again!" Rage filled Lilith. She rose from the ground and glared at him with clenched fists. Adam enjoyed her humiliation and smiled with delight. She wiped the mixture of her blood and his seed from her thighs. His smile left him as she flung the mix of their warm fluids in his face. The fluids stung his eyes, and he tasted his seed. He cried out in disgust and anger. She lunged at him before he could open his eyes or move. Her fingernails sank into his chest and drew blood as she raked them downward. He cried out in pain and struck her on the cheek with the back of his hand. Lilith stumbled backward and almost fell. She rubbed her cheek and glared at Adam. Then she rebuked him, "You are not worthy of having me! You are no better than the beasts of the field which force themselves on the females of their species!" Before he could reply, she leaped into the air and uttered the unspeakable name of God.

Heaven and earth became silent in response to Lilith's actions. She had uttered the sacred name of God she had heard at her creation. Instantly, she became a succubus as her anger transformed her. Wings sprang from her back and horns rose up from her scalp. Adam watched her transformation in horror. In the rage of what she had become, she screamed at him. He covered his ears and looked into her rage-filled eyes as the blood-curdling scream threatened to burst his eardrums. Fear drove him to the ground, and he dared not look at her. He heard her wings beating the air into submission, and then there was only silence as all of God's creations cowered in silence.

Lilith found a home in a cave near the Red Sea and there she gave herself to sexual perversions with the beasts of the field and sea. Her lusts were insatiable. Soon she became bored with the creatures because she could not bear children to them. So, she returned to Adam while he slept each night. She landed near him and blew the blue breath of deep sleep into his nostrils. The blue haze of sleep took hold of him, and she had her way with him over and over because he could not wake. As she took him, she whispered twisted thoughts of pleasure into his mind. His dreams became vivid, twisted, lust-filled expeditions of joy. Lilith always reached orgasm before him because it aroused her to take him unaware. Then, with his stolen seed deep within her, she rose and returned to her home.

Adam's dreams caused him to wake each morning with lustful cravings, but he had no wife, and his hand failed to satisfy his desires. In frustration, he took the beasts of the field to fulfill his urges, but the guilt of his sinful pleasures weighed heavily upon him. Time and time again, he failed to control his lust, and then in his despair, he realized man should not be alone. He needed a mate.

Adam fell upon the ground and prayed to God. "Oh, master of the universe, Lilith, the woman you created for me has run away." God appeared before him and replied unto him, "Adam, I see your need for a companion and mate! Man's nature is to marry and raise a family. Therefore, when a man finds a wife, he finds a good thing. That man shall have my favor!" Adam pleaded to God for Lilith to return because he desired her, and he wanted his favor.

God honored Adam's request. He sent three of his angels, Senoy, Sansenoy, and Semangelof to force Lilith to return to Adam and submit to him. Senoy, Sansenoy, and Semangelof found her as she flew near the Red Sea. The angels said, "God has commanded you return to the garden and submit to Adam as his wife!" She refused, "I will not return unto Adam. I take what I need from him while he sleeps and as for your God, where was He when I cried out as Adam defiled me against my will?" God knew Lilith's evil heart, and he gave the angels the power to impose his judgment upon her if she didn't obey. The angels spoke unto her saying, "If you do not return with us this day, your children will die each day. You will only bear a child when you have stolen the souls of one hundred children." Lilith refused them again, saying, "I will not return to the man who took me against my will and refuses to treat me as his equal." Then she cursed Adam, the three angels and God himself. She vowed, "I will never return to be his wife unless he submits himself to me!"

The angels cursed Lilith because she would not return. The child she carried in her womb fell from between her thighs and did not draw a single breath. It was hideous and deformed, half-demon and half-human. As they looked upon the horror of her child, they said, "This curse will be your burden for eternity! Your quest to collect souls will be hard because you will have no power over children protected by our mark!" Then they returned to God and Adam with their terrible news.

CHAPTER 20

God received the news of Lilith's disobedience from the three angels, and he did not want Adam to be alone. Samael corrupted the first woman, so God decided to make a woman from Adam's flesh. Dense fog engulfed Adam, and he fell into a deep sleep. God called his servant Sur-Juh to him and said, “Take a rib from Adam so that the Holy Spirit can make a woman from it.” Sur-Juh replied, “Yes, Lord!” He knelt beside Adam and touched his lower rib. The tip of his finger slid across his ribs. His flesh split open, and Sur-Juh plunged his hand into the open wound. A wet cracking sound echoed through the air, and then he raised Adam's bloody rib from the incision. Sur-Juh slid his glowing hand across the incision, and it closed.

The Holy Spirit took the rib from Sur-Juh. It floated in the air, and a bright light grew from within it. Dark particles formed in the air and spun around it. The rib disappeared into the spiraling ball of light as it started taking the form of a woman. When the woman was whole, God breathed life into her. Her blue eyes sprung open with the shock of sudden life. Then God said unto Adam, “She is born of your flesh, and she shall be your partner in life.” The woman's beauty pleased Adam. Her hair was a soft shade of red, her eyes were blue, and her milky skin embraced her delicate features.

“Name your bride,” God said to Adam. The woman looked at Adam in anticipation, and then he said, “I shall call her Eve.” Eve pleased God because he knew she would serve Adam as he served God. Adam and Eve were of one accord. Eve submitted to Adam during sex, and both were satisfied. They strolled through the garden, hand in hand, and communed with God and the animals. Their days were bright and happy, and their nights were peaceful, but we lurked in the shadows waiting for an opportunity.

Satan and the select among the Fallen Ones watched Adam and Eve and became jealous of how God communed with them. He communed with them as if they were his brethren and gave them dominion over the garden. In anger, Satan called Aym to his earthly throne and said, "Aym, take a handful of your faithful and whisper in Eve's ear. Make sure your words fill her ears as she sleeps and when she is alone. They will germinate and grow inside of her, like a seed in fertile soil. She will become curious, and then we can tempt her to disobey God, and she will!"

Later that night, as Adam and Eve prepared for their slumber, they heard a young fawn crying for its mother. They searched for the fawn and found it alone. Adam said to Eve, "The fawn has lost its mother, but she will return." Eve replied, "We will comfort the animal until its mother returns. Tonight, we will share our bed with this poor creature because it should not be alone." They laid down upon their bed, and Eve embraced the young fawn as if it were her child.

Adam, Eve, and the young fawn drifted off into a peaceful slumber as the cold night air danced over them. Adam and Eve slept well because they had never known fear, but Satan watched them from the shadows. Rage seethed from him as he thought of how God loved them.

Adam and Eve were in a deep sleep when the fawn's head spun around and faced back towards Eve. Its eyes sprung open, but they were not the bright, innocent eyes they saw earlier. Instead, the pupils glowed with an ominous red-light that swam in a pool of impenetrable blackness. Its gaze was like a dagger piercing unprotected flesh. As the fawn, Aym whispered into Eve's ear as she slept. His words slithered into her mind and wove themselves into her thoughts. The seeds took hold and grew. Not sin, but a curious and challenging nature that sought enlightenment and challenged authority.

Her nature would lead her to sin against God.

The bright morning sun flickered through the branches above their bed. Eve awoke startled, the fawn was no longer in her arms. She turned towards Adam, she was alone. Her eyes searched for the fawn in the garden around them. She let out a sigh of relief when she saw them. Fifty yards away, the fawn drank from her mother's bosom. As Eve rose to her feet, mother and fawn turned towards her. They tipped their heads as if to say thanks, turned and disappeared into the garden. Happiness welled up inside of her. Satan smiled as he turned and walked away. His plan was working!

God continued to commune with Adam and Eve like he never did with the angels. Humanity's relationship with God sickened him. Adam and Eve frolicked around the garden, flaunting their relationship with God and playing with the animals. Many days passed, and Aym continued to plant his seeds within Eve's mind. Before long, Eve strayed from Adam as he communed with God. She found reasons to wander through the garden, playing with the animals, smelling the beautiful flowers or bathing in the clear waters that fed the garden. Aym and his select visited her more and more as she strayed. They appeared as animals, whispers hidden in the breeze or spoke to her through the rustling trees and plants. She explored the outer edges of the garden and sampled all the gifts God gave them.

Many times, Satan himself visited Eve as a great serpent. Serpents intrigued her, and he used this advantage to gain private audiences with her. In these times he led her further down the path to fulfilling his plan. One day, following one of her long adventures, she stopped at a pool she frequented. As she bathed in the calm waters of the small pond, he swam near her.

Unaware of Satan's presence, Eve floated in the soothing waters, basking in the sun. She enjoyed how the sun warmed her face while the cool water brushed across her body as it rippled in the breeze. Many creatures frequented the pool. Fish and other marine life brushed up against her or nibbled at her fingers and toes, but she enjoyed the serpents' visits the most. They brushed up against her with a delicate touch and coiled their long tails around her arms or legs. She was excited by the unusually large serpent which joined her as a swimming companion today. The snake's black and yellow bands were bright and vibrant. Its' colorful scales glistened in the water as if it emitted light of its own.

As the serpent, Satan swam closer, and her heart raced with each passing touch. Her excitement rippled through the waters of the pool. *It is time to test Eve,* he thought. He swam underneath her and let the tip of his tail glide along her leg from the ankle bone. She shivered with pleasure as the snake's tail slowly ran up her inner calf, knee, and then even slower up her inner thigh. Just as she thought the snake might pleasure her as Adam did, it dove deeper into the pool and left her wanting.

After several moments, Satan surfaced near the crown of her head. He ran his fingers through her red hair. Her hair floated on the surface of the water like a fan of fire. His body was under hers now, and only a fraction of an inch separated them. She craved his touch and moaned in anticipation as her body tingled with excitement. The serpent's tail glanced across her hip, and she flinched. Its' tail rose from the water and extended towards her ankle as she watched. Her eyes followed the tip of his tail as two inches of length arched ninety degrees from its body. It touched her ankle and slid up the outside of her leg with the precision of a skilled lover.

Eve's muscles tightened as she neared orgasm. The serpent's tail was wet, soft, and textured like the tongue of a playful animal. Until this moment she hadn't realized that she could experience such pleasure apart from Adam. The serpent's tail slid up her leg and across her knee as it moved towards her inner thigh. Her heart fluttered as it approached her delicate womanhood. Adam had pleasured her many times with his manhood, but he never used his tongue. The thoughts of Adam pleasuring her with his tongue excited her even more. She imagined the serpent's tail as Adam's tongue and moaned loudly. The snake let out a low hiss of excitement as he parted the red veil that protected the entrance to her womanhood. The serpent's "hiss" sent a wave of horror through Eve as she realized, the serpent was pleasuring her! She pushed herself away from the serpent and rose from the water to face it.

So close, Satan thought. Eve rebuked the serpent, "STOP, God made me from Adam's rib. I am his, and he is mine!" Satan laughed, "Your beauty is like the stars in the night sky, and no man should own you. I only live to serve you, my queen! Is there a better way to serve one's master than to pleasure them? Does God forbid pleasure? Should you only receive pleasure from submitting yourself to your husband? Do you not pleasure yourself?" Eve interrupted him, taking offense at his accusations, "I do not pleasure myself!" Satan pressed on and continued questioning her. He wasn't looking for answers to his questions, but instead, he planted more doubt within her. "Why would God withhold pleasure from his children? Does God also forbid you from knowing the other secrets and mysteries of this world? No father should keep his children in the darkness, but instead, he should bring them out into the light of day!"

When Satan stopped speaking, Eve responded to his words, "God is mighty! We are his children and must obey! He has forbidden us to eat of the Tree of the Knowledge of Good and Evil, but he has given us dominion over all the other animals, insects and plants of this garden." Satan replied, "Do you know why he does not want you to partake of this forbidden fruit?" Eve replied, "No." Satan smiled and ended his conversation by saying, "He forbids you to eat of the fruit because he does not want you to be like him!" Satan had planted many seeds of doubt and questions within her, and he knew they needed to grow. So, he said unto her, "I am hungry, and I will leave you now so that I may find food. We will meet again soon, very soon."

Her mind raced with thoughts of her experience with the serpent. She searched for words to refute the serpent and found none. The vile snake had brought her to the pinnacle of ecstasy just before she pulled away from him. She wondered if her orgasm would have been a sin against Adam or God. Was God denying her pleasure by making her submissive to Adam's desires? Did God care about the pleasures of the flesh? What of the forbidden fruit? Could the forbidden fruit make her like God? Would she have the power to make others like her and Adam? She had often imagined having others like her in the garden. What if I was like God? Her thoughts bounced from question to question as she walked home.

Adam saw her as she broke into the clearing. He rose from the shade of his favorite tree to welcome her. She embraced him and took a deep breath through her nose. His scent filled her nostrils as she thought about him pleasuring her with his tongue. She became wet and desired for him to finish what the serpent had started. *If I had not stopped the serpent before it touched me*... she thought. Eve squeezed Adam and enjoyed the comfort of his embrace for a moment, and then she pulled him to the ground and kissed him passionately.

CHAPTER 21

In Heaven:

The messenger angel of God, Raziel recorded all that God said and did in a book. The cover of the book was pure gold, and the binding and pages were leather. Sapphire adorned its pages. A blue glow rose from the pages of the book.

Raziel knew the troubles that man would face, and he said unto himself, "I will go to the garden and show mercy unto Adam by giving him my book. Secretly, I will meet with him and teach him the understanding of all things written within its pages." So, Raziel descended unto the earth, and the Garden of Eden with the book and God was unaware.

In the garden, Adam lay under a shade tree, eating a piece of fruit. Raziel appeared before him. Adam fell on his face before Raziel and would have worshiped him, but Raziel begged him to rise. Raziel spoke unto Adam, "I have brought you a most special book. This book contains many secrets, and it can unlock many mysteries. You shall take this book and learn from it. I will meet with you daily to teach you from it, but you must not tell God. Your lessons shall be a secret that we shall share." Adam gladly accepted the book from Raziel and agreed to keep the text and their meetings a secret.

That afternoon when Raziel was not there, Adam opened the book. His eyes strained against the blue hue that came from the words written upon the leather pages. Like a child trying to understand complicated things, Adam struggled with the book and became confused. Adam became frustrated because he could not decipher the meaning of its words. Raziel saw his struggle and came to help him understand the book.

Raziel and Adam met daily to study the book, and Adam slowly began to understand the simple things written within its pages. Adam enjoyed his time with Raziel because they discussed many things that he was afraid to ask God about. Each day at the appointed time, Adam took the book from his hiding place, and after their lessons, he would return it.

After many days, two angels came from Heaven with evil intent. Semjaza and Azazel were part of a sect of angels in Heaven which bowed a knee to humanity as God ordered but did so only to appease him and stay in Heaven. These angels believed that humankind should not exist and that angels were vastly superior to them in every way.

One day, Semjaza and Azazel secretly watched Adam and Raziel as they studied the book. They heard secret words written in the book as Raziel explained them to Adam, and they saw the beauty of the book, and they were jealous. "How could God send Raziel to teach mankind secrets God did not share with them?" they thought. In anger, they proclaimed, "Man is not worthy of having the book of Raziel. We shall rise and take the book in the night. We will prevent humanity from learning the secrets of the book by throwing it into the sea. Humankind should not have such power!"

That night, the two angels snuck back into the garden and took the book from its hiding place. Azazel held the book tightly in his arms and desired to look upon its pages, but Semjaza was insistent that they get rid of the book. Azazel refused to throw the book into the sea without reading it. The two angels were at an impasse, but then Semjaza compromised with Azazel and said, "Let us take the book unto the sea and there you can read it until one hour has passed. When the hour is gone, you will throw the Book of Raziel into the sea, and we will return to Heaven without being missed." Azazel agreed with his proposal because he was afraid that God or one of his angels might catch them committing mischief against him.

Azazel and Semjaza sat by the sea enjoying the cool breeze as Azazel read from the book. The words written within its pages captivated Azazel. Azazel did not speak or hear anything until Semjaza yelled, "An angel is approaching!" Azazel came back to reality and saw an archangel approaching in the distance. So, Azazel begrudgingly threw the Book of Raziel into the sea for fear that they would be caught with the book.

Azazel and Semjaza rose into the air and flew towards Heaven, but the angel stopped them. Gabriel inquired of them, "What were you doing by the sea?" Semjaza replied, "We were sitting by the sea enjoying the cool breeze as it came off the waters." Many angels did this type of thing from time to time, so Gabriel had no reason to doubt them and sent them on their way.

The following day in the garden, Raziel came to visit with Adam and teach him the meaning of the things written in the book as was their custom. He found Adam sitting near the tree where he hid the book. There were tears in his eyes. Raziel asked Adam, "Why do you weep?" Adam replied, "I came this morning to retrieve the book so that I might learn from you the secrets of God, but the book was gone." Raziel's heart sank. He left Adam without a word and immediately took flight towards the throne of God. God would not be happy when he found out what Raziel had done, but that wasn't what worried him the most. The book was a powerful tool or weapon, and he did not know who had taken it!

In Heaven, Raziel went quickly to the Throne of God and requested an immediate audience with Him, and his request was granted. Raziel entered the throne room and threw himself on his face before God. God asked him, "Raziel, my faithful servant, what troubles you?" Raziel told God how he took his book and gave it to Adam. He explained how he tutored Adam on its' meanings and how someone stole it. Then he waited for God's response in the silence of the throne room.

After several moments of silence, God spoke and commanded his angels, "Go out and search for the Book of Raziel. Inquire of all of Heaven's hosts and find out where the book is. When you find it, bring it to me, and we shall return it to Adam." A murmur rumbled through the congregation of angels within the throne room. *How could God give humanity such power?* they thought. God did not chastise the angels, but instead, he commanded everyone except Raziel to leave his presence.

When only God and Raziel remained in the throne room, God said, "Raziel, your intentions were good in giving the book to Adam. He and his children will use the book's knowledge and wisdom to lead their people. One day, they will be a great nation because of the book. Therefore, once we have the book, you will give it back to Adam and make sure it stays hidden from those who would use it for evil or personal gain." Raziel bowed before God and replied, "As you have commanded, so shall it be." Then he asked God, "Master, may I continue to tutor Adam and his descendants?" God replied, "You may." Raziel departed from God's presence.

CHAPTER 22

Samael flew through the skies with the grace and elegance expected of one of God's most impressive creations. He was on a mission. A mission to find his bride to be, Lilith. His blood ran through her veins and destined them to be together. They would rule this world together. He had seen a vision of her and their children, but he had seen nothing beyond that. She was hiding somewhere below him. Then he saw the cave.

The cave's entrance was in the shadows, high in the rocky cliffs above the Red Sea. A perfect place to live for someone who didn't want uninvited guests. There was no trail or easily accessible route from the ground to the entrance. Only the most agile beasts could reach the cave's entry from the beach. Then they would have to contend with the creature that called the cave home. Lilith's dark presence grew stronger as he drew closer. A dense cloud of dark despair and death lingered around the cave. Her presence called to him like a siren luring a ship into the rocks and certain death. It was intoxicating, and she might even frighten him if he was not the Angel of Death.

He landed near the cave without making a sound, but Lilith knew she had company. Unlike the other angels she encountered, he seemed somehow familiar. Without fear, Lilith came out of the darkness and confronted him. Samael watched as she exited the cave. The light glistened off her dark, blood-red hair. Her eyes shone like emeralds and seemed to pierce his soul. Light brown skin, like an almond toasted in the mid-day sun, adorned her shapely body. She was beautiful and yet frightening. His loins stirred with an unfamiliar sensation as they stood silently facing one another.

Samael's appearance smote Lilith. He was powerful, beautiful, and yet he had something else. She sensed her likeness in him, *NO it is his likeness in me! How? Did not God create her?* Her questions faded from her thoughts, replaced by an irresistible urge to have him. The delightful thought of tasting him caused her thighs to become wet. Throwing caution to the wind, she let her desires guide her. She would have him, here and now!

Samael opened his mouth to speak, but she lunged at him. He instinctively reached for his sword, but quickly realized she did not intend to harm him. Her eyes were wild and filled with lust, and he was not sure what to do. Samael did not know the pleasures of the flesh, but today, he would taste them for the first time. She leaped on him. Her arms wrapped around his neck, and her thighs gripped tightly around his waist. She stared into his eyes for a moment, and a fire erupted within them. She could feel his member throbbing in anticipation of something he had never experienced. Lust overcame him, but he wasn't sure what to do next.

She kissed him passionately, and he followed her direction and mimicked her movements. Their tongues became intertwined in a battle of sorts, probing and coiling together like newborn vipers in their nest. Lust and sexual desire overwhelmed them. She loosened her grip of him and lowered herself to the ground as she unclasped his belt. His sword and undergarment fell at his feet, and she took him into her mouth. Her actions sent ripples of pleasure through his body. *How could such joy be a secret? Did God willingly keep this pleasure from his faithful?* The fulfillment of sexual desire rivaled the satisfaction he received from taking another life.

Samael's muscles tightened as an explosion welled up inside of him. Every fiber of his body erupted in pleasure, his cheeks flushed warm, and his temperature rose. His heart threatened to burst out of his chest, and he thought he might die from the pleasure of her actions. She felt his excitement and pleasured him faster in anticipation of his release. Suddenly there was an explosion of pure ecstasy within him. He was powerless against the pleasure that took hold of his body as he shook with every spasm of his ejaculation. The echoes of his gratification reverberated through his entire body, and then he fell motionless. He had never lived before this moment. One time would not be enough! Lilith realized that she could have an orgasm while pleasuring another, and this excited her more. Adam didn't deserve such treatment, but Samael was different.

Lilith's orgasm left her wanting more. She needed him between her thighs. So, she took his hand and pulled him down to the ground with her. He willingly submitted to her, and she rolled over on top of him. She guided his member between her thighs as she lowered herself onto him. Desire flowed from her and ran down her legs. A shiver of ecstasy shot up her spine as he fully entered her. He made her whole. It was as if the two of them made one whole part. She reached new heights of delight as she rode him. As she looked into his lust-filled eyes, she bit her lip and blood trickled down her chin. They were like glass, clear as the cleansing waters that fed God's garden. She could see into his soul, and pleasure was his countenance.

Samael reached up and grabbed her firm breasts. His fingers instinctively pulled on her erect nipples. He twisted them between his fingers, and she cried out in pleasure. Then he pulled her breasts to his mouth and kissed them. After a few moments, another explosion welled up within him. He would control his climax this time.

Forcefully, he rolled Lilith over onto her back and thrust himself into her. She moaned with the pleasure and the pain of him forcing her to submit. Unlike Adam, Samael was worthy of her submission. He would be hers, and she would be his forever! He thrust himself into her as if he sought to split her into two. The combination of blissful pain and total ecstasy drove her to a point where she thought she could take no more, but she refused to make him stop. She passed the threshold of pleasure and felt her soul rising from her body. Then, violently, her soul rushed back into her as she shuddered in orgasm repeatedly.

With each orgasm, her thighs tightened upon his member. Her cries of pleasure excited him, but he continued to thrust himself violently into her. Then Lilith's body became rigid, and she shook for what seemed like a hundred orgasms in succession. Her womanhood clenched his member and threatened to tear it from his body. He could take no more. Without warning, the pleasure of orgasm took hold of him. The intensity of his gratification caused him to cry out, "God..." He collapsed onto her as his body finished the spasm of release deep within her. She wrapped her arms, legs, and wings around him and pulled him into her bosom. Samael laid his head upon her breasts and savored their warmth upon her thighs.

Several moments passed with only the sounds of their erratic and heavy breathing. The sweet fragrances of their sweat and body fluids filled Samael's nostrils and threatened to revive his passion once more. He raised his head and looked into her bright, piercing eyes. She was completely satisfied, and he shared her contentment. He rose from her thighs and offered her his hand. She took it, and he effortlessly pulled her to her feet.

Then Samael spoke his first words to Lilith, "What do you have to eat in this place?" She replied, "Many beasts are here for your pleasure. What you find you may eat. I will go and refresh myself in the sea. When I return, we can speak about God and how you and I came together." Samael nodded in agreement and said unto her, "You will learn much from me in the days to come." Then he descended from the cave in search of food, and she leaped into the sea.

CHAPTER 23

As the days passed, Adam continued to commune with God, but Eve explored the garden in search of adventure and new things. Her experiences often became a hunt for the black and yellow serpent which she had not seen since their encounter in the pool. During one of her wanderings, she found a small, bright red serpent, and she took it as her familiar or pet. The serpent went everywhere with her. She loved it and treated it as if it were her child. Sometimes she even thought it spoke to her like the black and yellow serpent did.

Aym and his trusted servants continued to whisper to Eve, and each day she drifted closer to her place in Satan's plan. Satan, however, spent much of his time eavesdropping on Adam and God as they communed and fellowshipped together. God sickened him! *How could he take man as his most treasured confidant? He forced us to worship him, but with an inferior creation such as man, he shares everything. God placed me above the other angels, but now because I refused to bow down to humankind; I am a castaway.* His blood boiled with rage. In his heart, he believed God gave humanity the Garden of Eden to spite him. *He cast us out, left us deformed and in the darkness of this world for thousands of years, only to give everything to humankind.*

Satan couldn't watch them anymore. So, he left in search of Eve. He cursed God as he walked down the path towards the Tree of the Knowledge of Good and Evil. Along the trail, he passed a small patch of colorful and exotic flowers. *God's handiwork,* he thought as he looked down at the flowers. Then, without warning, he tore the flowers out of the ground and screamed profanities into the air. In an angry fit, he ripped the flowers to pieces, petal by petal, leaf by leaf, and stem by stem until they were a pile on the ground. He looked at the remains of the flowers that once possessed such beauty, but still possessed vibrant colors, and he stomped them into the ground until nothing recognizable remained. *I will not rest until I destroy all of God's handiwork. Especially, his precious man and woman!*

In the distance he saw Eve sitting under the Tree of the Knowledge of Good and Evil. The tree provided the best shade in all the garden. When the heat of the noonday sun was upon the garden, many of the animals sought shelter there. Eve sat under the tree, caressing her serpent as it slithered between her fingers. Satan laughed because he knew her affection for serpents came from his encounter with her at the pool. Eve was fair and beautiful to look upon, but she was inferior to him and the other angels. *Why did God not see they were superior to humankind?*

Disguised as an angel of God, Satan, walked out into the clearing. Eve saw a beautiful angel walking towards her. She welcomed him, saying, "May God's peace be upon you heavenly one." He returned her greeting, "God's peace be upon you as well. May I join you in the cool shade?" She replied, "Yes," as she slid over and made room for him near the base of the tree. He sat down in the shade beside her. With curious eyes, she studied him. "What is it like to fly?" she inquired. "The cool breeze is always upon your face, and God's beautiful creatures frolic below you," he replied. Eve asked, "What beautiful creatures?" "I have seen many beautiful creatures, but none compare to your beauty!" His reply caused Eve's cheeks to flush warm with embarrassment because she had never received a compliment from Adam. Satan continued playing to her beauty by saying, "If it were lawful, I would take you to be my wife. You would live with me in heaven. The other angels would admire your beauty and worship you. They would be envious of me for your sake!" Eve responded, "Do not speak of such things because I am Adam's wife, and he is my husband.

God created me for this purpose."

Satan shifted his line of questioning, "Why does this tree bear such succulent fruit?" Eve replied, "God forbade us to partake of the fruit!" Satan questioned her again, saying, "Why would God give you this garden and tell you not to partake of a single tree in it?" Eve replied, "God said if we eat from this tree, we will die." Satan answered, "You shall not die, but instead, you will be like God. You will know the difference between good and evil!" Then Satan glanced upward and selected the most appealing piece of fruit. He plucked it from the tree and retrieved a small blade from his belt. Eve watched him with great interest as he cut the fruit in half. Sweet juice flowed from the fruit and pooled in his hand. The intoxicating aroma of the fruit caused Eve's mouth to water with anticipation. Her eyes followed drops of juice as they fell from his hand as if they were in slow motion.

The fragrance of the fruit invited her to partake, but she resisted. *I almost have her; she needs a little push*, Satan thought. He placed his knife back on his belt and took one half of the fruit and ate it. "MMMMM..." he moaned with delight as if he was in the throes of pleasure. When he finished the piece of fruit, he dramatically wiped the juices from his mouth. Her eyes were wide with desire. Satan smiled as he offered the remaining half of the fruit to her. "There is no fruit like this! It is delicious, ripe, and sweet. Take the fruit and eat." Eve reached out to take the fruit from his hand and nearly had it, but Adam called to her from the trees. "Eve, where are you?" She jumped up, turned, and ran towards him. "I am here!" she yelled without looking back. As Eve ran to Adam, she thought, *Adam almost saw me with the angel! He cannot know how close I was to partaking of the forbidden fruit*

CHAPTER 24

In the weeks to follow, Samael and Lilith left their lair only to eat. They enjoyed the passionate embrace of the flesh and left very little time for anything else. In the other times, Samael shared the ancient ways with Lilith. She learned about God, the Great War in Heaven, Satan, and the Fallen Ones and the powers of this world. The power of God is the power God gave to the divine and humankind, and the power God that is in nature.

Samael told her about God's plan and how he thought if man multiplied long enough, God would become weak. He shared his thoughts, and she shared hers. Soon they agreed about destroying Adam and Eve's relationship with God. He was confident that God would not allow them to harm his precious children, but if they sinned against him, he would have no choice, but to drive them from his presence and then they would be vulnerable. Finally, Samael told Lilith the story of his banishment from Heaven and his battle with the Fallen Ones on earth.

Lilith listened as Samael explained his conflict with Bael and the Fallen Ones after his fall. He told her how God spoke, and it was, and how he spilled his blood. His life's essence, to bring her into the world. He told her how he couldn't imagine how perfect she would be when he spilled his blood upon the ground. After hearing his words, the desire to have him inside of her again overwhelmed her. She kissed him, and they made love until the sun rose the next morning.

Two days later, Samael sat on the narrow ledge at the entrance to her lair. He marveled at the beauty of another sunrise; *God is quite an artist!* His admiration for God's handiwork passed through his mind as quickly as the morning breeze carried the salty air off the sea. A tinge of excitement and revelation came to him. *Today is going to be a good day.* He rose and returned to Lilith. He woke her and said unto her, “Let's see how Satan fares with his temptation of Eve.” She rose from her slumber, and they flew to the garden God created for humanity.

Satan, Aym and his select few met them in the garden near the Tree of the Knowledge of Good and Evil. Aym and his select immediately lunged at Samael and intended to kill him for his part in their fall from Heaven. Satan knew they stood no chance of beating him in combat. “STOP!” Satan said in a raspy voice which echoed as if it came from hell itself. They froze in place and cowered back to Satan's side. Samael almost felt sorry for them, seeing Satan and the Fallen Ones in their disfigured forms was like witnessing something worse than death itself. They were deformed, burnt, and they reeked of rotting flesh, but they could not die from their wounds. They kept their original form only because Samael knew who and what they were.

Satan glared at Lilith as she stood at Samael's side facing him. *How had they joined forces*, he wondered? Samael bent a knee to the image of humankind instead of joining their cause because he saw a vision warning him of Satan's defeat during the First Great War. Satan didn't know about his vision and couldn't understand why Samael had not fought with them in Heaven. He didn't trust Samael or like him, but he hoped that his presence meant that he was not following God's agenda anymore. Several moments passed before Satan broke the silence and asked Samael, “Have you come to drive us from this place also?” Samael replied, “No, I am here to ensure that you don't fail this time! I went to great lengths to ensure the Tree of the Knowledge of Good and Evil was in the garden. My blood nourished it, hence its opposing nature. I killed one of God's faithful servants to keep the tree a secret, and God cast me out of Heaven for it!” Satan replied, “You should have shared your plan for mankind's fall with us from the beginning."

Samael replied, "You are a fool!" Satan fought back the rage that boiled up within him because he feared Samael might kill him and become the leader of the Fallen Ones. Samael spoke again, "You and the Fallen Ones were doomed to fail, even if I fought with you! We did not possess the strength to defeat God then, and we do not possess the strength now!" Satan defiantly replied, "We could have killed him." Samael replied, "Your desire for revenge clouds your judgment. Do not obsess with winning the war, but instead focus on winning the day. We will strike when he is weak and distracted. Lilith will help you ensure that Eve falls to temptation and eats of the Tree of the Knowledge of Good and Evil. Then, her guilt will cause her to lead Adam astray." Samael wanted Satan to understand his plan, but he wasn't ready to hear it, so he didn't waste his time trying to explain how God placed a part of himself in each man or woman he created. As humankind multiplied, God would grow weaker. That was tomorrow's concern. Today they needed to focus on the first step, the fall of Adam and Eve.

Satan considered Samael's words; what did he see that he didn't? Reluctantly, he said unto Samael, "After their fall, we will have our revenge. God will forsake them, and then we can kill them!" Samael replied, "How will killing them help us defeat God?" Satan answered, "I will have my revenge, and I will kill them!" Samael grew tired of trying to explain his plan to Satan who had spent thousands of years in pain, only surviving by his desire for revenge. Perhaps someday Satan will have rational thoughts, but until then, we only need to ensure that Adam and Eve sin against God.

Lilith would take great pleasure in helping Samael and Satan because she was jealous of the love Adam and Eve shared. *It should have been me*, she thought. Samael turned towards her and glared at her as if he had read her mind. His glare snapped her back to the reality of this situation, and she immediately regretted her thoughts and reassured herself. *Samael and I are meant to be together.* Satan needed her help, and she would gladly give it to ensure that Adam did not interfere with their plans. Eve must sin first. If Eve fell, Adam would follow, and God would forsake them!

CHAPTER 25

William almost jumped out of his seat when someone started pounding on the front door. It tore him from the pages of Satan's book. He hurried to his feet, got up too fast, and became lightheaded. His hands frantically searched for something to steady himself; they found the end table before he fell. The pounding continued while he took a couple of deep breaths and regained his faculties. Finally, Margaret called to him from outside, "William, my hands are full! Can you open the door, please?" "I'm coming," he said as he made his way to the front door. He opened the door, and Margaret pushed past him towards the kitchen. He tried to get the rest of the groceries from the car. "Don't even think about it! I will get the rest of the groceries, and you can help put them away," Margaret said. Defeated, he turned around and followed her to the kitchen to the kitchen. The screen door rattled and then squeaked as it was opened again. So, he turned back to see who was coming in.

"Close the kitchen door," he yelled to Margaret when he saw the large dog standing in their foyer. "Why..." trailed off her lips when she saw the dog. She slammed the kitchen door in horror. The dog stalked William with a deep, bone-chilling growl. Drool fell from it snarling mouth onto the floor as it approached him. William stared into the dog's black lifeless eyes. *I hate dogs, and this dog does not seem right!* His hatred for dogs came from numerous childhood dog chases, two of which ended in dog bites and emergency room visits. One of them even ended in rabies shots because the dog was a stray and ran off. *Dogs were his worst fear, and this was no coincidence!* He needed something to defend himself with, but he couldn't find anything.

The dog slowly backed into a corner and was close enough to pounce on him now. He knew he only had seconds, but he could not find anything big enough to defend himself. The dog was huge! The dog leaped at William. He tried to evade, but the dog was much faster, and he fell under its weight. He struggled to hold the dog's head away as it snapped its massive jaws a fraction of an inch from his face. Over and over, it thrust its powerful jaws towards his face. Warm drool sprayed across his face with each of the dog's attempt. Suddenly, William heard a clanking sound; the dog wined and fell limp on top of him. It took everything he had to roll the dog off his chest. When the dog fell away, he saw Margaret. She stood in front of him with an aluminum baseball bat. "Are you okay?" she asked in a familiar voice that was not her own. He tried to reply, but adrenaline and confusion only allowed him to mumble. "How...." The strange voice interrupted him, "I had to borrow your wife's body to save you. Her fear allowed me to possess her, and it's lucky for you that I did." William recognized the voice, *Amon!* "You wouldn't have to possess my wife if you protected me!" Amon replied, "I told you it is complicated! My intervention puts me and Satan's plan in danger." William responded, "I don't give a rat's ass. If your boss wants me to read his book and potentially help him, he'd better protect my family and me from whoever or whatever is trying to kill us. Now get the hell out of my wife's body and my house!" Amon tried to console him, "I will speak to Satan, but he is protecting you more than you know!"

William could tell the instant Amon left Margaret's body; she shook her head as if she was clearing the cobwebs and gave him a confused look. Then she said, "It was like a dream. I was in the kitchen sitting on the floor crying when something came over me." He stood up and hugged Margaret. "It's all right, you saved me," he said as he squeezed her tightly.

Twenty minutes later, animal control arrived to take the dog away. The owner had shown up and protested the dog's detention. They claimed the dog was a gentle giant and had shown no sign of aggression. A medic treated the claw marks on William's arms while the owner continued to plead for his dog's life with animal control. William believed the owner, but he didn't want to share his concerns with his wife. *Someone or something is trying to keep me from reading this book! Was God willing to kill me to keep the book a secret or was Satan behind it all?* The book caused conflict within him. His parents had always instilled in him a sense of good and evil, but Satan's book appeared to show something else. The lines between good and evil were becoming blurry. *I am in real danger!* Finishing the book seemed like his only hope, so after dinner, he sat down in his chair and began reading.

CHAPTER 26

Adam woke to the sound of birds singing and playing in the trees overhead. The sunlight danced between the branches, providing the perfect amount of light to bring them out of their peaceful slumber. Adam smiled as he admired his sleeping wife. He kissed her neck and ran his hand through her hair before tracing his fingertip over her ear. His finger glided over the top of her ear and down to earlobe. He squeezed it between his forefinger and thumb playfully. Eve woke and reached behind her and pulled him closer. He slid in behind her. Their bodies became joined in passion as they moved to the rhythm of the garden and their desire for pleasure. Their erotic symphony ended in a climactic release which echoed their delight throughout the nearby trees. In satisfaction, they drifted back into a peaceful slumber.

Adam woke to Eve kissing his cheek. "Sleep on, my love, I am going to the pool," Adam mumbled a drowsy reply and went back to sleep. Eve planned to swim in the pool for a short time, but her real intent was to find the great serpent. If the black and yellow serpent was not at the pool, she would search the garden until she found it. She needed to see it!

Eve strolled down the trail that led to the pool. She sat on the side of the water and soaked her feet in the refreshing waters. It was teaming with life. Creatures of all sizes and shapes moved around the pool and nearby garden, but she did not see the serpent. Her mind recalled the pleasures she received from its touch, and she found herself wet with excitement. She thought about what the serpent had said about pleasuring herself and allowed her hand to drift towards her thighs. Just as her hand pierced her red veil and entered the warmth it protected; the bushes rustled. Startled by the noise, she turned and saw the yellow tip of a serpent's tail. Her heart raced with excitement. *The serpent*, she thought as she rose to her feet and ran after it. She was determined to catch it.

Earlier in the garden:

Lilith watched as Aym whispered into Eve's ear as she slept. His words were evil and corrupt. They slithered into her ears and pierced her thoughts, nurturing her sinful desires. Adam's poor wife didn't stand a chance! Aym scurried off when Eve stirred. As soon as her eyes opened, she kissed him on the cheek, whispered into Adam's ear, and left in search of the serpent. *Everything is going according to plan!* Lilith laughed as she imagined Eve's fate. She rose from her hiding place and glided over to Adam as she transformed herself to appear as Eve. As Adam slumbered, she laid down beside him. Adam did not stir or wake as Lilith wrapped her arm around him and placed her head on his shoulder in a loving embrace. Out of habit, he moved in response to her actions, placing his hand upon her arm. Her hand drifted down to his manhood, but he did not wake even though her actions pleased him. She continued until sleep lost its hold on him. He awoke on the verge of showering his seed into the air. As he struggled to shake the grogginess from his eyes, she rolled over between his thighs and took him into her mouth. He groaned with delight as he left his seed within her.

Adam pulled Lilith up from his manhood and rolled her over. He smiled at her as he ran his fingers through her hair and down her breasts. Still, in the disguise of Eve, she looked up at him, encouraging him to have his way with her. His hands danced over her body until they came to rest between her thighs. His fingers danced upon and within her, and she moaned in response to his actions. Lilith encouraged him to take his time. There was no rush.

Present time, on the other side of the garden:

Eve burst out of the underbrush of the trail into a small clearing near a familiar tree. The Tree of the Knowledge of Good and Evil rose high into the air before her. It seemed to be calling to her. Aym and his select few were hiding high in the branches of the tree, calling to her in ancient voices carried upon the breeze. The fruit of the tree sparkled in the sunlight, and each one seemed perfect in her eyes. She recalled the sweet fragrance of the fruit when the angel had offered it to her. The juice that fell to the ground had seemed like a sinful waste. Before she realized what she was doing, she found herself under the tree, looking up, longing for the fruit that called out to her.

In the form of the black and yellow serpent; Satan perched himself in the tree, just out of her sight. He watched, wondering if he would need to do more for her to partake of the forbidden fruit and sin against God. Eve's eyes blazed bright with desire; she longed for the fruit. *I must have it!* Her mouth watered at the thought of eating the appealing fruit. Suddenly, she fell to her knees, willing herself not to succumb to her desire to have what she should not. *God has forbidden us to partake of this fruit! I will die if I eat the fruit, just as God has said.*

With his head and arms over one side of a branch, Satan lowered himself. He coiled around a tree branch to support himself, and with his tail, he picked the most appealing piece of fruit from the tree. He lowered it down within her reach and swung it from side to side. Her eyes followed the piece of fruit as it swung like a pendulum of pure temptation before her. The serpent's presence heightened her sexual desires, but she couldn't take her eyes off the fruit. Satan raised his tail just out of her reach and took the fruit in both of his hands. He spoke to her in a soft and soothing voice, "Eve, take the fruit and eat. There is no sweeter fruit in the entire garden. Do not fear; you will not die! This sweet fruit will make you like God."

Eve paused as if she was examining his words, and then she said, "I cannot." She spoke with the sorrow of someone who grieved the loss of a family member.

Satan split the fruit into two halves with his hands. A single drop of juice fell downward, as if in slow motion, and landed on the back of Eve's hand. She stared at the drop of juice on her hand. The sweet smell of the fruit rose from the drop like an intoxicating perfume, calling to her. It glistened in the light, and she could feel her skin absorbing the sweet juice. Satan took one half of the fruit and bit into it. As he ate the fruit, he made sounds as though he had never eaten before. He moaned, and she watched him until the fruit was gone.

He wiped the sweet juice from his lips with a sigh of satisfaction. Then, he took the other half of the fruit with his tail and lowered it within reach. He turned the fruit so that Eve could see the succulent meat inside. The fruit, which was only a few inches from her nose, filled her nostrils with its irresistible scent. Her mouth watered even more, and her stomach growled in anticipation. Satan whispered to her, "Take the fruit, eat and be satisfied." Then he lowered the fruit more and said again, "Eat and be satisfied."

Every fiber of her body wanted, no, needed the fruit. The serpent brought the fruit closer to her mouth. She took the fruit from the serpent with a hand on each side of the fruit. Her heart pounded with fear and excitement. She raised the fruit to her lips and inhaled the sweet aroma once more. Aym and the select few continued to whisper to her, "Eat and be satisfied." Satan said unto to her again, "Eat and be satisfied."

The juice flowed over her tongue like a refreshing stream as she bit into the fruit. It was as sweet as she had imagined. Pure satisfaction filled her as the fruit melted in her mouth. *How could such a lovely fruit harm me*, she thought? The rich flavor of the fruit was incredible. She wiped the excess juice from her mouth with a lustful moan, and then she licked it from her hand. As she finished the last bit of the fruit, she savored it. She had consumed the whole piece of fruit without pause. Suddenly, the fruit soured in her mouth.

Horror filled Eve, *What have I done?* She looked down at herself and realized she was naked. Ashamed of her nakedness, she hid in the branches of a nearby fig tree. She considered her actions and trembled in fear. Then she heard the evil, echoing laughter of Satan, Aym and his select few. Their laughter echoed through the trees of the garden, and her body trembled in the rhythm of it. Eve broke through the dense foliage in a dead sprint, with a fig branch in each hand. She covered herself with the branches as she ran in terror towards Adam.

On the other side of the garden:

A smile formed on Lilith's lips and her eyes opened as she heard Satan's triumph. She knew Eve sinned and ate of the forbidden tree. Eve's horror brought her great joy. Lilith had little time now, and she would have her revenge. Violently she rolled Adam over on his back and mounted him. He protested her violent actions until her womanhood constricted upon him. With a moan of pleasure, he laid back as she drew his seed from him. Each of her movements heightened his pleasure and drove him towards a climax. Moments later, his body shook and trembled as his muscles tightened. He opened his eyes and looked up at his wife as his seed flowed into her. Horror filled him as the last spasms of his seed left his body. *It is Lilith who is upon me!*

Lilith's evil laughter echoed through the trees. Birds and other creatures fled in terror. She dug her claws into him and drew blood as she pressed his shoulders firmly onto the ground. Her wings fluttered in triumph as she continued to ride him, seeking to pleasure herself. A wicked smile of pure satisfaction formed on her lips as her body shook with delight. She held him down, on his back, in submission, and glared down at him. Her hips rotated viciously on top of his thighs as she fulfilled her lusts. Then she arched her back, stretched out her wings, and dug her fingernails into his chest as she screamed with delight.

Adam was furious! Lilith wrenched his head to the side and slowly licked his cheek in a display of control. He groaned in anger and fought against her. She turned his head back, kissed him and bit his lip, drawing blood. Her fingernails drew blood as her hand constricted on his neck like a snake upon its prey. Adam thought, *She is going to choke the life out of me!* As he struggled to pry her hand from his neck, she wiped the blood from his lip with her other hand and licked it from her finger. She stared into his horror-filled eyes. Oxygen deprivation set in and his sight became tunneled, and he saw stars. He realized he was powerless against her. She smiled in delight because she knew his thoughts, and then she wrenched his head to face her and smashed her lips upon his cheek in a loveless kiss.

She released him and laughed as she rose to her feet. Adam remained on the ground, panting for air, tears of anger formed in his eyes and rolled down his cheeks. Rage welled up within him and propelled him up towards her, and he thought, *I will strangle her*! She taunted him as she rose into the air and out of his reach. He yelled at her, "You EVIL WITCH!" She suddenly stopped laughing and replied unto him, "Careful, good husband, your wife is coming. What will you tell her about how you allowed me to take your seed, not once, but twice?" As she rose up through the trees, his mind cleared, and he remembered Eve leaving in search of adventure earlier that morning. He fell to his knees and wept, *What have I done?* Eve broke through the trees with the sound of breaking branches and stopped in the clearing before him. He lifted his head from his hands and turned towards her. Adam's eyes met Eve's in a mutual gaze of absolute horror, and she fell to her knees and wept with him.

CHAPTER 27

Adam struggled to wrap his mind around what he had done. Images of Lilith stealing his seed flashed before his eyes. Rage and sorrow welled up within him, so he wept. Eve embraced Adam as he rose. They held each other for several moments, each seeking comfort from the other. Adam stopped crying as his rage subsided. His mind raced with unrealistic scenarios of him taking revenge against Lilith. Several moments passed before he realized Eve was still sobbing. He extended his arms, pushed Eve away from him so that he could look upon her. Her red, tear-filled eyes conveyed deep sadness, and she did not know about Lilith yet. He watched as a wave of embarrassment washed over her. She reached down and picked up the fig leaves which fell when they embraced. She covered herself with the leaves and looked at him with shame in her heart. "Why are you covering yourself with those leaves?" he asked. Eve replied, "Because I am naked!"

Adam knew she was different somehow, but he did not understand. He asked, "Eve, what happened to you?" She replied, "I ate the fruit which God forbade us to eat." Adam looked at her in horror and disbelief. *She ate the forbidden fruit!* Adam opened his mouth to speak, but the words left him. He communed with God daily. God had shared many of life 's secrets with them. He allowed Raziel to teach him ancient secrets from the pages of his book. His encounter with Lilith seemed like a distant memory now. *Eve's news was deeply troubling, this was terrible!* Fear washed over Adam, "What are we going to do now?" Eve did not have an answer for him, so they stood and embraced in silence.

Finally, Eve broke their long silence and said unto

Adam, "I was reborn when I ate the fruit." Adam looked into her eyes. The tears were gone, and her eyes were bright and vibrant again, but she was hiding something. She wanted and needed him to eat of the tree because she feared God 's wrath. "Let's go to the tree. You can partake of the fruit, and you will be reborn as I am. You will know as I know." He was not convinced, but he agreed, "Let's go to the Tree of the Knowledge of Good and Evil!" Eve took Adam's hand and led him down the trail to the tree. After several minutes of walking in silence, they broke through the underbrush, and the tree stood before them.

The tree rose high above the rest of the trees as if it were the king of the garden. Its lush fruit hung like decorations and seemed to call out to him "take and eat." Without hesitation, Adam walked over to the tree and looked up at the fruit. The sweet fragrance of the fruit rose into his nostrils, and his mouth watered in anticipation. A battle raged within him. He wanted to eat the fruit, but God said they would die if they ate it, and yet Eve stood beside him, healthy and alive.

Eve saw the battle raging inside of Adam. *I cannot be the only one to disobey God! God will have mercy on us if we both sin!* Satan and his Fallen Ones tempted me, and I fell, but they were not here now. *It is up to me now*, she thought. She reached up and picked the most appealing piece of fruit from the tree. She stretched out her arm, presented it to him, and said, "Eat and be satisfied!" Adam's gaze drifted from her eyes to the fruit in her hand, but he did not take it. Eve raised the fruit to her mouth and bit into it. As she ate the fruit, she held it up to him. The pleasant aroma was even stronger now, but he still did not partake. She took another bite and exaggerated her enjoyment of the fruit with soft moaning sounds she thought might arouse him.

Adam's inner conflict grew with each temptation. Many times, God told me, "You will die if you eat the fruit." Eve was still alive. Adam wrestled with his desire to eat the fruit as he watched Eve eat the fruit. Eve finished half of the fruit but did not swallow the last bite. Instead, she kissed him. He resisted and kept his mouth closed. Her hand slid down past his rippled abdomen and caressed his manhood, enticing him to return her kiss. Adam could not resist her temptation any longer, and he kissed her back. As they kissed, her tongue entered his mouth, and the sweet fruit went with it. The fruit was intoxicating, and he savored it. The taste of the fruit overwhelmed him, and he forgot her hand upon his manhood. When they finished with their kiss, he took the other half of the fruit, and he ate it. The sweet fruit delighted him. It wasn't until he swallowed the last bite of fruit that he realized Eve was kneeling between his thighs. As his seed left him, the fruit juice soured in his mouth.

The skies above the Garden of Eden turned dark and ominous before his muscles stopped trembling from orgasm. Lightning flashed through the air and struck a nearby tree. The tree split in two, and the thunder crashed like an explosion echoing through the trees. Adam took Eve's hand and pulled her to her feet. They covered their ears and trembled in fear as lightning and thunder ravaged the garden around them for the first time. Adam and Eve ran in terror back to the place they called home.

Adam understood why Eve covered herself after she partook of the fruit. He was naked and felt ashamed. So, they sewed fig leaves into garments to cover their nakedness. The dark clouds came, and lightning flashed ever since Adam ate the fruit, *It must be a sign that God knows of our sins*, they thought. They trembled and hid from God and his angels.

Raziel watched from the shadows. A single fell from his cheek, and a white lily sprang up from the ground. God had sent him to deliver the book, and the news about his continued education, but their fall from grace changed everything. Adam and Eve had done the unthinkable. They had sinned against God and done that which he forbade them to do. Raziel could not give Adam the book now and did not want to be in the garden when God's wrath fell upon them.

So, he left the garden and returned to heaven without making himself known to Adam and Eve.

CHAPTER 28

The next day God descended in the evening to commune with Adam and Eve according to his custom. He called out to them, "Adam and Eve, where art thou?" Adam and Eve did not answer him because they were ashamed and hid in the trees. They trembled in fear as God called for them a second time, "Adam and Eve, where art thou?" After God called out the second time, Adam finally replied: "We are here, Lord, but we did not answer because we are ashamed to be clothed with fig leaves!" God inquired of them, "Why are you wearing garments made of fig leaves?" Adam answered, "Lord, we were naked, so we fashioned garments to cover our nakedness." God replied, "Who told you that you were naked?" Adam replied, "No one, we realized we were naked!" God asked them, "Did you eat of the fruit of the Tree of the Knowledge of Good and Evil?" Adam replied, "Eve forced me to eat!" Eve interrupted them and defended herself by saying, "I did not force him to eat the fruit. He took it from me willingly!" Adam was desperate to free himself of blame, "She passed the fruit when she kissed me." Eve replied, "You knew the fruit was in my mouth and you wanted the fruit before I kissed you. You are the one that said, 'Let's go to the tree!'" God asked, "Eve, why did you eat the fruit which I forbade you to eat?" Eve responded, "Satan tempted me three times, and I had no strength left to resist. In the end, he came as a serpent, tempted me, and I ate!"

God became angry with them, "Did I not tell you that if you ate of the Tree of the Knowledge of Good and Evil, you would die?" Adam replied, "Yes, Lord, but we did not die, and unless you kill us now, we will not die." God responded,

"When you partook of the forbidden fruit, your natures became sinful. You are no longer immortal, and now you shall be hostages to the struggles of sin in this world. I cannot commune with you because sin is within you. You shall not have the gift of heavenly sight because of your sin." Adam and Eve's sight grew dim, and they could no longer see into Heaven, and they could only see supernatural beings if they showed themselves.

Then God cursed the serpent saying, "Upon your belly, you shall crawl! You shall eat the dust of the earth until this world burns." Then he turned to the Tree of the Knowledge of Good and Evil and cursed it, "You shall no longer be a bountiful fruit tree. You shall be a vine that crawls upon the earth like the serpent. Man shall despise the serpent, but your fate will depend on humanity. Humankind will trample you under their feet unless they choose to lift you off the ground. Your fruit shall be a grape which withers in the sun. Man shall make your grapes into wine and drink. Some men will become belligerent and hateful, and others will sleep and be slothful. They shall fall to drunkenness and ruin because there is no good left in you!"

Then God cursed Adam and Eve, "You are both subject to the pain of this world. You will work the earth and hunt for your sustenance. It shall not be easy for you. Eve and her daughters shall endure pain and suffering during childbirth because she fell first and then tempted Adam to eat. You will multiply and have children, but with each child will come pain, blood, and suffering. During childbirth, you will say unto yourself, 'I will die bearing this child!' and yet you will not die. This garden is no longer your home, and you may never return. NOW LEAVE MY SIGHT, SINNERS!"

When God finished his words, he called unto the Watchers from Heaven. One of the Watchers descended to serve his purpose. The giant angel held a great fiery sword in his hands. The angel drove Adam and Eve from the garden. As they left the garden, they saw God's curses fulfilled. The Tree of the Knowledge of Good and Evil became a barren vine lying upon the ground. The serpents slithered from the garden on their bellies as they hissed with shame. When Adam and Eve were a short distance from the garden, the mighty angel sealed the gate to the garden and stood guard before it. Then God commanded his spirit, and the garden became impenetrable except for the entrance. Humankind would never enter the garden again because of their sins. With a heavy heart, God returned to his throne in Heaven. Humankind separated themselves from him with their sin. He sat down on his throne and turned his gaze away from the earth. As he stared into the darkness of space, he mourned humanity's future. His beloved children would know great pain and suffering because of their sins, and he wept for them.

CHAPTER 29

Satan watched God curse Adam and Eve and drive them out of the Garden of Eden. Their sins separated them from God, and their eyes were no longer bright with the sight of God. Adam and Eve struggled with the heat and rough terrain of the earth. Their journey was difficult, and they knew the struggles of life for the first time. They stumbled and fell to the ground as the rocks and briers cut the bottoms of their feet. There was no pain, fear, or despair before their fall, but now nothing was easy for them. Satan's heart leaped with joy as he sensed the hopelessness and fear growing within them. It had been a long time since he enjoyed a victory, and this was only the beginning of the pain he wanted to cause humankind. Death was coming for them, and then God would know defeat!

Gabriel saw Satan's treachery and had mercy on Adam and Eve. He interceded with God on behalf of his children. Reluctantly, God sent his angels to lead them to safety and to bring them garments and sandals made of animals' skins. God blessed the garments to protect them from danger. The angels led them to a suitable dwelling place as God commanded them. They found a cave to protect them from the harsh environment their sins created. Adam and Eve accepted God's gifts, and they praised him for his mercy. God received their praise and rewarded them by commanding the animals not to harm them. He commanded them to provide for them until Adam's death. Only the serpents refused God's command and desired to kill Adam and Eve.

God's blessings raised Adam and Eve's spirits, but they still mourned the loss of their life in the garden. In the garden, they had true fellowship with God, but now there was an emptiness in their hearts. Despair, pain, and loneliness overwhelmed them like a mother mourning the loss of her child. Their mortality haunted them for the first time. *We can die at any moment*, they thought.

Adam and Eve decided to pray and fast for three days and three nights so that God might forgive them, but God remained silent. On the fourth day, they emerged from the cave because they said in their hearts, we will not die alone in this place. The bright sun stung their eyes, and they covered their eyes as they struggled to recover from the darkness of the cave. When their eyes cleared, they saw the gate of the garden and the great angel standing guard. They remembered the peace and happiness they experienced in the garden, and they became depressed.

Satan rejoiced in their despair and descended from a rock high above their cave and whispered to a nearby serpent. It obeyed and slithered onto a rock in front of Eve. She wailed and threw herself to the ground. Adam leaped between the snake and his wife as it struck. The great serpent struck Adam's chest, but the garment which God provided unto him protected him from the serpent's bite. The snake fell harmlessly to the ground in front of him. Adam picked up a large rock in anger and smashed the serpent's head before it could recover. Over and over, he struck it until he did not have the strength to lift the rock. Then he fell on his backside and cried out unto God with his head in his hands, "God, forsake not your children, but have mercy on us for our sins. We cannot bear to live apart from you!" God remained silent.

Adam and Eve walked to the garden and desired to enter, but the great angel prevented them. He drove them away because God commanded that they should not come into the garden again and that they should suffer if they try. After the angel beat them and drove them away, they wandered around the outside of the garden until they found a pool that fed the roots of the Tree of Life. The refreshing water reminded them of what they had lost. Eve fell to the ground as she remembered her time in the crystal pools of the garden. She remembered her encounter with the serpent and became ashamed.

Satan seized the opportunity and appeared before them as an angel of God. He said unto them, "Your sins have separated you from God, and there is no means on earth by which you can regain your fellowship with him. Cast yourselves into the waters and know fellowship with him again in the afterlife." Adam and Eve heard his words, and because of their despair, they jumped into the water. Satan watched as they remained under the water until they were dead. Their lifeless bodies floated to the surface of the water. He laughed and reveled in another victory as he thought, *This will bring God down low!* Satan rejoiced and left them for dead.

In Heaven, Gabriel showed God Adam and Eve lying face down in the water, and he had mercy on them. He sent an angel to them, and he pulled them from the water and laid them on the seashore, but they were dead. The angel returned to God and said, "I have done as you requested, but they have breathed their last breath!" God would not allow those created in his image to perish before their time, so he sent the Son of God out from the light. The Son of God descended from Heaven and blessed their garments a second time. The garments restored Adam and Eve from the dead.

Adam and Eve mourned their return to life because they hoped to be back in God's presence. The Son of God became angry with them and said, "Death will not restore your fellowship with God. God has a plan for your lives, but since you have taken your own life by the water, he places another curse upon you. From this day forth, your bodies will require water to survive. You will fight with the creatures of the earth to find water, because like you, they must have water to survive." When the Son of God finished speaking, he departed from their sight. As soon as he left them, a great thirst came upon them.

Satan sat in the cool of the day and enjoyed his victory

over Adam and Eve. As he celebrated, one of the Fallen Ones brought him the bad news. The Fallen One said unto him, "Satan, my king, God sent his son and raised Adam and Eve from the dead." Satan became furious with God and screamed curses into the air. The birds and the beasts trembled and fled from his presence like creatures fleeing a fire in the forest. In anger, Satan commanded the serpents to kill Eve. If he could not kill them both, maybe God would allow Eve to die because she caused Adam to sin. Then Adam would suffer the loss of his second wife.

An enormous snake, with black and yellow rings, came upon Adam and Eve first. It rose from the ground and stood on its tail to the height of Adam. Its neck flared, and a hood formed around its head. Its eyes were blood red and the snake intended to kill. Adam saw that the great serpent intended to kill Eve. So, he grabbed it by the tail because he had no weapon to kill it. The snake was too powerful for him. It knocked him down and coiled around both Adam and Eve. Now, it intended to kill both. The snake tightened its grasp, "God cast all of us out of the garden because of your sins!"

Adam and Eve's garments protected them from the serpent's grasp, and it could not crush them. A mighty angel appeared and grabbed the great snake. He wrestled Adam and Eve free of the reptile's grip. Then, he tied the great serpent in a knot and hurled it in the air, far away from them. The angel cursed all of the snakes in the name of God saying, "Cursed you were for your part in the fall of man, slick and crawling on your bellies was your fate. Now, because you tried to kill God's children, you shall not speak a word! Man shall know you by the hiss of your tongue!"

Several days passed, and no angels, nor the Son of God came to commune with Adam and Eve. Loneliness drove them into severe depression, and they mourned their lost fellowship with God. In their hearts, they said unto themselves, *If only we could be in the garden again, we would not have sweat upon our faces, and our flesh would not burn as if it were on fire.*

Satan watched them and drew strength from their despair. He visited them and carried them off to a high place. They sat upon the summit of a great mountain overlooking the gate of the garden.

Satan said unto Adam and Eve, “Throw yourselves from this mountain, and God will have mercy on you. Surely, he will let you die this time. In the afterlife, you will sit at the right hand of the Father in Heaven.” Adam and Eve considered his words, but they remembered his deceitful words before God resurrected them from drowning themselves. Satan knew their doubts, and he said unto them, “Free yourselves from the chains of this world and cast yourselves down from the rocks. Is this not your life? Can you not choose if you will live or die?” Adam and Eve considered his words again, and because their nature was sinful, they took comfort in them. Adam threw himself from the highest point of the mountain. He bounced off the rocks and tumbled end over end until he landed on the ground below. Adam lay at the bottom of the canyon, his face clinging to his skull by a thin strip of flesh. His flesh split open, and his muscles and organs spilled onto the ground. Bones impaled his body like a man on a wall of bone spikes. The last glimpses of life passed from him as he choked on his blood, and his body spasmed in a pool of blood.

Eve wept over Adam as she watched him fall to his dreadful fate. She gazed down upon his broken body and said, “To live without him, is not to live at all because I am his and he is mine. He has done this thing because I sinned first and then led him into sin.” Then she jumped from her high perch upon the rocks. She regretted her decision before she landed flat on her back on the rocks below. Blood spewed from her lungs as she coughed with each breath. Satan’s smile was visible to her as she looked helplessly up at him. Her final resting place was only a few feet from Adam’s lifeless body. She used the last of her strength to turn her head and look upon her husband one last time. The darkness came for her as she looked into his lifeless eyes.

Satan knew his victory was short-lived when a familiar twinge of God's power rippled through the air. Even before he turned to walk away from the perch where they jumped, he knew God saved them again. The blessed garments which God gave them made them whole again. He watched as the Son of God appeared and chastised them for tempting God by trying to kill themselves a second time. He said unto them, "Oh Adam, you and Eve have brought this despair on yourselves by disobeying the commandments of God. Stop trying to kill yourselves. God will not allow you to die before old age takes your lives. His plan is for you to be fruitful and multiply." Adam and Eve fell to the ground and wept because of their sins. God would not allow them to take their own lives. So, they had no choice but to suffer for their sins. Satan left them in a fit of rage.

CHAPTER 30

After the fall of Adam and Eve, Samael and Lilith returned to the cave by the Red Sea. Lilith was pregnant from her second union with Adam, but she miscarried the demon child just as the three angels said she would. She desperately wanted to bear children to Samael because he was a worthy mate and because he needed an army. "With an army, he could lead them to victory over God. They needed to wait and be patient," Samael told her over and over.

Lilith listened as Samael explained his reasoning. "Every living creature has the spark of God; a piece of God's energy, the essence of life itself. When humankind's numbers are like the sands of the seas, God will become weak. He will become silent, and his interactions with humanity and the earth will decrease because of his weakness. Then we will steal the rest of his power by turning his faithful against him. We will conquer this world while he is powerless to stop us. He created humankind in his image, and they shall be the key to his destruction. When our army is strong, we will destroy his kingdom and kill him." Lilith considered his words.

In the days that followed, Samael and Lilith discussed how they could overcome God's curse so that she might bear living children. After much deliberation, Samael presented her with a plan to defeat the evil God placed on her. Samael said unto her, "You can bear children unto me if you have over one hundred per day. The Filarial worm will enter your blood upon an insect's bite and receive nourishment from you. The worm will multiply and each new worm will bring you closer to giving me a child. The worms alone will not be enough to defeat the curse. So, fleas shall live between your toes, and you will sustain them. When they have matured, the cycle will begin again. In a few days, you will bring forth enough of these infestations to bear a child unto me." The thought of insect infestation being her only means to produce a living child disgusted her, but she was desperate. *This plan is my only hope*, she thought.

Lilith bore the insects, and they matured and multiplied, and Samael was right. She conceived a demon child unto Samael. Being more than a normal woman, the child reached full term in only seven days. In the next two months, she bore Samael six sons and two daughters. They were children of the night, demons born to terrorize humankind. Samael watched as his demon children grew stronger each day. He was pleased, but he would not reach the throne of God by increasing the army of darkness at a rate of one per week. They needed to multiply their numbers many times over if they were going to defeat God.

CHAPTER 31

To get back in God's good graces, Adam and Eve built an altar. Then they cried out and begged God for forgiveness and mercy. An angel appeared unto them with a lamb without spot or blemish. He said unto them, "Offer this lamb upon the altar as a sacrifice to God for your sins!" They obeyed the angel, and God heard their prayers. He sent the Son of God to them, and he communed with them. His fellowship comforted them. The Son of God blessed their cave, and it became holy ground. Satan watched them, he saw him bless their cave, and he became angry with God again.

The following evening Satan and several of the Fallen Ones transformed themselves into angels of light. They tried entering Adam and Eve's cave, but the blessing stopped them. When they could not go inside, Satan sat outside of their cave on a throne with his followers, and a great light shone into the cave. Then Satan said to the Fallen Ones, "Adam and Eve, come outside to greet and fellowship with us."

Inside the cave, Adam and Eve woke to a great light which they perceived were angels sent by God. They covered their eyes, headed towards the sunlight and would have exited the cave, but Adam was afraid. An angel of God appeared unto them in the cave and blocked their way. He said unto them, "You are right to be afraid, Adam. Why would the angels of God be outside and not enter this holy place?" Adam saw the logic in his words. So, he questioned Satan and his followers from within the cave, "Why don't you enter this holy place, which God has given us to protect us from evil?" Satan replied, "There is no room for my throne and the heavenly host, which serve me within the cave!" Adam pondered his words and found them to be contrary to God. *What angel would sit upon a throne, except God himself*? he thought.

In fear, Adam prayed to God. "Oh Lord, you have the power to create the angels of light. Have you sent these angels unto me?" God did not answer, but the angel appeared unto them again. He said unto them, "These are not angels from God, but it is Satan and his host trying to deceive you once more." The angel brought Adam and Eve from the cave, and they looked down upon Satan and his followers. As they watched, the power of God descended on Satan and his host of Fallen Ones. God stripped them of their disguises. The Angel pointed at Satan and the Fallen Ones and said, "These are the Fallen Ones who God cast out of Heaven. They bear the marks of their sins in their deformities." Then the angel drove Satan and his host from them and said unto Adam and Eve, "Fear not, God will protect you."

Satan and the Fallen Ones fled until they were out of sight. Satan sat down upon a large rock alone and deliberated with himself. In anger and frustration, Satan questioned himself. *Why was God faithful to humankind, even after they sinned? What would it take for him to turn his back on them forever?* Satan struggled to find answers to his questions, but he lived only for revenge. He detested his failures, but he wasn't sure what he should do next. *I will make them sin again, but how much will it take to separate them from God? When will God forsake humanity? My revenge requires a better plan!*

Later at Satan's lair, a Fallen One called Letum asked for an audience before Satan. Satan granted his audience. Letum approached Satan and said, "We made you our leader in Heaven, but now we are castaways and vagabonds. Our brethren have chosen me as their voice." Satan glared at Letum and considered killing him. *Is he proclaiming himself the new leader of the Fallen Ones?* He didn't outright say he was taking over, but he did declare himself to be their voice. Day and night, Satan had plotted and schemed to destroy Adam and Eve. His need for revenge consumed him, that was not a secret, but it had angered some of the more powerful Fallen Ones.

I should not be surprised, Satan thought. Letum spoke again, "Oh master of darkness and all that is evil, are you not worthy of rest from your labors? Are we not your servants? Do we not have power? Let us bear your burden and tempt Adam and Eve for a season. We shall trouble them and cause them to sin again." Satan considered his words. He did not believe they would succeed, but he needed time to come up with a better plan of his own. Plus, their failures would allow him to dismiss any future challenge of his authority. So, he said unto them all, "Do your worst!"

Led by Letum, the Fallen Ones troubled Adam and Eve, night and day. They tried and tried again, but each time God delivered his beloved children. Adam learned from their malicious attempts, and he called out to God anytime he sensed mischief. Each time Adam called, God sent his angels to deliver them and comfort them. After a season passed, Letum returned to Satan's lair in defeat. He fell on his face before Satan and begged him for mercy.

Letum lay upon his face before Satan and said, "Oh great and terrible master of this world, we have failed to lead Adam and Eve into sin." Satan laughed in a deep, evil, and sarcastic tone, and then he rose from his throne. He grabbed his sword, which rested against his throne. He didn't lift it off the ground but drug the tip across the stone floor. The sword made a heavy scraping sound as it left a trail carved into the rock.

Satan stopped and stood over Letum with his blade resting on its tip. He asked Letum, "What am I to do with your failure? Am I to turn a blind eye to your incompetence? How can I rule the Fallen Ones and this world if I allow such failure?" He allowed Letum a moment to find his words in reply, but no words would change his mind now. Letum would become an example for his brethren. The Fallen Ones must understand that failure is not an option! In his time of rest, Satan realized that he could not succeed on his own. He needed the Fallen Ones, but those who failed to accomplish their assigned tasks would pay a heavy price for failure.

Letum's mind raced. *Surely, he won't kill me. He has failed many times, remind him of his failures! That will get me killed. Just keep quiet,* he thought. Letum laid prostrate before Satan as his mind continued to search for something, anything that might save him. Satan shook his head from side to side and made a snickering sound. Then, without a sound, he raised his sword high above his head.

Letum heard a groan of exertion as Satan brought his blade down with all his might. He tried to look up at Satan, but he never saw him. The blade sliced his head from his shoulders, and the sword hit the stone floor below him. Sparks jumped up from the metal blade as it hit the stone floor and then Letum's head rolled from his body. It rolled, end over end, four times before coming to rest. Letum's head stopped face up, staring back at the congregation of the Fallen Ones. A surprised look was on Letum's lifeless face. Satan bent over and placed his finger in the pool of blood that was now forming on the floor where Letum's head had been seconds earlier. Horror filled the room as Satan placed the blood-soaked finger in his mouth and tasted the essence of Letum's life, *Sour, very interesting,* he thought.

CHAPTER 32

Satan grew tired of God saving and protecting Adam and Eve, so he devised a new plan. He called Haures unto him and said, "Go out into the world and use your power to cause the heat and humidity to rise. Adam and Eve will leave the protection of their cave because of the heat. Then we will kill them." The opportunity excited Haures, but Letum's execution was still fresh in his mind. *Failure isn't an option*; he thought as he left to do Satan's bidding.

Haures used his gift to influence the sun, it scorched the earth, and the temperature rose until it became unbearable for all living things. Creatures large and small hid or lay in the few remaining pools of water during the day and searched for the cool breeze upon their face at night. Adam and Eve suffered in the cave, but they refused to leave its protection because they feared Satan. Haures grew concerned that his efforts might be in vain and became desperate. So, he caused a dry, hot wind to blow into the cave until the heat threatened to kill them. Adam and Eve became delirious from the heat, and they did not inquire of God. They left the cave and found a cool place to sleep, but it offered no protection.

Satan watched them leave the cave and a smile formed upon his twisted lips. *Today, I will kill them*; he thought as he gathered the strongest of the Fallen Ones. Satan and the Fallen Ones went high into the mountains and chose a huge, flat slab of rock. Then, they threw the rock down at Adam and Eve as they slept. They watched in anticipation as the great rock fell.

Just as the rock was about to smash Adam and Eve, God's voice rumbled as it did in the days of creation. The Spirit of God moved, and the rock transformed into a dome of protection over them, but there was no door in the rock. Satan and the Fallen Ones could not harm Adam and Eve. Satan threw himself on the ground in a fit of anger. He cursed God and flailed about like a spoiled child. The Fallen Ones fled from him in fear, saying, "If God does not kill us, Satan will!"

The earth shook from the impact of the rock and Adam and Eve awoke in fear. They cried out because of the darkness. Adam thought the worst and said unto Eve, "God has placed this rock over us to plague us and imprison us. He must be angry because we left the cave that protected us from Satan without his permission." They wept and prayed for salvation.

Hours passed, and then the Son of God appeared unto them. He said unto them, "Oh, Adam, who told you to leave the cave God gave unto you?" Adam replied, "Lord, no one counseled us. We thought we would die from the heat, so we left the cave." The Son of God replied unto him, "If you could not stand the heat of the cave, you will not survive the fires of hell for eternity." His words cut Adam and Eve's hearts like a sharp blade. They fell to the ground and begged for forgiveness. The Son of God spoke again, "I will visit your children many generations from now. I will perform miracles and mighty works in the name of God, and yet the elders will crucify me. They will place my body in a tomb-like this. My body will rest there for three days and three nights. Then, God will resurrect me. My selfless act will save all of humanity from their sins! Like me, you will live within this rock for three days and three nights to atone for your sins. After three days, I will return and free you from this place." When he finished his words, he left them.

Three days and three nights passed before the Son of God returned unto Adam and Eve. When he returned, he struck the dome-shaped rock, and a door opened. Adam and Eve stepped into the light and the sun-washed over them. Their skin was dry, and their bodies were devoid of water and nourishment. God saw they were almost dead. So, he had mercy on them and forgave them of their sins. He sent his angels, and they brought them water and nourishment.

God also sent Gabriel and Raphael to the mighty angel who guarded the entrance to the garden. The angel allowed them to enter because God commanded Gabriel to bring back sweet-smelling incense and Raphael to bring back myrrh. He sent another mighty angel to the Indian Sea, and he brought back goldenrods. God commanded the angels, and they placed the treasures in Adam and Eve's cave. Then, he named their home the Cave of Treasures because of the gifts he gave them. The sweet aroma of the incense and myrrh reminded Adam and Eve of the garden. The gold represented the light of God. A symbol that God would always be with them if they remained faithful unto him.

When Satan saw God's compassion for humanity, he cried out in anger again. His latest attempt to kill Adam and Eve resulted in the forgiveness of their sins once more. God healed them and sent his angel to serve them. The angels gave them gifts to remind them of the garden and a future with God in heaven. God's generosity sickened him! *How could he love such feeble and insignificant beings as these?* Satan could not understand God's love for humankind because there was no love in him. He returned to his lair in despair.

In the years that followed, Satan and the Fallen Ones did everything within their power to cause Adam and Eve to fall. Every time they experienced success, God redeemed Adam and Eve. They tried to kill them by water, fire, snakes, and rocks, and yet they lived. Satan tricked them into taking their own lives twice, and again, they lived. Once, as an angel of light, he convinced them to follow him, and the Fallen Ones set the grain fields God gave them on fire. He led them into the wilderness for eight days until they perished from hunger and thirst. Before he could celebrate his victory, the Son of God came and raised them from the dead.

He wanted to kill God more than ever because he showed endless mercy to Adam and Eve. Adam and Eve's faith in God grew stronger with each of Satan's failed attempts.

Adam devoted himself to fasting, praying, and making daily sacrifices unto God. Satan feared his faithfulness might lead God to commune with him as he did in the Garden. To make matters worse, Eve agreed to fast and pray with Adam for forty days. No attempt to break their fasting and prayer succeeded. At the end of the forty days, an angel came unto them and prophesied unto them. The angel said unto them, "I bring you good tidings and great joy. God has seen your renewed devotion, and he sent me to bless Eve. You shall know your wife, and she shall conceive and bear children unto you!" The angel blessed her, and then he departed from them. Thoughts of having children strengthened their will and bonds with God.

God rewarded their fasting and sent his angels to help them. The angels brought a vessel of fresh water and a basket filled with nuts, berries, and fruit for them to eat. When they regained their strength, Adam came to Eve as he had in the Garden. They embraced, and she knew the pleasure of having him within her once more. Then, both of their bodies trembled in the joy of their union as Adam released his seed into her. The angel's prophecy echoed in their ears, and she conceived children unto Adam. Satan watched them from the shadows. *This news changes everything,* he thought. He left them for a season and considered a new plan for Adam and Eve's demise.

CHAPTER 33

Adam and Eve enjoyed a time of peace as they devoted themselves to worshipping God. Many days passed without temptation from Satan, and they enjoyed each warm embrace of the flesh without fear. They continued to pray, but with each passing day, their prayers became shorter and less sincere. Soon their prayers became rehearsed, and they held no meaning unto God. After several more weeks, the routine prayers even became less frequent.

Left to their own devices, Adam and Eve became driven by their passion and their lust for the pleasures of the flesh. They sought sexual gratification over fellowship with God. God became angry with them and sent an angel to warn them. The angel said unto them, "Why do you tempt the Lord your God by placing earthly pleasures above him? Do you not understand that God should be the center of all things?" Eve replied, "Did you not come unto us and say, 'Embrace each other again so that you can bear children?'" The angel answered, "Yes." Adam opened his mouth to speak, but Eve spoke over him, "We have followed the commandment God gave unto us by you. We have not ceased to pray and offer sacrifices unto him. What is it to God if we enjoy the pleasure of the act of creation? Does he not want me to bear children unto Adam?" The angel replied, "God does not want your empty words and works of service alone. Works and deeds done in the name of God cannot save you. You must devote yourself to him." The angel had said what God desired of him, so, he departed from them.

Adam and Eve sat in the cave considering the angel's words. After a few moments, Eve grabbed Adam's chin and turned his head towards her. She gazed into his eyes and kissed him. After a long kiss, she asked him several questions without pause, "My heart desires to bear children unto you and what of the pleasure that comes with our union? Did God create us, only to deny the pleasures of the flesh? Take me now, and tomorrow, we will make a glorious sacrifice unto God. Our sacrifice will satisfy God, and he will commune with us as he did in the garden." When she finished speaking, she leaned in and kissed him again. He returned her kiss, and the angel's warning fled from him. They fell to the ground in a passionate embrace and knew the pleasures of the flesh again. Their hearts were not with God, and rage grew within him. God turned his back against them because he couldn't bear the sight of them any longer.

Adam and Eve laid in their filth upon the floor of the Cave of Treasures. The smell of sweat and flesh drowned out the sweet fragrances of the incense and myrrh which God gave to them. Several days had passed since the angel visited them, and Adam and Eve had not made a sacrifice. The pleasures of the flesh clouded their minds. Finally, Eve rose from their filthy bed because of the stench of their lusts. She said unto Adam, "I will journey to the stream and fill the vessel which God has given us because we have no water to quench our thirst. I will bathe and refresh myself while I am there." Adam replied, "Should I go with you and bathe myself also?" Eve answered him, saying, "Rest and I will bring water for you to refresh yourself." Adam didn't want to go. So, he agreed with her, "I will pray for God to protect you from Satan and his host." Eve replied, "I do not need God's protection, his angels or yours. Satan and his host have not tempted us for a long time!" Adam agreed with her words and took them to heart. Eve left the cave, and Adam fell back into a deep sleep.

Samael grew weary and restless because he spent all his days with Lilith and their children. He loved Lilith and his children, but he longed for adventure and conflict. So, he said unto Lilith, "I will go and see what those made in the image of God have accomplished since their fall." He knew they were alive because Satan had not celebrated his victory over them. Lilith replied, "Go then, and do your worst!" The fresh air rushed over him as he flew through the sky in search of Adam and Eve. Just after he passed the mighty angel guarding the gate of the Garden of Eden, he saw Eve. Her garments and the water vessel were lying near a pool. She was floating naked in the clear, refreshing water.

He looked upon her nakedness as he approached and found himself aroused by her beauty. Eve's red hair flowed to the middle of her back. Her milky, ample breasts rose like snow-covered peaks out of the water. They called to him like a mother's bosom calls to a hungry child. His gaze drifted down to the crimson veil, which hid her womanhood from him. He imagined the treasures hidden there. Thoughts of her thighs wrapped around him caused his loins to throb with anticipation. His eyes drifted down the contrast of her shapely snow-white hips, and then along her long sun-drenched legs. Her pale torso bore witness to her nakedness uncovered and only increased his desire for her. Samael wondered if her beauty aroused God also. *He must enjoy the beauty of his creations, but who knows the heart of God?*

His member ached for her. As he drew closer to her, something about her seemed different or strange to him. He cautiously searched the area around the pool. *Was this a trap?* Adam was not standing watch over her, and no angels were protecting her. He peered into heaven and saw tears rolling down the face of God. God gave Adam and Eve protection from Satan and the Fallen Ones during many temptations and attempts on their lives, but it was gone now. He wondered, *What has changed?* He considered these things for several moments and then said unto himself, *Only a fool would waste this opportunity!*

Samael hid in the shadows of a nearby tree and pleasured himself as he watched Eve playing in the water. She eventually became bored and rose from the pool. The water rolled off her body, unveiling God's masterpiece. At that moment, he envied the water because it touched her bare flesh. The sun glistened off the droplets of water, and she seemed to glow like the sun. She tilted her head to the side and rang the water out of her hair out as she walked towards her garments. Lilith willingly showed him pleasure, but he would take comfort from Eve. His lust-filled eyes became fixed on the crimson veil which hid her womanhood from him. Eve turned her back to him and reached down to pick up her garments. He leaped out of his hiding place and was on her before she could retrieve her clothes. With one hand around her waist, he lifted her off the ground and with the other hand, he covered her mouth, so she could not scream.

He threw her to the ground under a nearby tree. His legs forced hers open, and he knelt between her shapely thighs. Her eyes were wide with terror, and tears began to form in them. Tears started running down her cheeks as she watched him take off his belt and leather girdle of armor. Samael tossed them on the ground next to him and smiled at her. He slid his hand up her thigh, pierced her red veil, and entered her. Then, his eyes widened with surprise. *Eve was pregnant with twins, one male, and one female!*

Samael pulled back from her for a moment, but he continued to hold her down with his body. *Her pregnancy changed everything, or did it?* He considered his options; forceful sex might kill the children and her. Plus, she might not bear children again. An idea came to him. If he was careful not to damage her, his seed might corrupt the children in her womb. *Would she give birth to demon children like Lilith?* The children were from Adam's seed, so he doubted they would be like Lilith's offspring, but their nature would change as Lilith's did. Thoughts of how he corrupted the first woman brought a smile to his face.

Eve's eyes grew wide with horror as he entered her. The circumference of his member threatened to split her open. His pleasure seemed to overwhelm him and cause him to thrust his member deeper inside of her. Eve tried to cry out but managed only to groan in protest of his painful actions. Her muffled groans brought Samael back to the reality of his plan. He refocused himself and took care not to harm the children or to damage her womb and therefore prevent her from giving birth to the children. He closed his eyes in concentration to prevent her beauty from overcoming his control. The pleasure of being inside her was almost unbearable. She was powerless to stop him from ravaging her, and that aroused him even more. *Focus*, he thought, *slow and gentle. Her children will be thorns in God's side, and some shall become soldiers in our war against God.*

A few moments earlier:

Eve shook in fear as he tossed her to the ground. She looked into the massive angel's lust-filled eyes. *Leaving Adam was a mistake!* The angel upon her was like unto God himself. Unlike the Fallen Ones, he was beautiful, powerful, and terrifying all at the same time. She struggled against him as he forced her legs apart and placed one of his large fingers inside of her. Horror drowned out any feeling of pleasure she might receive from his actions. Then, he suddenly stopped and looked at her with wide eyes. *He knows that I am pregnant,* she thought!

She looked up at him and feared what he might do to her unborn children. A look of determination came over him, and then he did the unthinkable. *The angel is inside of me!* All her hope for escape faded from her. She thought he might tear her in two as he slid himself into her flesh. He was massive, yet he was purposefully gentle, which only made his act of violation seem worse. She struggled against him and wished she was anywhere else but underneath him.

Samael pulled her arms over her head and pinned her wrists to the ground with one of his large hands. His other hand released her mouth and moved to her breast. He cupped it in his hand and squeezed it while pinching her nipple between his fingers. She cried for help, screamed in pain and horror until only a raspy exhale came out, but no one came to her aid. Adam was too far away to hear her cries, and God did not answer. Defeated, she fell silent under his powerful thrusts. His horrific actions held no pleasure for her. Tears streamed down her face even with her eyes closed. Suddenly, an irresistible urge to open her eyes came over her. She fought the craving with all her might, but her eyes opened, and she unwillingly met his gaze.

His eyes were like crystal waters swirling around bright rings of fire. They spiraled downward with no end, and she couldn't look away from him. *I am under his spell!* Panic rushed through her as she realized her body was no longer her own. Eve struggled to move, but it was futile. Each of his thrusts sent a ripple of horror through her mind and yet her body craved his next thrust. Her thighs grew wet with pleasure, and her mind screamed in terror. Blood rushed to her cheeks and her loins throbbed with delight. Dread filled her mind, but her body craved her impending orgasm. It loomed like a mighty storm on the horizon. In her mind, she prayed for it to stop, and yet she heard herself say, "Harder, take me! I am yours, spill your seed inside of me!" Her words begged him for orgasm, and yet her mind pleaded for him to stop. *Look away from his eyes*; she cried to herself. *NO*, her body suddenly shook with hundreds of powerful, unwanted orgasms in succession. Her muscles tightened under and on him as her body trembled in pleasure. She was powerless to stop herself from orgasm, and then she realized he had released her hands. Unimaginable horror filled her again as she felt her hands upon his backside. *I am pulling him deeper into me!*

Samael smiled as he looked into Eve's eyes as she shook with orgasm. He sensed the terror and pleasure within her. He had control of her body, but her mind was in turmoil. Her shapely thighs constricted upon him, begging for his release. He could sense the conflict within her as her mind realized that she was pulling him deeper into her flesh. As she cried out in pleasure and pain, he thrust himself fully into her, and his seed flowed from him. With each spasm of his loins, his sense of accomplishment and victory grew. He looked down into her helpless eyes and knew she felt the warmth of his seed within her.

Eve's mind writhed in agony and horror as he spilled his seed within her. Her hands still grasped his backside even though she cursed them for not moving. His seed seemed to have a life of its own. It slithered within her, searching for its unsuspecting prey. She felt one of the children convulse within her as his seed found its intended victim. In satisfaction, Samael released his hold on her body and rose from her wet thighs. Eve closed her eyes and curled up in the fetal position. Samael smiled with a sense of accomplishment as he retrieved his girdle and sword.

Eve sobbed with guilt as she relived the pleasure and horror she received from the angel's vicious act. She laid on her side and unwillingly relived his actions several more times in her mind. Anger rose within her because he gave her unimaginable pleasure. Samael snatched Eve up by the arm, and she flailed trying to free herself, but it was hopeless. She feared he might have his way with her a second time, but instead, he pressed her garments into her bosom. Then, he said unto her, "Get dressed, woman." He laughed at her as he watched her tremble and grimace in pain as she put her clothes on.

When Eve finished dressing, he picked up her and the vessel of water. He leaped into the air and flew towards the Cave of Treasures. They landed outside the cave. He set her feet on the ground and placed his hand under her chin and made her look up at him. She opened her tear-filled eyes. When their gaze met, he said unto her, "The children in your womb are healthy, but I have corrupted one of them!" Fear swept hope from her eyes. Then he spoke again, "Both of your children shall be thorns in your side!" Then he leaped back into the air and flew away. The shock of the events overcame

Eve as she watched Samael fly away. She fell on the ground in horror, wept and cried out to Adam.

CHAPTER 34

Adam awoke from his slumber and looked around the Cave of Treasures. The setting sun painted the cave walls bright orange, and yet Eve was not back from the pool. It would be dark soon, and it was not safe to travel after dark. Adam became concerned. So, he clothed himself and left the cave in search of his wife. Outside, Eve called out to him a short distance from the cave. He ran towards the sound of her sobbing and weeping.

A moment later, he found Eve. She was laying on the ground with her head in her hands. Their water vessel lay on the ground beside her. Adam knelt beside her and pulled her upright to him. He asked her, "Woman, why are you crying?" Eve looked up at him with sorrow in her eyes, but she did not answer him. He tried to pick her up, but she pulled away from him. She buried her face in her hands again, cried and wailed even louder than before. Adam placed his hand on her back and asked a second time, "Why are you crying?" Eve did not raise her head, but spoke unto him in a broken voice, shaken with tears. She said unto him, "We should have listened to the Son of God and devoted ourselves to him! As I rose from the waters after my refreshment, a mighty and terrible angel fell upon me. He desired me and took me against my will. I cried out to you and God, but the distance was too great for you, and my words never reached God's ears because of our sins. God no longer protects us! The angel ravaged me and spilled his seed in me. He knew I was pregnant, and his seed corrupted one of the children forming within my womb." When she finished speaking unto him, she wailed and cried out to God for mercy.

Adam's heart fell, and he tore his clothes. He fell to his

knees and prayed, "Almighty God, forgive us of our trespasses against you." God did not respond, and no angels appeared, but he hoped his words reached God's ears. With a troubled heart, he said unto Eve, "Woman, rise from the ground and go with me to the water at another pool and wash the angel's filthy seed from your thighs. I will stand guard until you finish and afterwards I will cleanse myself. We will fill our vessel with water and use it to cleanse our filth from the Cave of Treasures. When the sun rises tomorrow, we will go into the field and find a pure sacrifice. We will offer it to God with pure hearts, and he shall forgive us of our sins and return unto us!" Eve agreed with his words.

They cleansed themselves and the Cave of Treasures, as Adam suggested. When they finished, they fasted and prayed unto God so they would find a worthy sacrifice for their sins. They did not sleep but prayed until the sun rose in the morning sky. Then, they went out and searched for a worthy sacrifice. As they passed by the altar, Adam built unto God; they came upon a ram. The ram struggled to free itself from a thicket but could not. After a few minutes, it stopped struggling because it had no strength left to fight. Adam praised God for giving them a worthy sacrifice, and he took the ram and bound its legs. Then he carried their sacrifice to the altar on the hill.

Adam and Eve placed the ram upon the altar. Adam used a sharp rock to cut the ram's throat and drained its blood into a bowl that Eve placed at the altar. Then, they cried unto God, "Lord God, take this sacrifice which you provided unto us and accept it for our sins." The ram burst into flames upon the altar. They fell to their knees and praised God as the fire consumed their sacrifice. Happiness filled their hearts, and they returned to the Cave of Treasures.

CHAPTER 35

Satan watched Adam and Eve make their sacrifice unto God. As expected, God accepted the sacrifice they gave them. God was long-suffering with Adam and Eve. *Where was God's mercy when he cast us out of Heaven?* Satan didn't want forgiveness, but he detested his grotesque form. An idea came to him.

Before his fall from Heaven, Satan was smart and cunning. His anger and rage corrupted him, and he challenged God, which was a mistake. The season he spent away from tempting Adam and Eve helped him regain a part of himself. His thoughts were clear again, and he felt like he could control his angry outbursts. Satan still longed for revenge, but his time away had also caused him to miss an opportunity against Adam and Eve when God turned his back on them. The Fallen Ones had brought him news of Samael's encounter with Eve and how he had corrupted Adam's seed. Samael was a problem, and he needed to find a way to deal with him. So, Satan came up with a plan.

In the seventh month of Eve's pregnancy, Satan requested an audience before God. God granted Satan's first audience since his fall. The Archangel Michael transported him to Heaven. It hurt Satan to take a knee before the throne of God, but he needed to appear humble. As soon as he knelt, God asked Satan two questions. "Why do you come before my throne, and why should I listen to your words?"

Satan replied unto God without answering his questions, "Oh mighty God, how is it you cast your servant Samael from heaven, and yet he bears no scars from his fall?" God replied unto him, "Samael is my servant, and he must remain as he is." Satan answered again, "Oh mighty God, Samael has killed one of his brothers, and he nourished the Tree of the Knowledge of Good and Evil. The tree caused those created in your image to sin. He also corrupted the first woman, Lilith, and took her as his mate. Together, they defeated your curse on her, and now they are raising a demon army against you. Samael also took advantage of you again when you turned your back on Adam and Eve because of their sins. He raped Eve and corrupted Adam's seed and the heirs to your kingdom. Don't Samael's crimes outweigh ours? Samael mocks you while he remains free and unpunished!"

None of this was news to God, but for the sake of justice, he considered Satan's words. After several moments of deliberation, God replied unto Satan, "Your words bear the truth, and because I am a fair and just God, I will take action against Samael. Not for your sake alone, but for the sake of justice itself!" When he finished his words, God commanded Michael to transport Satan back to the earth.

When Satan was back on earth, and the Archangel Michael was gone, he smiled with satisfaction. He could not defeat Samael in open combat, but he could beat him with cunning. The punishment of God would serve as Satan's weapon against Samael. *Well done Satan, well done indeed,* he thought!

CHAPTER 36

Samael returned to the cave by the Red Sea and Lilith following his corruption of Eve. Lilith accepted his infidelity as a necessary part of their overall plan, and she continued to bear many healthy demon children unto him. Samael tutored his children in all the secrets of this world, and they grew more powerful each day. One morning, Samael sat outside the entrance to Lilith's lair, enjoying another beautiful sunrise when he felt them coming. He sensed several angels descending from Heaven. Their intent was contrary to him. So, he went back to the cave. Lilith met him at the entrance to their dwelling because she knew something was wrong. He said unto her, "Go, take the children and flee into the wilderness. I will come to you when I defeat them. Go NOW!" Lilith didn't argue with him. She gathered the children, and they fled deep into the wilderness. Samael watched them leave and then waited for the angels who were coming for him. *They will not have my children*; he thought as he watched his enemies' approach.

The angels approached from the east. They flew low and used the sun to obscure their numbers. Samael senses were too good for such a ploy to work, but he knew the angels had standard practices for battle. There were twenty-seven angels, and the Archangel Michael was leading them. Most of the angels were from the elite warrior class. They were the strongest and most powerful among all God's angels. Samael smiled and shook his head. *God sent Michael!* Samael and Michael fought hand in hand as brothers in the war against Satan and the Fallen Ones. Michael was Samael's confidant before God cast him out. He was the only one of God's buffoons he didn't want to kill. A wave of sadness flowed over him because he would likely have to kill his friend and all the other angels to survive.

A strange foreboding came over Samael as he watched the angels' approach. At that moment, he realized he would not be victorious, but he would not go quietly! As that thought passed, he set his resolve to make this the greatest battle in history. A plume of dust and rocks rose from the overhang as he shot upward. He left a vapor trail in his wake as he propelled himself faster than sound towards his target. Samael crashed into Michael's chest with both feet. He did not slow down, and Michael was not expecting his attack. Michael wanted to speak with Samael because they were once like brothers. Samael chose surprise instead of meaningless insults or one of Michael's famous "come peacefully" speeches. Michael fell from the sky like a meteor and hit the water flat on his back. Their collision left Michael broken and unconscious, but he was still alive.

Samael watched Michael hit the water, and he turned to face his next opponent. Two angels grabbed his left arm before he could react. He swung his sword with his free arm. It cut through the air with speed and precision separating both angels' heads from their bodies in one smooth and deadly efficient motion. The angels succeeded in their task before they fell. Samael looked at the shackle and chain in disbelief. His eyes followed the dead angels as they fell, and he saw the four angels standing on the ground, holding the chain attached to his arm.

Suddenly, the sea below Samael exploded, sending water spraying hundreds of feet into the air as Michael flew towards Samael. Samael raised his sword in defense, and they locked blades high over their heads. When Samael and Michael's swords came together, two of the other mighty angels grabbed Samael's right arm, one on the bicep and one on the forearm. With both arms, they grasped him as if they were wrestling a mighty serpent. On the ground, the four angels pulled the chain to his left arm rendering it helpless. Samael let out an angry battle cry and drove his forehead into the head of the angel on his bicep. The blow came with such force that the angel's skull split open, and his lifeless body fell to the ground.

Another mighty angel replaced the fallen angel, and yet another wrapped both arms around Samael's head to prevent another fatal head butt. Six more angels grasped his wings to prevent their use for escape or as weapons. The angels on his right arm fastened the shackle and pulled the chain tight as they retreated downward. Michael wrestled Samael's sword from his hand, and it fell to the beach. The blade came to a rest hilt deep in the sand.

The angels holding his wings took hold of their hooks and drove them through his wings. Samael cried out in anger as they retreated, pulling the chains downward. Samael mustered all his incredible strength and kicked Michael in the center of his chest. The force of his blow sent Michael falling end over end into the sea. He was unconscious for a second time. Four of the remaining angels latched onto his massive legs to prevent another kick, and the last of the angels attached the shackles to his ankles. Then the angels retreated down the chains and pulled them tight. Together, all the angels pulled the chains with all their might.

Samael hit the ground with a great thud. As he hit the ground, he exhaled in an attempt to protect his lungs, but it did not matter. The angels spread out and pulled him in four different directions. They pinned Samael to the ground, and he could not move. "Release me. Fight me like warriors," he cried! Uriah, chief among the warrior class angels, placed his foot upon Samael's forehead driving his head back into the sand and laughed at his challenge. "Why should we die at your hands as individuals? We defeated the great Samael," Uriah said. All the angels laughed at his defeat.

Michael walked out of the water and traversed the surf to the beach. He shook the water from his wings as he approached Samael. He drew Samael's sword from the sand without stopping. In anger, Michael commanded one of the angels, "Take hold of his member and stretch it out from his body!" Samael's eyes widened in horror as he realized what Michael intended to do. The angel obeyed Michael's command and snatched his member from under his garment. He pulled it out until Samael thought he might tear it from his body. Samael struggled, screamed in anger and protested. "Don't do this brother," he said as Michael raised Samael's sword. Panic set in and Samael yelled, "You can't do this!"

Michael stopped his blade in mid-air as he stood over Samael. Then he replied unto him, "You have determined your fate, brother! YOU caused those made in the image of God to sin. YOU fornicated with Lilith and raped Eve. YOU corrupted their seed, and now YOU will pay the price for your crimes!" Samael closed his eyes as he heard the blade cutting through the air. There was a wet slicing sound and then the sound of the sword hitting the sand. As the pain registered in Samael's mind, Michael took hold of Samael's testicles and squeezed them. Then, he separated them from his body as well.

Samael was bleeding profusely and writhing in pain, but the angels did not release him. Instead, Michael raised his sword into the air, looked towards Heaven, and said, "It is done, according to your will Lord!" Lightning came from heaven and struck his sword. The blade glowed with the heat of the strike. He lowered the smoldering red blade and placed it on Samael's loins. The hot blade sizzled as it seared his flesh and closed his wounds. He cried out with a renewed vigor. Rage and disgust filled Samael as the smell of his burnt flesh stung his nostrils. Animals and birds scattered into the air from the rocks above the water as his horrible cries echoed through the cliffs. Michael turned to the angels and said, "The great Samael is defeated and helpless. Will anyone save him?" Michael paused for a moment of silence to add a dramatic effect to the question. Samael's groans were the only sound until Michael said, "It is as I thought. No one will stand for Samael. He is no longer anyone's brother." Michael looked down at Samael, and they locked gazes, "You are disgraced and alone!"

After several minutes, Michael was sure Samael would live. So, he said unto him, "Samael your sins have brought you to this place. God has commanded us to bring you back to heaven, but not for redemption. You shall be a prisoner because God can't trust you on earth!" Samael remained silent, but his rage flowed out from him. Michael looked at Samael and remembered the friendship they once shared. A wave of sadness came over him because God took away Samael's will to fight.

Samael thought about other things as he lay on the ground, utterly defeated. He would never know the pleasure of a woman again. *That was eternal damnation*, he thought. *To live without the pleasure of the flesh is not to live at all.* He wished God would have killed him! The angels lifted Samael from the ground and wound the chain around him so he could not escape. They placed a great lock upon the chains, lifted him into the air, and took flight towards heaven. In Heaven, they imprisoned Samael in an inescapable prison cell and shackled him to the floor by his ankles. Two mighty angels with swords of fire stood guard over him until God needed his services again.

CHAPTER 37

In the ninth month of Eve's pregnancy, Eve said unto Adam, "The time for me to birth these children unto you is near. Since we have cleansed the Cave of Treasures, I would not see it defiled by childbirth. Let us go up to the dome cave where Satan tried to kill us, but God saved us. I will give birth there, and we shall make it our home. The Cave of Treasures shall be pure from this day forth; a temple dedicated to God. A holy place where our family may fast, pray, and worship the almighty God!" Eve's words were like honey in Adam's ears, and they took their things, except the goldenrods and the sweet-smelling gifts which God had given them and went up to the domed cave.

The time came for Eve to bear the children, and she screamed in the agony of childbirth because of her sin in the Garden of Eden. She wailed, cried, and squeezed Adam's hand as if she intended to break it. There was no comfort for her. Her labor continued all night, yet no child came. Adam watched her suffering and thought she might die before she birthed the children. He prayed unto God to have mercy upon Eve, but she continued to suffer for several more hours.

Eve labored in agony for a full day and passed out from exhaustion and appeared to be dead. Adam wailed before God with his face on the floor of their dwelling. He prayed to God, "Lord God Almighty, ruler of all that is and will ever be, have mercy upon your servant Eve. Breathe life into her so she might bear these children. She set aside the Cave of Treasures as a temple unto you. Have mercy on her, so our family may worship in your temple!" Eve's eyes opened, and she said unto him, "The children are coming now!" Their son came first.

When the male child was born, Eve cried out in fear because Samael corrupted her children while they were in the womb. She thought her children might be monsters or demons. So, she asked Adam, "Is the child an abomination that we should slay it at birth?" Adam held the boy up for her to see and said, "He is beautiful." Then Eve writhed in pain as the second child left her womb. Again, she asked Adam, "Is the child an abomination that we should slay it at birth?" Adam held the female child up so Eve could see it and said, "She is beautiful."

When she saw that both of her children were healthy, she cried out and praised God. God delivered her children into this world without deformity. Adam cut both of their cords and rinsed them clean with water from the vessel that God gave unto them. Then he thanked God for them. Eve named the male child Cain, which means hater because she said, "He is angry with this world, and he fought with his sister in the womb!" The female child she named Luluwa, which means beautiful because her features were delicate, and she was more beautiful than Eve.

Adam looked at the children as they lay in their mother's arms and was pleased. So, he said unto her, "You have done well to survive the birth of these children. They are strong and healthy like you. I will pray unto God and give thanks unto him, but I will not go to the Cave of Treasures. Instead, I will pray outside of our dwelling to protect you and the children, lest Satan come and devours you and them." As he spoke these words to her, an angel of God appeared to them in the cave. The angel said unto them, "Go now and worship God who has delivered your wife from childbirth and given you these healthy children! I will stand guard over your family until you return!" Adam did as the angel suggested. He kissed his wife and their children, and then he departed to the Cave of Treasures to worship God.

The following morning, Adam returned to the cave, intent on offering a sacrifice unto his first-born before God. Eve agreed with his words and said unto Adam, "Go now and offer a suitable sacrifice unto God for the birth of our first-born son, and on the eighth day we will go together and offer a sacrifice for our daughter." Eve finished nursing the boy, and Adam took him up to the altar of God.

When he arrived at the altar, he found a young sheep, pure and without blemish, standing near the altar. Adam took the animal and laid it upon the altar. He cut its throat and drained the blood into a vessel. An angel suddenly appeared at the altar, dipped his finger in the blood and drew a cross upon Cain's forehead. Adam did not question the angel but held the child up before God. He called unto God and said, "Lord God Almighty, accept this sacrifice in honor of our first-born son." Fire came from heaven and devoured the lamb and the blood. The bloody cross on Cain's forehead turned to ash. Adam was happy that God accepted his sacrifice, but he wondered what the ash upon the child's forehead symbolized.

CHAPTER 38

After three days and three nights in the wilderness, Lilith and her children returned to the cave by the Red Sea. They searched the cave and the surrounding areas, but Samael was gone. The only clue they found to his whereabouts was blood on the rocks at the beach. Lilith scraped the dried blood from one of the stones and placed it upon her tongue. As soon as the blood hit her tongue, she saw images of Samael's horror and pain. Sadness rushed over her, but not for Samael. She was sad because she would not know the pleasure of him within her again. She retreated to her cave and mourned her loss. Her children gathered around her like a flock of bats and tried to comfort her.

Lilith took no comfort from her children. *How will I bear children again*? she thought. There was only one logical conclusion; steal Adam's seed again. So, she sealed her children in the cave with a magical spell she learned from Samael. The magic closed the entrance of the cave and hid it from sight. Only her blood could break the spell.

When she was satisfied that her children were safe; Lilith took flight towards the Garden of Eden. Samael told her Adam and Eve dwelt a short distance from the gate to the garden. As Lilith flew over the Garden of Eden, she considered trying to enter, but she saw the mighty angel with a fiery sword standing guard. So, she continued past the pool where Samael took Eve, and she soon found the Cave of Treasures. As she approached the cave, a strange nauseous feeling came over her, and she realized this was a sacred place. Her senses told her that Adam and Eve were not inside the cave. So, she tried to enter, but an unseen force prevented her. She tried the ancient secrets Samael taught her, but she could not break the spell or enter the cave.

Frustrated by her failure, she looked around for signs of Adam and Eve. A few minutes later, she caught their scent and followed it higher up the mountain. Ahead of her in a mostly flat, rocky area, she noticed a sizeable domed rock that seemed out of place. Adam and Eve were inside of the domed cave, but there was something else. New flesh, the first human children lay inside of the cave.

Lilith's black heart raced with excitement as she considered what she might do with the innocent children. The sweet metallic smell of new blood filled her nostrils, and like sweet wine, it called to her. Her emotions fluttered, and her mind flooded with possibilities. *Would she eat them, bludgeon them, take them as slaves, or perform a ritual with them?* There were so many possibilities, and they all sounded delightful, but first, she had to take them. She approached the entrance to the unprotected cave. Light snoring echoed out of the cave. *They are asleep!* She bent her head around the corner and investigated inside.

Adam and Eve lay in the center of the cave on animal skins, and their children lay between them. Like a deadly predator, she crept into the cave. Her eyes adapted to the darkness and caught a glimmer of something shiny lying near the head of the children. The sweet aroma of the children overwhelmed her senses and distracted her from the flash of light. She froze as Adam moaned and rolled over on his side. The children slept peacefully, unaware of her presence. She moved closer to them and reached out to take them. Before the tips of her fingers touched the male child, a great light blinded her. The object at the children's heads was an amulet made of solid gold. Upon it were the names and images of the three angels God sent to curse her. Lilith suddenly remembered how Senoy, Sansenoy, and Semangelof decreed that she would have no power over children protected by the mark of the three angels.

Earlier that morning:

An Angel of God gave the amulet bearing the three angels' names and images to Adam and Eve as a gift unto their children. The angel said unto them, "This amulet will protect the children against terrible creatures that want to harm them or use them to create mischief against God." Adam and Eve did not question the angel of God. Instead, they thanked him for the gift and placed the amulet in the bed where the children slept.

Present:

Lilith stumbled from the cave and blindly scurried onto a high rock, feeling her way about in the darkness. As she sat perched on the cliff, she cursed the angels and God for protecting the children and feared her sight might not return. Her eyesight slowly recovered, but at first, there were only shadows in dim fuzzy light. She screamed into the air in frustration. Her bloodcurdling cry echoed through the rocks. Then, rumbling laughter came from behind her. Lilith quickly turned around in fright and fell on the ground. Embarrassed by her clumsiness, she stood up and gathered herself. A shadowy figure was sitting on a rock a short distance from her.

As Satan continued laughing, he took in her beauty. Lilith found no humor in his laughter and spoke first, "Why are you watching me?" Satan replied to her, "They took Samael from you, and now you require another companion!" She replied, "I do not need a companion!" He responded, "You are lying to yourself and me. You lust for sexual pleasures, and you desire to have offspring. Did you not infest yourself with vermin to bear children unto Samael?" She acknowledged him, "Yes, but I desired him. Your flesh is burnt, deformed, and, rotting."

Satan transformed himself into an image like Samael, "What say you now?" His transformation pleased her. So, she asked, "Would you keep this facade forever to have me as yours or just to take me now?" Satan responded, "I would have you as my bride for eternity! Your children shall be servants unto me until the day of God's reckoning when we shall triumph over him as Samael prophesied to you!" Lilith replied, "Samael thought he would defeat God one day, but now he is defeated and disgraced." Satan responded to her, "Samael is alive, but God has him in shackles until he requires his services. Samael thought I was a fool because my lust for vengeance blinded me, but now I have returned to my cunning ways. God will die, or I will bind him in chains for eternity!" Then Satan told Lilith about his plans, and she considered them.

Lilith agreed with Satan's plan but only considered being his bride. "What if I refuse to be your bride or play a role in this plan of yours?" Satan smiled at her for a long moment and then responded to her by saying, "I will have the Fallen Ones take you! They will bind you in shackles and chain you to the wall beside my throne. We will have our way with you! Afterward, I will take your blood and release the spell you cast to protect your children. I will kill your male children in front of you. We will not only rape you, but also your female children until you bear our children. My servants will then take the children from you. You and your daughters will be our slaves for eternity!" When Lilith heard him, she knew he meant every word. So, she gave in to him for the sake of her children and to remain free to torture Adam's descendants.

She replied unto Satan, "I will be yours, and my children shall also serve you! I will collect them, and we shall come to you at your earthly throne. We shall consummate our arrangement when I return, but only if you come to me in this facade. I will never have you inside of me if you are burnt and decaying or if I can see your deformities." He longed to sample Lilith's delights. So, he said unto her, "Return to me before the sun sets in the night sky. Then we will consummate our agreement!" Without delay, she left to retrieve her children from the cave by the Red Sea. He watched her fly away until she was out of sight, and then he turned towards his earthly throne with a smile upon his twisted face. As he entered his lair, he thought, *My revenge against Samael will be complete once I take his precious Lilith as my bride!*

CHAPTER 39

God saw Adam and Eve's renewed devotion and called the angel Raziel unto him. Raziel reported to God's throne and bowed before him. God said unto him, "I am pleased with Adam because he has repented and devoted himself unto me. Therefore, take the book you have written and return it to him so that he might learn its wisdom and secrets." Raziel's heart leapt with joy because he knew Adam would prosper from the words written upon its pages. So, he answered God, saying, "According to your will, Master." Then he departed from the throne.

Raziel retrieved the book and left Heaven for the Cave of Treasures. As he flew towards earth, he noticed two angels were following him. They wore black and hid their faces with hoods. He reached out with his senses, and they hid their true natures from him, but he sensed their intent. They wanted the book and were prepared to do whatever it took to get it. He called out to God, but his message never made it to Heaven.

Azazel and Semjaza desperately wanted the book of Raziel. Azazel used the knowledge he learned in only one hour with Raziel's book to block his communication with God. *Indeed, the book contains many more powerful secrets*, they thought! They sensed the concern in Raziel as he flew towards the Cave of Treasures. *Why did Raziel think the cave would provide him refuge*, they wondered?

Desperation overcame Raziel, and he shot downward at breakneck speed. The two pursuing angels were still closing in on him, despite his efforts. *They will kill me to get the book because they must be the same angels who stole the book from Adam. They must have learned how to stop my communications with God from its pages!* There was no way for him to reverse their spell because only the person who cast the spell could lift it. Killing the one who cast the spell could also break it, but there was no chance a scribe could beat these angels. Adam was his only hope!

Despite their best efforts, Azazel and Semjaza would not catch Raziel before he made it to the Cave of Treasures. They considered why he fled to the cave and then it came to them, *Adam!* God protected Adam, and when he prayed, God heard his prayers, and they could not sever those communications. As Raziel entered the Cave of Treasures, they gave up their chase. They shed their disguises and continued to block Raziel's connection with Heaven as they returned to Heaven in defeat.

Adam was praying unto God when Raziel burst into the cave. Adam cried out, "God, save me!" Raziel slid to a halt in the middle of the cave and immediately explained himself. "Two angels tried to steal my book," Raziel said as he held out the book. Adam prayed to God for deliverance from the mischievous angels, and the Archangel Uriel appeared before them. Raziel said unto Uriel, "Two angels pursued me to the cave. They blocked my communication and hid their true presences from me. The angels must have learned these secrets from my book. They must have been the ones who stole the book from Adam." Uriel comforted Raziel and said, "Fear not! There are no angels outside. I will return to the Throne of God and tell him about your encounter with the angels." Uriel immediately departed for heaven.

Raziel gave the book to Adam, and then said, "Keep the book hidden in the Cave of Treasures until you have learned its wisdom. I will visit you and teach you from the book as we did in the garden." Adam rejoiced with Raziel's words because he missed the fellowship they had in the Garden of Eden. That afternoon, they studied the book for a few hours, and then Raziel departed for heaven. Adam hid the text in the Cave of Treasures and returned unto his wife and his children.

In heaven, Raphael protested God's decision to return the Book of Raziel to Adam with his brethren saying, "Man should not possess such power!" Many of the angels agreed with him, but most of them feared God and refused to stand with Raphael. The Archangels called for Raziel, and he appeared before them. He told them what he knew about his pursuers. Gabriel agreed with Raziel's assumptions and said, "They must be the ones who stole the book."

After Raziel left their assembly, Gabriel expressed his concerns about Azazel and Semjaza. Based on Raziel's logical conclusions, if they stole the book the first time, then they were also his pursuers. However, the archangels had no proof, so they agreed to keep their suspicions to themselves for the time being. They decided that Gabriel would accuse them privately and try to rattle them. *If they are guilty, they might make a mistake*, they thought. Gabriel agreed to this, but stated he would claim he held their beliefs that the book was too powerful for humankind. The other archangels decided to keep an eye on Semjaza and Azazel and see how they reacted. They wondered if their guilt would cause them to kill Gabriel, or would they deny their mischief?

CHAPTER 40

Adam and Eve remained faithful unto God for three years after the birth of Cain and Luluwa. During that time, Adam communed with Raziel and learned from his book while Eve cared for the children. One day, as Adam and Eve prayed in the Cave of Treasures, a messenger angel appeared unto them. The angel said unto them, "Thou good and faithful servants, God has seen your faithfulness. Go up to thy home and embrace one another in a union of the flesh, and Eve will conceive and bear children again." Adam and Eve rejoiced and did as God commanded, returning to the cave they called home.

When they got to the cave, an angel caused a deep sleep to fall upon Cain and Luluwa, so Adam and Eve might embrace without the children being in want. The fear of falling into the sin of the flesh again had caused them to make a vow of abstinence to God since their children's births. They enjoyed the renewed opportunity to explore each other's bodies, but they felt like they were strangers again. Adam was gentle and kind as he took his wife. The rhythmic union of their love washed over them and revived their passion for each other.

Eve had last experienced pleasure when Samael took her, so she struggled with the repressed memories of that tragic event as they rose to the surface of her mind. She wept as Adam entered her. Her tears were a mix of joy and sadness. His warmth soothed her, yet her thoughts of the past haunted her. After several minutes, she opened her eyes and looked up at him. His countenance was that of sheer pleasure. Seeing his desire caused her face to flush with the familiar warmth of an orgasm, as waves of pleasure flowed over her.

Adam missed making love to Eve. He knew they needed to find a balance with enjoying the pleasures of the flesh and their service to God! Eve's thighs and arms pull him closer as she neared orgasm. The blissful pleasure of climax fell upon them both with the magnificent release of his seed. She squeezed him tight as she tried to make it last forever. Soon the tremors of pleasure subsided and became faint aftershocks of their bliss. As Adam rose from her, a second orgasm overwhelmed her, and she pulled him back to her again and he matched her passion with a second release of his own.

They collapsed in each other's arms and laughed with the giddiness of young lovers. With a sly smile on his face, he looked down into her eyes. She tried to blow the hair out of her eyes, but it was damp with sweat and clung to her forehead. Adam brushed it to the side for her and smiled. She smiled back, they laughed, and then she smacked him playfully on his chest.

Adam rolled off Eve and lay beside her with a sigh and a long exhale. They embraced and vowed to share their love more often. Their embrace ended when Luluwa cried. Eve kissed him softly on the lips and rose to care for the child. She brought Cain, who remained asleep, laid him down beside Adam and placed the amulet above the child's head, kissing the child's forehead. She took Luluwa up to her bosom and after she fed the child, she placed her beside her brother, and the child drifted off into a peaceful slumber. Adam pulled Eve to him once more, and they kissed. They looked upon their sleeping children and smiled at each other with happiness in their hearts. Then, Adam and Eve joined their children in a peaceful sleep.

The next morning, they awoke to the bright sun shining into their humble home. An angel appeared unto them and said, "Eve is with children as God has promised." The angel's words pleased Adam and Eve. So, they went out and found a large sheep that was without spot or blemish. Adam took it to the altar of God and sacrificed it. God accepted their sacrifice because they had enjoyed the pleasure of the flesh without forsaking him.

CHAPTER 41

Lilith returned unto Satan before the sunset, as promised. He took her children and gave one to each of the most powerful of the Fallen Ones. Then he said unto them, "These demon children are yours to instruct in the dark arts and the old ways of this world. Use them to cause trouble to those which God has created in his image. Treasure their usefulness because they will play a vital role in our plan to bring God to his knees." The Fallen Ones screamed, shouted, and howled in celebration of his words. One by one, they took the children and disappeared into their lair. When only Satan and Lilith remained, she grabbed his hand and led him in search of a suitable place to consummate their relationship.

In the throne room, Lilith pushed him onto his throne. She smiled at him with a childlike playfulness, and then bent over as if she would kiss him passionately on the lips. Her lips were so close he almost felt them upon his, but she didn't kiss him. Instead, she whispered, "You will know what pleasure is today!" She lifted her arms and placed her hands on the top of his shoulders. As she looked at him with her piercing emerald eyes, she dragged her hands down his chest. Blood rose in the wake of her fingernails. He clenched his teeth and groaned in the pleasure of her seductive acts. Her hands glided down to the buckle that fastened his leather girdle. His heart raced in anticipation as she unbuckled the girdle and tossed it on the floor next to the throne.

Her skillful hands slid down his powerful thighs until they rested just above his knees. She looked up into his lust-filled eyes and smiled as she shoved his legs apart. His member fell from on top of his lap onto the edge of the throne where he sat. She smiled with surprise and delight when she saw his girth. Their eyes locked and he stared into her devious, penetrating eyes as they drew him into a world of seduction.

Lilith lowered herself between his thighs as she looked into his eyes. When she took him into her mouth, he writhed in pleasure. In the garden, he had watched Adam and Eve, and Lilith and Adam have sex, but his wildest dreams paled in comparison to this pleasure. As her tongue danced upon him, he realized how sex could be a tool for controlling one's partner. Satan had only sampled its ability to control others during his temptation of Eve. *How much more powerful it must be when that person achieves sexual fulfillment*? he thought. His head fell back on the throne, and he groaned with pleasure. *Lilith will try to control you with sex, but if it felt this good, she could try all she wanted*, he thought. As she continued, Satan wondered if God knew such pleasures were possible. *He had to know, didn't he? If he did, why did he hide this from his angels?* His thoughts drifted away as the flickers of his first orgasm rose from his loins.

Satan was massive, but she kept going. She dug her fingertips into his thick muscular thighs as they tightened with his impending climax. His muscles started to spasm as something profound rose to the surface. A violent storm erupted inside of him and searched for release. He thought he might explode and then a powerful surge of energy shot out of him, as he spilled his seed into her. The tremors of his pleasure intensified as she took all of him and held him tightly until the tremors of pleasure subsided. He had no words for the sexual gratification that she gave him.

When his seed stopped flowing, she pleasured him again until he was erect. Then she rose and mounted him. He looked into her lust-filled eyes, and she said, "My turn," as she impaled herself upon his member. She lowered herself upon him and groaned with delight. Her appetite for sex was veracious. As a creature stalks its prey, she sought orgasm. Her hips gyrated and moved as she drew his seed from deep within him. Lilith's cries echoed through the cavern, heightening Satan's pleasure.

She is fantastic; Satan thought as Lilith guided them into ecstasy. Her actions reinforced his earlier thoughts of how sexual pleasure could manipulate someone into doing their lover's bidding. Then it came to him. Sexual gratification would be his greatest weapon in the war against God. Humanity did not know what their future held, but Satan had a new threat that would bring humankind to their knees and cause them to sin.

He grabbed Lilith's head, pulled her close, and kissed her. After a long passionate kiss, she pushed him away, and drove herself down upon him with a renewed vigor. Then, her muscles tightened upon him as she shook with the pleasure of her orgasm. Lilith threw her head back, arching her back, and spread her wings as her body quaked with delight. Multiple orgasms rippled through her loins and out her extremities. Her fingernails dug into Satan's chest until blood flowed again.

Satan grabbed her shoulders, pulled her downward, and thrust himself into her. His evil seed flowed into her as another orgasm swept through them. Satan looked into Lilith's eyes as they shivered in pleasure. When they finished, he smiled at her and ran his fingers through her long, dark red hair. Satan asked her, "Why would God hide this from me?" She shook her head from side to side and said, "I don't know!" They shared another passionate kiss.

After their kiss, she rose and said unto him, "I will refresh myself in the Red Sea near the cave that was my home." Satan replied, "Be refreshed, I will go and see what has become of Adam, Eve, and their children. I need to study their ways and figure out how we can cause the pleasures of the flesh to cause strife and conflict between them and their God!" When he finished speaking, Lilith left his lair and took flight towards the Red Sea. Satan went to see those made in God's image.

CHAPTER 42

Adam and Eve enjoyed a time of fellowship and devotion to God. They did not fall into the temptation of Satan and the Fallen Ones. Cain and Luluwa grew older and were healthy. Then, the day came for Eve to give birth again. She called Adam and said unto him, "Go to the river and get water so I may bathe myself and the children after their birth." Adam left the cave to get water his wife requested. When he returned to her, she was already in the pains of labor. Adam remembered how she almost died during childbirth with Cain and Luluwa. So, he prayed that God would have mercy upon Eve and bring the children into the world without suffering.

Despite his heartfelt prayers, anguish and the pains of labor fell upon Eve. She believed she might die. Satan watched them and took pleasure from her suffering. He tempted Adam and Eve, "Where is your God in your time of need? Swear your allegiance to me, and I will end your suffering!" Adam replied unto Satan, "Get thee behind me Satan. You are evil and have brought this suffering on her through your temptation!" Satan laughed and said, "You sinned of your own free will! God continues to punish you because of past mistakes despite your renewed devotion to him. Follow me and be free of his tyranny." Eve cried out in pain. Adam tried to comfort her, but she suffered despite his efforts. She begged for mercy, "Save me, Lord!" God did not answer or send his angels to comfort her.

Satan spoke unto Eve, "The lowest of God's angels could place his finger upon you and take away your pain. If you ask me; I will end your suffering. Pledge your allegiance to me, and you will suffer no more!" Eve cried out because her pain was more significant than her first childbirth. In great sadness, Eve succumbed to her suffering and said to Satan, "I pledge..." She passed out from the pain before she could pledge herself to him. Adam feared she would wake and devote herself to Satan. So, he prayed to God, "Our suffering is the penance for our sins, and we accept this punishment but deliver us from Satan's temptation lest we sin again!" As soon as he finished his prayer, an angel appeared and cast Satan out of their dwelling.

Eve awoke and endured great suffering for several more hours before the first child came. The first child was a boy, and they called his name Abel. The name Abel means "Breath," because the boy had a peaceful countenance. A second female child was born, and they called her Aklia. Eve named her Aklia because the name had no meaning and suited her because she was ordinary with dull eyes.

Adam and Eve thanked God because both of their children were healthy. They bathed the children and wrapped them in animal hides. Eve nursed the children while Adam prepared a bountiful sacrifice unto God. When he finished his preparations, he took Abel from his mother's bosom and offered a sacrifice unto God for the child's sake according to their custom. A great light came from Heaven, and fire consumed the sacrifice before him. God accepted his sacrifice, and Adam brought the glad tidings unto Eve.

On the eighth day, they went to the altar and prepared another sacrifice for Aklia's sake. Again, a great light came from Heaven, and fire consumed the sacrifice they presented to God. Then Adam and Eve said, "Let us go unto the Cave of Treasures and bless the children with the gifts that God gave unto us. We will pray unto God and give thanks for them. We shall praise him because we have four healthy children." At the Cave of Treasures, they blessed the children and prayed unto God and gave thanks for his mercy. They returned to their home in peace. Satan was not pleased.

CHAPTER 43

Cain was three years old at the time of Abel and Aklia's birth. He was an unusual boy because Samael's seed corrupted him in the womb. Luluwa, his sister, escaped Samael's corruption and she stayed by her mother's side, but Cain loved to wander in search of adventure. Adam and Eve often found Cain playing in the corner of the cave or outside in the rocks with spiders, scorpions or snakes. He found strange and deadly creatures intriguing and loved them, but they never harmed him. The animals and insects seemed to enjoy his company as much as he enjoyed theirs.

One day, Cain woke before his family and left the cave. A short distance from the cave he saw a black and yellow banded snake slither into a small patch of trees. Cain ran after the snake, falling several times along the way. He peeked into the trees looking for the snake, but he couldn't find it. Instead, he found a young boy only a few years older than himself. The boy sat on the ground, playing with a giant scorpion. The scorpion parried and dodged a stick as the boy jabbed it. Cain watched as the scorpion grabbed the wood with its claw and pulled it away from the boy.

Cain wanted to play with the scorpion and entered the trees. He sat across from the boy with the scorpion in between them. The boy and the scorpion continued to play and paid no attention to him. After several minutes, the scorpion turned towards Cain and danced as if it wanted to play with him now. He picked up a small twig lying beside him and jabbed the scorpion, as the other boy had done. It responded to him in the same manner, and he lost track of time playing. Suddenly, Cain jumped backward in reaction to the violent scene that unfolded before him. The other boy became angry because the scorpion played with Cain. In a fit of rage, the boy raised a rock above his head and smashed the scorpion. Over and over, he slammed the rock down upon the scorpion. When the scorpion was unrecognizable, he stopped. The boy's breathing was heavy, and he panted with exhaustion. Cain looked at the boy with tears in his eyes. He had not mastered speech, but he asked the boy, "Why did you kill?"

Satan, in the image of the boy, responded to him, "I killed the scorpion because it left me to play with you!" Cain tried to understand what he witnessed and the boy's words, but it was foreign to him because he was still a child. He saw his father kill for food, but no other reason. Adam had told him, "God gave us dominion over all of the creatures of this world, but we have a responsibility to kill only what we need to sustain our own lives." His young mind could not comprehend how you could kill for any other reason before now.

Adam woke, startled by Cain's absence. He ran out of the cave and yelled for his son. "Cain, where are you?" Cain heard his father's voice and jumped up. He left the patch of trees slowly with his head down because his parents forbade him from leaving the cave alone. Adam's heart leaped when he saw Cain emerge from the trees. "What are you doing outside?" Cain did not answer, but he ran to his father. When Cain was within reach, Adam scooped him up into his arms and hugged him. Cain wrapped his small arms around his father and tucked his head into the nape of his neck.

After a few moments, Adam pulled Cain away from his shoulder and looked into his eyes. Then he asked Cain, "What were you doing in the trees?" Cain replied, "Playing with my friend." At the time, his answer did not seem strange because Cain loved to bring his *special friends* home to scare his mom or sister. He put the boy on the ground facing the entrance to the cave and smacked him on his backside. "Go inside to your mother." Cain did as his father suggested and skipped into the cave.

Adam knew his son was curious, but he wondered what he was doing in the trees. Curiosity got the best of him, so he walked over to the patch of trees. He pushed the branches apart and looked inside. Nothing was there except for a rock sitting upon the remains of something unrecognizable. *Had Cain killed whatever that used to be?* Adam had not seen Cain harm another creature, but he could not think of another explanation. As he considered the matter, he turned and went back to the cave while making a mental note to ask Cain later.

In the months and years that passed, Adam and Eve continued to worship God and were faithful unto him. They raised their children in the ways of God, and they grew stronger each day. Satan continued to commune with Cain in secret. He schemed and used smart words to lead him further away from the teachings of God. Cain became selfish and envious of his brother Abel because he was like his father and sought God. His brother prayed several times a day and made sacrifices unto God with his father, even as a young child. Adam and Abel were inseparable.

Cain was not like Adam or Abel. He believed in God, but he did not want to spend his time in prayer and offering sacrifices unto God. On one morning, Satan came to Cain as the young boy who played with the scorpion, as was his practice. Satan asked, "Cain, your sister Luluwa has grown into a beautiful young woman. She is voluptuous and ripe before my eyes." Cain rebuked him, "She is my sister?" Satan responded, "Do you not look upon your sisters and mother as they bathe in the pool? Luluwa's beauty rivals your mother, and yet your sister, Aklia, is plain to look upon." Cain considered Satan's words because he was coming of age and had feelings and desires which he did not understand.

Satan saw Cain's heart and the sexual desires of his youth and asked him, "Have you not wondered why you wake in the morning with your manhood reaching for the heavens?" Cain's cheeks flushed with embarrassment, "I do not know why these things happen, but I cannot control them." Satan replied, "This is desire welling up inside of you because Lilith whispers to you in your dreams. She wants you to experience sexual gratification!" Cain replied, "Who is Lilith? I have not heard her name, seen her, or heard her voice." *Adam and Eve had not told their children about Lilith!* Satan wondered if telling him about Adam's first wife was the right thing to do, but decided against it. *I will save Lilith's story for another time.* So, he replied, "The wind carries Lilith's voice to your ears because you are coming of age!" Cain drifted off into deep thought as he considered Satan's words. Adam and Abel met Cain as they walked up the trail to make their sacrifices unto God. Satan departed as they approached, knowing he had planted his evil seed in Cain's young mind. Adam saw Cain standing alone; looking into the fields and felt a shiver climb up his spine. *Why is my son out here alone*?

CHAPTER 44

Adam called out to Cain, "Come here, my son." Cain went to his father and his brother, who joined them. They had just returned from making their sacrifices and worshiping God. Adam looked upon his son Cain and said, "You shall be a tiller of the field. I will teach you the ways of the field as the angels of God have shown me." His words made Cain immediately angry because he knew God cursed the ground when his father and mother fell from God's grace in the Garden of Eden. *Working in the fields is hard work*, Cain thought. Before Cain could speak out in protest, Adam turned to Abel and said, "You will tend to the animals of the field so that they may grow strong. You will help me pick the best of them to sacrifice unto God on the altar." Cain's rage boiled over until he could not hold his tongue! "I am your eldest son. I should be the one who watches the animals. He should till the hard ground in the heat of the day!" Adam replied in a harsh tone, "I have made my decision, and you will obey your father's words!" Cain turned away from his father and left in anger while Abel stayed with Adam, joyous with his father's decision.

When Adam returned to the cave, he sent Abel to tend their flock, and his sisters to gather wood and berries so that he might speak to Eve in private. Adam said unto Eve, "Our children have grown strong and tall and are coming of age. The time for them to marry is upon us! Since there are no others, but our children, Cain should marry Abel's sister Aklia, and Abel shall marry Cain's sister Luluwa!" His words pleased her, and she agreed they should marry when the youngest children, Abel and Aklia, came of age.

Satan overhead their conversation and went straight to Cain, who was tending the field as his father commanded. Cain was sitting in the shade of a tree near the field he had just tilled. He was so angry that he plowed half of the area in the heat of the day. His body ached, and his hands were bloody and blistered. The heaviness of sleep weighed on him as he rested in the shade. Satan came to him as a young man carrying a vessel of fresh water.

Satan said unto Cain, "Greetings, how does your work go?" Cain replied to Satan, "It is hard, but I will finish it after I rest!" Satan offered him the water, "Drink! Wash your hands and feet and refresh yourself." Cain accepted his offer because he had no water. Satan spoke to Cain as he washed, "How is it that the eldest tends to the field, and yet the youngest sits in the shade and watches his father's flock?" His words stoked Cain's anger again. Cain replied, "Abel stole my father's bosom from me, and there is no room for me there!" Satan answered, "I have seen how your father and mother love him more than you!" Cain's raised his voice in anger and replied, "My mother does not show Abel favor over me!" Satan laughed at him and said, "I just overheard your parents speaking in the cave. They have agreed that your beautiful sister, Luluwa, will wed Abel and you shall marry Aklia, who is plain to look upon!" Satan's words stung his heart because he knew that he was right. Cain rose without a word and tilled the rest of the field in anger. Satan watched him from the shade until he was sure that his words took hold of Cain. Only then did he leave him.

When Cain finished tilling the field, he went to the cave his family called home. When he got to the cave, his mother was alone. Adam and Abel were fasting and praying unto God in the Cave of Treasures, and his sisters were bringing water from the stream. When Eve saw Cain was angry. She reached out to hug him, but he knocked her arms away and refused her embrace.

Cain spoke to his mother with anger, "Why have you and father conspired against me so I should be a tiller of the fields? Why have you determined I should marry Aklia and my brother should marry my sister, Luluwa? I should get to choose!" When he stopped speaking, Eve replied, "Son, your father thought that you should marry your sister Aklia because you did not share the womb with her!" She wasn't lying, but deep within her heart, she did want Abel to marry Luluwa. Abel was gentle and kind, unlike Cain. She also favored Luluwa because she was beautiful and clung to her bosom.

Suddenly, Cain backhanded his mother without warning. A loud clap rang throughout the cave. Her head swung awkwardly to the side as she spiraled down to the ground. She propped herself up with her forearm and covered her injured cheek with her hand. Her cheek burned, and a red handprint rose to the surface. Then, Cain kicked his mother. His foot impacted her midsection before she recovered from the first blow. The powerful kick drove the air from her lungs. She looked up at him in horror as she struggled to take another precious breath.

Her short gasps echoed in the cave. She writhed in pain on the ground as Cain loomed over her. His rage emanated from him like a rock gives off the heat of the day, well into the cool of the night. Visions of the creatures he killed with his friend flashed before his eyes. A voice whispered in his ears, *Kill her! Kill her and your father because they betrayed you! No,* he thought, *this is Abel's fault. If it weren't for him, my parents would love me. It is Abel who must die! If I kill my brother, I will be their favorite again! Then, they will give me Luluwa's hand in marriage!*

He tried to grab his mother's arm and help her up, but she flinched when he touched her. "Take my hand," Cain said as he held out his hand. Eve took it, and he lifted her off the ground. Cain hugged his reluctant mother like a small child embraces his mother. Then, she said unto him, "Go now, back to the fields and spend the night there so your father will not punish you when he sees what you have done to me. If you are here when he sees the mark upon my face, he will be angry.

I will make intercession with him for you until his anger has passed!" Cain listened to his mother, returned to the fields, and made his bed under a large tree.

CHAPTER 45

Adam returned unto Eve in the cool of the evening after he had finished his prayers and fasting unto God. Abel remained at the Cave of Treasures because he desired to pray until the sun rose. Cain's sister Luluwa would tend the flock until Abel returned. She was beautiful and delicate, like a rose and was not well-suited to work in the fields. Aklia, on the other hand, liked hard work and would help Cain in the field except he did not want ther, preferring to work the fields alone. So, Aklia helped her mother gather herbs and other plants from the rough mountainous terrain. These herbs and plants provided remedies for their illnesses and injuries. However, Adam was not pleased that Eve had not yet returned from gathering the sphagnum moss that grew high up on the mountain, "I will have my wife when I return!"

When Eve finally returned from gathering, Adam saw the bruises upon Eve's body. He became furious with Cain, but Eve made intercession for him and then distracted him. She offered herself unto him before their children returned. Eve kissed Adam, then she said, "Take me," as she bent over a stool. Adam mounted her like a beast in the field. He reached around her and cupped her ample breasts, pulling her to him as he thrust himself into her warmth. She moaned loudly in response to his thrusts of passion. Her cries of pleasure heightened his arousal. They knew Aklia would return soon and they didn't have much time. His pace quickened, which only served to bring Eve more pleasure. After a few moments, Adam reached the peak of his climax and released his seed within her. The warmth of his seed caused Eve to reach orgasm, and both were satisfied.

Aklia entered the cave and immediately knew something was going on because her parents scurried from their embrace, like rats brought into the sudden light. The lust of the flesh was something she clearly did not understand yet and did not want to see what her mother and father did! She turned her back on them and said, "Have mercy on your child and cover yourselves!"

After they dressed, Adam said to Aklia, "Daughter, sleep because before the sun rises, I need you to go to the field and tell your brother Cain to gather a bountiful sacrifice for God and bring it to the altar. Then go to the Cave of Treasures, tell your brother Abel to pick a sacrifice from the flock that is without spot and blemish and bring it also to the altar. Aklia did as her father asked.

The next morning, she rose before the sun and took her father's words unto her brothers. Cain watched the sun rise as he planted the remainder of his field. He hoped that his hard work would pay off and that his harvest would be plentiful so that his parents might be pleased with him. Cain had woken before sunrise because he feared his father might still come to the fields and beat him for hitting his mother. He was constantly looking over his shoulder and down the path to their home as he continued to sow seeds in the field. Then, in the distance, a figure walked down the trail, and his heart leaped with fear. His eyes focused on the path until he saw it was his friend and not his father, and a sense of relief washed over him.

Satan spoke to Cain, "Greetings unto you!" Cain replied to him with the same words. Then Satan said, "I know that your father's decision for whom you should marry angers you." Before he could finish his words, Cain interrupted him, "Why do you care about this matter?" Satan replied, "Have I not been your friend since you were a child? I come to bring you good news. If you can convince your parents to allow you to marry Luluwa, I will bring you to my land, which is to the north. In my country, I will give you a lavish marriage ceremony. You will have fine wedding robes, gold, silver, and a wonderful dwelling laden with my gifts unto you. My servants will also be your servants, and you will not have to tend the fields or the flocks, but they will do everything for you. You will know wealth beyond measure, and you will not need your father's God because I will be like a God unto you. You will want for nothing!" Satan's words were sweet in Cain's ears, and his heart was eager to know the pleasures of his friend's kingdom. Then, his friend said unto him, "Go now, unto the pool and look upon your future bride Luluwa as she bathes there." Cain heard his words and gladly left for the pool.

CHAPTER 46

Cain approached the pool where his mother and sisters usually bathed, using the cover of the trees and the foliage to find a vantage point. He found a spot that allowed him a close view of the pool, but provided concealment, so his sister would not catch him watching her. Cain had never gazed upon his sister Luluwa without clothes or any other woman, for that matter, and he wondered what she looked like naked. His mind raced in anticipation as a strange warmth rose up from within his loins.

A few moments later, his sister approached from the well-worn trail that led from the cave that was their home. She looked around the pool as she drew near to make sure there was no one nearby. When she was content that she was alone, she let her garments fall to the ground and waded into the pool. Cain watched intently from her left side. Her hair glistened in the morning sun long and flowed down her back. Her limbs were long and shapely, and her ample breasts stood proudly upon her chest. Her nipples became erect as she waded into the cold waters. Between her legs, a veil of hair rose to hide her womanhood from his view.

His loins stirred, and his manhood rose from under his garments. He shifted his position to restore his view of Luluwa as she waded into the pool, and his hand accidentally grazed his manhood. His touch sent a ripple of pleasure through his body. So, he began to rub himself as he watched her. He became lost in her beauty as he pleasured himself.

Suddenly there was another hand on his manhood, but this one was under his garment! He struggled to see who took hold of him and would have screamed, but the person also covered his mouth from behind. A female voice whispered in his ear, "SHHH, she will hear you. Your sister is beautiful. Look at her as her hand lingers between her thighs. She is pleasuring herself, but she does not understand her body yet. She is like a newborn fawn trying to stand and walk. She is clumsy within herself. I will teach you how to satisfy her!"

Cain did not understand who this woman was or what she was doing to him or why it felt so good, but at that moment, he didn't care. As her hand moved upon him, he drew closer to his first orgasm. He had no idea what was building within him. A strange warmth filled him, and every muscle within him began to tighten slowly. After a few moments, he thought his muscles might tear away from his bones, as the warmth within him searched for a means of escape. His eyes blinked as spasms rose from deep within his loins. Cain looked at his sister exiting the water, saw the red veil between her thighs and his seed burst from within him. When the spasms ended, he was alone at the pool. He looked down at his seed, lying on the ground in front of him. *What have I done?*

Lilith whispered in response to his thoughts, "You are becoming a man, and this is only a small taste of the pleasures I will show you in the coming days. Soon you shall taste your sister's pleasures too." With that, she pulled his arm around behind him and placed it between her thighs. The woman was not like his sister. There was no veil hiding the pleasure between her legs. She held his hand on top of his fingers and pleasured herself with his hand. She moaned softly in his ear. Then she pushed his fingers inside of her. Her warmth excited him, and he became erect again. She whispered in his ear one more time as she reached around with her other hand and began to stroke him softly, "Tonight, I will meet you by the large tree at the field, and you shall learn what it feels like to have this," *She squeezed his manhood,* "inside of this." Then she pushed his fingers inside of her once more. He groaned with delight, and then she was suddenly gone!

CHAPTER 47

William closed Satan's Book and set it on the end table next to him. *Lilith*, every time he read about her, he found himself aroused. He still was not convinced the book was real, but there was something about her exploits that resonated within him. "So, you like to read about me, William?" The woman's seductive voice startled William, and his eyes frantically searched the unlit side of the room for her. Then, in a dark corner, he saw two piercing emerald eyes glaring at him from the shadows. "Who are you?" he asked, but he was afraid that he already knew the answer before he asked it. Lilith stepped out of the shadows and replied, "William, you know who I am." "Lilith..." trailed off his tongue in disbelief. "I came to see Satan's chosen voice for myself! When I saw how aroused you got reading about me; I decided that I should pay you a personal visit!" William could not take his eyes off Lilith. Satan's Book did not do her justice. She was seductive, beautiful, and terrifying, all at the same time!

One second, she was standing in the dark corner, and the next second, she was standing directly in front of him. He could feel the warmth of her body; she was so close. Her warm breath brushed across his lips as her hand rested upon his erect member. He was not sure when she took hold of him or when he became erect, but he groaned in delight as she kissed him. They shared a passionate kiss, and then she looked into his eyes. Her penetrating green eyes captivated him as her skilled fingers danced upon his member. Suddenly, they were naked, and he was looking up at her. Her head swung in coordination with her hips which gyrated upon him, drawing him deeper inside of her. Images of her taking Satan upon his throne came to his mind from the pages of Satan's book. Her fingernails sliced into his chest as if she knew his thoughts. He groaned with delight and the sweet agony of pleasure. She looked down at him with a wry smile on her lips as he felt the heat rising from deep within his loins.

Her hips moved upon him, and her warmth constricted as the spasms of orgasm echoed through his body. Suddenly, Lilith stopped and dismounted him. *Is she going to leave me at the verge of release*? William wondered. Suddenly, she was kneeling between his thighs, and his question vanished. Seconds later, he spilled his seed into her. He watched as she took all of him and then she allowed some of his seed to run down his glistening member. He looked at the red-haired demon as he shook with orgasm. Her wings fluttered in delight as she drained him. Then, she lifted her head and looked up at him with his member still inside of her. He held her gaze as she teased him with her tongue, coaxing the last of his seed from him. When nothing remained, she rose until she laid upon him. She kissed him, and he tasted himself for the first time.

Suddenly, her erotic spell lost its hold of him, *Margaret!* He prayed this was a dream or nightmare, but Lilith was still on top of him. *I cheated on my wife with a demon*! he thought. Lilith loomed over him, staring into his eyes. "Margaret? Are you worried this will hurt your relationship with your wife?" She laughed as she grabbed his jaw with her hand. He struggled as she squeezed until his mouth opened. In horror, he watched as she pinched her nipple and sprayed a putrid green liquid from her breast. The liquid burned his mouth and lips. Total paralysis quickly took hold of him, and he could not move. Lilith released his jaw and stood up. His head fell to the side, and drool rolled down his cheek onto the floor. She looked down at him, smiled, and said, "Don't worry William. I plan to make sure your wife enjoys herself too!" Horror filled him as she turned and walked away. He silently screamed as he watched her turn the corner to the stairs, and he listened to her footsteps, climbing the stairs to their bedroom where

Margaret slept.

William's mind suddenly seemed foggy. It lasted for what appeared to be a long time, but he could not be sure. The fog eventually rose, and then he remembered how Lilith went to Margaret. William realized that he could move again, and he leaped to his feet in a panic. *That was a mistake*! The room spun violently, his vision tunneled, and he fell flat on the floor. He took several deep breaths and propped himself up. After a few more deep breaths, his vision cleared, and he slowly stood up. His legs were shaky, but the room was not spinning. William never made it upstairs. As he passed the kitchen door, he smelt bacon and eggs. *How long was I out,* "Margaret," he called as he went into the kitchen? "William, come in and sit down. Your breakfast is almost ready." His mind raced as he pulled out his usual chair and sat down at the table. She put a cup of coffee on the table in front of him.

William sipped his coffee as Margaret bounced between the stove and island counter, humming a song, he did not recognize. As she finished making breakfast, he wondered, *Was it all a dream?* If not, *What had Lilith done to Margaret?* She set a plate down in front of him and sat down across from him with a plate of her own. William said, "Thanks." She smiled back at him and took a bite of her eggs. "Needs more salt," she said as she grabbed the saltshaker off the table. She was humming again as she salted her food. Finally, he asked, "Why are you in such a good mood?" "Promise you won't make fun of me?" she asked. He couldn't hide his curiosity as he replied, "Sure, I promise that I won't laugh at you."

"I had a dream last night. Several vivid dreams!" William was curious now, "What kind of dreams?" She gave him a look that implied they were sexual, and he said, "Oh!" Then, she explained her dreams, "A tall, beautiful redhead was in my room. We had sex, and it was amazing! I was still wet and horny when I woke up this morning. My vibrator got one hell of a workout. I had to change the batteries!" William stared at her in disbelief. She had not openly talked about masturbation or another woman in years. When they met in college, Margaret was dating another woman. She was a free spirit back in those days. "Did your dream make you wish you stayed with Carla and not me?" William asked. The three of them lived together during their junior year of college, but she decided they should be monogamous and get married. Margaret replied, "I miss her sometimes, but I would never trade you, my love." She smiled after she said the last part. He knew she was kidding, but the next thing she said surprised him. "Let's pick up a woman some time and try a threesome again."

William's eyes were like saucers. He could not believe what he was hearing! He loved to watch Margaret with another woman as much as he liked to join in on the fun. The birth of their children had changed their life. He had no regrets, but their kids were adults now. "Maybe we should," he said as he returned to his breakfast. *What a strange morning,* he thought. Margaret finished eating and put her plate in the sink. She kissed him on the forehead and said, "I'm going to take a shower, and then I need to go shopping. Would you like to come with me?" William replied, "No, thanks, I only have four days until I go back to work, and I want to finish the book that I am reading." She was glad he did not want to go because she hated taking him shopping because he did not like browsing and would pout like an unhappy child the whole time. *It is better for me if he stays home with his precious book*, she thought as she headed upstairs.

William rinsed off his plate and poured himself a second cup of coffee. He added a splash of milk in, and he headed back to the den. "Goddammit," William said as he entered the room and found Amon sitting on the couch. "Do you guys have a supernatural doorbell or something? One of these times, I am going to have a heart attack!" Amon laughed; *Humans could be such drama queens*! Then he asked, "So, Lilith paid you a visit last night?" "She did, and my wife too," William replied.

"Margaret had several *wet dreams* last night and woke up so horny she spent the morning pleasuring herself," William said. Amon replied, "Lilith has that effect on both angels and humankind. How are you doing with the book?" "I have four days until I have to go back to work, but I should finish the book before then." "That's good," Amon replied. William asked, "So, what happens when I finish the book?" Amon replied, "I guess Satan will give you the second book, and then your daughter can read the first one. Satan has not discussed it with me." Then, Amon vanished, and William was alone again. *Not even a goodbye? Typical,* he thought as he shook his head. He took a sip of his coffee and set it down on the end table. Then, he picked up Satan's Book and started reading again.

CHAPTER 48

Cain replayed the events at the pool in his mind as he returned to the field. He thought about his sister's voluptuous body, the mystery of the strange woman, and the pleasure she showed him. When he got to the field, he found Aklia sitting under a tree. Before he could speak, she said unto him, "Father has commanded that you bring the best of the field and make a sacrifice unto God!" Cain replied, "Why should I let my hard work go up in smoke before God? Can't God make a sacrifice unto himself? Won't his sacrifice be greater than mine?" Aklia said, "That is between you, our father, and God!" She left Cain and went to tell Abel about their father's command.

Rage filled Cain and threatened to consume him like a fire consumes dry wood. He was not pleased with his father's request, and even worse, he did not know Adam told Abel to make a sacrifice unto God as well. Cain was tired of being second to his brother. Their previous sacrifices were all rams or sheep that were without spot or blemish. He wondered, *Would God accept grain, nuts, and fruit as a sacrifice?* So, instead of giving his best sacrifice unto God, he took the fruit which had fallen from the trees and bushes as a sacrifice. The stench of his sacrifice drew flies and bugs which tormented him on the way to the altar of God.

He arrived before his brother and placed his sacrifice upon the altar. When Abel arrived, there was no room for his sacrifice upon the altar. So, he built a makeshift altar beside the old one and placed a great ram upon it. The ram was fat and without spot and blemish. Cain glared at Abel with hatred in his eyes. *He brought the perfect sacrifice! Our father probably helped Abel pick that ram out of the flock*, he thought. Abel's sacrifice overshadowed Cain's. Adam spoke to his son, "Cain, I have called you here to sacrifice unto God with your brother, so you might ask God to forgive you for the harm you inflicted upon your mother. I hope you and your brother will become closer because of your shared sacrifices."

Then Adam prayed, "Lord God Almighty, you know the hearts of my children. Accept their sacrifices and forgive their sins. Let the spirit of brotherhood be upon them, so they will not be adversaries!" When he finished speaking, fire came from heaven and devoured Abel's sacrifice because he gave it with a pure heart and no ill intent. Cain's sacrifice remained on the altar, untouched by the flames from heaven. Suddenly, there was a loud buzzing sound filled their ears as a dark cloud approached them. A swarm of locusts fell on Cain's sacrifice and devoured it because he had not offered his best unto God. Cain's heart was not pure because he did not love his brother, and he did not want God to forgive him. *My parents, brother and even God are all against me,* he thought. Cain left the altar in anger and vowed he would not live with his family anymore.

Cain arrived at the shade tree near his field at the hottest part of the day. He rested in the shade until the heat of the day passed. As he laid there, he saw a raven flying overhead. The raven landed near him, and it had a small rodent in its beak. Cain paid no attention to the bird and fell asleep. He woke to the sound of scraping on the rocks near him. He opened his heavy eyes and looked towards the sounds. The bird had set the rodent on the ground and was digging with its beak. It scraped the ground until there was a small hole. Then, it picked up the rodent and dropped it in the hole. The bird covered the hole with dirt and stomped on top of the soil to pack it down. The raven looked at Cain, squawked loudly three times and flew away. Cain considered the meaning of what he witnessed for a moment but then fell back to sleep.

A few minutes later, Cain woke to the sounds of movement, crunching and chewing. When he opened his eyes, he saw his brother's sheep eating the tender sprouts from his field. Anger filled him, as he walked over to the flock, seeing his brother sitting unaware in the shade. "*ABEL!*," thoughts of killing his brother like his friend had smashed the dancing scorpion brought a smile to Cain's lips. He needed to do something about him. *I will kill him!*

The beginnings of a plan came to him as he walked towards his brother. When Cain reached his brother, he sat down beside him and asked, "Brother, why does your flock eat of my planted field?" Abel rose in horror because he did not realize that his herd had ventured into his brother's field. "Brother, my mind wandered. I thought the flock was still grazing in the wild grasses next to your field. I will help you replant it." *You make me sick because you are perfect,* Cain thought. Cain used his brother's apology as an opportunity to fulfill his desire to kill him.

So, he spoke unto Abel, "Brother, I realize that I have not been gracious to you because I have hated you since your birth. Your relationship with our father has made me jealous. Today at the altar, I was angry with myself for not bringing a proper sacrifice. When I returned to the field, I prayed for forgiveness and sought peace between you and me." Abel was happy, hugged his brother and said, "Praise be to God!" Abel had prayed many times for peace between him and his brother.

After they embraced for a few moments, Cain spoke to his brother again saying, "Tomorrow you shall go with me, and I will show you a place with lush green grasses for your flocks and cool shade trees for your rest." His words pleased Abel, and he said, "Tomorrow then!" He left with the flock and whistled a happy song as he returned home.

The ease by which his lies rolled off his tongue surprised Cain. He smiled and thought, *Tomorrow my brother will be dead. I will kill him and bury him in the wilderness!* Great joy filled him as he completed his plan. The details came together with ease. He even rehearsed the words he would say before he killed him. Cain thought about his brother's death with delight in his heart. He whistled a happy song as he built a simple wooden shelter to be his home. In his mind, he saw himself smashing Abel's head over and over with a rock. *Tomorrow is going to be a great day!*

CHAPTER 49

Cain finished his primitive dwelling before sunset, and built a fire to keep the night chill away. His mind replayed images of this morning's encounter as he watched the fire. *Who was she? Would she keep her word and come to him tonight?* Lilith's seductive and authoritative voice echoed through his head as if it traveled upon the winds in response to his questions. The memories of their early morning encounter caused his loins to stir again.

Lilith startled him when she spoke from behind him, "Child, are you ready to become a man?" He spun around to face her. "I am ready," Cain replied. Thoughts of the treasures her body held excited him. Lilith wore a simple, white linen gown. It hugged her hips and fell just above her knees. Her dark red hair looked like hot coals smoldering under the surface of a fire. Tanned skin adorned her voluptuous body, a body which called for him. His gaze met hers. Her eyes were like emerald flames, which produced a light of their own. His loins trembled in response to her beauty. He could not resist her even if he wanted to.

Lilith sensed a hint of Samael's darkness in him, and thought, *This must be the child which Samael corrupted in Eve's womb.* Memories of Samael heightened her desire to corrupt Cain and intensified her need for sexual gratification. Thoughts of being Cain's first lover, caused her thighs to become wet in anticipation. His eyes blazed with desire for her. She reached up and pulled her dress off her shoulders. The dress fell, hugging her body as it slithered to the ground. Cain's eyes followed its descent, gazing at the revelations it unveiled on its downward journey. She lifted her feet out of the dress by raising her knees towards her chest and extending her long legs in an exaggerated motion. Then, she stepped towards him. Her beauty captivated him, but her power enslaved him. His eyes saw her perfect breasts, accented by nipples hardened with her desire to have him. His focus shifted to the glisten of passion, which formed between her thighs. He remembered how warm and wet she felt at the pool, and he moaned softly.

Like a predator, she gracefully stalked Cain. With each step, his body twitched in anticipation. His body ached for her next step towards him. A moment later, she stood before him, face to face, gazing into his eyes. Her eyes were like gateways to a passion-filled world. The wondrous delights she offered caused a warmth to rise within him and sent a shiver of anticipation throughout his body. Her beauty left him in a trance until she kissed him. He did not respond to her kiss until he tasted her soft, wet, and intoxicating lips upon his. Then, he closed his eyes and followed the movements of her lips and tongue. A hunger rose within him, as he kissed her passionately.

Lilith knew he lacked the stamina of a skilled lover. So, she took his hand and led him to his shelter. She lowered herself to the ground and pulled him down on top of her. He stared into her eyes, and nothing else existed but them. She pushed his head down until his lips rested on her erect nipples. Then she whispered to him, "Take them into your mouth!" He did as she desired and kissed her breasts and nipples. "Bite them," she said. He obeyed until she wanted more. She pushed him further down until his face was between her thighs.

Cain followed her direction and willingly moved down until he kissed the warmth between her thighs. Her hands grasp the back of his head, and she pulled him in until his tongue danced within her. In his mind, he felt her encouraging him. She was like honey to his lips. Deeper and deeper, he probed her until he found the center of her pleasure. His lips and tongue danced upon and within her until she shook in orgasm, but he didn't stop. His desire and excitement grew with each of her orgasms.

His eagerness and willingness to obey her made up for his inexperience. She gave into him and giggled in response to his enthusiasm. She pulled him up from her thighs, and kissed him passionately, savoring herself upon his lips. Cain submitted to her as she rolled him over and straddled him. She guided Cain's erect member into her warmth. His eyes rolled back in his head with pleasure, and he groaned with delight. Every nerve ending in his body screamed her name, *Lilith!* She had another orgasm in response to her thoughts, and then he showed his inexperience and lack of stamina.

The pleasure of his release rivaled their morning encounter. As soon as he thought there was no greater pleasure, he achieved a new level bliss between her thighs. It was like a tidal wave passed through the eye a needle. She sat upon him until his seed stopped flowing. His thoughts cleared, and he wondered, *Who is this Lilith?* Adam told him once, "God made them in his image, but spoke of them only." *She was real, alive, and like them, so who made her?* There was something different about her. He wasn't sure what it was, but he liked it! He wondered, *Does my father know Lilith?*

Lilith sat on top of him for a few moments looking into his eyes. Conflict and uncertainty swirled in his mind, but there was something else. *Murder!* His hatred for his brother drives him to murder. She wondered, *What will God do when one of his children kills his brother, especially one as beloved as Abel. Would God condemn Cain? Would he raise Abel from the dead?* Tomorrow they would see what God would do, but today she would have her fun with Cain.

She bent over, kissed Cain, and asked him, "Has your father mentioned his first wife?" His eyes grew wide with surprise as he thought, *His first wife?* He opened his mouth to speak, but she placed her finger on his lips, "Shhhhh..." She looked deep into his eyes, and he became stiff once more. His eyes closed, and he groaned in appreciation, as her hips danced upon him once more. Moments later, Cain left his seed in her and immediately drifted off into a deep sleep. Lilith looked down at him and smiled at the young man as he slept peacefully. "Sleep now, young Cain, because tomorrow is going to be a hell of a day," she said! Then, Lilith rose from Cain and dressed. She stole one last look at him as she spread her wings in flight. *Satan needs to know about Cain's plan*, she thought.

CHAPTER 50

The next morning Cain awoke with a smile on his face, but sorrow pushed away his happiness because Lilith was gone. He wondered if he would see her again, but she said nothing about coming back. Lilith had given him a taste of the pleasures of the flesh, and it was glorious. His thoughts turned to his sister naked at the pool. He wondered, *Will laying with my sister result in the same pleasure I experienced with Lilith? I will find out, but first, I must kill Abel. Then Luluwa will be mine!* He whistled a sweet melody as he went to the pool and bathed himself. Along the way, he found a large branch and fashioned it into a heavy staff. Then he said unto himself, "With this staff, I will strike my brother down!"

He returned to the field and ate a breakfast of nuts and berries as he waited for Abel to come. After a short time, Cain saw Abel approaching with his flock. Cain's heart leaped with excitement. When Abel was close, Cain said unto him, "Place your sheep in the field next to mine, and they can graze there until we return. I will show you the path to the plentiful fields of grass, and then you can bring the flock when you know the path." Abel trusted Cain because he believed he had repented and changed his ways.

Cain and Abel walked for a long time, deep into the wilderness. They walked until they reached a place where Cain knew his father had never been. The land did not have plentiful grasses as Cain described to Abel, and he became fearful. So, Abel asked Cain, "Why do you take me into the wilderness? Do you intend to kill me?" Cain replied truthfully, "Yes, today you shall die!" Then, Cain hit Abel on the crown of his head with his staff.

Abel fell to the ground, stunned by his brother's blow. Rage filled Cain as he thought about the favor that Adam showed Abel. He beat him upon his arms, legs, and torso, but he did not want to kill him yet. Cain wanted to savor his brother's death slowly. So, he beat him until his body was bloody, bruised, and broken. After many blows, Abel lay in the fetal position upon the ground. He cried out unto Cain, "Strike me dead if you intend to kill me. Take a large rock and smash my head until my spirit leaves my body!" Abel's words pleased Cain because he remembered his friend killing the dancing scorpion with the rock. So, he grabbed a large rock, struck Abel's head and said, "Goodbye, sweet brother!"

Blind rage flowed through Cain as flashes of the boy smashing the scorpion and him smashing his brother's head became intertwined. Over and over, he continued until he could not muster the strength to lift the rock. He fell to his knees and searched for breath as he looked down at his bloody hands, holding the stone. His heavy breaths echoed in his ears, and his vision tunneled. As his breathing slowed, his eyes drifted from the pooling blood below the rock where his brother's head had been. Now, unrecognizable pieces of flesh, brain matter, and bone fragments lay in a twisted pile at the top of Abel's shoulders. *I have won!* As soon as that thought passed, the earth quaked and shook. His mind raced with fear as he thought, *The ground beneath me will split in two and swallow me up because I have killed my brother!* Cain was not sorry, and he would not repent, but he did not want to die. He trembled in fear of death as the earth shook. The earth quaked because Cain spilled Abel's innocent blood.

When the earth stopped quaking, and Cain was still alive, he remembered the raven. *The raven buried the dead rodent!* He grabbed his staff and the rock. Then, he dug the first grave within the earth. Killing his brother and digging the grave left Cain exhausted. He struggled to roll his brother's lifeless body into his grave. Once Abel was in the grave, Cain threw the rock that he killed his brother with inside also. The stone hit Able in the middle of the back with a dull thud. He examined the staff and found none of his brother's blood, so he kept it as a trophy. Then, he filled the grave and packed it with his feet. When he finished, he picked up the staff and left.

Cain was only a couple steps away when a cringe of fear ran down his spine. He turned and looked back at his brother's grave. Horror filled him because Abel's lifeless body was resting above the ground with the bloody rock beside it. Cain's heart raced as he dug another grave and buried his brother a second time. He packed the soil harder this time by stomping his feet and jumping upon the loose ground. When he finished, he gathered his things again and left. Another chill ran down his spine. He turned around, and his brother's body was lying on top of the ground with the bloody rock beside him once more. Cain trembled in fright and tore his clothes because of his brother's body. He quickly buried his brother a third time and packed the ground by jumping up and down upon it. *This time the earth will hold him*! He picked up the staff and turned once more to the grave before he left. Again, he saw his brother's body and the bloody rock lying on top of the ground. Panic filled Cain as a raven squawked three times from the tree above. He buried his brother three times, but the earth refused his innocent body each time. Finally, he abandoned his brother and returned to his field. His brother's lifeless body and the bloody rock remained upon the ground in the wilderness.

CHAPTER 51

Cain hurried back from the wilderness because he did not want his parents to find him away from the field. His mind replayed the events of his brother's murder over and over. Try as he might, he could not bury his brother, and that worried him. At the field, he heard his brother's flock grazing nearby, and he went to scatter them. Cain stopped in his tracks. *Luluwa is gathering Abel's sheep!* He returned to his field without Luluwa seeing him and started tilling the weeds. After some time, Luluwa came to him and inquired about Abel by saying, "Cain, have you seen our brother, Abel because when I arrived, the flock was unattended?" Cain replied unto her, "Am I my brother's keeper? Why don't you ask his father or mother instead?" She left him, took the flock to their cave, and told her parents that Abel was missing.

Later that evening, Adam, Eve and his sisters returned unto Cain at the field. Adam asked him, "Where is your brother, Abel?" Cain replied, "Who can say, am I my brother's keeper?" Adam and Eve wept for Abel because he had a gentle nature. *Mischief must have fallen upon him*, they thought. The whole family, to include Cain, searched all night for Abel. When the sun rose, and they had not found him, Adam and Eve fell to the ground and wept for Abel. Adam called out to God, "Lord, deliver our son and bring him home to us again!"

The Son of God appeared and greeted them. Then he turned to Cain and asked, "Cain, where is your brother Abel?" Cain replied unto him, "I am not my brother's keeper!" The Son of God cursed Cain because he knew he killed his brother. He said unto him, "Cain, you have killed your brother and tried to hide his body in the earth! The earth will no longer bear fruit unto you because you spilled innocent blood. You have killed your brother Abel because he was pure of heart and your father promised Luluwa to him, as a wife. Because you hated him and desired her, you took his life." Cain trembled and shook because of his words. The Son of God spoke again saying, "You shall tremble and shake all of your days, as a sign you killed your brother!"

Cain replied to the Son of God by saying, "Your curse is more than I can bear!" Then the Son of God said, "Fear not Cain, your days upon this earth shall be many." The Son of God struck Cain upon his forehead, and a mark rose to the surface. "A mark shall be upon you all the days of your life. No man or beast will dare kill you because a curse will be upon them if you die. If any man should kill you, he will die a thousand painful deaths before he sees the afterlife." Cain's heart sank because there was no place for him among his family. The Son of God cursed him again, saying, "The Mountain of God is no longer your home. You shall not abide here, lest you suffer in pain and torment!" Then the Son of God departed from them.

Adam's heart fell with the news of Abel's murder because his love for Abel was more significant than his passion for any of his children. Abel worshiped God like Adam. Their hearts were of one accord in all things concerning God, as they were both devoted to serving him. Neither Eve nor his daughters could comfort Adam. He tore his clothes and ran naked up into the mountains. He intended to throw himself from the highest peak and take his life. Eve followed him, but lost him upon the rocky cliffs.

Aklia and Luluwa stayed there mourning and wailing for the loss of their brother Abel. Cain seized the opportunity to take his bride with him because the Son of God commanded him to leave the Mountain of God. So, he snatched Luluwa by her arm and pulled her to her feet. She continued to weep as he pulled her to him. Cain said unto her, "You will be my wife!" Fear overwhelmed her, and she did not reply or protest. Aklia protested for her sister, but she was happy not to be his bride and let him take her. They left the Mountain of God before Adam and Eve returned. Cain and Luluwa traveled many days down from the mountain to the northeast.

Eve returned to Aklia at the fields when she could not find Adam upon the steep mountainside. When she saw Aklia alone, she asked, "Where is your sister, Luluwa?" Aklia wept as she replied, "Cain took Luluwa to be his wife." Eve fell on the ground. She cried and mourned the loss of both her son and her daughter. "Cain took both of them from me," she told Aklia. Aklia mourned with her mother, but they did not cry for Cain. Instead, they said, "His punishment is not harsh enough. God should have killed him!" They prayed for Adam's safe return.

CHAPTER 52

After Abel's murder, Eve and Aklia dedicated themselves unto God for thirty days in the Cave of Treasures, but Adam did not return. On the thirtieth day, an angel came unto them and said, "Get up onto your feet and bring Abel's body home! God has sent an angel to keep his body from decay and to protect it from the wild beasts. Follow the raven to the place where Cain killed Abel. Bring Abel's body back to the Cave of Treasures and wrap it with strips of cloth and with sweet-smelling spices and myrrh. You shall carve a resting place for him within this cave because he was without blame before God. Abel was a humble and gracious servant unto him!" The angel gave them strips of cloth, sweet spices, and myrrh. Suddenly, a raven squawked outside of the cave.

They obeyed the angel's words, followed the raven, and traveled to the place where Abel's body lay. Horror filled them because Abel's head and face were unrecognizable. Eve fell to her knees and wept before God. God had mercy on her. The angel who stood guard over Abel's body touched him and restored his face and head so that Eve might have one last memory of her son's fair countenance. She thanked God for his mercy, even though he did not restore his life. Eve and Aklia took Abel's lifeless body and hoisted it over their shoulders and journeyed back to the Cave of Treasures.

Satan appeared to them along the way and said, "Eve, why do you weep for your son? Has your heavenly Father not revived him?" Eve replied, "Abel is dead, and God has commanded us to bury him in the Cave of Treasures!" Satan answered, "Join me, and I will restore his life!" Eve's heart leaped with joy, but then she remembered how Satan tricked them so many times before. So, she asked him, "Why should I trust someone who caused us to sin?" He laughed and replied, "I did not cause you to sin. You sinned of your own accord. I only presented you with the opportunities to choose your path. Is it my fault that God will not allow you to be free? Your jealous taskmaster condemned me and my brethren because we wanted free will!" Eve refused to listen to him any longer and said, "Leave me, deceiver. I have no time to listen to your lies!" Her words held no power over him, but he left because she was not willing to betray her God.

It took Eve and Aklia three days to carry Abel's lifeless body back to the Cave of Treasures. When they arrived at the cave, they were exhausted. Despite their weak condition, they obeyed God and cleansed Abel's body without delay. They dried the body and placed sweet spices and myrrh upon it. They wrapped it with the cloth that the angel gave them. When they finished preparing his body for burial, they looked and found no tool to carve out a place in the rock for Abel's body as the angel commanded them. They used hard stones from a stream to create a crypt in the cave, but their progress was slow. In frustration, they cried out in anger and complained amongst themselves, "Why would God give us this task without the tools to complete it?" Satan sent his servant Amon unto them.

Amon could not enter the Cave of Treasures because God's spell protected it. So, he called out to Eve and Aklia from outside the cave. "My master has sent me with gifts to ease your labor!" *Why would Satan give us gifts to ease our labor?* They feared it was another trick, so they stopped at the entrance and did not leave the protection of the Cave of Treasures. Amon held out two golden cups, and they took them from his hand because they thirst. He took a pitcher of water from the ground beside him and filled their golden cups with the freshwater. They quenched their thirst with the cold water, and he filled the cups a second time. When Eve and Aklia' strength returned, Amon presented them two hammers and two chisels made of the best wood and metal. He held them out before Eve and Aklia and said, "My master would not have you suffer in the labor of burying your dead. Take these tools as a gift from Satan and use them to cut a fine tomb for Abel in the hard rock of the Cave." Eve took the tools from him and replied, "I will take these tools to make our labor easier, but I still serve God alone." Amon smiled and replied, "These are gifts given to you with no ill will or obligations. Satan seeks only to make your labor of sorrow less burdensome!" When he finished speaking, he left them alone with the tools, the cups and the pitcher of fresh water. They took Satan's gifts and returned to their labor.

Eve and Aklia finished Abel's tomb with the help of Satan's tools and placed his body in its final resting place. Then, they said unto themselves, "Let us go back unto our home and tend to the field and flocks again." Adam had not returned, so they agreed to travel to the Cave of Treasures one day a week to pray and fast for his safe return. They devoted the rest of their time to tending the flocks and the fields because they had no one else to help them. God blessed their labors, and their animals grew large and fat, and the earth bore bountiful harvests unto them.

One night, as they prepared to take their rest, Aklia said unto Eve, "I will die of old age, never having known a man, the pain of childbirth or the love of a child!" Her words pained Eve, and she replied, "Pray unto God. Ask him for a husband and children!" Aklia raised her voice in anger, "My prayers will fall on deaf ears as yours have. Every morning and every evening, you weep and pray unto God when you think I am asleep. I hear you sobbing and begging for my father's return and yet, where is he?" Eve placed her head in her hands and wept. Aklia felt sorry because she made her mother cry. So, she said unto her, "Let's pray together and believe God will answer our prayers." In the shadows outside of their dwelling, Satan smiled. *Their impatience gives me another opportunity to separate them from God!*

High up on the mountain:

Adam sat perched upon a large rock overlooking the valley below. *The whole world lies before me, and yet I wish I were dead!* Sorrow hung from him like a heavy chain. Many days passed since Abel's death, but his suffering continued without relief. His appetite and sleep fled from him, and he wished God would let him die. *How could God allow a child to die before his father? Did God have no compassion?* Adam had not prayed or spoken to God since Abel's death because God allowed his beloved son to die. *Abel's death has left a void in my heart that not even God can fill*, Adam thought.

Lilith smiled with delight as she watched Adam from a safe distance. She listened and waited for Adam to reach the lowest of lows as she thought, *Then, I will comfort him!* Many days passed and Adam finally reached his lowest point. He was malnourished, exhausted, and long past his time of fellowship with God. *He is helpless!* Lilith had not visited Adam since the day of Eve's fall. She had tricked him that day, but not today. *Today he will submit to me!*

Adam laid on the rock on the edge of a cliff, as he was close to death. Lilith approached him, but he did not move or stir. She bent over him and whispered into his ear, "I cannot stand to see you in pain, my love. Let me comfort you." Adam did not raise his head or respond to her words. Again, she spoke unto him, "Let me ease your pain and bring comfort to you." This time as her words trailed off, she reached down and rubbed his chest.

Adam was numb to this world, and her hands felt like a distant dream upon him. His body was weak; he remained silent and did not move under her touch. *I will have to try harder!* Lilith's hand drifted down his chest. She gently massaged his loins, and he groaned, acknowledging that he was still alive. Several minutes passed, as the pleasure of her actions pushed the sorrow of his loss down within him. With each stroke, his spirit rose from the murky depths of unconsciousness.

Adam's almost inaudible moans let Lilith know she was stirring the embers of passion again, so she knelt between his thighs. He moaned louder now, but his eyes remained closed. A few minutes later, the flames of passion engulfed his loins. Adam cried out, and his seed sprang from him. Lilith's tongue danced upon him as she savored every drop of him.

Adam's body trembled like the first time Lilith drew his seed from him. When his eyes finally opened, he saw Lilith and protested, but he was too weak to fight her. The pleasure of her actions drove his sorrow away and took his mind off the loss of his son, and that was all he wanted. "Take me," she said. "I do not have the strength," he replied. She smiled, and he watched as she bit the end of her finger. Before he could object, she stuck her bloody finger between his lips. Her blood tasted sweet, and it somehow energized him. He sucked on her finger like a child on his mother's bosom, and her blood revived his lifeless limbs. The sound of him sucking on her finger echoed through his mind and time seemed to stop. Her blood was like a powerful drug, and he could not get enough. "STOP, that is enough," Lilith proclaimed with a harsh tone as she pulled her finger from his mouth.

Adam looked up into Lilith's eyes. Lust filled him, and he had to have her. His mind tried to object and find a reason not to take her. Eve and his children came to mind, bringing a wave of sorrow with them. He did not want to think about his family or God because Abel was dead. *God had allowed him to die!* In despair, Adam sought refuge between Lilith's thighs. He took Lilith with violence and passion, as Samael had taken her. She writhed in the pleasure of the mindless sexual beast he had become. In every powerful thrust, Adam sought to drive his sorrow away.

In the days that followed, Adam and Lilith only rose from the embrace of the flesh long enough for Lilith to revive him with her blood. After seven days, she found herself lacking the strength to continue. So, they rose in search of food. They killed and ate the beasts which lived among the rocky high places and their vigor returned.

Lilith became pregnant because God's curse held no power over her union with Adam when he willingly gave himself to her. Seven days later, she bore three children unto him. The children appeared to be healthy, but were more demon than human. The male child she named Djinn. The first female child she named Piznai, and the second she called Lilitu because she bore a striking resemblance to her.

When Adam saw the children, he remembered his family with Eve. His heart opened, and Lilith's hold on him faded. He looked at Djinn, Lilitu, and Piznai, and he said, "You are the bastard children born of a demon and sin!" Lilith sarcastically replied, "But my Lord, are not these your children? Conceived during a willful union of the flesh? You willingly took me as I submitted myself to you, for all of these many days?" When Adam heard her words, they pierced his heart like a dagger of fire, because he knew they were right. He fell upon the ground and cried out to God, "Lord have mercy on me and forgive me for my sins!" God heard his prayers because he also mourned the loss of Abel.

Lilith had known that her time with Adam would not last. So, with great satisfaction, she snatched up her children and laughed at Adam. As she left him, she said, "Farewell, my husband, until we meet again." She laughed again and flew away from him with her children in her arms. Adam sins troubled him, but he did not wallow in them. Instead, he immediately rose and journeyed down from the high places back unto the mountain of God. He went straight to the Cave of Treasures. At the cave, he washed his body and prepared himself before God. Then, he went up to the altar. Near it, he found a great ram that was without spot or blemish. He took the ram by its horns and wrestled it to the ground. Then, he tied the ram's legs, threw it over his shoulders, and carried it up to the altar. There, he offered the ram as a sacrifice for his sins. God accepted his sacrifice and forgave him.

Aklia had fallen asleep in the shade of a tree as she

watched the flock. She awoke frightened because she smelt burning flesh. She searched the area near the sheep but found no fire. Then, she saw smoke rising from the altar of God. *Is my mother making a sacrifice to God without me?* She ran up to the altar. There, she saw the burnt sacrifice, but not the person who made it. *Who could have done this?* she wondered. She looked around the altar, and down the trail to Cave of Treasures. Aklia's heart leaped with joy. Her father was entering the cave. She turned and ran to the fields were her mother was working. Excitement fueled her as she sprinted into the morning sun. When she reached her mother, she stopped and struggled to catch her breath. Only mumbling came from her lips as she tried to tell her mother the good news.

Panic filled Eve as Aklia ran towards her. She feared something terrible had happened to the flock. Her fear faded quickly away when she saw the joy in her daughter's face. *What was so vital that she ran to me?* Eve fought back a rush of panicked thoughts as she tried to decipher Aklia's mumbling. As Aklia caught her breath, Eve recognized one word, "Father." Excitement filled Eve, but she could not allow herself to believe Adam was back. It was easier for her to think that he was dead. Finally, Aklia spoke clearly, "I was tending the flock when I smelt burning flesh. I saw smoke rising from the altar. When I approached it, I found no one, but I saw father entering the Cave of Treasures."

Adam had decided to devote himself to God and prayed at the Cave of Treasures before he returned to his family. He would go to Eve and his daughter after he fixed his relationship with God. As he prayed for Abel's spirit, Eve entered the cave, wide-eyed and winded from her journey. Eve met him on the ground, hugged his neck, and cried. Adam comforted her and explained how his sorrow overcame him when he lived upon the mountaintop. He did not tell her about Lilith and the children she gave birth to in the wilderness. She kissed him and clung to his neck because she did not want to let him go.

Adam and Eve talked, and they enjoyed each other's embrace. Then, Adam explained to Eve how he promised to commit himself fully to God. "I have devoted myself to serving God in the Cave of Treasures." His words made her sad because she loved him and wanted another son. "When will you return to us?" Adam replied, "I will come home tonight, but I will return to the Cave of Treasures tomorrow before the sun rises and devote myself to prayer and fasting for seven days." Adam paused, "Wait, why did you say daughter? We have two daughters!" Eve's expression became sad. "Cain took Luluwa with him while I searched the mountains for you!" Adam's countenance fell, but he would not allow himself to fall into sorrow and depression again. *I will make intercession with God on her behalf!* Eve set her mind to convince him to spend his days with her. For now, she would take the time he gave her. Together, they went up to their home, and they celebrated his return with their daughter, Aklia.

CHAPTER 53

Cain and Luluwa came down from the Mountain of God, and they searched for Cain's friend and his people. After many days, they found no man, and Cain realized it was a lie from Satan. Then he said unto Luluwa, "I am a fool because I trusted a man who is not a man. Satan has betrayed me!" Luluwa did not reply. She was still afraid of Cain because he killed their brother. Satan's betrayal meant nothing to Cain, except they had no home. He had wanted to kill Abel because he was his father's favorite son, and that had nothing to do with Satan. His only regret was that his parents, especially his mother, were dead to him.

As they walked further down the mountain, he said unto Luluwa, "I killed Abel because I couldn't bear the thought of you being with him instead of me! I love you!" Luluwa was glad to hear he loved her, but she mourned her brother's death. She considered his words as she continued walking with him. Abel was meek and devoted to God. *Would Abel have loved her as Cain will?* She thought, *Cain, will be the better husband, because he will place me in the center of his life, instead of God. Who wants a husband who spends his days fasting, praying, and making sacrifices unto God? Abel's death might be the best thing for me!* Adam had spent most of his time away from their mother, and she had no desire to live as her mother and father did. So, she replied unto Cain, "You should not have killed our brother because it is contrary to the ways of God, but as for your love for me, we shall see!"

They continued their journey east of the Garden of Eden. Three days passed before they found a suitable place to live. The ground was flat, and the water was clear. Fruit trees were abundant, and great cedar trees were plentiful. Cain smiled with satisfaction and said, "We will build a city for our children here." There were no caves because the ground was flat and Luluwa asked, "Where shall we live?" Cain replied, "We shall sleep by a fire under the stars tonight. In the morning, I will rise early and build a suitable dwelling of strong timber. I will improve our home every day until it is suitable for one as beautiful as you!" His words satisfied her, and she replied, "It will do for now!" She did not want to seem too pleased, so he would keep his word and build them a lavish home.

The next morning, she woke with only the fire's warmth. Chopping sounds echoed through the trees, so she assumed Cain was gathering wood. He had risen before the sun and fashioned tools for his labors. Then, he gathered the wood and other materials he needed. Healthy vines to tie lumber together. Large pieces of bark and small-leaved branches covered with mud would make a roof to protect them from the sun and rain. The morning was half over when he began construction of their home. As the sun beat down on him, he finished a simple fireplace made of rock and clay. He used sand from the river as mortar for the bricks. As the sun became unbearable, he laid the pine needle floor under the shade of the roof.

Cain labored until it became too hot to work. Luluwa admired his hard work, but she enjoyed watching his muscular body in the sun as he worked on their home. At noonday, he found shade under a large tree and rested. She brought him sweet berries and water in a gourd which she hollowed out. As he devoured her offering and drank of the cold water, she smiled at him. Cain looked into her beautiful eyes, and they shared a moment of satisfaction. He loved hard work when it suited his purpose, and his beautiful Luluwa was a great reason to work hard. He placed his hand upon her cheek and gently rubbed it with his thumb as he looked into her eyes. He found no fear or sadness left in her eyes. Refreshed, he returned to building their home before it got dark.

As the sun disappeared behind the mountains, he finished making a door of long, stripped branches tied together with vines. He looked at his handiwork and was pleased with his first day. Luluwa stood beside him, and they admired their home together. He turned to her and said, "Let's gather wood for a fire, so the night chill does not devour us as we sleep." They gathered wood and placed it next to their makeshift fireplace. She smiled and kissed him on the cheek. Cain built a fire and sat down across from her on the large fur blanket which he brought with them. She smiled at him, and he smiled back. He had wanted to consummate their marriage along the way, but he would not take her against her will. Now, he wanted her again, but he thought, *She must offer herself to me!*

Cain asked her, "Will you take off your garments so that I can look upon your beauty?" Luluwa replied unto him, "Haven't you already looked upon me as I bathed in the pool during the morning sun?" Cain blushed because her comments surprised him. *She knew I was watching her.* "How did you know I was there?" She replied, "I heard you in the throes of passion as you watched me touching myself!" *What?* Memories of her bathing and Lilith flashed before his eyes and his manhood stiffened. *I cannot tell her it was Lilith's actions that brought me to climax!* So, he smiled and said, "I do not remember what you did that day. Show me how you touched yourself." She gave him a sly smile and said unto him, "You remember, but I will refresh your memory because you built us this home!"

Luluwa stood up and danced for him. Her hands glided over her body, and she laughed as his eyes grew full of desire. She seductively untied the strap which held her garments and let them fall to the ground, but she kept dancing. Her beauty left him speechless. He was about to pull her to him when she suddenly stopped dancing and turned to face him. Her eyes were wild with lust. He watched as her hand slid down between her luscious thighs. She stood just out of his reach as her fingers parted the veil which hid her womanhood from him. As he watched her moan with the delight of her touch, her delicate flesh called to him and drove him beyond his restraint. *I must have her!*

Cain rose, picked her up, and raised her lips to his. He stared into her eyes, and then he kissed her passionately. She wrapped her arms around his neck and her legs around his waist and returned his kiss. When their kiss ended, he raised her until her erect nipples met his lips. She arched her back in pleasure as he squeezed one of her perfect breasts in his hand and kissed and playfully sucked on her nipple. She pressed her warmth upon him and rubbed herself against his erect member until he could wait no longer.

He turned and laid her gently upon their fur hide bed. Then, he kissed her lips, neck, and breasts before drifting down between her thighs. She moaned with delight, encouraging him to continue. His tongue pierced her warmth, and she screamed with pleasure. She arched her back and ran her fingers through his hair as she pulled him deeper between her thighs. *I must thank Lilith for teaching me this if I ever see her again*, he thought as Luluwa shook with orgasm.

Luluwa had pleasured herself before, but it was nothing like this. *How had Cain learned to do such acts of pleasure, or was he born with this gift?* The questions fled from her mind as waves of pleasure rippled through her body. She pulled his hair, drawing him deeper into her warmth, and she felt him respond with even more vigor. He smiled within himself as she writhed in the ecstasy of his actions. *It feels so good,* she thought. Words could not describe what she felt next. Every muscle in her body became taut, and her toes curled up to the sky. Then, she exploded with the most powerful orgasm of her life. She had achieved climax with her hand, but that did not compare to this. Luluwa shook as the quakes of her pleasure flowed throughout her body. His hands gripped her thighs tight, and his fingers dug into the flesh as he drove her to new heights of pleasure. Her hands instinctively pulled him closer, and he obeyed.

When the last tremor of orgasm passed, Cain rose from her thighs with a sly smile. He stared into her passion-filled eyes as he moved upward until he pierced her warmth. She bit her quivering lip as she reveled in the pleasure of having him within her. Her nails drew blood, and she gasped with a tinge of pain when he was entirely within her. With each delightful stroke, she moaned, encouraging him to continue. Soon, her breaths were shallow as her muscles tightened in preparation of her climax. The pain of his actions fled with her impending orgasm, and she encouraged him to speed up the pace of his thrusts. She cried out in pleasure in response to his actions. Her hands drifted down to his firm buttocks, and she dug her fingers into him as she pulled him deeper inside of her. Without warning, he felt her muscles tighten on him, and his seed flowed into her warmth. He collapsed on top of her.

Cain and Luluwa held each other in a lovers' embrace until the sun rose the next morning. She would conceive from their first union! Before the sun rose, Cain kissed Luluwa, and she smiled with the lingering satisfaction of their passion and her newfound love for him. Then, he said unto her, "Let us rise and bathe in the stream, and then I will continue to work on our dwelling while you pick fruit and nuts from the nearby trees. The bounty of your labors will give us the energy to repeat last night's actions." A sly smile formed on her lips as she replied, "I will gladly spend all day gathering if you can repeat last night's pleasures!" Any reservations she had about Cain left her forever.

CHAPTER 54

One day, Eve said unto Aklia, "Take the flock to graze in the field next to the one Cain planted. As the sheep graze, you can clear the rows between the crops of the field. When you are away, I will have a chance to convince your father to lie with me so that I can bear another male child. A child that will come of age and marry you while you can still bear children." Aklia obeyed her mother and left with a joyful heart because she wanted to have children before she died barren!

Aklia cleared the rows of the field while the sheep grazed. The heat of the mid-day sun beat down upon her until she had to seek shelter. She took refuge in the dwelling which Cain built under the tree. Her eyes grew heavy as she watched the sheep from the cool shade. Before long, she fell into a deep sleep. Lilith and Satan found her asleep in the dwelling.

Satan looked at Aklia and said unto Lilith, "Shall we defile her while she sleeps?" Lilith looked at her and replied, "She is unattractive and ordinary, but she is pure. We should defile her!" Satan considered Lilith's words and smiled as he did when he had an idea for mischief against God. Lilith watched Satan with expectation, until he said, "Speak to her dreams, and she will become wet with desire! I will go up to Eve and whisper a new plan into her ears. A plan to deceive Adam and gain both of their heart's desire!" She did not know what exactly he had in mind, but she had learned to trust him because he was intelligent and cunning. So, she agreed with him, "I will place lustful thoughts into her dreams."

As Aklia slept, a vivid dream came unto her. In her dream, she stood over her mother's bed as her mother lay sick with a high fever. Eve refused Aklia's attempts to comfort her and cried out for Adam, but he did not come to her. He was at the Cave of Treasures serving God. In desperation, Aklia left her mother alone and ran to the Cave of Treasures. She found Adam praying and worshipping God, which was his custom. Aklia took a moment to catch her breath, and then she said unto him, "My mother, and your wife, is sick with a high fever and is dying! She cries out for you, but you do not come to her. Come, pray for God to comfort her, and save her!" Adam went to his wife.

When they reached the cave, an angel of God was standing at the entrance to it. The angel turned unto them and said, "You are too late! Eve has perished from her fever. Take your daughter as your wife, so your seed shall live on as God has promised!" Adam heard the angel's words and wept. He tore his clothes from his body and cried for God to raise Eve from the dead. He mourned his wife and did not want to lay with his daughter. The angel of God spoke again, saying, "God has spoken!"

Adam obeyed the angel, rose with tears in his eyes and turned to face his daughter. He was naked, and she looked upon him. Aklia had not seen her father or brothers naked, but she could not lift her eyes from the sight. His manhood was like a snake hanging between two thick branches, and two pieces of ripe fruit hung beneath it.

With tears in his eyes, he walked over to his daughter. He ran his hand through her hair, pinning it behind her ear. With his other hand, he untied the cord, which held her gown upon her. She covered herself in shame as it fell to the floor. Her body was ordinary, and her skin was white as snow. Adam shared her embarrassment, but he obeyed the angel and laid her upon his bed. As her father mounted her, she awoke in a terrible fright.

Aklia's dream disturbed her. *It was only a dream, but it seemed so real! Have I seen the future?* She shivered with disgust at the thought of having her father inside of her. Memories of her father's nakedness filled her thoughts. She cringed as she thought about how he felt between her thighs, and she became wet and nauseous at the same time. *That is my father!* She needed something else to occupy her mind! Without wasting another minute, she rose and gathered the stray sheep back into the fold. When she finished with the flock, she plucked the weeds from Cain's field. When there was no more work to keep her busy, she sat down upon a large rock. As she watched the flock, trying to keep her mind off her dream, she thought, *It is useless*. Images of her father's nakedness flooded her mind once more.

In the distance, Aklia saw a young man approached from the northeast. When he got to the field, he spoke to her. "I am Cain's friend, but he has left without telling me where he has gone!" Aklia replied unto him, "Cain killed our brother Abel and God cast him out of our lands. I do not know where he lives or if he is dead!" The young man tore his clothes and wept. He called upon God, "Lord, let Aklia's words be untrue!" She comforted him, "I am sorry for your loss, but I swear my words are true."

Aklia and the young man sat under the shade tree next to Cain's dwelling. She told him of the evil Cain did unto his mother and Abel. Then, she asked him, "What is your name?" Satan replied, "My name is Kokab, which means star, because my father said, 'My son is like a star falling from Heaven!'" Aklia gazed into his crystal blue eyes. They called to her as they sparkled like precious gems. Lost in his beauty, she didn't even hear his words until he spoke again. "Let us go unto the pool and escape the heat of the day!" Aklia considered his words. *How can I go with him? He is beautiful, and yet I am unattractive. Why would he want me?* He smiled, reassuring her, held out his hand, and she took it. They walked to the pool together.

When they arrived, Kokab turned to face her with his back to the pool. He smiled and took off his robe. She looked at him in disbelief but could not look away from his nakedness. His skin was without spot or blemish, and there was no hair upon him, except for the hair on his head. His manhood rivaled that of her father's in her dream because it hung down to his mid-thigh, and it called to her as if it had a voice of its own. She wanted to have him inside of her and to please him, and somehow, she knew that she would accomplish both! Lust rose within her, and she wanted him.

Kokab begged her, "Drop your robes so that I might look upon your nakedness." She blushed and protested, "I cannot because I am plain and nothing to look upon!" Kokab disagreed, "You cannot see your beauty, but I see all of you!" After a few moments, she untied the cord that held her gown. It fell to the ground, but she covered her breasts with one arm and her womanhood with her other hand. Kokab was in the water up to his shoulders and smiling at her. "Why do you cover yourself?" She replied, "Because I am ashamed of my body!" "Why? Show me your beauty and let me be the judge!" She hesitated for a moment longer, and then she dropped her arms to her sides.

Satan smiled at her and said, "You are beautiful, and I will prove it to you. Join me in the cool and refreshing water of the pool." Her cheeks flushed with embarrassment because she had never received a compliment because of her appearance or features. She smiled because his words pleased her. Aklia waded into the pool's cold water. Chill bumps rose upon her body, and her nipples became erect. Satan became aroused as the innocent Aklia waded towards him.

Kokab reached out and took her in his arms. He pulled her in tight unto his chest. His muscular body was hard as stone. She looked into his deep blue eyes which flowed inward as crystal clear rivers flowing into eternity. His eyes captivated her, and she found herself lost in them. She was not sure how he got so close, but his lips pushed against hers in her first kiss. Her lips parted in response to his tongue, and she followed him into a passionate kiss. A strange lust came over her, and she bit his bottom lip. His eyes opened wide with surprise. In response, he grasped one of her breasts in his hand

and squeezed as he kissed her. His other arm wrapped around her waist and drew her in close until their bodies came together. She felt the warmth of his member pressing against her flesh and wanted him between her thighs.

Lilith could watch no longer, so she waded into the pool unnoticed. She reached around Aklia, from behind, and cupped her right breast in her hand, tweaking her nipple between her thumb and index finger. She squeezed her backside with her other hand. Aklia did not realize Lilith was with them but became lost in their acts of pleasure, as they overwhelmed her senses. Several moments later, she realized, *Someone is behind me!* She spun around and found a beautiful woman standing in front of her. Her hair was like fire, and her seductive emerald green eyes seemed to pierce her soul. The woman's beauty took Aklia's breath away. Lilith smiled, "Are you enjoying my husband's embrace?" Her words surprised Aklia, and she gasped, but the woman's beauty and her smile drove the shock and horror of her announcement away. Lilith kissed Aklia, and Aklia heard thoughts of pleasure within her mind. Satan wrapped his arms around Aklia and Lilith, pinning Aklia's arms around Lilith's waist. He drew close and nibbled on her earlobe. Aklia felt his warm breath on her neck, leaned her head back towards him, and closed her eyes as she enjoyed the pleasure of his actions.

Lilith pressed her body against Aklia. Her tongue teased her other ear lobe, and she thought about driving her fangs into her snow-white neck, but she resisted the urge. Lilith's lips drifted down her throat and onto her breasts. Her hand found the warmth between Aklia's legs. She was wet with anticipation. Aklia welcomed Lilith's advances with soft moans of approval. Her fingers slid inside of Aklia, and she groaned with pleasure. Seconds later, Aklia shook with her first orgasm. *She has never pleasured herself or received pleasure from another*, Lilith and Satan realized with child-like delight. Before the wave of Aklia's first orgasm stopped, another began. The second orgasm struck as Satan entered her from behind while Lilith's fingers yet danced inside of her from the front. Aklia gasped for breath as the pleasure and pain of their acts drove her deeper into ecstasy. Pleasure rippled through her like electricity. Every muscle shook and vibrated with the tremors of her passion. She lost count of her orgasms as her mind, spirit, and soul surfed on a torrent of pure pleasure. It was not until he spilled his seed that she realized he was in her backside. The warmth of his member and his fluids inside of her, combined with Lilith's actions, drove her to her most powerful orgasm yet. His throbbing member spasmed a second time, in response to her powerful orgasm, and Lilith's skillful fingers reaching deep within her warmth. The pleasure of their violations was too much for any human to bear, and darkness engulfed Aklia. She woke hours later, laying on the shore of the pool. *I am naked! What happened to me?* Her thoughts were foggy and unclear as she struggled to her feet.

CHAPTER 55

Eve came to Adam in the Cave of Treasures during his prayers and distracted him. He rose, and with a harsh tone, asked her, "Why do you come while I am in prayer?" Eve replied, "You haven't laid with me for two years, and my thighs crave your touch. Also, I want to bear children to you again!" Adam wanted her, but he feared the lust of the flesh might separate him from God again. *I cannot bear the loss of another child!* After a few moments, he replied unto Eve, "I will not lie with you unless God tells me our child will survive this sinful world." Eve replied unto him. "Let us pray together, so God may have mercy upon us and command us to lie together and bear children. Our children will serve and worship him!" Her words were pleasant unto his ears, and they prayed together.

God sent an angel unto them. The angel said unto them, "God has heard your prayers. Adam, God wants you to go to your dwelling and know your wife, Eve, again. You shall bear children again, and the male child shall be a great servant to Him!" His words pleased Adam and Eve's heart leaped with joy because she would know her husband again, and the angel promised she would bear another son. In happiness, Adam and Eve rose and went to their dwelling.

When they arrived, passion overtook them, and they embraced in the pleasures of the flesh once more. They enjoyed each other's embrace, and Adam left his seed within her, before drifting off into a deep slumber. As Eve laid next to Adam, she had joy in her heart because of the promise of bearing children again. Her thoughts drifted unto her daughter, Aklia, and sadness fell upon her. Eve heard a voice within herself, ask, "What about Aklia, doesn't she deserve to have children before she is old?" The question echoed in her ears several times. *Poor Aklia*, she thought. The sun was setting, and she had not returned from the fields. As Eve thought about Aklia's barrenness, she entered the cave.

Eve saw Aklia's turmoil even though she was trying to hide it from her mother. She could see both happiness and confusion within her daughter, and she wanted to help, but how? An idea sprang up in her mind as if someone whispered it into her ear. So, Eve asked Aklia, "Do you want to bear children before thou art old?" Aklia replied, "With all of my heart!" Eve opened a simple clay jar and took a handful of herbs from it. She handed the herbs to Aklia and said, "Make a strong tea from these herbs." Aklia obeyed her mother without question. When the tea was ready, Eve woke Adam and said, "Your daughter returned from the field and saw you at home. So, she has made you tea!" Adam drank the tea. The herbs in it caused him to fall into a deep sleep. Eve shook him to make sure he would not awaken.

Then Eve took Aklia by the hand and said unto her, "I will cause your father's loins to stir, and then you will mount him. You will pleasure yourself upon him until he spills his seed within you. Then you will bear children!" Her mother's request sickened Aklia because she remembered her dream and she did not want to obey. Her heart cried out for children of her own, but this seemed wrong. *There are no other men!* So, she did as her mother suggested. Eve took Adam's manhood and caressed it. Aklia watched in disgust as Adam's flesh responded to her mother's touch. Eve turned to Aklia, "Place your hand between your thighs and caress yourself. Your father is almost ready." Aklia obeyed her mother and touched herself as Lilith touched her at the pool. Moments later, Eve turned to Aklia and said, "Straddle your father, and you shall bear children!" She climbed onto the bed and sat upon her father's thighs. Eve guided Adam's flesh into Aklia's warmth, and then she left her with him.

Aklia closed her eyes and felt the warmth of her father's

flesh within her, *Disgusting*, she thought. She whimpered in disgust and pleasure as she moved upon her father's manhood. As she rode him, disgust overshadowed the joy of her actions. Tears streamed down her cheeks as she rotated her hips and prayed for his seed to spring from his loins and end her torment. Several minutes passed as she pressed herself down upon him. *Please, let this be over!* Finally, he lost his seed within her, and she wept in sadness and hope. When his spasms ended, she looked down at her sleeping father. Shame filled her as she thought, *What have I done?* Aklia rose from her father and left his bed. Without a word, she went to her bed, laid in the fetal position, and cried herself to sleep.

Eve was not ashamed by her actions because she thought, *Aklia deserved my help!* She laid down beside her husband and drifted into a peaceful sleep. Dreams of her children and Aklia's children playing together filled her rest. Outside the cave, Satan turned away from the door where he was watching Eve and Aklia's treachery. He smiled and whistled a sweet melody as he returned to his lair. *I cannot wait to tell Lilith about this!*

When the sun rose, Adam woke Eve and said unto her, "I am going back to the Cave of Treasures. At the cave, I will commit myself again to God until the birth of our children." Eve smiled and kissed her husband goodbye. In the days that followed, both Eve and Aklia conceived from Adam's seed and became great with children. Eve kept Aklia busy in the fields and made excuses for her absence when she visited Adam at the Cave of Treasures. Adam remained unaware of his daughter's pregnancy.

At Satan's Lair:

Before the birth of Aklia's children, Satan called his best craftsman to his throne. When all of them were present, he said unto them, "Gather the finest marble, gold, silver, and gems from the earth and construct an altar worthy of me. Soon we will have a human to sacrifice." They did as he commanded them.

When they finished the altar, they called Satan to examine it. The sides of the altar had images of Satan, the Fallen Ones, and ancient symbols of power. Precious stones and gems adorned the sides of the altar. The concave sacrificial slab was polished black marble, and it had a golden drain made in Lilith's image in the center. A massive golden chalice adorned with huge rubies sat in a hollowed receptacle at the base of the altar below the golden drain tube. The altar pleased Satan.

Back at Adam and Eve's dwelling:

Aklia felt the pains of childbirth before Eve. Her children pressed on her, and they refused to stay in the womb any longer. Eve told Aklia, "This is good because we can deliver the children without Adam's knowledge. He will not know they exist, and when they are older, he will love them and not harm them because they are his seed." Eve's words pleased Aklia. Aklia endured the curse of labor for many hours, and then she gave birth to two children. She had one male child and one female child, and both children were healthy.

Eve turned to Aklia and said, "We cannot sacrifice on the children's behalf because your father will learn of their birth." Aklia agreed with her mother. So, they cleansed the children before God, but they did not sacrifice. Aklia named the boy Abe after her slain brother. She called the girl Luluqa because she looked like Luluwa. Aklia and Eve watched the beautiful children sleep on the blanket between them. Then they both fell into a peaceful slumber because Aklia had children of her own.

CHAPTER 56

Satan told Lilith about Eve and Aklia's betrayal, and then they waited for the children to be born. After Aklia gave birth, Satan spoke to Lilith. "They fulfilled my plan, and Aklia has borne two children unto Adam. He is unaware of their betrayal and the children's existence. The children do not have God's blessing because they did not offer a sacrifice for they feared Adam would see the smoke from the altar and discover Aklia's children." Lilith laughed and said, "Shall we tell Adam and expose their malicious deed?" Satan answered, "No, Adam will discover their betrayal in his own time. The children are unprotected!" "What shall we do, to them?" Lilith asked. Satan replied, "The amulet which the angel gave to Adam to protect his children from you is not in their dwelling. It is in the Cave of Treasures with God's other gifts because Adam doesn't know about the children. The children are ripe fruit hanging from the branch. Go to the cave and steal the children while they sleep. You may take one child for yourself, but the other one is mine. Bring the child to me, and we will sacrifice it in my name." Lilith's piercing green eyes sparkled with excitement. She leaned over to kiss him but paused before their lips met. Her hand slid between his legs, found his member, and squeezed. He groaned with delight as she said, "I will give you a proper reward when I return with the child." Then she pressed her lips against his in a kiss and left without another word.

As Eve and Aklia slept, Lilith crept into their cave. The horror of her last attempt to steal children from their dwelling made her second guess Satan. Her eyes searched the darkness for any sign of the amulet, but she found none. *Satan was right; the charm is not here!* Lilith's heart leaped with joy because the children were unprotected. Cautiously, she reached down and took the children into her arms. As she rose with them, she looked down at Eve and Aklia. They slept, unaware of her presence. "Thanks for the special gifts," she whispered. They didn't stir or wake. Lilith turned and left the cave with a smile.

A safe distance from the cave, Lilith laid the children on the ground and admired them. She laughed because she had no motherly instincts. The sweet smell of the newborn children was like a drug to her. Her mouthed watered in anticipation. *Which child should I choose?* She snatched the male child from the ground. The child let out a blood-curdling cry as her fangs tore into his tender flesh. She fed on the child's blood, tissue, and bones until nothing remained. The child invigorated her like nothing before.

Lilith struggled against the temptation to consume the second child and her stomach growled in protest. *Eat the child, and do not return to Satan.* She laughed; *He will hunt me down and torture me for eternity.* It took all her strength to resist her urges as she picked up the female child. She looked down at the wailing child. "GGGRRRR," she groaned as she leaped into the sky and flew towards Satan's throne.

Lilith landed a short distance from the entrance to Satan's lair. She admired the young child once more. Her mouth watered, remembering the first child. *The child's blood was so satisfying!* Her cravings seemed worse now. She couldn't resist the child's sweet blood, but she feared the repercussions if she consumed it. *Maybe I could have a little taste!* Her fangs pierced the female child's neck, but she did not drain the child or consume its flesh. *This child's blood is sweeter than the first child's*, she thought. It was like a fine wine, thick in her mouth and bitter upon her tongue. She sensed the child would die if she continued. So, she withdrew her fangs from the child's neck with sadness. Satan might kill her if she did not bring the child to sacrifice unto him. Begrudgingly, she licked the wounds on the child's neck and then she watched as they healed before her eyes. She wondered when another opportunity like this would present itself as she took the child into Satan's lair and gave it to him.

CHAPTER 57

Aklia woke to the sounds of birds chirping and a gentle breeze whistling into their dwelling. She wiped the sleep from her eyes as she rolled over to look at her sweet children. Horror filled her, *Where are they?* Her mind raced in search of some reasonable explanation for her missing children. She frantically rummaged through the fur blankets even though they were not there. *Did my father return, find the children, and take them in anger*? she wondered. There was no blood or any sign of a wild animal taking them. *They are just gone*, she thought as all hope left her. She fell to her knees on the blankets and wailed for her lost children.

Eve woke to the sound of weeping and turned to see Aklia crying and holding the empty blankets to her bosom. She tried to understand Aklia's incoherent mumbling, but it was gibberish. Then, she realized her daughter's children were gone. Eve grabbed Aklia by her shoulders and turned her to look into her eyes. "Where are your children?" Eve asked. Aklia yelled at her mother in a broken and bitter tone. "You brought this pain on me. You made me take my father's seed so that I could bear children unto him without his knowledge or God's consent!" Aklia did not give Eve a chance to respond before she spoke again, "I pray that your children are torn from your womb and given to the beasts of the field for your transgressions against your husband, your God, and me!"

Aklia's words struck Eve as if a spear pierced her heart. She thought the children would bring her daughter happiness, but she was wrong! Eve fell on her face and begged God for forgiveness. She could not imagine what happened to Aklia's children, and now she feared for her unborn children's lives.

She prayed for God to protect them. Aklia became enraged as her mother begged God for her unborn children's lives. She raised her hand and slapped her mother's face. Anger flowed through her, and she beat Eve upon the face, arms, and chest. *She is going to kill me,* Eve thought. She scurried on the floor in search of refuge, but found none. Over and over, Aklia beat her and screamed obscenities at her. Eve searched for something, anything to defend herself from her daughter. Finally, her hands found a piece of smoldering kindling in the firepit, and she struck Aklia with it. The half-burned piece of wood sent sparks flying into the air as it collided with her daughter's temple. Aklia went limp and landed awkwardly on the hard floor, unconscious. Eve paused and watched to make sure her daughter was still breathing. Then, she ran out of the cave and into the wilderness. *I must protect my unborn children*, she thought.

CHAPTER 58

Satan rose from his slumber on the day of his sacrifice. "Today will be a great day," he said aloud as he thought about the night's events. The thought of sacrificing one of God's precious humans excited him. *A human child sacrificed in my name*, he thought as a smile formed on his twisted lips as he imagined God witnessing it. The child's blood would consecrate his altar, increase his strength, and intensify the natural powers of the harvest moon. The ritual mocked God and celebrated Satan's power over humankind. He could not wait for the festivities to begin.

The full moon hung as a centerpiece in the star-filled sky. Satan admired it from the entrance to his lair. Minutes seemed like days as thoughts of the child sacrifice made him giddy with anticipation. He turned when he heard the footsteps of someone coming out to join him. "Master, it's time to prepare yourself for the ceremony. Everything is in place, and your congregation will gather at the altar soon." Amon's words pleased him. "Very well," Satan replied as he turned and went into his lair.

When he arrived at his private chambers, Lilith's daughters were waiting for him. They had a voracious appetite for pleasure, but this was not the primary purpose of their visit. As he entered the room, they took him by the hand and led him to the bath. A sweet fragrance infused the steam that rose from the bathwater. They disrobed him and helped him into the tub. He closed his eyes, sank into the water, and leaned his head back. The beautiful demons caressed his body with their sponge-filled hands. He was not surprised when one of the young demons discarded her sponge and slid her hand between his thighs. Groans of pleasure echoed through his chamber as they bathed him.

Lilith's voice stopped the young demons, "Rise, my lord." Satan opened his eyes. Lilith stood before him wearing a white silk gown. A golden crown sat atop her flaming red hair. When he reached his feet, she raised her dress, knelt before him and finished what her daughter had started. He groaned with pleasure as he looked down into her emerald eyes. *There is something about her eyes*; he thought as she took his seed. When nothing remained, she rose and motioned to her daughters. They dried him off and dressed him in fine linen. Then they placed a crimson robe over his shoulders and a golden crown upon his head. Lilith nodded with approval. He smiled, and they walked hand in hand to the throne room.

The congregation bowed as they entered. Satan sat down on his throne. Lilith sat on his lap in symbolization of Satan's reign. A rein of lust, pleasure, passion, and sex. The desire of the flesh was a crucial weapon in his plan for those made in God's image. *God's most faithful servants will struggle with the pleasures of the flesh and their lusts for another, man or woman. Then, without God's protection, humankind will fall. With each loss, God will become weaker, and I will grow more powerful. God draws strength from the sacrifices of his followers, but the sacrifice of his precious humans will strengthen me*, he thought.

"Rise, my faithful servants," Satan said as he motioned to Bael. Bael was his powerful second in command and not-so-secret adversary. Satan gave Bael this task to play to his ego and desire to rule the Fallen Ones. Bael commanded his servants, and they brought Aklia's child to him. Bael extended his arms and raised the child over his head. He held the child up so Satan and the congregation could see her. Then Satan said, "Sacrifice the child unto me!" Bael passed the child to one of his servants, and he placed the child on the sacrificial altar. The child cried for its mother, but Aklia could not save her. God heard the child's cries, but he refused to deliver the innocent child because it was the product of sin and deceit. Satan called Bael forward and presented him with a ceremonial dagger. Bael drew the golden knife from its jewel-encrusted scabbard and waved it before the congregation. They cheered and said in unison, "Sacrifice the child unto Satan!" As the Master of Ceremonies, Satan gave Bael the honor of sacrificing the first human child upon this earth.

Bael walked over to the altar and stood over the crying child. He looked at Satan and raised the dagger over his head with his palms facing downward. The congregation fell silent, and only the child's cries echoed in the chamber. Satan nodded, and Bael sliced both sides of the child's neck with the blade. The child shrilled in agony. Then as if it accepted its fate, the child's cries became a faint whimper. The crimson flow of its lifeblood drained into the image of Lilith and flowed into the golden chalice. When the blood stopped flowing, Bael raised a vessel of sweet-smelling oil. He poured it upon the child's lifeless body. His servant took a torch from the wall and presented it to Bael. Bael took the torch and placed it on the child's chest. The oil ignited, and flames sprung to life and consumed the child.

When the fire consumed the child's body, Bael wiped the blood off the ceremonial blade and sheathed it. Then, he took the ceremonial chalice to Satan. He knelt before Satan and handed him the chalice, "Master." Satan accepted the cup and held it up before the congregation. As Bael and the Fallen Ones knelt before Satan, they said, "Take strength from the child's blood," three times. After they spoke the third time, Satan drank the blood. Lilith watched him with envy as the sweet smell of the child's blood filled her nostrils. She remembered how the child's blood tasted, and her mouthed watered. Satan took strength from the sacrificial blood, but he knew his wife's thirst. So, he did not consume all the blood but saved her some. He handed her the cup, and she drank what remained. She held the empty chalice up before the congregation. When they saw it was empty, they cheered, "Hail Satan," three times. The ceremony culminated in a feast and orgy that lasted until the sun rose the next morning.

CHAPTER 59

Eve woke to the bright light of the full moon which hung in the sky above her. She covered her sleep filled eyes with her hands, trying to shield them from the sudden brightness of the light. *Where am I?* Eve thought while surveying her surroundings, but she did not recognize anything. *I ran into the wilderness, and now I will die!* Her heart raced with the sudden realization she was alone and lost. *Why didn't I go to the Cave of Treasures and tell Adam everything?* Eve cried out to God, "Lord have mercy on me and send an angel to show me the way to my husband!" God ignored her cries and turned His back on her because of what she helped Aklia do to Adam.

The moon was already setting, and she wondered, *How long was I asleep?* A dry twig snapped in the underbrush near her. Her heart raced even faster now. In the shadows, the creatures of the night lurked because she had no fire to drive them away. *I will die before my children take their first breath*, she thought. She prayed to God for deliverance, but He did not deliver her. Finally, she tried to reason with God, but He did not listen to her. "Lord, Adam has no living son, except Cain who you cast out. If I die and his male heir dies in my womb, who will serve you when Adam dies?"

Satan and Lilith sat upon a high perch, near Eve, and watched her beg for her life. They listened as she prayed for Adam's unborn son, and yet she had two children within her womb. They talked amongst themselves and wondered, "Is Eve so consumed with having another male heir that she would sacrifice one child for the other?" They plotted and schemed, considering what they should do.

Darkness fell upon Eve, and vicious beasts tormented

her throughout the night. *Stay awake, or they will devour you and your children*, she thought. As the hours passed, she grew tired and delirious from hunger. Her thoughts became irrational, and fear took hold of her. Real and imaginary creatures threatened her from all sides. She swung a large stick wildly and screamed threats into the air, defending herself against an unseen monster. Satan and Lilith laughed at her pathetic actions. Suddenly, a great light shone down from heaven, and they became paralyzed and blind. They fell from their perch and landed on the hard ground.

Satan and Lilith cursed God for blinding them and interrupting their entertainment. They laid motionless on the ground and had no choice but to listen to the messenger of God. "You will not harm the male child or kill Eve. She conspired against Adam and God, and therefore, the female child is yours to do with as you will. The loss of her daughter will be a punishment for her sins!" When he finished his words, the angel disappeared, and their sight returned. They sprung to their feet as soon as the paralysis ended. Satan said to Lilith, "This is an unexpected blessing. Let's take this child and..." Lilith smiled at the thought of consuming another child or at least tasting its sweet crimson nectar, so she interrupted him and said, "Eat the child?" Satan knew her desires, but he had no patience for her lusts in that situation and slapped her across the face. The blow was unexpected, and she fell to the ground. She held her cheek and looked up at him in surprise. He glared at her and said, "No, you will not consume the child, and I will not sacrifice her. Instead, you will teach her the black arts, and when she has mastered them, we will send her to torture and kill her mother. We will teach her all that we know and focus her rage until she is a holy weapon; we can use to make Adam and Eve suffer. Then, God will also regret the gift He gave unto us." Lilith was angry and disappointed that she would not get to feed her hunger, but she had to admit Satan's plan was good.

Eve woke in a panic as the pains of labor came upon her.

She had no strength to rise and laid upon her back with her knees bent skyward. The agony of childbirth caused her to cry out in pain. With each contraction, her fear grew stronger. *Can I deliver my children alone in the wilderness?* Satan and Lilith watched her and drew strength from her pain and anxiety. Eve's suffering lasted for a day and a half. *God has deserted me,* Eve thought. All her physical strength left, and she could not cry out for God or Adam anymore. Tears stopped flowing down her cheeks because her body was devoid of moisture. Satan and Lilith drew closer to her and laughed audibly at her weakness. Their evil laughter sent waves of panic through her body, and adrenaline invigorated her cries for help, but nobody came to save her. *Satan has come to kill me and steal my children!* Lilith interrupted her thoughts, "When you die from the curse of childbirth, I will cut your children from your womb and devour them. I wonder if their blood will be as sweet as Aklia's children." Horror consumed her because she realized what Lilith had done. Satan laughed; *Lilith is evil! We are the perfect couple.*

At the Cave of Treasures:

Adam earnestly prayed in the flickering light of a dying fire. As he prayed, an angel of God appeared to him. The angel said, "Your wife has sinned against you and God. Eve listened to Satan's treacherous words and conspired with Aklia to steal your seed while you slept." Adam spoke harshly unto the angel for his wife's sake. "Surely your words have no truth in them!" The angel placed a vision of the events within Adam's mind, and he fell onto the ground and wept in sorrow.

The angel spoke a second time, "The male child which your wife delivers shall fulfill God's prophesy, but you shall not have the female child. Your daughter shall become a weapon in Satan's hand because of Eve's sins against you and God. The plan was Eve's, and Aklia's heart was not in her terrible deed. So, when the male child is of age, they shall marry, and Aklia will bear grandchildren and great-grandchildren unto you." The angel paused, and then he said, "When the time comes for the male child to be born, I will call upon you, but there is nothing you can do to save the female child from her fate." The angel's words tore Adam's heart into pieces because one of his children would pay for Eve's sins.

Back in the wilderness:

Satan and Lilith stood over Eve. They yelled for her to push the children out and end her suffering. She fought the urge to push because she feared they might take her children from her. The pains of labor tormented her, but she would not concede the children's birth into the world. When she refused to birth them, Satan and Lilith tormented her with terrible visions of what she had done. Over and over, she watched herself place Adam's unwilling member into her daughter's flesh. She saw herself encourage Aklia to drain his seed, and then she helped her deliver the unclean children. When Eve thought, *This is the most horrible vision*; she saw an image of Lilith stealing Aklia's children. She saw her devour one child, and then she saw the other die as Satan's sacrifice. *God's divine plan is going to die with my children and me!* Shame filled Eve, and she sobbed, but she couldn't cry. Finally, she surrendered and said aloud, "I deserve this fate because of my sins!"

Satan and Lilith tirelessly mocked her. They even re-enacted the theft of Adam's seed in their perverted sexual performance while lying beside Eve. Finally, Eve reached the point where no amount of willpower or physical strength could prevent the children's birth. Satan and Lilith gathered over her thighs as the first child sprang from her womb and drew its first breath. Eve wept as she heard the child's innocent cries. In her previous births, the male child came first, but the female child came early this time. Lilith slashed the umbilical cord, and Satan snatched the child from between Eve's thighs. Eve did not see the child because Satan blocked her view. She could not tell if the child was male or female, but she assumed it was as her previous births. Satan held the child up to Lilith. Finally, Satan turned so Eve could see. Lilith looked into Eve's tired eyes and smiled as she cleaned the child by licking it. Satan looked at Eve and said, "God promised us your daughter because of your sins. Since we have our gift, good luck delivering your heir!" Satan and Lilith turned their backs to Eve and left her in the wilderness alone.

Eve's heart sank because she lost another daughter. Then, the agonizing pain of childbirth ravaged her body once more. She cried out in labor, and the creatures of the wilderness howled in delight. She trembled with fear because the wild beasts no longer hid in the shadows. The scent of her blood and fear drew them closer until they circled her and growled. After a few moments, one of them lunged at her. It snatched her daughter's afterbirth from between her legs and dragged it away. The other beasts gathered, fought, and tore the flesh into scraps. The sight of them eating the afterbirth sickened her.

When the flesh was gone, another beast came closer. It snarled as the smell of Eve's bloody thighs filled its nostrils. She kicked at the creature, and it bit her foot. Eve cried out as its teeth tore her flesh. A fresh rush of fear and adrenaline drove the second child from her womb. She screamed in agony as the child's head ripped her flesh as it left her. The first group of beasts finished their feast and stalked her and the male child. She pulled the bloody child up to her bosom, and it took its first breath. The child cried, and she pulled it in tight. Darkness engulfed Eve and her vision blurred until only shadows circled her. The last sound she heard was animals scurrying to a feast. *The animals are going to kill me;* she thought as consciousness left her.

Pain snatched her out of unconsciousness. She frantically kicked at the wolves that nipped at her bloody legs. Several small bites and scratches littered her legs and thighs. Bael watched from the shadows and laughed at her suffering. Satan and Lilith left with the female child because God said they could not take the other child, but he did not share their obedience. His eyes flickered with a red glow as he encouraged the wolves to attack Eve. They snapped at her face, snarled and growled at her. The baby cried, and Eve remembered the child. She was thankful they were both still alive. Suddenly, a wolf jumped between her legs. Its sharp teeth protruded from its blood-stained muzzle. Eve thought, *The animal is going to tear into my flesh!* She breathed a sigh of relief as the wolf leaped over her thighs with the second afterbirth in its teeth. Then she realized there was a problem.

The umbilical cord!, Eve thought as she saw the game of tug of war begin. Eve pulled against the wolf with all her might. Adrenaline fueled her exhausted body as she kept the wolf from pulling her child from her arms. Another wave of relief surged through Eve as the child's cord split in two, and the wolf pulled the placenta away. Eve quickly tied the child's cord in a knot and tucked him back into her bosom. She watched the wolves fight over the scraps of the placenta and knew that her victory would not last long. *God help us!* Bael smiled in anticipation as the wolves started back towards Eve and the child.

Suddenly the wolves turned and ran into the wilderness. Eve panicked, *Where are they going? Is there an enormous beast looming behind me?* She tried to turn and see what was behind her, but she was too weak. So, she let her shoulders fall flat on the ground and tilted her head back as far as she could. A mighty angel stood behind her! Eve's eyes closed as she let the feeling of safety was over her. She opened her eyes and looked back at the angel. He stood with his arms crossed, and his wings spread wide. Then he said, "God sent me to protect you because he promised Adam, he would save you and his heir." Eve thought about her lost daughter. The angel knew her thoughts and said, "The daughter you lost will devote her life to your suffering because of your sins!" Bael left in disgust as the angel stood guard over Eve.

CHAPTER 60

When Satan returned to his lair, he sent three of the Fallen Ones to torment Aklia. Sitri, Caym, and Ose gathered at the entrance of Adam, Eve, and Aklia's dwelling. They could hear the young woman weeping and praying to God, begging him for forgiveness and mercy. Ose, the bringer of insanity, went in first and used his powers to disrupt Aklia's prayers. Aklia suddenly found herself back at the pool with Kokab and his wife. She felt them inside of her and immediately shook with the pleasure of a powerful orgasm. This time the blackness came for her, but she remembered what happened at the pool during the orgasm she thought caused her to blackout.

Aklia closed her eyes as she tilted her head back towards Kokab. Waves of pleasure rattled her body like the sea pounds the shore. He was kissing her neck and nibbling on her ears, and she loved it. His wife's fingers danced within her warmth and heightened the pleasure of Kokab's member, which violated her backside. His actions should be vile, but she cried out in the joy of multiple orgasms. Amid her intense pleasure, Aklia opened her eyes to look at the woman. The shock and horror of what she saw, overwhelmed her senses. She saw Satan and Lilith as they were. Lilith's emerald eyes penetrated her soul. Her dark and ominous beauty sent a shiver through her body. Satan's hot breath was upon her neck, and she turned her head to look at him as he continued to drive his member into her. Fear caused her body to become rigid when she saw his evil, twisted face. The stench of his burnt and rotting flesh caused her to vomit. Lilith's laughter filled her mind as she violently heaved into the pool. Satan and Lilith's actions became a violation of her as the darkness overcame her.

Suddenly, she found herself floating in the air over the pool, watching the horrific scene unfold. They continued to violate her even though she was unconscious and pinned between them. Satan's blood-curdling cries of pleasure echoed through the air as he spilled his seed deep inside of her for a second time. Lilith stopped violating Aklia, leaned over her drooping head, and kissed Satan passionately. Satan continued thrusting himself into Aklia as he kissed Lilith.

His abuse continued for several minutes, as Aklia watched in horror. Then Satan suddenly arched his back and threw his head backward in his third climax. Aklia found herself back inside of her body as Satan spilled his seed. His vile seed oozed out of her backside as he withdrew his member from her. Her last memory of the pool was the stench of his seed as she felt it on and within her.

Aklia found herself back in her dwelling. The horror of the events at the pool caused her stomach to churn until vomit spewed from her mouth and splattered on the floor. The disturbing memories haunted her. Satan and Lilith brought her to the highest levels of pleasure, but now she fought off the gut-wrenching memories of the actual events. Ose left Aklia, and Sitri entered the dwelling.

As Aklia wept, Sitri cast a spell upon her. As she knelt in a pool of her vomit, she realized how good her hands felt upon her flesh. She rubbed her thighs with both hands, and her fingers danced like electricity upon her flesh. *STOP* echoed through her mind, but her fingers found the warmth beneath her thin garments. A ripple of pleasure flowed through her.

Aklia moved to her bed, disrobed, and laid down. She spread her legs and thrust her fingers into her wetness. Thoughts of the pool filled her mind as she pleasured herself. Only moments ago, Satan's stench and his true nature caused her to be sick, but now she relived the events and took pleasure from them. Her mind wanted to stop, but she was powerless. Suddenly, she felt the warmth of his seed within her as she pleasured herself. Then Aklia experienced her most powerful orgasm yet. As the waves of pleasure subsided, she looked down at her thighs and watched his seed flow out of her onto the bed. *How can this be?* she wondered.

Aklia's body became her own again. She sat in a pool of filth and wept. As suddenly as the fit of lust came, it vanished. The guilt of her actions gnawed at her insides. She was distraught and cried out to God, but no answer came. She prayed and wept for hours, but God did not respond to her cries. "Kill yourself," echoed through her mind as if it was her voice. "Kill yourself," the words trailed off her tongue. She ran out of the cave and up the mountain. When she reached the highest point, she stopped and sat down upon a rock. *I should jump and end my miserable existence!*

As Aklia considered the reasons why she should end her life, something moved, and the rocks shifted behind her. She turned, too fast, and lost her balance. Her terror-filled eyes looked down at the ground below. In response, her hands desperately searched for something, anything to prevent her fall. Panic rushed through her body as she teetered on the edge of the cliff. Then she saw the wolf. She screamed, and it lunged at her as she fell backward. *I am going to die*; she thought as she tumbled over the edge. To her surprise, the wolf latched onto her garment with its powerful jaws and pulled her back up to solid ground.

Caym spoke to her as the wolf. "Why do you want to kill yourself by leaping to your death?" Aklia replied, "I know two ways by which I might take my life. My mother and father killed themselves by throwing themselves off a high place and by drowning. God raised them both times, but I hoped he would let me die because I am worthless to him!" Caym knew God intended to continue Adam's lineage through her. God would raise her from the dead as he did for Adam and Eve. They needed to try something different. "There is another way. I know a man who has mastered death itself." "Where is this person?" Aklia asked. The wolf turned and said, "Follow me, and we will journey to the place where Stolos dwells. He will show you a way to end your suffering." Aklia followed the wolf, but wondered, *Who is this Stolos?*

Aklia followed the wolf down through the wilderness for a day, and then she realized they were no longer on the mountain of God. A tinge of panic overcame her, and she thought, *Turn around and run home to your mother and father.* Images of Lilith and Satan taking her in the pool suddenly replaced her desire to run. She shook her head and tried to think of something else as she followed the wolf. Just as the sun was setting in the sky, the wolf stopped at a cave hidden amongst the rocks upon a ridgeline. He turned to her and said, "Stolos waits for you inside." She turned towards the cave and saw a faint flickering light within the cave. She turned back to the wolf, but it was gone. A foreboding voice called to her from the cave, "Aklia, I am waiting for you." She cautiously walked towards the entrance.

Before Aklia entered the cave, a bright light shone down upon her from Heaven. Then Gabriel appeared and said, "My child, the place which you are about to enter is Satan's Lair. True evil resides within the passages and chambers of this place. Fallen angels, demons, witches, and evil beasts dwell here. You will not find the peace you seek inside. The creatures within this lair want to make you their prisoner and torture you for their amusement. They want to harm God by killing and torturing those whom God created in his image. Turn away from this place, and I will carry you upon the winds back to your home. There, you will cleanse yourself and offer a sacrifice unto God. He will forgive your sins because He has a plan for you."

Aklia's heart leaped as Gabriel finished speaking. She thought God had forsaken her, but now she knew He had a plan for her life. So, she said, "I will go with you, and do what you suggest." Gabriel smiled and took her up in his arms. They soared through the air, carried by his mighty wings. In only a few moments, they traveled the distance it took her a day to walk. She was envious of Gabriel and wondered, *Why don't we have wings?* He landed at Aklia's cave and placed her upon her feet. Then he said unto her, "Go, cleanse yourself and make a worthy sacrifice unto God." Aklia did everything that Gabriel suggested. God accepted her sacrifice and forgave her sins. Satan's angry screams echoed throughout his lair.

CHAPTER 61

The angel returned to Adam at the Cave of Treasures and led him to his wife in the wilderness. As they approached, Adam saw Eve and the baby lying on the ground. Another mighty angel stood guard over her. The angel who led Adam said unto him, "Go and take your wife and child to the cleansing waters of the pool. Gather a great sacrifice unto God for the boy's sake and yours, because God had mercy upon you and has given unto you another heir!" When he finished speaking, both angels departed from them.

When Adam reached Eve, he bent down and took the child up in his arms. Then he said, "His name shall be Seth, which means strength." Adam held up the child to the heavens and thanked God because he delivered his son and his wife out of their affliction. He took Eve by the hand and led her to the crystal waters. After they bathed, they went to the Cave of Treasures to retrieve the amulet given to them by an angel of God. When they arrived at their home, he placed the amulet in their bed.

Adam saw Aklia sitting alone. She did not speak to them because of her indiscretion and because she was still angry with her mother. He was not sure what to say or do with her because she obeyed Eve's plan to steal his seed. As he thought about it, anger rose in him. He left the dwelling without speaking to his wife or daughter. Adam went to the flock and took the two largest sheep that were without spot or blemish. He bound the sheep and placed them upon the altar. Then, he returned to the cave and took Seth from his mother's arms. Adam took the boy to the altar and held him up before God and offered the sacrifice unto him. Fire descended from heaven and devoured the sheep and the blood. God accepted his sacrifice, and Adam left the altar.

With joy in his heart, Adam took the boy up to the Cave of Treasures. He blessed the boy in the name of God, with the gifts given unto him by God. Then he prayed and made intercession for his son until the boy cried for his mother's bosom. Adam rose and took the child into his mother so she could nurse him. When he had placed Seth upon his mother's breast, he said unto Eve, "This is my SON! You will protect him with your life and keep him from sin. If you fall into sin or lose the child, I will cast you out from this mountain, and you shall live with Cain and his lot. Seth will not go with you, because I will keep him upon the mountain!" When she heard his words, she wept for her sins, and because he thought she would not give her life to protect their child. She mourned for herself because Adam did not trust her and probably would not lay with her again. *What is life without a husband's love?* she thought.

Before Adam returned to the Cave of Treasures, he approached Aklia. She would not stand before him or lift her gaze to meet his because of her shame. He commanded her, "Stand up for your father!" She rose and looked at him with sadness in her eyes. He watched as tears welled up and ran down her cheeks. Then, he said unto her, "An angel showed me the immoral deed you and your mother did unto me to get children within thy womb. I know you did this thing out of desperation, and the plan was your mother's. Have patience, and you will bear children unto Seth when he comes of age. Your children shall be as the grains of sand by the sea, innumerable! Now, devote yourself to God and prepare yourself for this honor." Aklia heeded her father's words and purified herself a second time unto God. She prayed for God's mercy and strength.

When Adam finished speaking with Aklia, he turned back to Eve. Then he said, "God will have to persuade me, NO, he will have to command me to lie in your bed again. I cannot trust you to obey God's laws. Instead of God's ways, you seek the pleasures of your heart. Repent from your sins and turn back unto God so that he can give you refuge." When he finished speaking, he left without giving her a chance to respond to his words.

At Satan's Lair after the birth of Eve's daughter:

Satan and Lilith placed Eve's female child within a crib made of bones and wrapped it with fur blankets to keep it warm. Lilith would rather eat the child than tend to her. So, Lilith and Satan agreed that one of her daughters born from her union with Samael would raise Eve's daughter as her own. Lilith chose her most gifted daughter, Seraphiella. Seraphiella nursed the child from her evil breasts, and the child grew strong. When the child was only eight years old, she appeared to be a beautiful woman of marrying age. The child's hair flowed down her back like a golden mane, and her eyes were like blue oceans piercing through the darkness. She was a quick study with a gift for the dark arts. Her skills rivaled Seraphiella, and many of the masters already.

Seraphiella named the girl Naqama, which means to avenge or take vengeance. Eve failed as a mother, and God gave the child to Satan. So, Naqama wanted to watch her mother suffer and bleed at her hands. She wanted to watch her die, but not right away. Naqama wanted to hurt Eve, both physically and emotionally. All Naqama's time went to the discovery of new ways to torture her mother. She always smiled and appeared calm, but on the inside, the flames of hell raged and threatened to engulf her. Her desire for revenge brought focus to her learning and training. *Someday I will kill Eve and have my revenge. I live only, to torment my mother and end her life*, she thought.

CHAPTER 62

William set the book down on the table and rubbed his eyes. Satan's book was entertaining, but it had not done much to change his mind about the status quo of good and evil. If the story is true, Lucifer tried to help his brethren and rebelled to overthrow God, who he claimed is a dictator. "So, you don't believe Satan and the Fallen Ones are the good guys?" Amon asked. "Goddammit, seriously, you can't keep doing that! You are going to give me a heart attack!" Amon did not respond to William's comments but asked about the book. "Put yourself in our position. What would you do if you were an angel and God cast you out of Heaven because you refused to bow down before humankind? Wouldn't you try to destroy Adam and Eve to get revenge?" William responded, "Why are you still trying to destroy humanity?" "We aren't, well not all of us, anyway. Bael and his followers want to destroy all of humankind; the rest of us are seeking redemption by overthrowing God. We believe that humankind is the key to victory. Every human that turns their back on God is a soldier in our fight against him. Our war against God started before we were cast out, but the final battle is drawing near." William did not reply. Instead, he headed towards the kitchen for his second cup of coffee. "Would you like a cup of coffee?" he asked with a chuckle. Amon's response surprised him, "Do you have any espresso?" "Sure," William replied as he shook his head. *Of course, fallen angels like expresso. Why should that surprise me?*

Amon and William sat at the kitchen table and sipped their coffee and espresso. Amon finished his expresso and said, "Satan placed Orobos to watch Monica. He is concerned for her safety." William replied, "Everything about that sounds wrong, but I am grateful. After all, you and Satan put us in this situation when you gave me the book. I had to save the book and nearly died because of it." "Sorry, we did not expect Bael and God to move against us so quickly. It appears that they are working together in some way!" William's voice elevated as he replied, "You said you were at WAR! What did you think was going to happen?" Amon started to reply but quickly vanished as the door opened and Margaret walked into the kitchen.

"Are you talking to yourself again?" Margaret asked as she looked curiously at the empty espresso cup sitting across from William. *Amon left me holding the proverbial bag,* William thought as he replied to his wife, "I was reading aloud." "Where's the book?" she asked. *The book is in the other room. Dammit, think fast, PHONE!* He picked up his cellphone and said, "I was reading something on GOOGLE. Something the book referenced, but I wanted to research more. You know how my mind works. No stone left unturned." *Nice save,* he thought as she laughed. Margaret took a coffee cup from the cabinet and poured herself a cup. *That does not explain the espresso cup William,* she thought. *Maybe he has an imaginary friend.* She smiled and imagined him having coffee with a big pink bunny or something equally entertaining. "Okay, I will leave you to your research then," she said and walked out of the kitchen and went back upstairs with her coffee

William tipped his cup again, and when he put it down on the table, Amon was back. He picked up the empty expresso cup. "Mind if I have another cup?" "Sure," William replied as he made another shot for him. "Are all of the Fallen One's caffeine addicts?" Amon replied, "Like humans, we have vices too."

Their discussion turned back to the book as William handed the espresso to Amon. "What happens to Eve's daughter? The one Satan and Lilith took." Amon replied, "I am not going to spoil that for you, but since you mentioned it. If God is so merciful, why would he give the girl to Satan and Lilith? The Bible also talks about God commanding the Israelites to kill their enemy's women and children several times. Despite those holy scriptures, most Christians claim God does not approve of abortion!" William replied to his original question, "Because she sinned, and their enemies worshipped other Gods?" William's reply was more of a question than answer. Amon pressed the issue, "According to the Bible; humankind was born into sin after Adam and Eve's fall. Has he turned his back on all of humanity, or does he only care about Christians because they worship him? What about their families? Face it, William, God, is a hypocrite! Where is he when a child dies of cancer or gets sexually assaulted? What about when some poor schmuck's family dies in a tragic auto accident? Where is the self-proclaimed God of love in those times? Satan, the Fallen Ones, and the Watchers gave science and medicine to humankind because they wanted to help humanity. Then God tried to take it from them with the flood!" William replied, "The Bible says the flood was punishment for mankind's sins."

"I have said too much already. You have not gotten to that part yet. Finish the book, and you will learn many things about God and our war against him. Thanks for the espresso," Amon said before vanishing again. William shook his head and thought, *Amon, is quite the character*. He went back into the living room, sat down, and opened Satan's book. Amon had left him with more questions than answers.

CHAPTER 63

Cain finished their home just before the torment of Eve's curse fell upon his wife. He held her hand and tried to comfort her, but her suffering was too much. She turned to Cain and said, "God is killing me because I carry your seed within me." Cain didn't reply and thought, *She might be right.* His heart ached for her because he thought *My wife's suffering is more significant than our mother's.* In desperation, Luluwa prayed to God, "Save me, Lord, deliver me from this torment!" God did not answer her, and He did not send an angel to comfort her. *Why would he answer me?* she thought. As her pain grew worse, she begged God for death, saying, "End my suffering, Lord!" The sun rose the next morning, and she still hadn't given birth. With each passing hour, she suffered more. Finally, she turned away from God and begged Cain, "Take my life! Cut the children from my womb and let my suffering end!" He replied, "My life holds no meaning without you! I cannot take your life. Our children will come soon, and then joy will wash your pain away." She did not speak or pray anymore. Cain placed a damp cloth upon her forehead and hummed a sweet melody, but Luluwa continued to whimper as the agony of childbirth raged within her. Her suffering lasted for three days and three nights. Then she gave birth to two healthy children.

The first child born to Cain was a son. Cain named him Enoch and said, "I will build a great city in his name!" The second child was a female child, and they called her name Jilani. Jilani was fair and beautiful like her mother. Luluwa could not travel to a place to cleanse her children. So, Cain went to the crystal waters and brought back water for his wife and children to bathe. He did not offer a sacrifice unto God for his children's sake because God cast him out and because He did not ease his wife's suffering during childbirth.

Cain prospered in the land of Nod, but his fits of shaking grew worse because of God's curse. Luluwa worried about him. She feared he might choke on his tongue and die. God had forsaken them, so she called out to another. "Satan, lord of the earth and keeper of ancient secrets. Hear my prayer for my husband, and we shall serve you forever!" Satan had left Cain and Luluwa alone and focused his efforts on Adam, Eve, Aklia and Seth after God cast them off the Mountain of God. When he heard Luluwa call his name, he came to her as Cain's friend.

Satan asked Luluwa, "Why have you cried my name in prayer?" She replied, "We have no God, and Cain's fits are becoming more violent. I am afraid he will die and leave me alone in the wilderness." "What can I do," he asked? "Heal him," she said. "I cannot undo God's curse, but I can treat the condition. I will send a servant back to you with a special potion. The fits will stop if he drinks one vile each morning." Luluwa smiled and hugged his neck. Her touch aroused him, and he said unto her, "What will you do for me?" Luluwa pushed him away and looked alarmingly into his eyes. Her mind flooded with horrible thoughts as she considered what he wanted. Satan knew her mind and a sinister grin formed on his lips, "Isn't your husband's health worth a gift of gratitude?"

Luluwa's naïve mind pushed back the horrible things he might want, and she focused on simpler things. *An offering of fruits, and or nuts; perhaps, Cain loves them. Maybe a burnt sacrifice such as the ones their father presented to God.* "Master, if you do this thing for us, my husband will build a mighty altar in your name. We will make a great sacrifice in your honor." Satan liked her idea, but he wanted more. He smiled and said, "I accept your offer, but I also want to taste your pleasures." Luluwa was visibly distraught and surprised. She crossed her arms as if she was protecting herself. He saw her reluctance and said, "I am sure your husband will be fine without my help. Good luck." His abrupt words struck her like a physical blow. She watched him turn and walk away. "No wait," the desperate words flowed out of her mouth just as Satan knew they would. He turned back to her and smiled with delight.

Satan took Luluwa on the ground outside of her home. She kept her eyes closed and tried imagining it was Cain thrusting himself into her flesh, but Satan's massive instrument took her breath away. Waves of unwanted pleasure rippled through her body as he filled her. She opened her eyes and looked at Satan. The illusion of Cain's friend flickered as he took her. Flashes of his true self caused her mind to drift between horror and pleasure. His pace quickened, and she dug her fingernails into his back as his warm seed flowed within her. The warmth of his climax sent her into a violent orgasm of her own. She wept as she realized she had not been with her husband since the birth of their children. *I gave myself to him for Cain's health*, she thought, as he rose from her thighs.

He looked down at the beautiful woman and reveled because she willingly gave herself to him. *A deal is a deal*, he thought. "Let my seed remain inside of you. Go unto your husband and take him. Our seed will mingle within your womb. Three wondrous daughters will come from our joint union." His words lifted Luluwa's spirits. She rose and clothed herself. He watched her dress and then he said unto her, "Tell your husband about the burnt offering only! Do not tell him about our shared embrace. Make the sacrifice at sunrise, and my servant will bring you a week's supply of the potion. I will keep sending the potion as long as you remain faithful to me and sacrifice on the first day of the week." Luluwa replied, "We will do as you have said. Thank you for your kindness, my lord!" Satan smiled and thought, *You are welcome, my sweet child.* He left without another word.

After the birth of Enoch, Cain began working on the city walls. He cut down mighty cedar trees and cut them in fifteen feet sections. The work was hard, but Cain promised to build a great city in his son's name. Mighty walls would protect his children and his beloved wife from the beasts of the field. As he worked, Luluwa came unto him. She brought him sweet berries and cold water. As he ate and drink, she said unto him, "My body craves your touch. Our children are safe and sleeping in our home. Take me here, and now, so I may know the pleasure of you inside of me again."

He choked on the berries in his mouth. His wife's abruptness surprised him, but his body shivered in anticipation. Cain loved teasing Luluwa. So, he asked her, "Shall I stop my work so that I can pleasure you? Shouldn't I finish my work while the sun still hangs in the sky?" He had no intention of continuing before he took her among the trees where they sat. He saw the irritation on her face as she mocked him, "Let's wait until you have returned to our home? When dinner is upon the table, and the children are crying for the warmth and comfort of their mother's bosom?" He laughed, and she realized he was playing with her. She leaped on him and knocked him to the ground.

They kissed for a few moments, and then their desires overcame them. Luluwa took off Cain's garments and pleasured him as she looked into his eyes. He writhed in the delight of her touch. When he could not take her playing any longer, he rolled her over and pulled her garments from her body. He held himself above her for a few moments admiring her beauty until she pulled him down upon her.

Luluwa exhaled with delight as he entered her. Cain's labors not only built them a home and city walls, but the hard work chiseled his body into a powerful work of art. She dug her fingernails into his rock-hard chest, and his thrusts became more vigorous. He smiled down at her, and she wrapped her legs around his waist, pulling him closer. Luluwa felt the warmth of his flesh within her as he spilled his seed. They collapsed in each other's arms and shared a lover's embrace for a few moments. Then she rose, dressed, and said unto him, "I must go to our children because they will wake soon." She bent down and kissed Cain passionately. Cain bid her farewell as she departed from him, "Be safe, my love!"

Luluwa told Cain about Satan's promise and the altar that evening. Cain woke early the next morning and built an altar worthy of Satan. Then, he found a wild ram and performed a blood sacrifice upon the altar. Satan saw the sacrifice and kept his promise to Luluwa. His servant brought the potion to Cain, and his fits of shaking stopped. From that day forward, they served Satan as their God. *Our Father's God cast us out and left us alone in the wilderness, but now we have a true God,* Cain thought. Cain and Luluwa worshiped Satan, the mysteries of the earth, moon, and sun. Satan accepted their worship, protected them from harm, and caused their labors to be fruitful.

CHAPTER 64

Whispers of Lilith's mischief spread throughout heaven, but none of the angels dared speak of her in God's presence. The Archangel Michael was the first to accuse her before God. "Why have you requested an audience with me, Michael?" Michael, who knelt on one knee before God raised his head and answered, "Master, the angels whisper of Lilith's evil deeds. She birthed thousands of demon children unto Satan because of her scheming with Samael. The vile demon stole Aklia's children, the seed of Adam. Lilith consumed the male child, and then offered the second child as a sacrifice to Satan in a mockery of Adam's sacrifices to you." God replied, "You speak the truth. She was the first woman, and wife of Adam, but perhaps I am too merciful!" God's light blazed a brighter orange. Michael knew God was angry. Seeing his opportunity, Michael asked, "Shall I slay the evil hag?" "No, you will not kill her yet, but she shall not be free of her curse, and another curse I will thrust upon her," God replied.

On earth, Lilith flew through the night skies basking in the brightness of a full moon. Suddenly, a great light shined down from heaven and blinded her. She closed her eyes and screamed as she lost control of her flight. Seconds before, she was soaring through the skies with grace and elegance; now, she was tumbling downward in a tangled mess of wings and limbs. Lilith crashed into a group of trees, bouncing from branch to branch as she fell. Her arms and legs frantically searched for anything to slow her fall. Finally, her hand found a tree branch, but it snapped without slowing her descent. Her body made a loud thud as she landed upon the rocky soil below. The air rushed out of her lungs as a result of her violent impact.

Lilith writhed in pain and cursed God because this had to be His doing. Her lungs burned as she tried to breathe. Fear filled her as she fought for breath. It seemed like an eternity before her lungs finally expanded. She took several shallow breaths, wincing in pain, and rubbing her eyes as she gathered herself. Then she heard their voices, Senoy, Sansenoy, and Semangelof. *The filthy angels who cursed me when I would not return to Adam*, she thought. With a bitter tone in her voice, she asked them, "Why has God sent you to torment me?" They replied, "Your wickedness and treachery are known. You conspired with Samael to defeat God's curse. Your demon children went out into the world, and God has seen their lewd and sinful acts. You stole Aklia's children, the seed of Adam, consumed one, and offered the other as a sacrifice unto Satan." Fear rose in Lilith as their accusations against her mounted. *God's wrath is upon me*, she thought.

Her vision slowly returned, and she looked at the angels. They appeared to be standing in a fog. The angels smiled when they realized she could see them. They said unto her, "A second curse is upon you. No creature or vermin will receive nourishment from you. Even the milk of your breasts shall be poison unto those who consume it." The worms in her blood burrowed out of her flesh and fell upon the ground. Fleas leaped from between her toes and searched for another host. She screamed into the air, a horrible, terrifying scream as she felt her child dying in her womb. Blood oozed from the microscopic holes left by the worms. Anger overwhelmed her, and she screamed a second time as she wiped the blood from her face. The pains of labor engulfed her as the child died. *My unborn child shall not take a breath in this world. His destiny of greatness, taken from him by God and these three wretched angels.*

Lilith fell to her hands and knees as the pains of childbirth ripped through her. She was powerless. Her tears turned to blood and rage boiled up within her heart. The angels taunted her during the height of her suffering. "Because of your wicked deeds, God's curse is upon you a third time. You shall dwell in darkness. The light of day shall be like the fires of hell upon your flesh!" As the angels left, they mocked her suffering once more. She screamed in pain and anger as she pushed with all her might. The dead child sprung out from between her thighs and landed on the ground with its lifeless eyes looking up at her. She looked at the child with disgust and slashed the cord which bound them together. Lilith rose from the ground, leaving the unborn child for whatever creature might find it. *Children are only numbers*, she thought, but she reminded herself; *They are numbers in an army that will rise against a cruel God.* Someday she would have her revenge and that day couldn't come fast enough!

CHAPTER 65

Satan grew tired of tempting Adam. Adam's devotion to God was unwavering, and God was quick to deliver him from harm's way. So, Satan shifted his focus to Seth. He transformed himself into an angel of light and met Seth on the road leading to the Altar of God. Seth was only seven years old when Satan met him. He had just finished making a sacrifice unto God. Seth communed with God and was mature beyond his years because his father had started teaching him the ways of God before he could even speak. On that day, Seth sang praises to God as he strolled back home from the altar. Suddenly, a great light appeared before him, and an angel stood in it.

As an angel of light, Satan said unto Seth, "Seth, my son, I will take you from this world of sin. You will ascend with me to Heaven. There are other men and women there, created in our image. You will live with them, and when you are of age, you will have your choice of the fairest maidens. Their beauty rivals your plain sister, Aklia, who your father has said you will marry." Seth heard his words and considered them, but he was not old enough to know the urges of manhood.

After considering Satan's words, Seth replied, "What is a maiden's beauty? I live to serve my God and my father." Satan countered his words, "If you come with me, you will live as God lives in Heaven." Seth answered him, saying, "Your words please me because my family has known the turmoil of sin." Satan pressed the advantage of Seth's willingness, "Then come with me, and I will take you to my home. A place where sin does not exist!" Seth thought about Satan's promises because they seemed too good to be true.

Several minutes passed, and then Seth replied, "I will go to my father and tell him where I am going. I do not want them to worry about my safety." Satan quickly replied, "There is no time for you to tell them. Come, while the door is open." Satan's insistent tone caused Seth to doubt his words, and his conscience warned him of Satan's temptation. So, he turned away from Satan and would have run home, but Satan blocked his way.

Seth knew he was in trouble when Satan disposed of his disguise. He could not pass by him because the trail was narrow. Satan reached out to take hold of him, and Seth ran away. He ran back towards the altar of God. "Stop, there is no escape," Satan yelled. The boy beat him to the altar, and before Satan could grab him, he threw himself on the altar. Seth cried out to God, "Lord God Almighty, take my life as a sacrifice upon this altar. Do not let Satan take me into his arms and pull me unto his bosom!" Satan dared not lay his hands on the boy because he knew what would happen next. He departed from the altar in disgust.

The Archangel Gabriel descended from heaven, saying, "You did the right thing by throwing yourself upon the Altar of God when Satan pressed you. Lean not unto your strength when you fight evil, but instead, have faith in God. God will send his angels, and they will save you from the darkness." His words pleased Seth, and he praised God for his salvation. Gabriel spoke again, saying, "Go to your father and mother because Satan has left you and God's angels shall protect you." Seth turned to see his path was clear, but instead of going home, he went to his father at the Cave of Treasures.

Seth told Adam about the encounter with Satan and the altar of God. He explained how Gabriel spoke to him and praised him for turning to God when he faced Satan's temptation. Seth's victory caused Adam to regret his failures when Satan first tempted him. He smiled at his son because he was proud of him. Then Adam said, "Do not take pride from your victory because it is God who saved you." Seth considered his father's words and returned unto his mother and sister to help with the chores of the day.

CHAPTER 66

Luluwa looked at her protruding stomach, and thought, *I am much bigger this time.* The children pressed on her womb, and she went into labor early. Cain joked with her and said, "Our son will be like a mountain!" She laughed but knew that she would not bear a son. A forceful contraction drove the laughter from her. Luluwa's labor was hard, but it did not last long because there was no room for the three children who shared her womb. As the sunset in the evening sky and the full moon rose, she gave birth to three daughters. The children shared identical features, except for the color of their hair. One child had red hair, one had black hair, and the third girl had blond hair. Their beauty was evident even as they entered the world, and their first cries were as angels singing a beautiful song.

Cain smiled as he looked at his daughters. He named them Parthenope, Ligeia, and Leucosia. At sunrise, after their mother fed them, Cain and Luluwa took them to the crystal waters. Luluwa washed herself at the side of the lake while Cain bathed the children. With three children in his arms, Cain dipped them into the water. When he raised them from the lake, the Fallen One, Vepar stirred the waters. The children flailed in fear as the cold water splashed upon them. Cain struggled to maintain his hold of the children, and all three of them fell into the troubled waters.

As he cried out in fear, Cain leaped into the water after the children. Luluwa panicked and dove into the water after him. Several minutes passed, as they searched for the children, but they could not find them. In desperation, they cried out, "Satan, save our children!" Vepar appeared before them in the form of a mighty angel, holding the three babes in his arms. As he stood amid the swirling waters, he spoke unto Cain and Luluwa. "Your children are dead, but they may live again! If you pledge your souls to Satan for eternity, he will raise your babes, and they shall never die again."

Cain and Luluwa saw no other choice. So, Cain said unto him, "What is it to us if we should follow Satan for eternity because God has cast us from his presence?" Vepar replied unto them, "You shall seal this contract in blood, and then the children can return unto their mother's bosom." Satan appeared before them with a golden knife. He took the golden blade and handed it to Cain first. Then, he said, "Cut your palm with this blade and say before God and all the world, my blood seals this contract with the one who heals my wound!" Cain did as Satan asked, and when the blood rushed from his palm, Satan took Cain's hand. Satan put Cain's hand to his mouth and drank the blood. Then, he licked Cain's wound, and it closed before their eyes.

Luluwa watched as she sobbed for her children. Satan handed her the knife, and without reservation, she sliced her palm, opening the flesh. As the blood pooled in her palm, she recited the words, "My blood seals this contract with the one who heals my wounds." As her blood rolled off her hand onto the ground, Satan took her hand in his. Then, he looked into Luluwa's beautiful eyes as he sucked the blood from the palm of her hand and licked it. Her wound also healed before their eyes. His gazed lingered with hers, and she remembered the pleasure they shared. Her cheeks blushed as her thighs became wet with desire.

Satan showed Luluwa what they could share again as she lingered in his gaze. He knew her desire and left her with the thought of them together. "Cain, place your daughters upon your wife's bosom and see their life return unto them. From this day forth, they cannot die, but instead, they will call men to their deaths with the sound of their voices." They stared at each other in disbelief as Satan departed. Cain wondered what his words meant, as Luluwa imagined Satan's warmth again.

Cain took two of his daughters from Luluwa, but she kept one. They held the children tight in their arms and thanked Satan for his mercy. Then, they remembered their other children, *Enoch and Jilani are alone!* Their hearts raced with a renewed fear as they quickly made their way home. When they reached their home, only silence greeted them. Panic set in and Cain shoved the large door open. The sound of the door woke Enoch and Jilinai. Their children's cries filled them with relief. *Praise be to Satan*, they thought.

A smile formed on Satan's twisted lips as he heard Cain and Luluwa's words. Joy filled him, as he allowed his mind to linger on the vision of the role Cain's daughters would have in God's defeat. Parthenope, Ligeia, and Leucosia cried as Luluwa fed Enoch and Jilinai. Their delicate voices filled Satan with delight, and he drifted off into his first peaceful slumber in years.

CHAPTER 67

Adam came to Seth while he was working in the field and said unto him, "Son, you have reached the age to take a wife and marry. Go up to our dwelling and take Abel's sister, Aklia, to be your wife." He said these words unto Seth when he was fifteen years of age. Seth did as his father commanded and went unto his mother and Aklia in the cave where they dwelt. He said unto them, "My father has said unto me, 'Take your sister Aklia to be your wife.'" I replied unto my father, "Let it be according to your words, before God's eyes." Seth turned to Aklia, "I will prepare a place for us to live because we cannot know each other's embrace with our mother lying beside our marriage bed. When I finish our home, I will return and take you to our home. We shall dwell there for all the days of our lives." When he finished speaking, he left them. His words pleased Aklia and Eve. Aklia's heart leaped with joy; *Finally, my time has come*, she thought.

Seth searched the Mountain of God for a suitable place to build his home. Then, he came upon the shelter which Cain built under the large shade tree. Seth said unto himself, *This is an excellent place to build a home.* So, he tore down the shelter and kept the wood to make furnishings for the home. Seth gathered large rocks and water from the pool. He poured the water upon a pile of loose dirt and made mud. Building a home from rock and earth was hard work, but several weeks later, he stood and admired his handiwork, *Perfect!* The stone dwelling rose from the level piece of ground like a fortress of rock. The thatched roof and stone floor kept the home cool for most of the day. A large oven and wooden furnishings accented the one-of-a-kind home. He placed a large animal fur blanket on their bed as the finishing touch and smiled.

As promised, Seth returned to Aklia and took her to their home. She admired the house he built for them, and it pleased her. Then Seth said unto Aklia, "I am young and have no experience with the pleasures of the flesh. Be gentle with me and instruct me so that I might become a gracious lover." She replied unto him, "I am older than you, but I am also ignorant in the ways of the flesh because I have never known pleasure from a man." She was not lying about being with a man, but she had known much pleasure from Satan and Lilith. The thought of their encounter made her wet again. Aklia hoped with all her heart that lying with Seth would produce the same pleasure.

Seth looked at Aklia with lust in his eyes. *What pleasures does she hold for me?* He untied her garments. They fell onto the ground around her feet, and she kicked them away from her. He looked upon her. Her hair flowed to the curved raise of her backside. Her skin was white as snow, and her erect nipples rose proudly from her large, ample breasts. His eyes made their way down along her hips, which curved outward from her small waist, creating an hourglass shape to her silhouette. A forest of dark hair rose from between her thighs, hiding her warmth from his eyes. He had never seen a woman naked, but her nakedness caused his loins to stir.

Aklia's heart leaped as she saw the smile form on Seth's lips. There was also a noticeable rise beneath his garments. She stepped closer to Seth and leaned up to kiss him. They kissed as she slid her hand under his garments and touched him. His kiss grew more passionate, and she feared that he might prematurely spill his seed. So, she stopped pleasuring him and took off his garments. A smile formed on her lips as she looked upon him. Seth's body was thin and muscular. She imagined God chiseling him out of granite. Her eyes drifted from his thick chest down to his rippling abdominal muscles. His lower abdomen was flat, and his hip bones protruded forming a "V" shape. His uncircumcised member rose out of a small forest of hair like a mature tree among seedlings.

Without warning, she shoved him down upon their bed and jumped on top of him. Seth moaned in appreciation as she kissed his neck. Her large breasts pushed upon his chest, and he felt the warmth between her thighs upon him. He thought he might die never knowing such a feeling again, but he was wrong. Aklia rose from his neck and straddled him with one hand upon his chest. With her other hand, she guided him into her warmth. They groaned with mutual delight as she lowered herself upon him. His manhood quivered within her and threatened to spill his seed. She knew he was close to climax. So, she looked down into his pleasure-filled eyes and said, "Wait for me." He was not sure what she meant.

Akila stopped moving and looked down at Seth until the moment passed. Then, she moved her hips in a circular motion, thrusting down upon him as if she meant to impale herself. A strange warmth flooded him as his muscles tightened. He was not sure what was going to happen, but it felt amazing. Aklia pulled his head up as she leaned into a passionate kiss. Then she threw her head back, arched her back and howled with delight, as her body shook with orgasm. Her cries grew louder and louder as she thrust herself down onto his erect manhood. His warm seed flowed into her as she shook with orgasm. She continued moving her hips upon him until the ripples of their pleasure stopped.

In exhaustion and satisfaction, she rolled off him. She sighed as she laid her head on his chest. Gently, she rubbed his chest and slid her fingernails across him from sternum to navel. As she looked up at him, Aklia asked Seth, "Are you pleased with me?" He smiled and kissed her. "Oh yes," he said, and then he suggested, "Let's go to the pool. The cool waters will refresh us." They watched each other dress, and then he took her hand, and they went to the pool.

CHAPTER 68

Samael sat with his head resting in his hands and thought about his time on earth. He could not even remember how long it had been since his last visitor came. Then, he heard Saphriael's voice. Saphriael was once one of his closest confidants. Samael watched intently as the guards opened the heavy prison doors, which squeaked in protest. Saphriael walked into the cell, and the guards shut the doors behind him. Samael longed for this day. The day in which a visitor came to see him. Any visitor would do, but an old friend was an exceptional gift. He longed for conversation. The silence was the worst part of his imprisonment, *Absolute torture!*

Saphriael looked at Samael and thought, *He is a shell of his former self, beaten in combat, castrated, and imprisoned.* "How are you?" Saphriael asked. "I've been better. Did you bring any wine?" neither of them laughed at Samael's failed attempt at humor. "Samael, my old friend, this is not a social visit. The question of how you ended up here has been nagging at me since they captured you. Can you explain how you ended up fighting against God?" Samael raised his head and looked at his old friend. After a deep sigh, he asked, "Don't you wonder if there is more to life than mindlessly obeying God?" Saphriael replied, "I serve God as he created me to do. You were his most feared servant! Now you have fallen into sin's deadly grasp."

Samael shook his head from side to side, "No, Saphriael, you are like a child without learning. You cannot even fathom the freedom and pleasures I experienced upon the earth. The essence of life itself rests between a woman's thighs. Life comes from the joining together of flesh. I have hundreds of children from my union with Lilith. Why do you think God hid the pleasures of the flesh and procreation from us?" Saphriael replied, "I do not know why God would withhold anything from us, but our place is still to serve our master." "Saphriael, does a master give free will to his children, only to restrict them from exercising it?" "You speak blasphemy, Saphriael replied with a harsh tone." Samael laughed, "Now I know what I used to sound like!" Saphriael rose in anger and left Samael as he considered their conversation.

Samael watched Saphriael walk towards the door. The guards started to open the door, but before he walked out, Saphriael turned and opened his mouth to say something. Samael cut him off and spoke first, "Go down to the earth, take a wife, and know the greatest pleasure of all. I cannot describe the pleasures of knowing a woman, but to say it is like a powerful storm passing through the eye of a needle. The pleasure of the flesh bears the fruit of life without God's manipulation! How can life come from something wrong?"

Saphriael stood in the doorway until Samael finished speaking. He listened to each word, measuring them to understand why his lifelong friend fell into sin. *Samael was once loyal to God!* Saphriael's mind raced with questions. *Did the union of flesh drive out rational thought? What if his words concerning free will and God keeping the secrets of pleasure from them are true? Why would God hide pleasure from us? Samael was in prison because of his other sins, wasn't he? Could life come from sin?* Saphriael turned and walked out of the door as he considered Samael's words and his questions. The guards shut the heavy door behind Saphriael, and Samael was alone again.

CHAPTER 69

For weeks, William's time and thoughts were on Satan's Book, but when his wife stepped into the room, he forgot all about it. Her tight, red, silk dress clung to her like a second skin, accenting her shapely figure in all the right places. A slit ran up her left leg well above mid-thigh, and he thought, *This is not our regular date night!* "You look amazing! Should I change into something nicer?" William asked as he assessed his decision to wear a decent pair of slacks and a simple collared shirt. He almost always went with jeans, good thing he picked out something better for tonight. "No need," she said, and they headed out to the car.

A few minutes later, Margaret's 2007 Audi glided down the road. He stole a glance at Margaret's exposed thigh and wondered if she was wearing panties. Ever since Lilith's visit, she seemed revived. It was almost like being twenty again; their sex life was amazing! The years stole much of the passion they once shared, but now it was back. He wondered, *Is this Lilith's doing or could it be the book? Maybe it was the dark influences he imagined swirled around it. Time will tell!*

He took advantage of the red light and placed his hand on his wife's bare thigh. She said nothing, but she put her hand on his, interlocking their fingers. *Shot down,* he thought. She pulled his hand up her thigh and through the slit in her dress. *No panties,* he thought as she guided his hand between her legs. The driver behind them blew his horn in protest, and William jerked his head around to see the light was green. He depressed the accelerator and put his hands back at ten and two. Once they were moving with traffic, he turned towards his wife. His jaw dropped, and his eyes widened, *Her hand is still in her dress*. She bit her lip and moaned softly. He watched her and the road until she shook with orgasm and cried out in delight. She opened her eyes and looked at him with a sly smile before slipping her wet fingers into his mouth. *God, why can't there be a place to pull over?*

Suddenly, a bright light filled the cabin of the Audi. Everything moved in slow motion as the front of a large commercial truck slammed into the passenger side of the Audi. Shattered glass floated in the air, reflecting light from the truck's headlights as the airbags inflated. The car rolled away from the impact of the truck. Ten rolls later, the mangled Audi came to a sudden halt against the short, brick retaining wall protecting the sidewalk on the other side of the intersection, and time returned to real speed. Steam and smoke rose from the front of the car which lay on its top. Glass, accessories, and parts of the car's exhaust system lay spread throughout the intersection as evidence to the violence of the crash.

Twenty Minutes Later:

Monica's phone rang, and she threw her body upward from the couch where she was sleeping. Her eyes strained to recognize the number on the phone. She didn't know it, but she answered anyway, "Hello?" A professional but soft voice asked, "Is this Monica Reynolds?" Her heart rate increased as she answered, "Yes, what is this about?" The voice replied, "Ma'am, this is Deputy Dwight Smith. There has been an accident." Monica's heart dropped. She knew her husband was asleep because she just talked to him from his hotel bed before she fell asleep. He was in California for a business conference. *It must be my dad. I told him not to read that damn book!* "What kind of accident?" "A commercial truck driver ran a red light and hit your parent's car," the deputy replied. Monica cut him off, "Are they all right?" "Yes, they are being held for observation." "You could have led with that! Why the hell wouldn't you lead with that?" He replied, "Ma'am, I am so sorry, but this is my first notification." "What hospital are they in?" "They are at Newport Hospital, in Rhode Island," the deputy replied. She did not even say goodbye before she hung up.

Monica quickly called her husband as she packed. He was half asleep but woke up when he heard the news. Her fingers swiped left, right, and pressed the screen of her smartphone as she searched for the first flight out while they talked. One hour later, she boarded a plane from the standby passenger list. Monica wanted a rum and coke to settle her nerves but asked for a warm cup of tea instead because she had to drive a rental car to the hospital. Satan's Book had almost got her father killed twice, and now her mother was involved, and she was angry!

Two hours later, Monica arrived at the hospital. Delayed on takeoff, backed up at arrival, and three rental car counters before she found something smaller than a full-size car or SUV. At the hospital, Monica pulled her mid-sized sedan into a vacant spot in the parking garage and shut it off. She placed both hands on the steering wheel and let out a stress-relieving sigh. Two deep breaths later, she grabbed the keys from the ignition and reached for the door handle. A startling voice stopped her from getting out of the car.

"We weren't responsible for your mother and father's accident!" Monica threw herself against the driver's door and pushed as far away as she could from the thing sitting in the passenger seat. The hooded figure turned to face her. Instead of a face, flames burned within the hood. Somehow, they didn't burn the hood, and yet they seemed real. The air in the car wreaked of burning sulfur. "We weren't responsible for your mother and father's accident," Amon said a second time. Monica overcame her fear and let her anger flow. "Maybe you're not responsible, but if you had not given him that fucking book, we would not be here!"

Amon let Monica ramble and vent. Humans are so tedious. *Awe, the good old days when Satan did not have the patience for their whining,* he thought. Monica wasn't one of the weak ones, though. She had a fire in her, and he appreciated that about her. So, he waited for her to tire herself out. *Finally*, he thought as she stopped talking. "Someone tried to kill your parents, but I saved them. They are fine except for the Audi. German engineering only goes so far!" Monica replied, "Is that a joke? Is this funny to you?" Silently he kicked himself in the ass for that comment. *I should have known better!* Their conversation was over, for now.

Monica exited the car, and it chirped as she depressed the lock button on the keyless remote. Amon laughed, to himself as he watched Monica stomp out of the garage and track through the half-frozen black sludge on the walkway to the main entrance of the hospital. Something about her caused a stir deep within him. He shook his head and said out loud, "Don't you even think about it, Amon!" It had been a long time since he had a relationship with a human, and the last one ended badly. It still came up time to time during some of the Fallen One's drunken ramblings. He watched as she entered the hospital.

Monica stopped, stomped her feet on the black floor mat, and pulled her hat and gloves off. She stuck them in the pockets of her long black coat. Amon appeared in front of her as her head was down. As a doctor in blue scrubs, he said, "Right this way, Mrs. Reynolds, I will take you to your parent's room." Monica was surprised by the sudden appearance of a doctor until she saw a flicker of flames in his eyes. "Let's go," she said with a snarky tone in her voice.

They took the elevators to the third floor without exchanging a single word. Monica was angry, but she was also working very hard to stay angry. *Humans,* he thought again. They exited the elevator and took another right turn about halfway down the hall. At the end of the next hallway, Amon opened the door on the left, Room 347, and motioned for Monica to enter, "After you." She gave him an angry look but mumbled "Thanks" under her breath. Amon smiled at her. *Another mistake on his part.* She shook her head in disgust as she entered her parent's room.

William and Margaret turned in unison as Monica and Amon entered the room. They were both sitting up in their beds with their respective tray tables in front of them. Green gelatin, milk, coffee, and a couple of blue hospital water pitchers littered their trays. Margaret pressed the mute button on the bedside remote, and the Family Feud soundtrack fell silent mid jingle. William spoke first, "We are okay! Our cell phones broke in the crash, and you were on the plane before we could get to another phone." "What happened?" she asked. Margaret replied, "Well, we were on our way to meet another couple for a private date night dinner..." Monica interrupted, "I don't need to know about your perverted sex lives. What caused the accident?" "An eighteen-wheeler ran the red light at a busy intersection and hit us! The officers told us the car rolled ten times before landing on its roof. It was a miracle we weren't killed or seriously injured!" Monica looked over at her father and gave him a look. He received her meaning loud and clear. *He owed her the rest of the story, but not in front of her mom.*

Amon addressed them, "Is there anything else I can do for you both?" William opened his mouth to speak, but Monica beat him to it. "I will have more questions for you later!" He pursed his lips as if to say "great" and replied, "I will be right outside if you need anything." Monica blurted out, "You'd better be!" Monica's rudeness towards the handsome young doctor was strange, but Margaret dismissed it as worry for them. William said, "Thanks" to Amon and watched as he left the room. He looked at Monica and said, "Where would we be without his help, huh?" Monica glared back at her father but said nothing. Instead, she thought, *Where indeed?* Margaret replied, "He seems like a great doctor."

A few hours later, Monica and William talked with Margaret's soft snoring in the background. "So?" Monica asked. William replied, "We were on our way to dinner, and a truck ran a red light. It was crazy! We should be dead. I remember a faint blue light around us as the car rolled. Later in the ambulance, Amon appeared as an Emergency Medical Technician and told me someone had possessed the driver of the truck. They tried to kill us by running the traffic light?" Monica asked, "Someone who? Isn't Satan supposed to be protecting you!" William replied, "He is, but there are other forces which don't want the real story to get out. God, His angels, Bael, and his followers, maybe even humans!" "What if this is Satan's plan? To convince you, God is the bad guy, and the Fallen Ones are good?" Monica countered. William paused for a moment, and then said, "The more I read the book, the more I understand why he can't be lying. It's hard to explain, but once you read the book, you will know too!"

It was evident to Monica that the book was affecting her father, but was it in the right or wrong way? *What if he is right?* Monica wanted to help her father, but she needed answers. "Get some rest. I want to see how much longer you and mom have to stay." William nodded and said, "Be careful!" "I will," Monica replied as she scooped up her purse, threw the strap over her shoulder, and left the room.

Monica walked to the nurse's station, but she didn't see her parent's "doctor." She didn't know what name Amon was using, but it couldn't be his own. The nurse raised her head from the chart and looked at Monica. "How may I help you?" she asked with a strong Boston accent. "My parents are in Room 347, is their doctor around?" "Yes, Dr. Alex Mon," she replied. Monica smiled and laughed, *Dr. A. Mon, Amon, wow!* "Is he still on shift?" she asked the nurse. "Ma'am, he went down to the morgue. He should be back any minute." "How long has he been gone?" The nurse looked at her watch, "Twenty minutes or so." "Is the morgue in the basement?" The nurse reluctantly answered, "Yes, 3B, but you can't go down there!" *Watch me*, Monica thought as she headed towards the elevator.

The elevator doors opened on 3B, and Monica stepped out of the elevator. *Something was wrong!* The flickering fluorescent lights made it difficult to read the sign on the wall in front of her. After her eyes adjusted, she saw MORGUE in capital letters with an arrow pointing to the right. She turned and looked down the long hallway towards the double doors at the end. Only the light above her and three fire lights spread out between her and the morgue entrance at the end of the hall flickered with light.

An involuntary shiver ran down her spine as she saw her breath. She crossed her arms in response to the sudden chill and wished she would have brought her coat. It was freezing, and she had seen enough horror movies to know it was a bad omen. The ding of the elevator doors closing sent a fresh rush of adrenaline through her body. She turned to stop the doors from closing, "SHIT," she said out loud as the doors shut. The hallway was even darker now.

Monica slowly walked down the hallway towards the morgue, sidestepping the debris from several fallen light fixtures. *All this debris makes it look like a war zone or the aftermath of a severe earthquake! What happened here?* She flinched at the unexpected sound of glass cracking under the fallen ceiling tile as she stepped on it. Her heart raced. *Why am I doing this? I need answers;* she reassured herself as she stepped over the remains of another ceiling light. *Halfway there...this is a long hallway! Is this hallway getting longer?* Only a couple minutes had passed, but her trek down the hall seemed like a never-ending journey. Her cellphone vibrated, and the light flickered. She stopped in a panic and looked at the screen. The low battery light was barely visible through the frost on the screen. *Great! What else could go wrong?* The world seemed to reply, "Challenge accepted!" A crashing sound came from inside the morgue, and the double doors swung slightly open before slamming shut again. She stumbled backward trying to avoid a ceiling tile as it fell in front of her. Her heel got stuck in the debris, she fell flat on her back, and her head bounced off the floor. The ground knocked the wind out of her and sent her cellphone flying back towards the elevator. Her head started throbbing, her vision became blurry, and then the blackness came.

She woke to the sound of an electrical short circuit and a shower of sparks from one of the few lights still attached to the ceiling. *How long was I out?* It was impossible to tell. The back of her head still throbbed. She felt for blood, but her hand came back dry. *Just a concussion*, she thought. Fear rolled over her like a wave of ice-cold water, and panic set in as another crashing sound came from within the morgue. *RUN*, she thought as she rolled over, pushed herself up, and tried to compel her legs to move towards the elevator. She got her hands down just in time to catch herself, but they were shaky too. Her face hit the floor harder than she would have liked. She lifted her face up and spat out a combination of ceiling tile dust and insulation. Her hand rubbed the debris from her lips as she checked for blood. No visible blood, but she had the familiar metallic taste of it in her mouth. Her tongue surveyed her teeth. All seemed in place.

Monica rolled over, sat up, and looked down the eerie hallway towards the morgue. *I came to get answers from Amon*, she thought with a newfound determination. The state of the hall worried her. She took a few deep breaths; her head wasn't throbbing anymore. Once again, she found herself slowly walking towards the double doors at the end of the hallway. Her hand found the metal plate on one door, and she pushed it inward. The door squeaked in protest before coming to an abrupt stop as it contacted something metallic laying directly behind the door.

She squeezed through the small opening between the doors, back first and immediately regretted it. Monica found herself unable to see into the morgue with her shirt caught on the metal door. Her back was facing whatever, or whoever was in the morgue. A renewed surge of panic washed over her as she frantically struggled to free herself. She tugged her shirt with both hands. The sound of ripping fabric didn't give her enough time to stop her backward descent into the morgue and its darkness. Pain shot through her arm as she landed on her funny bone. Her eyes strained to adjust from the flickering hallway lights to the darkness of two dim fire lights. One light hung over the door just behind her and one hung above the silver, metallic refrigeration doors which kept the bodies cold. *Dead bodies!* A chill ran down her spine as she saw one of the doors was open. Her eyes scanned the room for movement or another person, angel, demon, or anything out of the ordinary. Everything she knew about a morgue came from television or the movies. Monica had no clue what should be in a real-life morgue. However, she did notice a dark shape laying on the floor in the far corner. *Oh shit, this can't be good...*

Monica rose to her feet and made her way towards the figure lying on the floor. She skirted the outside of the room to avoid walking towards the open refrigeration drawer. As she approached the figure, she realized it was a man in scrubs. He was laying on his side, facing away from her. Cautiously she knelt beside the dark figure. She placed her left hand on the man's shoulder and rolled him back towards her. When the body's back hit the ground, Amon's head rolled over to face her. Her hand covered her mouth and muffled her scream. *Was he dead? He was a fallen angel, who could have killed him?*

A renewed wave of panic shot through her body. Monica swung her head around the room, scanning for any movement. She breathed a sigh of relief after she confirmed they were alone a second time. The cooler door was still open, but she was not going to check in there. "We need to get out of here!" Amon's almost inaudible words nearly scared her to death. Her eyes locked on his. The fire in his eyes was dim and flickered as if he was clinging to life. "What happened?" she asked with genuine concern in her voice. "I will explain everything when we get out of here. We need to get out of the hospital and make sure your parents and the book are safe!" Monica didn't like not knowing what was happening, but she feared for her parents, herself, and even a *fallen angel?* Monica helped him to his feet and even allowed him to put his arm around her to support himself. She wondered, *What am I doing?*

After what seemed like the longest elevator ride ever,

they made it to the floor where her parents recovered from their accident. "Go get your parents. I will fill out the release forms for them. We need to go," Amon said. "Are you okay?" she asked as she surveyed his eyes and facial expressions for any sign of his actual state. "I've been worse, help your parents get ready to leave." Without another word, Amon gingerly walked towards the nursing station to process her parents' discharge.

Relief washed over Monica as she entered the room and found her parents sitting up in bed watching television. William asked, "What happened?" Monica replied, "We need to get out of here; get dressed!" She turned away from her parents and stepped into the small bathroom to clean herself up. Her bloody and battered face looked back at her in the mirror. *I am so hot,* she jokingly muttered to herself. The water stung as it got into the split in the corner of her lip. She grabbed the small bottle of mouth wash off the sink and took a sip. *SON OF A BITCH*, she silently screamed as the alcohol hit the open wounds in her mouth. She spat the mouth wash into the sink, noted the red swirls of blood, and ran her fingers through her hair. A second look at the mirror, *Not great, but better!*

The hospital discharged William and Margaret in record time, and they left. Monica, William, and Margaret sped towards her parent's home in the rental car. Amon followed a safe distance behind, just in case. Amon intrigued Monica; her father described him as reluctant and even unhappy to be helping William. *What had changed?* Before they left the hospital, they planned to meet on the back porch of her parent's house after she confirmed Satan's book was safe and got her parents settled. She looked forward to getting answers to some of her questions. The morgue incident left her with even more questions than she already had.

Inside the house, Margaret fell asleep on the couch, and William sat down in the recliner and sipped a fresh cup of coffee. He looked at Satan's book and wondered if he should stop reading it. The book had changed his life, but Monica's involvement concerned him more than anything. If something happened to her, Margaret would kill him. She was, after all, their baby girl. He smiled as highlights of her childhood rushed through his mind.

Monica stepped outside and shut the door behind her. Amon stood with his back towards her looking into William's snow-covered back yard. "Where should I begin?" Amon asked. She savored the warm coffee for a second and then swallowed it. "What happened in the morgue?" Amon took a deep breath and said, "Someone tried to kill your parents. We believe one of Bael's loyal followers is to blame, but false accusations could start a civil war in hell and endanger all of humanity. So, I went to the morgue to identify the guilty party." Monica interrupted, "How could you find the person or thing that tried to kill my parents at the morgue?" When a deity, fallen angel or demon possesses someone, and they die a violent death, the possessor becomes trapped in the dead body for a time. That time varies, but some spirits could remain in their prisons of flesh for hours. I intended to confront the deceased truck driver's possessor when they came out of his body. Someone else ambushed me in the morgue while I waited. We fought, I lost, and the mortuary and hallway bear witness to the struggle."

Almost an hour passed as Amon answered Monica's questions. "How are you doing?" he asked. She gave him a look and said, "What choice do I have?" "To be honest, none. If it's worth anything, I questioned Satan's decision to choose your father and you. Now, I believe he made the right choice." Monica was not sure how to respond to his comments. "Thanks, I guess?" "I have to go, but my brethren will stand watch until I can return." His injuries were evident, and she knew he needed to tend to his wounds. She tried to imagine what that treatment looked like, but gave up because most of the options made her shudder to think of. Amon placed his hand on her shoulder, "You will be in good hands until I return. Thank you for coming for me in the morgue." "I did not come to help you! I wanted answers." "Nevertheless, Monica, you saved my life! My attackers fled when you got off the elevator. Otherwise, they would have killed me!" She saw the sincerity in his eyes. According to religion and the Bible, the Fallen Ones were evil, with no good in them. Yet, Amon stood before her displaying real emotions, and genuine concern for her family. Suddenly Amon was gone, and she was alone looking at her parents' snow-covered yard.

Inside the house, William finished his cup of coffee. He smiled as he looked at Margaret, sleeping on the couch. The back door opened and closed. Monica called out, "I am going to shower and get some sleep." "Okay, honey, I will be here reading." He opened Satan's book as he heard Monica going up the stairs. He placed the heavy book in his lap, put on his reading glasses, excited to find out what came next.

CHAPTER 70

Seth and Aklia shared the embrace of the flesh many times, but she did not conceive until Seth was twenty years of age. Aklia bore Seth a son and a daughter. They called their son, Enosh, which means "humankind" because he would be a father unto all of humanity. The daughter they named Afraima, which means "fertile" because she would bear many children into this world. Shortly after the birth, Adam visited their home, blessed the children, and prayed for God to protect them.

When the time for sacrifice came, Seth left his wife and took the fattest sheep from their flock. A sheep without spot or blemish and prepared it for a sacrifice unto God for Enosh's sake. He returned to their dwelling, and once she cleansed and fed the boy, he took him up to the Altar of God and offered a sacrifice for him. God accepted the sacrifice, devouring it upon the altar before them. When the sacrificial fire went out, he took the child up to the Cave of Treasures and blessed him with the gifts that God gave Adam and Eve after their fall. Then, he fasted and prayed unto God for the child according to their custom.

Satisfied that he had fulfilled his duties to God, Seth returned unto his wife and daughter and placed Enosh upon his mother's breast, so that she could feed him. He had joy in his heart and a smile on his face as he looked at her and his children. On the eighth day, he took Afraima to the altar and offered a pure sacrifice unto God for her sake as well. God accepted the sacrifice, and they traveled up to the Cave of Treasures and blessed her with the gifts from God. Then, they fasted and prayed unto God on her behalf, as was their custom. Seth and Aklia returned to their home with their children. They placed the amulet of protection at the head of the children's bed and thanked God for his protection. In the years that followed, Seth and Aklia had many more healthy sons and daughters.

In the land of Nod:

Cain feared for the lives of his children because he heard the story of Lilith from his father and mother. He no longer trusted in God and worshiped Satan, and he was not sure Satan would protect his children from Lilith. So, Cain spoke to his wife about Lilith and the three angels who protected children from her. His wife had a beautiful voice and often soothed Cain's anger with her songs. Luluwa decided to compose a song to sing unto their children at night to protect them from Lilith. Because Cain still feared that her song alone would not save their children, he sacrificed six young lambs, six white doves, and six serpents upon an altar and prayed unto Satan that the life essence of the creatures might bring power unto her lullaby. She sang her song as he took the lives of the creatures, and then they drank the blood, and the lust of the flesh fell upon them.

When Luluwa finished her lullaby, she looked upon Cain. The crimson blood of their sacrifices covered his body. Desire rose within her as she stared into his dark, lust-filled eyes. Driven by lust herself, she ran at him like a crazed person. He did not try to defend himself from her, but instead, he grabbed her from the air, and they fell onto the altar. She grabbed his wrists and pinned him upon the remains of their sacrifice. His blood-soaked lips met hers in a deep passionate kiss, which ended with her licking the blood from his face and neck. She aggressively bit his neck, nearly drawing blood.

Cain writhed in the painful pleasure of her bite. His lust overwhelmed him, and he tore her garments from her delicate body and rolled over on top of her. Cain discarded his garments on the ground beside the altar and grabbed a vessel which contained the blood of the sacrifices. Then, he poured it upon her naked body. The blood splashed onto her chin and flowed down between her firm breasts. She rubbed the blood onto her chest and arched her back in pleasure. He poured the remaining blood upon her chest, and it ran down her abdomen before parting into two streams as it met the veil which hid her warmth from him. Excited by his actions, Luluwa's hand grasped her breast. She ran her outstretched fingers down the trail of blood and parted her thighs. Her hands rubbed the blood into her tender flesh and she moaned with delight. Cain watched lustfully and bit his lower lip in anticipation.

Luluwa's hands danced on and within herself. She was wet with desire and the blood of their sacrifices. In the throes of orgasm, she looked up at Cain and beckoned him to take her. Driven by lust and his desire to pierce her heavenly veil, he moved closer. He forcefully grabbed her, and flipped her over onto her stomach. With one hand wrapped in her lengthy hair, he pushed her face down upon the altar and drove his member into her warmth. She cried out in pleasure as he grasped one her breasts with his other hand and pulled it back towards him with each powerful thrust. The sounds of their passion echoed through the trees.

Luluwa's cries overwhelmed all other sounds. She thought he might split her in two, but the pleasure of his actions overcame her, and her body tightened as an orgasm rose within her. Cain groaned loudly as her muscles constricted upon him. Like two powerful storms colliding, orgasm came upon her first and then him. As she cried out, he spilled his seed. Then, he collapsed onto her, breathed heavily, and whispered into her ear, "I love you." She replied, "I love you too!" When their breathing returned to normal, she said unto him, "Let's go and bathe ourselves in the cool waters of the river, so I can return to our home, and feed our children." Cain rose from her, lifted her to him, and kissed her passionately. They held hands and walked to the river in happiness.

CHAPTER 71

One day when the heat of the day was excruciating, Seth stopped working in the field. *It's too hot, and if I continue, I will die!* So, he went to the pool to find relief from the heat. When he got to the pool, he found a young woman already in the water. She stood in waist-deep water with her back to him. *Turn away,* he thought, but her beauty captivated him, and he could not look away. He watched as water splashed onto the small of her back as she played. She sank and disappeared below the water. A few seconds later, she emerged running her fingers through her golden hair, forcing the water from it as she tilted her head backward. His eyes drifted to her right side where her breast threatened to reveal itself. She turned and faced him without attempting to cover herself. He was a prisoner to her beauty.

Seth looked upon her perfect breasts, which sat high up on her chest. Her erect nipples called to his lips. His eyes drifted from her succulent breasts down to the dark, golden hair between her thighs. The dark hair hid her warmth from him, but his loins stirred. Entranced by her nakedness, he could not turn away from her. She continued to wring the water from her hair as she smiled at him, unashamed of her nakedness. Slowly she moved towards him. Her eyes were like a crystal blue sea with no end. He could see no escape.

He woke from her seductive spell as her cold, wet breasts pressed against his chest. Her lips smelled like fresh strawberries, and his mouth watered in anticipation as he thought, *Kiss her!* Her breath was upon his lips, but she didn't kiss him. After several moments, he gave into temptation, grabbed her shoulders, and pulled her into him. His lips met hers, and she returned his kiss. Their kiss lasted several passionate minutes before he released her. He asked, "Who are you?" as he opened his eyes. *Where did she go?*

Had the heat of the day caused him to hallucinate? Thoughts swirled through his mind. He almost dismissed it as a heat-induced dream, but the taste of strawberries was still on his lips. He could not explain what happened. So, he dove into the cold waters of the pool. The water shocked his body and refreshed him from the heat. He held his breath and swam beneath the surface of the water. The water rolled off him as he broke the surface of the water gasping for air. He pushed his hair out of his eyes as he rose from the pool. His mind raced with thoughts of the beautiful girl as he gathered his things and started his journey home.

At Satan's Lair:

Naqama rose from her trance and smiled at Seraphiella. "My brother could not resist my gaze, and he kissed me." She carefully wiped the poison from her lips with the cloth Seraphiella handed her. If the slightest amount touched her untreated skin, she might die like her brother, Seth. Seraphiella hugged the girl. Naqama hugged her back and buried her face in the young woman's cold bosom. Seraphiella was not her mother. She was more valuable than a mother because she was teaching her how to get her revenge!

The sweet fragrance of the fermented syrup they thickened over a fire only an hour earlier filled the room. It was a mixture of Devil's Berries and the root of the Nightshade plant. They found the simple ingredients near their home and mixed them into a deadly potion. Next to the bowl of syrup was a tub of beeswax. The fatal poison could not penetrate her wax-coated lips. Seth's death would be violent. It would start with horrible cramps and hallucinations followed by numbness in the limbs. Total paralysis would follow, and then his life would abruptly end. She smiled as she thought about her brother's violent death and the horror it would bring her mother, Eve. Naqama hugged Seraphiella tighter. *Today is a great day*!

On the road to Seth's dwelling:

Seth thought about the woman as he hurried home. *Who was she? Why did she disappear? What did it mean?* He smiled as he looked up and saw his house in the distance. Dust rose from the ground as he fell to his knees, grasping his midsection. Excruciating pain engulfed him. His abdominal muscles tightened in agony as he bent over, unable to rise from his knees. The roar of a wild beast gave him the strength to lift his head and open his eyes. He looked towards his home and saw a giant, fiery creature stalking towards him. The beast snarled, and drool fell from its massive teeth as it moved in for the kill. *It will devour me!* He pushed his face down on the ground and covered his head with his hands. Fear and pain surged through him. His heart threatened to burst from his chest as it beat faster and faster.

At Seth's home:

Aklia was mending a garment made of animal hide when an angel of God suddenly appeared. She fell on her knees before the angel. "Woman, rise and heed my words. Your husband will die on the road if you do not do what I say! Hurry to your husband with a mixture of warm vinegar and mustard seeds. Force him to consume it or he will die. The mixture will neutralize the poison!" *Poison?* Aklia rose in fear and did as the angel commanded her. Once she had mixed the things, she ran down the road towards Seth. She found him lying face down in the dirt.

He's dead! Aklia's heart raced with terror as she rolled him over. He was alive, but his eyes rolled back into his head. She opened his mouth and poured the mixture inside. Seth choked and convulsed. After a few moments, he stopped shaking, and his breathing became steady. She forced his mouth open again and gave him the rest of the mixture. He choked once more but regained his breath quickly. *I am helpless*, she thought, as she held him in her arms. An hour passed, and Seth did not regain consciousness. *I was too late!* Aklia fell to the ground beside Seth and cried out unto God in prayer. "Lord God Almighty, I have done as your angel commanded me and yet my husband has not risen. Revive my husband so that he might serve you again.

God didn't answer Aklia, so she dragged his unconscious body back to their dwelling. He laid near death for three days and three nights as he recovered from the poison. When he woke, he said unto Aklia, "I fell into temptation and kissed a woman who came in a dream or reality. I cannot be sure which! Temptation overcame me, and I fell into Satan's trap. I kissed her and nearly died for my sin. God's mercy and your willingness to obey the angel saved me. I pray you and God will forgive me for my trespasses against both of you." When he finished speaking, he went to the altar and offered a sacrifice for his sins, and God accepted his offering.

Back at Satan's Lair.

The scrying mirror flew across the room and shattered against the rock wall. "AAAHHHHHHHHHH!!!!" Naqama screamed and stomped her feet in a tantrum because she was unsuccessful in her attempt to kill her brother. She fell onto her knees and beat the ground with her fists. *Revenge was in my grasp! I need her to suffer as I have suffered. Is there no justice in this world?* Her thoughts became broken, and she wept uncontrollably.

Seraphiella heard Naqama's fit and came to her room. "Why are you screaming and crying?" Naqama replied, "God sent His angel to my sister, Aklia. They cured Seth and ruined our plan!" The hatred and tears in her eyes brought a smile to Seraphiella's lips. *I can use her anger!* She would use it to turn her into a powerful weapon. Seraphiella reached down and pulled Naqama up to her bosom. "Be still my child. Your day will come. We will keep trying until we succeed, and you get revenge! Eve will suffer soon enough!”

CHAPTER 72

Years passed after Eve and Aklia's treachery against Adam and God. Adam devoted himself to God and spent most of his time at the Cave of Treasures. Eve was lonely and relied on the occasional visit from Aklia and Seth to lift her spirits. Adam's unwillingness to lay with her or spend time with her frustrated Eve. So, she went to him. She found Adam on his face praying and fasting to God at the Cave of Treasures. *He will keep praying unless I intervene!* She interrupted his worship and said, "Adam, you are my husband, and I need you! You only come to our dwelling to eat the occasional meal or sleep. If you continue to neglect me, I will dry up and blow away like the chaff of the field." Adam stopped praying and replied, "I have devoted myself to God, and I will not dwell with you or lie with you again unless God commands me." Adam's words were harsh, and she wept. *I no longer have a husband,* she thought, as tears of sorrow rolled down her cheeks. In despair, she left him and returned to her home.

Saphriael had no interest in humans, but Samael's conversation about women left him with many questions. So, he descended to investigate humankind for himself. He flew over the earth and searched for humanity. On the Mountain of God, he watched a beautiful woman enter a dwelling made of stone. Curiosity got the best of him, and he landed near the house. Silently, he approached until he stood just outside the entrance. He heard the woman weeping inside the cave. Through a small opening in the door, he saw the woman sitting with her legs folded under her, and her head resting in her hands. The woman's red hair hung to the floor and hid her face from him.

"Why are you crying?" he asked. Saphriael's question

frightened Eve, and she leaped to her feet. She grabbed the staff she kept as protection against wild animals. Horror filled Eve's eyes. *Samael must have told him about me! He is here to rape me also!* "Are you here to defile me as your brother did," Eve asked? *What?* the angel thought. "I am not here to harm you! Stories of your beauty and the wonder of women filled my ears, and I came to see for myself. Why are you crying?" he asked a second time. She answered him in a shaky voice, "I cry because I have lost my husband. He devoted himself to God so that he might be free from sin." In response, he asked her, "Shouldn't it be a sin to forsake your wife?" She wondered, *Is it a sin to neglect your wife to serve God?*

She is beautiful, Saphriael thought, and then he said, "Woman, wipe away your tears. If you accept me as your husband, you will be content in all things." Eve replied, "How can I be yours when you are not a man, and I am married to another?" He asked her, "Are you married if the man forsakes you for another? You are right about me not being a man, but can't I love and pleasure you? If I lie with you, won't you conceive and bear children unto me?" Eve considered his words and replied unto him, "You are right to say my husband has forsaken me to serve God, but whether we can marry or if I can conceive and bear children unto you, I know not."

He spoke again, "I must return to heaven, but I will revisit you tomorrow. Before I return, go to your husband and make him choose between you and God. If he does not choose you, then make him give you leave from your marriage to him. If he grants you a divorce from him, I will take you from this place and build a home. We will live together with our children." Eve was not sure about being with the angel, but she agreed to make Adam choose between her and God because she thought, *I cannot be alone!*

The next morning Eve found Adam praying and fasting before God at the Cave of Treasures. She said unto him, "Adam, I am lonely to the point of death. You must choose between serving God fully or dwelling with me as your wife." Adam listened to her, and he was sad because his heart was God's, and he would not return to dwell with her. So, he replied, "Woman, I vowed to God, that no living thing, not even my body, would ever separate me from God again. I cannot dwell with you." Eve replied unto him, "If this is your heart's intent, then give me my leave from you, so that I may find another." Her words tore Adam's heart in two, but he would not break his vow. "Let God dissolve the marriage bond between us because I will serve him only." Once again, Eve left him with tears upon her cheeks.

Later that morning, Saphriael returned and found Eve tending the flock near Seth and Aklia's dwelling. He landed near her and Eve's heart leaped with joy because someone desired her again. It had been a long time since she felt loved. Saphriael opened his mouth to speak, but Eve spoke first. "My husband dissolved our marriage before God and gave me leave from him." Her words pleased him, and he drew close to her. He bent down and placed his hand under her chin, lifted it towards him, and kissed her. She returned his kiss, and a strange sensation welled up within him. His loins stirred for the first time. *Samael was right!* He said unto her, "I will take you to the land of Nod, near the place where your son Cain and daughter Luluwa live. In that land, I will build you a home worthy of your beauty." Her cheeks flushed with embarrassment and delight. *It has been a long time since someone admired me!*

"I will go with you, but first I must say goodbye to my son, Seth, and my daughter, Aklia," Eve told Saphriael. He stood outside and waited for her as she said goodbye to her children. Aklia hugged her mother and wept because of her parents' divorce. Seth was not sad and said unto her, "This is good for both of you! Now, my father can serve God with no reservations, and you are free to marry another." Aklia disagreed with him, "It is not good. What is life without a mate and marriage?"

Eve told her children, "I have more news. An angel came from Heaven and asked me to be his wife. He is taking me to the land of Nod. I pledged myself to him, and he promised to build a home for us. He is waiting outside for me, and we are leaving tonight." They cried and hugged her neck. Eve wept and returned their embrace. Then she stood over Enosh and Afraima as they slept and kissed them softly on their foreheads. She blessed them in the name of God, smiled at her children, and joined Saphriael outside.

Seth and Aklia watched Saphriael take Eve up in his strong arms. His mighty wings spread as he cradled her close to his chest. They sprang into the air and flew towards the land of Nod. Seth and Aklia watched them rise into the heavens and disappear. *I will never see my mother again!* Aklia wept for her loss and went back into their home. She stood over her children and cried because they would never know their grandmother. Seth stood outside for a few moments longer. *Did my father make a mistake? Was letting their mother leave a sin? Can a man serve God without a wife?*

CHAPTER 73

Saphriael kept his promise to Eve and built her a beautiful home upon a hill overlooking the land of Nod and the city of Enoch. Then, he left her in the house with all the stores she could desire and returned to Heaven because God had a task for him. While he was gone, Cain and Luluwa noticed the elegant house upon the hill. They brought gifts and went up to admire it and welcome their new neighbor.

Cain and Luluwa marveled at the house as they approached. The house had a peaked roof with high arches and large doorways. They considered what mighty angel or God might reside within the home and second-guessed themselves, wondering if it was such a good idea to present themselves unto their new neighbor. As they approached the door, Cain admired the craftsmanship, which included metal hinges and a decorative door knocker made in the image of a large brass ring within a great lion's mouth. He did not know such things were possible because there was no knowledge of metalwork upon the earth.

Cain and Luluwa stood at the grand entrance of the home, frozen in awe, because a man or some being three times their height could walk through the door. Cain looked upon the knocker on the door and gleaned its purpose. He reached out with both arms, stretched upward as far as he could reach, and barely took hold of the ring and slammed it against the wooden door. It thundered as it hit the wood and he wondered who had made such a thing.

After several moments the door began to open slightly. They looked upward expecting to see an angel or giant man. To their surprise, they looked down and saw their mother,

Eve, standing in front of them. Cain spoke first, "Mother, how it is that you now stand before me in this mighty dwelling?" Eve replied, "Saphriael, a great and mighty angel, saw that Adam forsook me to serve God, and he had mercy upon me. He asked me to be his wife, and after Adam divorced me before God, I went with Saphriael. He built us this home, and when he returns from his service to God, we shall marry." Cain and Luluwa could not believe her words and thought, *Can this be true?*

After Eve finished greeting them, she hugged both of her children and wept because she missed them. They embraced for several moments, and then Eve invited them into the home. She told them about her adventures, the stories of Adam, Aklia, Seth, her stolen daughter, Enosh, and Afraima. In turn, Cain and Luluwa told her of Enoch, Jilani, Parthenope, Ligeia, Leucosia, and their other children.

Cain, Luluwa and Eve enjoyed their reunion and vowed to let the past be the past so that they could be a family again. Eve wanted to see Cain and Luluwa's children, so they planned to return after a short time, so they could tend to their fields and flocks. They inquired of Eve's needs, but she had none because Saphriael had seen to everything prior to returning to Heaven. Cain and Luluwa shared another warm embrace with their mother and returned home with joy in their hearts.

CHAPTER 74

Saphriael returned to Eve in the cool of the night as she prepared for bed. Secretly, he watched as she combed out her long red hair, *She is stunning!* "You are beautiful." She jumped because she did not hear him enter the bedroom. Eve playfully asked, "I am?" She saw the desire in his eyes as he looked at her. Adam had not looked at her like that in years. She reached up on her tippy toes and kissed him. He returned her kiss and picked her up in a loving embrace. She felt happy and safe in the comfort and security of his arms.

"Take me, let's consummate our union," Eve said as she looked into his eyes. Saphriael smiled, but sadly replied, "I want nothing more than to know all of your pleasures, but I am afraid you will become pregnant. I am not sure that I can watch you suffer in childbirth because I love you with all of my heart." His words touched her heart, and her desire for him became even stronger.

Eve said unto him, "Saphriael, your love knows no bounds, and my love for you is equal. I will give my life for you. What are the pains of childbirth compared to death?" Saphriael replied, "As long as breath is within my body, you shall not die. I will protect you even at the cost of my life or imprisonment." She kissed him more passionately than before.

Saphriael returned her kiss, cupped his hands on her round backside, and raised her to him. She wrapped her legs around his waist, gripping him with her thighs. Her delicate lips moved passionately upon his, driven by her desire to have him. Her arms grasped his neck. His arms wrapped around her back, pulling her tight against his chest. Her ample breasts pressed upon him, and their passion grew hotter.

"Put me down and lie upon our bed," Eve said. He gently put her down and laid flat upon their bed, looking up at her. She stared into his eyes as she disrobed him. Then, she rose and kissed him again. Her lips explored his body as she kissed and nibbled on his neck. She moved down to his chest, kissing him as she went. Her hands squeezed his muscular chest as she moved further downward. She teased him with the light touch of her tongue across his chiseled abdominal muscles. Her fingernails scratched downward from his chest, his abdomen and came to rest on his hips as she took him. He groaned with delight as her tongue glided down the length of him. Then she took him into her mouth.

His thoughts drifted back to his conversation with Samael in Heaven. *How could God keep this from us?* The feeling was indescribable. His eyes met hers as she looked up at him without stopping her rhythmic motion. Her red hair interrupted their gaze as her hands took hold of him while her mouth took more of him. A growing warmth welled up from somewhere deep within his loins. She pushed her red hair out of her eyes so she could look into his pleasure-filled eyes again. His muscles tightened as she responded by taking him deeper inside of her. *He is close*, she thought. She swallowed the tidal wave of pleasure as he cried out in the delight of his first orgasm. The glossy look of satisfaction in his eyes caused her to smile even though he was still in her mouth.

Eve wiped her mouth as she rose from between his legs. She let her gown fall to the floor as she gave him a sinister smile. His mouth fell open as he looked upon her nakedness. She paused and let him admire her for a moment. Every curve of her body called to him. He stretched out his arm and, she took his hand. He pulled her down to him. They kissed, and then she pulled away from him. She sat upon his thighs, and she took hold of him again. He watched as she guided his erection through her red veil and into her warmth. She moaned with delight as she lowered herself onto him.

After only a few moments, she cried out in the pleasure

of her first orgasm with him. Eve's warmth constricted upon him and drew his seed from him. As his seed flowed into her body, she erupted into multiple orgasms in succession. When the waves of pleasure subsided, she collapsed onto his chest. They laid still for several minutes until Saphriael broke the silence. "That was amazing!" He wrapped his arms around Eve in a lover's embrace. "Absolutely!" she said, and kissed him.

Saphriael was even more upset with God now. The pleasure that Eve shared with him rivaled anything he had experienced, even in God's presence! *Samael was right! God purposely kept this from us, but why?* Eve rolled off him and drifted off into a peaceful slumber. He pushed her hair behind her ear and admired her delicate features. She seemed more beautiful now!

Gusoyn, a Fallen One, had secretly watched Saphriael and Eve until they were both asleep. Then he crept up to bed beside Saphriael and whispered in his ear. A horrible vision of the future came to him in his dreams. In his dream, Eve was in the throes of labor. He stood beside her and attempted to comfort her, but he could not help her. She was great with child because a giant grew within her womb. The giant was the unexpected offspring produced by the union of an angel and a woman.

Eve screamed in agony as the child struggled against her. Blood flowed from between her thighs and pooled around her. Saphriael cried out to God, but God did not answer. He searched his mind for a way to save her, but he found no solution. Tears of sadness and horror rolled down his cheeks. He wept and held her hand until she died. Her abdomen moved and contorted as their child fought to free itself from her oxygen-deprived womb. Several moments later, the child stopped moving and died too. Saphriael felt sadness for the first time, and he wept uncontrollably.

"Saphriael," Eve called his name for the second time, but he still did not answer. Panic fluttered in her until his eyes rolled back forward and he returned to her. He blinked a few times and met her gaze with sadness in his eyes. "What's wrong? I was so afraid that I lost you!" He searched his mind for the right words but couldn't find any. So, Saphriael told her, "I was deep in thought concerning our future." He was afraid of her death, but she didn't press him further on the matter.

A few weeks later, Saphriael's worst fears became a reality when the time for the curse was upon Eve, but no blood came. *She is pregnant!* Thoughts of bearing children to Saphriael pleased Eve, but he did not seem excited. He spoke about the child, but in his eyes, she saw only loss and pain. So, she questioned him about it, "Tell me your concerns. Why are you not happy that I am with child?" Saphriael replied, "I had a dream about our future. You and our child will die in labor because the child in your womb is a giant. I could not save you or the child, and I watched as you both suffered and died a horrible death!"

Eve's heart sank. She looked down at her belly, which was already showing a child. *I should not be this big already*, she thought with a rush of panic! Her stomach was more significant than it was with her previous children, and they were twins. So, she asked Saphriael, "What can we do to prevent my death and ensure our child's life?" "Eve, I don't know what we can do, but I will save you both, somehow!" He hugged Eve, and then he kissed her. She was afraid, but she believed in his love for her. *Saphriael will save our child and me.* He left her in search of a solution.

CHAPTER 75

Satan sat upon his earthly throne, thinking. *How should I tempt or inflict suffering on Adam and Seth next*? As he considered this question, Gusoyn, came unto him and said. "Oh, great master of this earth, I bring you good news from the land of Nod." Satan replied, "Let me hear your news, and I will be the judge." Gusoyn wasted no time and gave him the news, "Adam granted Eve a divorce. The angel Saphriael came from Heaven and took Eve to be his wife. They live in the land of Nod, and she is pregnant with his child." *What, how can this be true?* Satan thought.

Gusoyn watched Satan intently after he delivered his incredible news. Satan tried to destroy Adam and Eve's relationship with God many times, but now they did it on their own. Satan's mind raced with the information that Gusoyn gave to him. *Saphriael's involvement made the situation even more exciting. Adam no longer has a wife! What kind of child will she have with an angel? What will God do when he finds out?* He smiled as his mind raced with the possibilities. Then a final question came to him. *How can I capitalize on these recent events?*

A plan took form in his cunning mind. *First, I will make sure the news of Saphriael's unlawful fornication with Eve reaches God's throne. The abomination born of their union will enrage God! I need to request an audience. I want to deliver this news myself!* Satan looked up and realized Gusoyn was still standing in front of him. He was smiling like a kid waiting for a reward. "Get OUT," Satan roared! The smile fell from Gusoyn's face as he fled the throne room.

He was about to proposition God for an audience when

doubt entered his mind. *I have failed or fell into one of God's secret plans, so many times! I need a better idea.* A few minutes later, he smiled with satisfaction. *With the proper manipulation, this will be huge! I'll use Saphriael to cause more angels to fall and split Heaven once more.* Satan left to find Saphriael.

Satan found Saphriael sitting on the bank of a brisk stream near his home in deep thought. He sat down and wasted no time getting to his point. "So Saphriael, you took Adam's wife, as your own?" "I did not take her! She gave herself willingly to me because Adam forsook her to devote himself unto God." Satan faked interest in the angel's response and asked, "How can a man forsake the pleasures of his wife to serve God? Especially with a woman as beautiful and voluptuous as Eve. Why are you sitting here, perplexed, contemplating your despair? Why aren't you enjoying your bride's embrace?"

Saphriael replied, "Eve is pregnant, and I saw a terrible vision. Eve and the child will die because the child is too large to pass from her." Gusoyn's face appeared before Satan as he considered his words. *He caused Saphriael to see the vision*! Satan knew it would come true if something did not change. *Samael raped Eve and corrupted Cain, but she was already pregnant. So, it seems logical their offspring will be something new, something better if God allows it to live!*

Satan spun his web of mischief. "What will you do then? Will you let both mother and child die?" Saphriael replied, "How can I save either? I am not God. Do I have the power over life or death?" "Saphriael, God is merciful." Satan fought off the sting of his words as he paused for dramatic effect. "Go to Heaven. Request an audience with God, throw yourself down before his throne, and beg him for their lives. Profess your undying love for Eve in front of your brethren. God will have mercy on you." He fought back a smile as Saphriael shook his head in agreement. *God might kill this pathetic fool!*

Without another word, Saphriael rose and took flight towards Heaven. He landed at the throne of God and requested an audience. God granted his audience and asked, "Why have you come before me, Saphriael?" "Lord, I have traveled throughout the world of man, and I found a woman there. Her hair is like the flames upon the altar, and her beauty is unmatched in heaven and earth. Adam forsook her, so I took her in marriage." God was not pleased and asked, "Who told you to take a wife? Did I give you my blessing?" Saphriael began to question his decision to approach God with this problem, but it was too late to turn back. "You have not spoken of marriage with angels or forbidden us to marry. Nor did you acknowledged the pleasure we can experience when we join them in a physical union. Eve deserves love, or will you just cast her out like a worn garment?" Saphriael expected God to strike him down for using such words, but his love for Eve overshadowed his fear. The angels in the throne room braced themselves for God's wrath.

Several silent moments passed as the audience waited for God's reaction. Finally, God replied with a renewed sternness, "I created Eve because it was not good for Adam to be alone. They were not born for the heavenly host to use for pleasure or companionship. Man and woman marry and have children to worship me! I have not sanctioned the union of angels with man, woman, or beast." Saphriael replied, "I took Eve for myself, and now she is pregnant with my child. I saw a vision, and they are both going to die during childbirth." God replied, "Why should I care? You did not ask for permission to marry or inquire what abomination might come from your union. The design of woman is not to bear children unto angels, but to man only." Saphriael spoke again, saying, "I love her, and I would not see her or the child within her die. What can I do to save them?" God looked upon Saphriael with mercy. He knew love brought them together and not the lust of the flesh. His heart was also troubled because he sensed that Satan pushed Saphriael to confront him.

So, God said unto Saphriael, "I will have mercy on her because your heart is true. If you truly desire to be with her, you must relinquish your heavenly body and become a man of flesh and blood." Saphriael looked at God in disbelief. He had not considered God might say such a thing. With joy in his heart, he replied, "Lord, I will take human flesh and become a normal man because my love for her is true!" God heard his words and said unto him, "Go back to earth and find the Blue Cohosh plant. Grind it into a powder and make a strong drink for Eve during the third month of her pregnancy. She will give birth to the child before it is too large to pass from her. Saphriael, know that when your feet touch the earth, you shall become a mortal man." God's words pleased him. He would gladly give up his immortality and take on humankind's fragile nature. *I will give my life for one more moment with Eve!*

Saphriael landed a short distance from his home near a patch of Blue Cohosh plants. As his feet touched the ground, he felt mortality for the first time. His wings vanished, and he became a normal man. He willingly accepted the change. *Eve and the child will live! Now we can have a future together*; he thought as he pulled several of the plants from the rocky soil.

Eve sat on the porch waiting for Saphriael to return. In the distance, a man approached, and Eve feared for her safety. When the man drew near, she recognized his face, *Saphriael!* She ran to him and hugged his neck. "Saphriael, you are a mortal man! How can this be?" "God had mercy on me. I agreed to become a man so I could spend my life with you!" He told her about his audience with God and all he said. He explained the power of the plants and showed them to her. She wept for his sacrifice because she knew how much he loved her. They went into their home, and he tossed the plants on a table next to the door after he closed it. He picked her up and carried her to their bedroom. They made love and fell asleep in each other's arms. Their hearts were full of love and happiness.

CHAPTER 76

God blessed Seth and Aklia, and they had many children who followed God's ways, but Efrim fell from God because of his envy. Efrim was born three years after Enosh, and he envied his older brother because God favored him. Enosh kept the field, and it bore bountiful harvests. Everything he touched grew and bore fruit like it was in the Garden of Eden. He offered abundant sacrifices from the fields and orchards to God, and he accepted them.

To make matters worse, Adam also showed favor to Enosh. He took him as an apprentice and taught him to be a priest of God. Like Adam, Enosh devoted himself to God and took a vow of chastity. When Enosh was not serving God, he spent time with his sister Noam. When Enosh reached the age of manhood, a strange feeling stirred within him as he looked upon his sister. *I love my sister*, he thought, but he could not marry, because of his vows of celibacy and devotion to God. Efrim saw how Enosh and Noam looked at each other, and it made him more envious of his brother. One day, he found his sister Noam and said, "I see you have eyes for our brother Enosh, but he cannot marry! We should marry, or you will die without children." Noam listened to him, but she loved Enosh and would rather die without children than marry Efrim. So, she told him plainly, "My heart belongs to our brother, and I have no love for you!" *Enosh and Noam will suffer by my hands*; he thought as he left his sister.

Efrim prepared a sacrifice to God and prayed for permission to marry Noam. He took the fattest sheep, without spot or blemish according to their custom. Besides the sheep, he stole the sweetest fruits from Enosh's orchard because God favored his sacrifices. He laid the sheep and fruit on the altar. Then Efrim cried out to God and begged him for Noam's hand in marriage. A mighty angel appeared before Efrim and asked him, "Why have you stolen fruit from your brother's orchard and sacrificed them as your own? Is the sacrifice for your sake or your brother's?" Efrim opened his mouth to speak, but the angel spoke first. "God accepts this sacrifice for your brother's sake. He shall marry Noam, and out of their union, a savior shall rise!" When he finished speaking, fire came from Heaven and devoured only the fruit. The sheep died from the heat, and the meat instantly spoiled. Maggots crept out of its nostrils, eyes, ears, mouth, and anus. The stench of death filled Efrim's nostrils and caused him to gag.

Efrim looked at the burnt sacrifice and the dead sheep in horror. In anger, he cursed God, "May Heaven burn and God with it!" Suddenly, he heard laughter behind him. He turned and saw an older man, dressed in white robes, mocking him. His hair was like wool upon his head, and he looked wise. Satan spoke to Efrim in the disguise of the old man, "Your God gave the desires of your heart to Enosh." Efrim replied with bitterness in his words, "How can you know my heart?"

Satan replied, "I will give you the desires of your heart. Just pledge your allegiance to me instead of God." Efrim replied, "I do not know you. Who are you that I should pledge my allegiance to you? Are you a God?" Satan replied, "I am like God because I can also grant your heart's desire." His words pleased Efrim because he was angry with God and wanted his sister. "What would you have me do?" Efrim asked. Satan replied, "Bend a knee before me and pledge an oath to serve me." Efrim took a knee and bowed his head to Satan, "I pledge my life to you in exchange for my heart's desire."

Satan spoke to Efrim, "Go take Noam by force and leave the Mountain of God. A raven will lead you to a place which I have prepared for you among Cain's family. They have also pledged themselves unto me." Efrim agreed with Satan's words and went out to the field where Noam watched over the flock. He hid in the shadows and waited for her to come close to him.

Efrim watched her for several moments without her knowledge. *She is alone!* Noam was petite and small of stature and posed no physical challenge to him. Silently Efrim stalked her until he was close enough to grab her. A twig snapped under his foot, and she turned. Noam looked into his eyes and saw ill intent within him. She screamed and tried to run, but he leaped on her like a hungry beast upon its prey. Efrim bound his sister's hands and feet. Then he placed a cloth in her mouth so that she could not scream. He tossed her on his shoulder and looked up. A large raven took flight from a nearby tree and led him down the mountain.

Efrim followed the raven until it landed in a tree when the sun was low in the sky. He laid Noam on the ground and gathered wood and built a fire for warmth and protection. The raven left while he made the fire and returned after he sat down next to his sister. Light from the flames flickered off the branches. The wind rustled through the trees, and finally, the raven returned to roost in a large tree above them. The bird descended and walked a few steps toward Efrim. A large piece of bloody flesh hung from its beak. Efrim held out his hand, and the bird dropped the fatty meat into his hand. He took the meat and roasted it upon the fire. Then he removed the cloth from Noam's mouth, "Are you hungry?" She did not speak. Despite her silence, he gave her a sip of water and fed her the meat. She drank and ate but refused to talk to him.

After a long period of silence, Efrim asked Noam, "Will you remain silent forever?" She did not respond. "It does not matter if you speak or not. You are mine, and in time you will grow to love me." She flinched as he tried to brush her cheek. When she turned back towards him, he pushed the hair out of her eyes. She jerked her head away from him. In anger, he slapped her hard across the cheek. "You will submit!" Then he snatched her breast and squeezed until tears filled her eyes. She finally spoke, "I will never give myself to you!" He replied, "Then, I will take you against your will because you are mine." When he finished speaking, he tore her garments off and looked upon her nakedness for the first time. She looked into his lust-filled eyes until he rolled her onto her stomach. He straddled her backside and took his manhood into his hand. Horror filled Noam as she felt him trying to penetrate her warmth. "NO, God save me, PLEASE!!" Efrim forced her face into the dirt, silencing her cries. He groaned in delight as he touched her bare flesh. She felt his warm flesh upon hers and prepared herself to handle him inside of her, but suddenly, he was gone. She rolled over, expecting to see Efrim preparing himself or planning something even worse for her. Instead, she saw a mighty angel standing over her.

Efrim suddenly found himself disoriented and flying backward through the air. As he flew back, he saw the mighty angel standing over his sister. Before he could violate Noam, the angel snatched him up and threw him across the field. He hit the ground awkwardly. His shoulder popped with an audible cracking sound, and his screams echoed through the trees. Efrim writhed in pain, rolling on the ground. Noam stared at the angel in disbelief. A moment ago, Efrim was on top of her. Now a mighty angel stood over her with a clean dress in his hand. She took the clothing and covered her nakedness. The angel helped her up and made a strange clicking sound. A branch snapped to her left. She turned and watched as a pack of wolves ran out of the trees. They snarled and growled as they moved towards Efrim. He cried out in fear as the drooling beasts circled him. They attacked Efrim, biting him and tearing at his flesh, but the angel forbade them from killing him. The wolves would torment him until the sun rose. Then, they would leave him near death, bleeding, unconscious, and naked in the field as the angel commanded them.

The angel took Noam in his powerful arms and leaped into the air. He brought her to the Cave of Treasures where Adam and Enosh worshiped God. "Enosh, God says, take your wife, Noam. You shall serve God with your wife. She will bear many children unto you, and a savior shall come from their seed. The savior shall be your grandson, Noah. He will be faithful to God when he purges the world of unrighteousness."

They rejoiced at the angel's words, and Adam gave Noam to Enosh. He took her unto him, and they built a home near his father and Seth. Enosh knew his wife, she conceived and bore Kenan and Mualeleth to him. Noam was fertile, and she bore many other children unto him, but many of their children turned away from God and served Satan.

CHAPTER 77

In the third month of Eve's pregnancy, Saphriael ground up the root of the Blue Cohosh plant, brewed it in a tea and gave it to Eve. Eve drank the bitter tea, and the first contractions and pains of labor struck her. She suffered for two days, and then she gave birth to a great and mighty child. The child was not like any other child born upon the earth. At the end of the first month, the child weighed fifty-six pounds. Saphriael and Eve named the child Nephili because he was the first giant among humankind.

God was impartial to the child because Saphriael and Eve conceived the child without his blessing. He allowed Saphriael to become mortal for Eve's sake, but he refused to bless the child further. Nephili was the first of a race called Nephilim. Nephilim and men would always be at odds. The Nephilim would have insatiable appetites, great size, and many would wield strange abilities like angels. Nephili was unique and would not be like future giants. He had a gentle nature because of his parents, Saphriael and Eve.

Nephili grew strong, and his legend spread on earth and in Heaven. At only five years of age, he stood fifteen feet tall. One day, while returning from the field with his mother, a mighty lion attacked them. The beast sought to devour Eve, but Nephili grabbed the lion with a hand on each jaw. He ripped the lion's head into two pieces with his bare hands, killing it immediately. Nephili skinned the beast and wore its hide as a cloak for all to see.

Nephili's great feats amazed even Satan, and he often visited him. He used many temptations and tried to enlist his service, but he would not bend a knee unto him. When Satan realized he would never bow to him, he devised another plan. At Satan's lair, he called the Fallen Ones unto him. He said unto them, "Saphriael, the angel of God, took Eve to be his wife and she bore him a son, Nephili. He stands above all men and has no equal of those born on the earth. What is stopping us from taking wives from the children of God for ourselves? Then our children will be mighty warriors and do our bidding upon the earth!" The Fallen Ones cheered in delight of his words. So, they took wives from the children of Adam and Cain unto themselves and ravaged them. The Fallen Ones' children came into the world as lust-filled ravenous beasts. They were unruly and hell-bent on destroying humankind, just as Satan hoped!

CHAPTER 78

Naqama mastered the black arts long ago, but she remained patient in seeking her revenge upon Eve. She tried to kill Seth in her youth, but God foiled her plan because Seth was one of his chosen vessels. Several years passed, and she watched and waited. Then the time came for revenge. Eve married Saphriael, an angel who became mortal to be with her. Later, Eve bore the mighty Nephili to him. Naqama considered many options when she planned her revenge, but murdering Eve was not one of them because *She needed to suffer and know loss!*

One night as Saphriael and Eve slept, Naqama slipped into their bedroom. She watched as they slept in a peaceful embrace. Naqama moved to Saphriael's side of the bed and stood over him. She whispered a powerful curse on him. Then she reached for the pouch hanging from her belt and opened it. The sand spider moved out of her bag. It stopped on her palm and looked at her with its six dark eyes. She smiled at her treasured pet, it was one of her oldest companions. She raised it from a spiderling into a creature spanning over four inches in circumference. Its venom was a powerful hemolytic that caused massive necrosis and hemorrhaging from a single bite, and there was no anti-venom.

She continued whispering her death chant as the spider climbed the wall near their bed. It crossed the ceiling until it was above Saphriael. The pace of her chanting sped up as the spider glided down the silky line of web towards its intended target. It swayed from side to side and turned as it rode the soft air currents downward. The spider stopped and waited, fractions of an inch above Saphriael's closed lips. Naqama waved her hand with her palm facing out away from her body. He gasped in response to her spell, his mouth opening with a snort, and the spider dropped inside.

Two seconds later, Saphriael woke, clutching his throat. *I can't breathe*, he thought as a stabbing pain erupted deep in his throat. Two more sharp pains and he choked. His terror-filled eyes grew larger as he struggled for breath. His throat was swelling, but that was not the most terrifying part. *Something is moving in my throat!* His oxygen-deprived mind and his situation caused him to panic. Then he saw something even more disturbing. An ominous figure with glowing red eyes stood in the shadows in front of him.

Eve woke, startled by the commotion, and grabbed Saphriael's shoulder. She turned him around to face her and looked into his eyes. His face was red, and veins bulged out of his forehead. His eyes were huge, and his mouth was open, but nothing was coming out. *Something is in his throat*, she thought in a panic! Saphriael's face was turning blue, and there was a bulge moving in his throat. The lump moved inside his throat like an unborn child pressing on its mother's belly. She was looking into his haunted eyes when the coughing started. Blood and saliva flew from his mouth and into her eyes. Her hands instinctively went to her eyes, but it was too late. Blindness replaced the initial burning sensation as she realized, *It isn't just blood and saliva!* She could not see it, but she felt the spider crawling up her forehead and into her hair. Shivers of disgust and fear flowed through her as she screamed in horror.

The spider moved over her head and down towards her back. Eve yelled, panicked, and swatted at her head, trying to dislodge the spider in her hair. After several frantic tries, she struck the spider, but her wild swing caused her other arm to strike Saphriael across the face. He fell over on the bed, holding his throat. She heard the spider hit the floor and scurry away. Then she heard something hit the floor beside the bed, *Saphriael!* Eve frantically wiped her eyes with their blanket.

The sound of the spider's tiny feet rapidly clicking across the floor sounded like thunder in her ears. *It's coming back!*

Naqama watched the scene unfolding before her with great pleasure. She laughed out loud when Saphriael fell onto the floor. Her revenge was going better than expected. Eve fell silent as Naqama's laughter filled the room. Eve struggled to see the person that was laughing. Then, Eve saw Naqama's glowing red eyes in the dark corner near the bedroom door. The hooded figure opened a pouch hanging from their belt and made a soft clicking sound. Eve heard something move on the bed. A faint flicker from the fire reflected off the spider's shiny black eyes. *It was right in front of* me, she thought as a new rush of horror surged through her. The spider turned, scurried across the bed, and leaped onto the floor. Eve watched as the spider ran up the hooded figures robes, looked back at her, and went into the pouch. *Saphriael,* she turned towards her husband. Her eyes confirmed what she already suspected. Saphriael was lying face down on the floor. He was not breathing and looked like a statue frozen in horror. Her eyes burned again as the tears of sadness came, *Saphriael is dead!* A few moments later, anger drove away Eve's grief as she turned to face the hooded figure.

Naqama locked gazes with her mother. She saw the anger, horror, and loss in her mother's eyes and smiled. *Now it's time to take the next step in my revenge.* She lowered her hood, and her golden locks of hair fell over her shoulders. The girl's piercing crystal blue eyes replaced the glowing red eyes of the hooded figure. They stared into each other's eyes for several moments. Eve's sobs were the only sound in the room.

Naqama broke the silence, "I am your daughter, Naqama. The daughter God gave to Satan because of your sins!" Eve's heart immediately sank because she knew the girl spoke the truth. The scary and yet beautiful young woman standing before her was a painful reminder of her past sins. Naqama spoke again, "I have been waiting a long time for my revenge. Your sins kept me from knowing a mother's love, and now, I have taken the love of a lifetime from you." Eve was speechless. She watched as Naqama pulled her hood back up as she turned and left without giving Eve a chance to respond.

Eve fell on her knees and wept as Naqama left. After a few minutes, she crawled to the other side of the bed and laid beside Saphriael. Then, she mustered the courage to look at him. Her shaking hand reached for his shoulder and rolled him over. His body rolled over first, and then his head followed. She screamed in the horror of his appearance. His lifeless eyes bulged out of his disfigured and discolored face. He was almost unrecognizable to her. Eve wept because she loved Saphriael more than Adam, and now she was alone again.

Three days later, Cain and Luluwa found Eve lying next to Saphriael's decomposing body. His stench overwhelmed the room, and yet Eve held his cold hand. Cain forcefully took Saphriael's corpse from her dwelling and prepared it for the funeral pyre. Luluwa took Eve to the river and bathed her because she refused to care for herself. Cain returned to them later that evening at Eve's home. He found Luluwa sitting with her mother, who laid on her wedding bed sobbing. "I bathed her, but I cannot force her to eat." Cain looked at his mom with sadness in his heart and said, "Mother, we will burn Saphriael's body on the funeral pyre tonight. Are you going to pay your last respects?" Eve sobbed harder but did not answer. Luluwa told Cain, "I will bring your mother out when it is time." Cain kissed their mother on the forehead, and then he kissed his wife, "Thanks."

Later that evening, Luluwa walked Eve out to Saphriael's funeral ceremony. His linen-wrapped body lay high upon the funeral pyre. Cain held a burning torch in his hand. He offered the torch to his mother. She looked at it and Saphriael's body for a moment before turning back to Cain. When her sad eyes met Cain's again, she fell on the ground sobbing. Luluwa knelt beside her and hugged her. Cain faced his family, which gathered around them. "I consecrate Saphriael's body to the earth. To Satan be the glory, amen." He put the torch to the dry wood, and the fire raged. When the fire consumed the body, Luluwa walked Eve back to her home.

In the days that followed, Eve mourned her husband's death and refused her family's attempts to comfort her. Eve would not eat or rise from the floor for seven days. She mourned Saphriael's death for thirty days in all. Then she rose and returned to the living with a broken heart. Nephili returned from his adventures and tried to comfort his mother. She loved Nephili, but he couldn't fill the void left by her husband's death. He reminded her of Saphriael. Cain, Luluwa, and Nephili questioned their mother about Saphriael's death, but she spoke only about the spider. She did not blame Naqama because her estranged daughter's actions were her fault. *My sins cost me the love of a lifetime,* Eve thought.

Back at Satan's Lair:

Naqama returned to Satan's lair in high spirits. As she walked down the dark corridors towards her chambers. She passed several rooms and grew concerned because some of the Fallen Ones took wives from the children of Adam and Cain. They spoke of Nephili and how their offspring would be like him. Her pace quickened as she thought, *I am one of the few women upon this earth! Will they take me too?* The male figure, Fallen One, demon or humankind, disgusted her. The thought of the filthy appendages hanging between their legs made her stomach turn. Naqama loved females, demon or human. In contrast to the male body, the female body was one of God's few masterpieces.

The heavy door slammed shut behind her, and she quickly latched the door. The cold water invigorated her as it splashed out of her cupped hands and ran down her face. She wiped the water off with a sigh. *Today was a great day!* As she sat down on her bed, she heard footsteps but saw no one. The hair on the back of her neck stood up. *I am not alone.* She called to her unseen guest, "Show yourself, coward!" Bael became visible and stood in the corner near her bed. She covered herself with her blanket. "Why are you in my chambers?" Bael replied, "Satan told us to take the women of this earth and I chose you!"

Bael's words struck Naqama's heart. "I am not a sheep or cow! Who can say who I will marry?" She knew her words meant nothing to Bael, but she could not stand the thought of being with him. Bael ignored her comments and got to the point of his visit. "Lose the blanket so that I can look upon your nakedness." Her stomach churned as she thought about lying with him, but she knew disobedience would probably kill her. So, she stood up and let her blanket fall to the ground. *What choice do I have?* Bael grunted like a boar in heat. *Disgusting!* He commanded her, "Come and pleasure me." Naqama's mind raced, searching for a way out of her current situation. She slowly walked towards him, wishing she could save herself. *He was too strong to defeat by magic or physical force. It was hopeless!* He sat down in the chair, and she reluctantly climbed onto his lap. "Stop, use your mouth first," he said as he pushed her to her knees. She was visibly disgusted, and her stomach churned with the thought of taking his filthy appendage into her mouth. "What are you waiting for?" He seemed to enjoy her disgust. She grasped the base of his member and took it into her mouth as she gagged. A sour, metallic taste filled her mouth, and she vomited a little in the back of her throat.

Bael grabbed the back of her head and forced her to take more of his vile member. His decay and filth made the act even more disgusting. When his member was hard as a rock in her mouth; he let her rise and mount him. It was far less disgusting to her this way, but she hoped he would release his foul seed quickly. Unfortunately for her, he was not even close to climax. The drone of her unenthusiastic actions infuriated Bael.

Naqama bounced upon Bael's member without pleasure. She was relieved when he pushed her off his lap, but all relief vanished as he shoved her over the arm of the chair. His instrument of torment tore her flesh as he thrust himself inside of her with no regard for her health or pleasure. She cried out in pain, and he enjoyed her more for it. Over and over, he relentlessly drove himself into her flesh as he cried out in pleasure. Tears of anger and disgust rolled down her cheeks. Her knuckles turned white as she squeezed the chair with each violating thrust. She vowed not to give him the satisfaction of crying out again. Blood dripped onto the chair as he dug his fingers into her shoulders and violently pulled her back towards him every time, he thrust himself into her flesh. She was numb to the pain and just wanted him to finish. Finally, Bael cried out in pleasure as his vile seed plunged into her. His seed filled her until it flowed out of her flesh and ran down her legs. She looked down in disgust and disbelief as his fluids mixed with her blood pooled on the floor beneath her. He collapsed on her with another disgusting grunt of satisfaction. His sweat and filth appalled her.

She struggled for breath because his weight was upon her, and her lungs could not expand. She silently screamed as she waited for him to pull his vile member out of her. However, several minutes passed before he rose from her. Bael's gross appendage slithered out of her like a wet eel. More of his seed gushed out of her in its wake and splashed onto the floor. She shivered in disgust as what remained of his seed oozed down her legs. He dressed and said unto her, "I will be back tomorrow. Please try to show more enthusiasm, won't you?" He laughed as he left the room. When the door slammed shut, her psychological dam burst, and she wept uncontrollably.

CHAPTER 79

In those days, the children of humankind multiplied and became a vast multitude of people. A sect of angels known as the Watchers saw Saphriael's love for Eve, heard about the pleasure of sex, and bore witness to his giant child. They also knew of Samael's exploits on earth and heard how the Fallen Ones took women as wives. The Watchers looked upon the women of the earth and desired them.

The Watchers grew tired of God's rule. Semjaza, their leader, asked his followers, "Why does God keep us from knowing the pleasures of women? Let's take what we choose. We will be like Gods on the earth!" Their lust for women and power overcame their desire to worship God. When they could no longer obey his laws, they left Heaven. The Watchers did not oppose God in an open rebellion as the Fallen Ones did; they left Heaven of their own accord.

Semjaza led the Watchers to the earth, and they lived on the base of the Mountain of God, near the land of Nod. They demanded humanity worship them and gave in to their desire for sexual gratification. Humankind built images, statues, and temples in their likeness. Many of God's children stopped serving him and worshipped the Watchers instead. The women of the earth offered themselves to the Watchers, and they fulfilled their sexual desires.

God saw humankind worshiping the Watchers and fornicating with them. His anger filled Heaven and spilled over onto the earth. He cursed the inhabitants of his mountain and those who worshiped the Watchers. He cursed them, saying, "The people who worship my creations instead of me are cursed! They shall rise against their neighbor, and their lands shall be in turmoil." His curse caused brothers and sisters to fight against one another. War and chaos abounded, and the world knew no peace.

God sent an angel to the Watchers and commanded them to return to Heaven. Semjaza beheaded the messenger, and they refused to submit to God's rule. In anger, God forbade them from returning to Heaven and cursed them. The Watchers' celestial bodies changed. Their wings and skin became dark as night, and their eyes were like a snake, yellow and glowing like the sun.

To bolster his army, Satan sent a messenger to the Watchers imploring them to join him. Semjaza beheaded his messenger, and they chopped his body into pieces. They placed the pieces in a basket and left them at the entrance to Satan's lair. One of the Fallen Ones brought the basket to Satan's throne. "Master, the Watchers dismembered our brother Artemus and cut him to pieces." Satan was angry because they killed his messenger and refused him. The Watchers held themselves in higher regard than the Fallen Ones.

Satan sent a second messenger, but he returned with no arms. He gave Satan a message from Semjaza. "God cast you and the Fallen Ones out of Heaven. Your bodies bear the scars of rebellion and your fall from Heaven. The Watchers left Heaven of their own accord. Therefore, we reign above you and the Fallen Ones!" Satan killed his messenger after he heard their words.

The Watchers tormented God and humankind. So, Satan tolerated them for a season because they opposed God. They led humanity away from God's laws and that assisted his plan. Satan sat on his throne, sipping wine and pondered the future. *War is on the horizon,* he thought, *I will kill the Watchers because they refuse to follow me! They will be an example for future generations!*

CHAPTER 80

Among the Fallen Ones, a great blasphemer rose, and his name was Yatsar. Yatsar approached the entrance to Satan's throne room and motioned to the guard. The guard came to him, and Yatsar said, "I want an audience with Satan." The guard nodded and disappeared into the throne room. A few moments later, he returned and said, "Satan will see you!" Yatsar entered the throne room. He reminded himself that Satan killed many of the Fallen Ones during his angry outbursts. *Bad news, bad ideas, or inappropriate comments might cost you your life! Present yourself humbly.*

Yatsar knelt before Satan and waited for permission to look up or rise. After several moments, Satan spoke, "Rise, Yatsar. Why have you come before me?" Yatsar replied, "Master, I came to ask permission to take Echidna, Lilith's daughter for myself." His request intrigued Satan. "Why? I gave all of the Fallen Ones permission to fulfill their lusts with Lilith's children?" Yatsar replied, "Master, I want her to pleasure me, but I also want her for another purpose. As a descendant of God's original human creations, I believe she might be what's missing from my experiments. With her, some conjuring and gene manipulation, I believe that I can bring new vicious creatures into this world."

Impressed by Yatsar's creative nature, Satan told him, "Take her and do your worst. May your first creation be worthy of guarding the gates of Hell! But know, if you fail to produce such a beast, you shall suffer a terrible fate." Yatsar bowed his head and replied, "I will not disappoint you, master." He left Satan's throne and took Echidna by force.

A smile formed on his lips, and he laughed like a giddy

child as he looked at Echidna. She was not like Lilith's other children. Many legends and rumors of her conception echoed through Satan's lair over the years. He looked upon her with great anticipation. She had beautiful blue eyes and long golden hair. Succulent bosoms sat on her chest like ripe melons before giving way to her rippling abdominal muscles. Red scales began at her navel, and her lower body was like a great serpent. A large black rattle adorned her powerful tail.

She is the key, he thought. Yatsar knew she would be the mother of his monstrous creations, but he lied to Satan about wanting to have sex with her. He intended to force her to fornicate with all manner of abominable creatures. She would be the mother of his hideous and evil creations. The mere thought of taking her after that sickened him.

The next day, he brought a hellhound to Echidna. Hellhounds were an unholy union of demon and wolf. When a Fallen One died, their spirits roamed the earth in search of a body. The fallen souls often possessed giant wolves and became vicious creatures which Satan sent to kill on his behalf. He commanded Echidna to lie down and allow the beast to mount her, and she willingly obeyed.

To his surprise, Echidna cried out in pleasure as the hell hound penetrated her. He left them during their unholy union because it sickened him to watch. Yatsar returned with a great lion. As the hound spilled its seed in Echidna, the lion tore into the hound's neck and ripped him off her. The lion mounted her, and their seed mixed within her. As the lion and hound's seed yet slithered within her, Yatsar slit his wrist with a ceremonial blade. His blood flowed down onto her hands as she pleasured herself and pushed his blood, and the beasts' semen deeper into her flesh. He chanted the ancient words which God spoke at creation. The seed of the hellhound, the great lion and his blood mingled and fertilized Echidna's egg. Yatsar smiled with satisfaction; *She will give birth to a mighty beast worthy of guarding the gates of Hell!*

Echidna became pregnant, and each day Yatsar conjured

spells and manipulated the beast within her womb. The creature grew stronger and pressed on its mother's womb. When Echidna's time came, her screams echoed through the corridors of Satan's lair. She struggled to birth the massive beast within her. Satan, who sat on his throne, smiled and wondered, *What kind of mighty beast will spring from her womb?*

The beast burst from her womb with a deep snarl. It had a muscular tarsal with four sturdy legs like a lion. Huge lion claws protruded from its massive paws. A mane of deadly vipers rose around its necks. Three ferocious dog heads with powerful jaws and razor-sharp teeth sat on its shoulders. The beast's tail was like a serpent but had a scorpion's stinger on the tip. As Yatsar admired the creature, venom spewed from its tail and splattered upon his face. His eyes burned, and his sight diminished until he was blind. He fumbled to the table, found the water bowl,washing the poison from his eyes.

When Yatsar's sight returned, he saw Echidna nursing the beast. "Your name shall be Cerberus," Yatsar proclaimed. She nursed the pup until he was a full-grown beast which craved blood and death. Yatsar took Cerberus from his mother and presented him to Satan at his throne. Satan was rarely impressed by his subordinates, but this creature amazed him. Yatsar wanted to keep Cerberus, but he knew Satan would not allow it. Satan commanded his guards to chain Cerberus to the gates of Hell.

Satan watched as Cerberus entered the gates of hell, and then he turned to Yatsar. "Go back to your chambers and continue your work. Create more vicious and hideous beasts. So, we can release them into the world. They will torture and kill humankind and be a blasphemous mockery unto God. Let no creature be safe from your corruption and manipulation, not even humankind!"

CHAPTER 81

Bael returned to Naqama each day and forced her to lie with him and perform many deviant sexual acts. After a short time, she conceived his child. He continued to defile her until the third month of her pregnancy when the child was too large for her womb. Naqama ground the root of the Blue Cohosh plant and brewed it into a strong tea. She drank the tea, and the curse of labor fell upon her. The pain of Eve's curse was unbearable, and she fell on the floor in agony. Hours passed, and yet the child did not come. Bael approached her chambers and heard her screams. He took pleasure from her pain and suffering. His laughter drowned out her cries and echoed down the dark passages of Satan's lair.

Seraphiella returned from foraging for supplies, and she heard Naqama's cries and Bael's laughter. She went to Naqama and said, "Bael takes great pleasure from your torment. Hush now and suffer quietly, so he can't take pleasure from your pain. If you heed my words, I will help you as your midwife." Naqama shook her head and bit her lip as the next contraction came upon her. Her muscles tightened, and her body strained as it tried to push her unborn child into the world. Days passed as she struggled to give birth. Bael's child grew faster than those who came before him. She waited too long to consume the root. The child could not pass through her hips without breaking her in two. Seraphiella tried to comfort her, but there was no way to ease her suffering. She could not save her and the child.

Naqama cursed God and Bael as she suffered. Another violent contraction came, and blood ran down her legs. *I am going to die*, she thought. The child within her womb fought for its own life. It clawed and kicked at her belly. Images of Bael looking at her lifeless body with their child in his arms filled her with rage. She would not let him celebrate the product of his continuous violation of her.

So, Naqama conspired with Seraphiella to take her own life and get the power for one final curse. She cried out in agony, "Bring me my book." Seraphiella retrieved her Book of Shadows from the bedside table. Another terrible contraction came, and the child tore at her again. The pool of blood around her thighs grew larger. She cried as she rifled through the pages, looking for the spell she needed, "Got it!"

Moments later, Seraphiella passed her a ceremonial blade and lit the ceremonial bowl of fire. Naqama drove the knife into her eye and plucked it from her skull. She ripped the connecting tissues, severing it from her body, and held it over the bowl of fire. "AAAHHHHH," Naqama screamed and ground her teeth as her pelvic bone split in two. The child's hand sprung from between her thighs as it fought to leave her womb.

She spoke in the devil's tongue and said, "As I have taken my eye, let this child and all of those like him be cursed to see the world through only one eye. Their deformity shall make them villains unto all who see them." She let her hatred for Bael flow through her words. When she finished speaking, she tossed her eye into the fire. It popped, sizzled and hissed as the fire consumed the moisture and it turned black.

Naqama spoke again, "Let this child also bear another deformity, so that his father will remember how he took me by force, and I received no pleasure from his perverted acts." Then she drove the knife into her abdomen. The blade sliced the babe's cheek from lip to ear. More blood rushed from her stomach, but she would not die from this wound. She looked up at Seraphiella one last time and drove the blade into her chest. The sharp knife pierced her heart and sealed the curse forever. Her lone remaining eye blinked uncontrollably as her spirit fled from her. Her last glimpse of this world came as Seraphiella raised the bleeding child from her womb. She gazed into the child's hideous one eye and smiled as she exhaled for the last time. Seraphiella cut the child's cord, bathed it and wrapped it in cloth. Then she took it to Bael.

He did not rise when she came in with the child. *Children bring me no joy. I am incapable of love*; he thought as he took the child from her. He turned the child towards him so he could look upon it. "What have you done to this child?" he asked as he looked at its single large eye and a fresh scar that ran from lip to ear. Seraphiella replied, "Naqama cursed him and all the children of the Fallen Ones. They will all have one large eye." "What about the scar upon his face?" "She stabbed the child while he was in her womb, so you will remember she was unwilling."

Bael's dark, bellowing laughter echoed through the tunnels, chambers, and caverns of Satan's lair. He was impressed by her efforts but laughed because the scar and the child only served as a trophy of the pleasure, he stole from her. *The curse of the single large eye will bring horror upon the men of this world. Their children will fall upon humankind with great violence, and humanity did not stand a chance.* Bael looked forward to seeing what he would become.

He turned to Seraphiella, "The child shall be called Tsarebeth," which means scar. "You will take the child and care for it as your own. Do not teach him the dark arts because he shall be a brute monster. He will bring terror upon man and beast." She bowed and said, "As you have commanded, so shall it be." Then, she took the child from him and left his presence. Bael imagined the violence his offspring would bring to this world. A smile formed on his twisted lips as he watched the demon leave. *I will visit Seraphiella as I did Naqama*, he thought.

CHAPTER 82

Adam saw Seth's love for God and his wife, remembered Eve, and sadness fell upon his heart. He prayed unto God on her behalf. Suddenly, an angel appeared unto Adam and said, "It is good that a man should not take a wife and devote himself fully unto God if he can overcome the flesh. God sees the sadness upon you because there is still love for Eve in your heart. Seth's sister murdered Saphriael, Eve's husband, because she is angry with her mother. Eve is mourning his loss because his love for her was so great that he forsook his celestial body to love her as a man."

When Adam heard about the angel, he wept for Eve's loss. Then, he spoke unto the angel saying, "Is it lawful before God for me to marry Eve again so that I can care for her?" The angel replied, "It is lawful, but you must find balance in your life. A man's wife needs love. It is for this reason that God gave Eve unto you in the garden." The angel's words pleased Adam, and he left the Cave of Treasures and told his children about his plan. His plan made them happy because they longed to see their mother's face again.

Satan listened to their conversation from just outside the entrance of their home and could hardly believe his ears. *Had God become so soft that he allowed his precious children to do whatever they pleased? Adam pledged his life to God and then changed his mind because he was lonely, and God was fine with it? His former master cast him out of Heaven and showed him no mercy, but now God shows mercy to Adam without limitations!* Adam's desire to reunite with Eve did present Satan with another opportunity. Satan would conspire with Lilith to bring Adam to his knees once more. He returned to his lair and planned Adam's demise with Lilith.

Eve mourned Saphriael for more than thirty days, but she was still bitter. She no longer prayed to God because she could not comprehend how a compassionate and just God could have granted Saphriael the ability to become human only to allow Naqama to kill him. Eve blamed God more than her estranged daughter. *I cannot serve a God who allows such tragedy to fall upon his children*, she thought.

Suddenly, the thundering sound of the metal door knocker startled her. She opened the great door and found a young man standing before her. The young man appeared to have run a great distance. His breathing was heavy, and sweat ran down from his head as if he poured a vessel of water on himself. He struggled to catch his breath for several moments. Then he said unto her, "Come quickly, Cain and his family are sick with a high fever, and I am afraid they will die!" Eve cried out in fear and anger as she cursed God once more. *How could God be so cruel?* she wondered. She gathered her cloak, shut her door, and ran into the night towards Cain's house.

The young man watched as Eve disappeared into the darkness and then he, Satan, called unto Lilith. Lilith walked gracefully out of the shadows. When she stood with him, she lightly touched his thigh and then he kissed her passionately. He could still taste the blood of her last kill upon her lips. *There is no time for such things*; he thought as he pulled away from her and said, "Adam is almost here. Go into Eve's home and prepare yourself for him."

Adam journeyed down the mountain and found Eve's dwelling in the Land of Nod. He knocked on the door and patiently waited for her to answer, contemplating the conversation he would have with her. *I ignored Eve to devote myself to God! She begged and pleaded for my attention. I let her go, she found love again, but now he is dead. What words could he say to her? How could he win back her love?* He knocked harder the second time, and the door creaked as it opened slightly. He peered in and saw nothing, but the glare of a fire coming from another room.

He heard a soft melody coming from the well-lit room. Cautiously and quietly, he made his way to the office. His eyes strained to adjust to the light coming from the candles and the fire that burned brightly on the other side of the room. Then he saw Eve, and he was unable to look away from her. Eve sat with her back to him, and she was naked. She hummed a sweet melody and bathed herself with water from the basin in front of her. Her beauty caused his loins to stir with desire.

Lilith had heard him knock twice and enter the home after she nudged the door slightly open. Even now, she could feel his eyes upon her and his desire to have her. The intoxicating smell of the pheromones that he unwillingly produced heightened her arousal. She could hear his heart beating faster and faster, and with each beat, she wanted him more. The thought of taking him unknowingly again pleased her very much. She was surprised that the idea of having him again had caused her hand to drift down between her thighs. Lilith gently pleasured herself as she thought about him watching her.

As Adam watched Eve pleasure herself, he became aroused and moaned softly. He immediately realized that she heard him. In horror, he watched as Eve quickly turned to face him. Lilith half-heartedly covered herself with her arms and the cloth as she imagined Eve would do and put her best shocked and surprised look upon her face. "Why are you here?" she asked him. Adam replied unto her, "I have come to ask you to be my wife once more." She replied, "Take me, then." She lowered her arms, revealing her nakedness to him. Without a second's delay, he took her up in his arms and kissed her passionately. His hands wandered down her back until they rested on her backside. Their passionate embrace and kiss lasted for several moments.

Lilith could not conceal her desire to have him inside of her. She was wet in anticipation of knowing him again and skillfully took off his garments as they kissed. Suddenly, she pulled away from Adam and shoved him. His eyes were wide with surprise as he stumbled backward and fell back upon the bed. Surprise became wanting as she crawled on top of him and kissed him passionately. Lilith looked into his eyes and saw his delight as he entered her warmth.

It had been so long since he had felt such pleasure. A few minutes later, his muscles tightened as the first sign of his impending climax. He spilled his seed and shook with orgasm. To his surprise, Eve suddenly cried out in pleasure as her body shook with an orgasm of her own. Then, she collapsed upon him. As she lay upon him, her warm breasts pressed upon his chest, and he could feel her breath upon his neck. Lilith stayed on top of Adam for several minutes, relishing another victory over her poor husband. She expected him to be quick to orgasm because he had not known Eve for many years, but she was surprised by hers. *Why do I enjoy stealing his seed so much?* She did not have an answer, so she rose from him and said, "I will go to the stream and get us some water. I will warm it over the fire so that we can take a bath together." The suggestion pleased him, and he watched as she put her clothes on and left.

Lilith met Satan outside, and they shared a passionate kiss in the shadows next to the house. Satan looked upon his beautiful wife, who once again stood in front of him in her natural form. She saw his desire, knelt before him, and pleasured him. As she took him into her mouth, he thought, *Lilith is an incredible creature.* He looked down into her deep, emerald eyes. Lilith saw the familiar twinkle in his dark black eyes just before she tasted his seed. She pulled him deeper until he finished, and then she rose from him. With a seductive smile, Lilith looked at him and wiped her lush lips. He watched her wipe his glistening seed from the edge of her mouth and lick her finger clean. He wanted to take her right there, but he knew there was no time for that. Eve was approaching.

Eve's mind raced with the possibilities of why the young man deceived her *If he was a young man at all! Cain and his family were healthy and safe. What was the meaning or purpose of such deception?* She half expected to find her home destroyed or on fire, but everything seemed the same as she left it. As she entered her home, she saw light coming from her bedchamber. When she entered the room, she could not believe her eyes. Adam was lying naked on her bed. She stared at him in disbelief as he slept in peace. Confused and somehow angered by his presence, she yelled his name, "ADAM!" He leaped up startled from a deep sleep.

Adam strained to shake the sleep from his eyes as he looked at her. "Where is the water?" he asked. "What water and why are you here?" Adam gave her a puzzled look, "The water that you went to get so that we could take a warm bath, and you know why I am here. As I told you earlier, I am here to make you my wife again." Adam's words made no sense to her. "I have no idea what you mean! You were not here when I left to see Cain and his family. I just returned from their home to find you here naked upon my bed."

Adam told her of the events that led to him being upon her bed, and she again affirmed to him that it was not her. They realized that Satan and Lilith conspired this charade against them. They were both angry, but rage welled up within Adam. For the first time in his life, he thought, *I would kill her if I could! Cain murdered in anger, and God cast him out, but was it a sin to kill something evil?* He looked towards the heavens and asked God to forgive him for lying with that foul witch again.

Adam realized that he needed to explain the purpose of his journey. "Eve, I came here to make you my wife again and bring you back up to the mountain of God. I have seen the error of my ways, and I will not forsake you again." His words pleased Eve, but she was still angry with God because of Saphriael's death. Eve also remembered her loneliness on the Mountain of God. She worried that if she returned to him that he might forsake her again. So, Eve asked him, "How can I be sure that you will not forsake me again?" Adam replied, "I must find a balance between God and my wife. To forsake you again would be a sin before God. If you are my wife again, we will live together near our children." Eve thought about his response and said, "I will consider your request and give you an answer tomorrow. You can sleep in this room and I will rest somewhere else."

That night an angel of God appeared unto Eve. The angel said unto her, "Fear not Eve, take Adam as your husband because he has seen his mistake and will not forsake you again. God has a plan for you both and your son, Nephili. He will reside on the Mountain of God." Eve listened to the angel's words because they pleased her, and she still had deep feelings for Adam. She also worried that Nephili might fall to evil if he remained in the Land of Nod. The angel departed, and she had her first good night's sleep since Saphriael's death.

Adam woke before sunrise and prayed unto God. As he prayed, Eve came to him. He stopped praying when he heard her approach and rose to greet her. She told Adam, "An angel of God appeared to me last night. I heard his words and yours, and I will go with you, but I must say goodbye to Cain, Luluwa and their children. The angel also told me that my son, Nephili, must come to the Mountain of God because God has a plan for him." Adam joyfully replied, "Go unto them, but I cannot because they are dead to me because Cain killed his brother Abel." Eve was sad that Adam would not see Cain, Luluwa, and their children. In sorrow, she left him and journeyed to say goodbye to her children and their family.

CHAPTER 83

At Satan's Lair:

Satan sat upon his earthly throne, contemplating his next move. As he considered his options, one of the royal guards approached him. "Master, Aym has returned and is requesting an audience." "Send him in," Satan replied. Aym entered and bowed before Satan. Then he said, "Master, while I was spying on Eve, an angel came to her. The angel told Eve to return with Adam to the Mountain of God. He also told Eve that Nephili should go up with them because God has a plan for him." Aym's words sickened Satan. *Why doesn't God tire of protecting and showing mercy to Adam, Eve, and their children? Where was our compassion?* He fought back his anger and considered all his options with the skill and cunning of a master strategist.

Aym watched Satan and dared not interrupt his thoughts. After several minutes, Satan said unto him, "Where is Nephili, and when do Adam and Eve plan to make their journey up the mountain?" Aym replied, "Nephili is wandering the wilderness in search of adventure. Eve is visiting with Cain and his family. They sent one of Cain's children to find Nephili and tell him about his mother's plan to return to the Mountain of God and Adam. They will also tell him what the angel said about God's plan for him!"

Satan called the elite among the Fallen Ones to the throne. "What of the children born to the Fallen Ones. Bael spoke first, "Our children have grown strong, but they only have one eye." Satan replied, "I don't care how many eyes they have. Can they see? Will they kill our enemies?" Bael replied, "Yes, Lord, my child is only ten years of age, but he is already twenty-five feet tall!" "Good, send ten of the one-eyed giants into the wilderness to find Nephili. Tell them to kill him and bring me his head. Then, send ten more to kill Adam and Eve on their journey!" Bael left to send the giants out as Satan commanded him.

In the wilderness near the Land of Nod:

The first group of one-eyed giants went into the wilderness to find Nephili. They traveled in a pack and left a trail of broken trees and branches in their wake as they bulled through the dense foliage. The one-eyed giants were unintelligent, brute beasts focused on a single mission. *Kill Nephili and bring back his head.* Deeper and deeper, they wandered into the wilderness. When the sun set in the evening sky, they stopped and made camp until morning.

High above the one-eyed giants, Nephili sat upon a huge boulder. He watched the giants stop and make camp because the wilderness was treacherous in the darkness. *They are here to kill me,* he thought. Rumors of the one-eyed children of the Fallen Ones spread after they abducted several human women. They were awkward beasts who destroyed everything in their path. Nephili towered over the cyclops giants. He was thirty-five feet tall, but there were ten of them. He would have to use all his cunning and intelligence to defeat them.

Nephili woke before sunrise. He ate as he planned to defeat them. The wilderness was his home, and he knew it well. When he finished eating, he packed his things. With his plan complete, he stood in an opening above a steep, rocky incline. The lazy giants had not risen or nourished themselves, so now was the perfect time to start a fight. He yelled and howled down to the giants who slept below him. After several moments one of them woke and looked up at him.

The other giants woke and shook the sleep from their eyes as they tried to figure out why their comrade was yelling. They roared as they saw Nephili and rose from their slumber.

Without delay they rushed to the base of the incline, leaving their supplies behind. They shook the large timber clubs they wielded as weapons into the air. Nephili selected this spot because it would be difficult to climb with their clubs. It was very dangerous without equipment. He took one of the round boulders from the pile he had constructed. When the giants started their climb, he hurled the first of many rocks down at them. The rock bounced off the cliff several times before it crushed one of the giant's legs as he attempted to evade. He cried out in agony as his massive shin bent out at an unnatural angle. His suffering ended with a powerful blow from one of his companions. The club split his skull, and its contents spilled out like a ripe melon upon the rocks.

One down! Nephili didn't celebrate or waste any time. He continued to heave the massive rocks down at the giants. Left with no alternative, they abandoned their clubs and climbed faster. Another boulder glanced off a giant's head and shoulder, breaking his collarbone and ripping his ear from his skull. The giant lost his grip and died upon the rocks below. *Two down!* Another giant fell when a deadly viper hiding in the rocky cliff bit him. The fall killed him before the poison could. *Three down!*

The one-eyed giants soon learned to hug the walls to avoid Nephili's rocks, and they became ineffective. Three giants were dead, but seven remained. He could defeat three or four in hand-to-hand combat, but seven was an impossible task. He needed to improve his odds. Nephili's agility would be his next weapon because he was as graceful as a normal man. He had a distinct advantage if he confronted these brute beasts on uneven terrain.

The first one-eyed giant reached the top of the cliff and peered over the edge only to meet Nephili's club. The powerful blow sent him, end over end, down the steep incline. His lifeless body landed on a jagged rock formation about halfway down the cliff. *Four down!* The other giants crested the cliff together before they fell to Nephili's club too. Nephili was already running away from them. The six giants paused for a second, took a few breaths, and started after him.

Nephili's feet thundered on the ground as he ran. He traversed the narrow path up towards the next peak. Rocks rolled down the sides of the trail in his wake. The one-eyed giants chased him, but they labored clumsily behind him and could not match his pace. Most of them fell several times, sustaining bumps and bruises, but none of them stopped pursuing him. *My plan might not work*, he thought, but then one of his pursuers slipped on a loose rock and tumbled over a steep embankment. *Five down and five to go!*

When Nephili reached the next peak, he turned to survey the giants chasing him. The largest of his pursuers was several hundred feet ahead of the others. *I can kill him before the others catch up!* He watched the giants as he caught his breath. Water rushed from the wineskin into his mouth, *Ah, still cold.* He rubbed the excess water from his beard with the back of his hand as he watched the first giant approaching.

The one-eyed giant stopped in front of Nephili and took a deep breath. The giant's huge eye sat disturbingly in the center of his forehead. Nephili did not give him a chance to catch his breath. He lunged forward raising his club. The club missed its intended target and struck the giant's shoulder because he turned to avoid the blow. He staggered backward, but he regained his balance. The one-eyed giant lunged at him with a deep battle cry. Nephili sidestepped the giant, stuck his leg out and tripped him. His momentum sent him tumbling to the ground, face first. Before the giant could roll over, Nephili brought his club down on him. It hit just below his shoulder blades with a loud snapping sound. The giant threw his head back and screamed in agony. Nephili turned with his club to his side and swung again. It met the giant's face as he was rolling over. The giant's eye exploded. Pieces of tissue and fluids splattered into the air. Nephili wiped parts of the eye off his face as he watched the blood pool around the giant's lifeless body. *Four giants remain!* He started running again.

He was only a short distance away when he heard the remaining giants cry out in anger when they found their dead companion. Fueled by rage, they chased Nephili even harder. Nephili reached the cliff at the end of the trail. It was five hundred feet straight down, with rocks to the left and water to the right. He survived the leap once before, so that was an option, but only if the giants defeated him in combat.

The first of the four remaining giants reached him a few seconds before the others. He lunged at Nephili, who stood with his back to the cliff. Nephili sidestepped the awkward beast. With his empty hand, he pushed the giant, increasing his momentum. The giant tried to stop, teetered on the cliff's edge, and swung his arms to regain balance. He looked back at Nephili with one horror-filled eye and tumbled headfirst to the rocks below. *Three giants left, no time to celebrate!* Quickly, he moved further away from the edge to ensure that he didn't fall while fighting. The remaining giants stopped short of him and pulled three small trees from the ground to use as weapons.

The giants inched closer to Nephili, spreading out to keep him near the cliff and prevent his escape. They growled and grunted at him, trying to intimidate him. Nephili had killed seven of them and was not afraid of those who remained. *Let's finish this*; he thought as he moved from side to side, changing his fighting stance to confuse them. They moved with him until they were in striking distance. Nephili swung, and the first giant dodged, but the second was not as fast. The blow caught him in the side, and he tumbled into the third giant. Before Nephili could turn to defend himself, the first giant hit him with a powerful blow. The one-eyed giant's makeshift club smashed into his ribs, and he cried out in pain and anger. He pushed aside the pain and countered with a devastating blow to his attacker's leg. The giant's knee buckled, tearing his ligaments and he fell under his weight.

Nephili spun to face the other two giants just as they lunged at him. He was not fast enough. One giant hit him high, and the other one hit him low. The ground drove his breath from him. The giants were too close for clubs. So, they beat him and clawed at his flesh. Nephili's breathing returned, and he struck the giant on his chest in the side of his head. The punch stunned him for a second, and he capitalized with another more powerful roundhouse, which sent the giant tumbling to the ground. He looked down at the giant on his legs just as he struck a powerful blow to his groin. Nephili cried out in pain as his hand searched for his club. His fingers found the handle. "DIE," he cried as he swung the club towards the giant who punched him a second time! The momentum of Nephili's strike lessened the impact of the giant's punch to his groin. Nephili's club struck the giant's head, knocked him unconscious and sent him to the ground.

The giant that had been on Nephili's chest composed himself and rose to face him. Nephili swung his club with all the force he could command. The club drove the giant backward until he teetered on the edge of the cliff. His arms frantically searched for some invisible rope or handhold that would prevent him from falling. Nephili kicked him in the chest. The giant let out a horrified gasp as he fell to the rocks below. *Only two giants remained, and one could not stand,* Nephili thought. The giant with the injured knee laid on the ground and wept with pain and anger.

Nephili looked into the uninjured giant's eye and saw fear, anger, and determination. They jockeyed for position as they moved in a circle. Several seconds passed as they searched for weakness and an opening in their opponent's defense. Finally, the giant abandoned strategy and lunged at him. Nephili dropped to one knee, the giants club missed its mark and swung over his head. He thrust his club upward. The club struck the giant in the groin, and he fell to his knees, bent over grabbing himself. Nephili thrust his club upward a second time and rose while the giant was on his knees. The club struck his opponent under the chin. He hit the ground with a dull thud and did not move. Nephili grabbed his ankles and hurled him off the cliff. Then he turned to the giant with the injured leg. In horror, the giant tried to rise but fell again. His over-sized eye looked up at Nephili, begging for mercy. He showed the giant no mercy and struck him with a powerful blow. His neck snapped, and his head drooped backward until his lifeless body fell back upon it. Nephili fell on his backside and breathed heavily. *It is over*; he thought as he breathed a sigh of relief!

CHAPTER 84

At Satan's Lair:

Satan sat upon his throne, enjoying one of the many pleasures of this world. Seraphiella, Lilith's daughter, knelt between his legs. Seraphiella rivaled Lilith's skills in the art of fellatio. Her split tongue danced and constricted on his member in ways he could not comprehend. Plus, Bael desired her, and that's why Satan took her. As Satan neared orgasm, Aym barged into the throne room, saying, "Master, our giants failed to kill Nephili. He has killed all of them!" Satan cried out, not because of his news, but in pleasure as Seraphiella drew his seed from him. He grasped the armrests of his throne as he shook in pleasure. As the spasms of pleasure faded, his cries of joy turned into rage.

Seraphiella rose from between his legs and smiled with delight. The back of his hand caught her off guard, and she tumbled from the throne down to the stone floor. She wiped the blood from her split lip and scurried out of his presence. Satan was furious. Aym kept a safe distance to avoid being his next victim. Satan pounded on his throne, ripped down the wall tapestries and threw golden decorations across the room. His tantrum lasted several minutes, and then he stared at Aym in anger. *He is staring into my soul,* Aym thought.

After several long moments, Satan turned away from Aym and said, "Send Ayporos and four other Fallen Ones to join the giants who will attack Adam and Eve on the road. Tell them to kill them, and if Nephili joins them, kill him too! Make sure their deaths are painful. Show them the same mercy God showed us. Everyone that worships God shall suffer at our hands! I swear it upon my life." Aym nodded but didn't speak.

He left the chamber relieved that Satan did not kill him in anger.

Tsarebeth, the son of Bael led ten giants down the road leading up to the Mountain of God. Ayporos, Vepar, Haures, Amudusias, and Serephah joined the ambush, but they would not be part of the giant's formation. The Fallen Ones selected a narrow pass to the south of the giant's position. Their ambush position had the high ground on both sides of the road. They positioned themselves on the high ground, set a watch, and waited for their unsuspecting victims to pass by.

In the Land of Nod:

Eve finished saying her goodbyes to Cain, Luluwa and their children. She joined Adam at her home, and they prepared for their journey back up the mountain. However, Eve was sad because Adam continued to refuse to see his children,. "Cain is dead to me!"

That night they rested for their journey. Eve worried about Nephili because she had not heard from him. The next morning Adam and Eve walked outside to leave and saw a young man approaching. He greeted them, "My name is Bartholomew. I have heard about the Mountain of God; the Cave of Treasures and the gifts God gave to you." Adam considered the young man's words for a moment and said unto him, "I do not know who told you about these gifts, but I welcome any man who wants to know about God." They departed the city of Enoch together.

On the road to the Mountain of God:

Adam, Eve, and Bartholomew traveled for one whole day without incident. They found a suitable place to spend the night. Bartholomew built a fire to cook upon and drive the night chill from the air. Adam and Bartholomew discussed God's ways, but Eve pretended to be asleep while she prayed for Nephili. She only prayed because she thought *I might never see my beloved son again!* Nephili was only one of her sons, but he was special to her. His father, Saphriael, had become human for her, but died at the hands of her estranged daughter. Nephili was the gift Saphriael gave to her. Tears rolled down her cheek onto the ground, as she cried herself to sleep.

They woke before sunrise, ate, and packed for the second day of their journey. Adam and Bartholomew continued talking about God as they walked, but Eve worried about Nephili. When the sun was high in the sky and the heat of the day took their breath away, they stopped and rested under a large shade tree and slumbered until mid-afternoon. When the heat passed, they set out again.

Adam, Eve, and Bartholomew entered a narrow canyon along the road to the Mountain of God. They walked straight into the blinding light of the sun. The canyon offered no trees or caves for shelter, but Adam thought they would make it out of the canyon before darkness. Bartholomew and Eve agreed with his assessment, so they kept going. They shielded their eyes and strained against the brightness as they walked. Finally, Adam saw trees at the other end of the canyon.

Ayporos, Vepar, Haures, Amudusias, and Serephah lay on both sides of the canyon walls and watched as the giants marched towards Adam, Eve, and a young stranger. Adam and his companions could not see the giants because they were walking into the sun with Tsarebeth leading the giants directly towards Eve and her companions. Eve was his grandmother, but that only made him want to kill her more. His father, Bael, told him the story of how she abandoned his mother Naqama in favor of Seth.

Adam's eyes strained against the sun, but he swore the trees at the end of the canyon were moving towards them. He stopped and raised his hand to shield his eyes from the sun as he tried to get a better look. The sun was almost straight ahead of them now. After a few moments, Adam turned to Bartholomew and Eve and said, "Those aren't trees. Something is moving towards us." Bartholomew and Eve strained to make out the dark shadows, and then Bartholomew said, "They are moving towards us, and I think they are giants, not trees." Eve cried out in fear, but Adam fell upon the ground and prayed to God for protection.

Tsarebeth and his giants stomped towards Adam, Eve, and Bartholomew until they were only a hundred feet away. He called out to them as he continued walking towards them. "Satan, the Worthy One, has sent us to kill you. Throw yourselves down before us and beg for mercy. Then I will make your death quick." Adam did not reply but continued to pray. Eve cried because she thought *They are going to kill us*! Only Bartholomew stood against the giants as they approached.

When the giants were within fifty feet, they ran at Adam and his companions. The ground shook, the earth quaking under their massive strides. They raised their clubs into the air and let out their rumbling battle cries, "GGGRRRR!" Before they reached Adam, Eve and Bartholomew, a powerful invisible explosion sent the giants flying back through the air. They crashed to the ground, tumbled and rolled backward until they came to a stop twenty-five feet away. The giants groaned and cried out in pain as they rose to face their enemies again.

Ariel, the lion of God, stood before the giants with his sword in hand. Ayporos, Vepar, Haures, Amudusias, and Serephah expected God to defend Adam, but to have one of the most powerful angels in Heaven travel with them hidden in the form of a human was a new trick for God. Satan anticipated God's interference and sent them for this reason. The Fallen Ones started their attack. They tried to kill Adam and Eve by raining fire and wind down upon them, but Ariel successfully blocked them. He raised his sword over his head, and an invisible force pushed the flames out to their side. The fire shifted towards the giants. Tsarebeth and the other giants leaped backward as the fire singed their skin and hair.

Ayporos and his brethren dove from their perches high up on the canyon walls and landed on the other side of Adam, Eve and Ariel. They had enemies to the north and south! *The*

Fallen Ones rejoiced because Ariel could not fight on two fronts, could he? Ariel called out to the Fallen Ones saying, "Leave now and you may keep your lives. Attack, and you will die!" Ayporos replied, "You can't hope to beat us alone. Surrender to us, and we will make your death merciful!" Tsarebeth and his giants took advantage of their conversation and closed the distance between Adam, Eve, and Ariel.

Ayporos and his brethren stopped speaking and attacked Ariel. Amudusias conjured a powerful storm. Dark clouds hung ominously over the canyon. A bolt of lightning streaked out of the dark clouds and struck Ariel. His muscles spasmed as he ground his teeth, fighting the pain. The electricity drove him to his knees. When the strike ended, he rose to his feet and raised his sword in a defensive position. "Is that all you've got?" Before he finished speaking, Haures sent a fireball at his chest. Ariel knocked the flaming ball down with his sword and brought it back to a defensive position just in time. Amudusias' second bolt of lightning struck his sword and was deflected harmlessly to the ground.

Vepar lunged at Ariel before he returned to a defensive position. He lashed out with his claws, drew blood and left oozing marks on Ariel's thigh. His other hand swept through the air toward Ariel's unprotected throat. Ariel blocked his deadly attack with his forearm and countered by smashing the hilt of his blade into the crown of Vepar's head. He fell to the ground, unconscious. Ariel glanced at his thigh and groaned. Vepar was a vile creature whose claws caused wounds to turn gangrenous almost instantly. He cursed himself; *You are a clumsy, arrogant fool!* In anger, he raised his sword to kill Vepar, but Ayporos attacked. Ayporos leaped high into the air and brought his blade down with a powerful two-handed attack. Sparks from the clash of their swords showered down upon them. Before the last spark burned out, Ariel parried with a slicing movement across Ayporos' abdomen, opening a deep wound. Ayporos retreated as Serephah entered the fight.

Ariel turned to face Serephah, but it was too late. Blue waves of pure energy slithered from the tips of Serephah's trident and engulfed Ariel. The powerful blast sent him flying backward through the air. He landed hard on the rocky ground, and his sword bounced out of reach clanging on the ground as it went. His eyes widened in horror as the three prongs of Serephah's trident pierced his abdomen. "AAAHHHH," he cried until the energy of the trident coursed into him, rendering him silent. His eyes blinked uncontrollably as his body spasmed. Images of Serephah smiling as he pinned him to the ground flashed before him, then darkness overwhelmed him.

On the other side of the canyon, Tsarebeth held his grandmother by her throat, looking into her horror-filled eyes. He smiled and laughed at her, "I am Naqama's son!" Her eyes grew large with the horror of his words. "She is dead, but I am the product of her union with Bael. I am here to kill you, but I intend to enjoy your suffering first!" He squeezed her throat harder as she desperately pried at his hand with her frail, human fingers. One of his companions had Adam pinned, face down on the ground to his right. His huge foot pressed down on his back, forcing the air from his lungs. "Kill him," Tsarebeth said as he turned, so Eve could see him die. She watched in horror as the giant pushed his foot down on Adam. He couldn't scream but managed a painful groan as the giant forced the air from his lungs. Eve watched Adam until the darkness in her peripherals engulfed her and consciousness left her. The last sounds she heard were his bones breaking.

CHAPTER 85

A blinding light and a shrill whistling sound ripped William from the pages of Satan's book. He dropped the book, closed his eyes, and covered his ears in vain. "AAHH," he screamed as he fell to his knees on the living room floor. Time passed, but he could not be sure how much. He was not unconscious, but the pain of the high pitch sound and the brightness of the light made him wish he was unconscious. His stomach was rolling, and he could taste vomit, but he did not remember throwing up.

William opened his watering eyes and looked around. A glowing image stood before him, but the light reflected off his tears. He wiped his eyes and saw a bright angel standing before him holding Satan's book under his arm. *That's my book!* He tried to speak, but no audible words came from his mouth, *Or did they?* "It's Satan's perverted book," the angel replied! *Did the angel read my thoughts, or did I say the words aloud?* William could not trust his senses because of the disorientation he felt.

"We need to hurry. The extreme light and sound are a warning spell the Fallen Ones use from time to time. They are coming!" William fought through the confusion and suddenness of the situation. "Why should I go with you?" "I am the Archangel Michael, and God sent me to bring you and the book to him." William stared at him in disbelief. *Is the Archangel Michael really in my living room telling me God wants to meet with me?* "What does he want with me?" William asked. "You will know soon enough. We have to go NOW!"

Suddenly, there was a blast of energy. A powerful shockwave sent William tumbling back to the floor, and he lost sight of the angel. William opened his eyes, looked up from the floor and saw the Archangel Michael crash into the wall. Margaret's beloved cuckoo clock fell from the wall and broke into several pieces. Ironically, all William could think about was *Margaret is going to be so angry. They bought that clock in Bavaria when he was a private in the Army.* Michael lost his grip on Satan's Book when he hit the wall. The book landed on the floor on the other side of the room. Amon hit Michael with another powerful blast of energy and pressed his attack. William looked back at the book and decided to make his move. He did not bother to stand; instead, he crawled over to the it. He picked up the book, clutched it to his chest and rolled over to see how the fight was progressing. To his surprise, Michael had Amon on the ground. His left arm held Amon's collar, while his right hand punched him in the face several times. *Amon is in trouble*, William thought.

William used the table to pull himself to his feet. *Amon is getting his ass kicked! I need to do something*, he thought as he considered his options. William charged across the room and crashed, shoulder first into the Archangel. He succeeded in getting him to stop hitting Amon, but not much more. Michael turned towards William, who just bounced off him and landed on the floor. He looked irritated. The next thing William knew he was on the other side of the room sliding on his back across the hardwood floor. Michael rose from Amon and stomped towards William.

"NO," Amon yelled from across the room. William looked past the approaching angel and saw Amon rising to his feet. Suddenly, three more beings appeared next to Amon. William assumed they were Fallen Ones because they immediately drew their swords and moved towards Michael. "Leave him alone," Amon said sternly. Michael turned and saw that Amon was no longer alone. Then, he quickly moved to William. William looked into the angel's eyes. He was not sure what the angel was about to do, but he did not expect what happened next. The mighty angel gently grabbed William's shoulder, and he saw a blinding flash of light.

A few moments later, Amon bent down and knelt beside William's body. He was still clutching Satan's book in his arms, but Amon feared the worst. William was alive, but Michael took his spirit out of his body and escaped to Heaven. He would remain in a coma until his spirit returned. *Satan is not going to be happy!* Amon thought as he plucked the book from William's arms. *Shit, Monica is going to be angry!* He had been on the receiving end of Satan's rage more than once, and it was never good, but a pissed-off woman was almost as bad. He was not looking forward to their next conversation.

An hour later, a handsome young doctor stood beside William's hospital bed explaining to Margaret and Monica, who was on speakerphone, how William was in a coma, but they could not provide a medical explanation for it. "What do you mean all the tests are negative, and none of the scans show any reason why my husband is in a coma?" "We will continue to run tests, but we cannot explain why he is unconscious. Everything seems normal." Monica chimed in from the phone, "Thanks for your help doctor. Please keep us informed." He put a reassuring hand on Margaret's shoulder, "Please let the nurse's station know if you need anything." Then he left the room. "Mom, I can't get there until tomorrow morning. Are you going to be okay?" Margaret replied, "I will be fine. Get here when you can, and be careful. I love you." "I love you too," Monica replied as she hung up the phone! "AMON," Monica yelled at the top of her lungs, "AMON!!!!"

In Heaven:

William looked at the multitude of angels gathered around the throne in front of him. He could not imagine how many there were. All the angels bowed before the throne, a bright light shining from it. He realized the light was God. Michael turned towards William, "I live here, and it still amazes me!" William could only think of one word to describe it, "Awesome!" Suddenly, a voice thundered through Heaven, "Worship!" All the angels fell to the ground and cried out, "Holy, Holy, Holy!!!" William felt an irresistible urge to join them, and he fell with them, saying, "Holy, Holy, Holy!!"

Made in the USA
San Bernardino, CA
13 May 2020

71447891R10212